I0825830

THE RUBY HEIRESS
The Adventure Continues

DEDICATION

I have been so blessed in my life to be surrounded by family and friends who truly love and care about me. From my earliest recollection, my paternal grandmother Lucia inspired me with her strength of character and filled my heart and my mind with stories from her youth. My Nona taught me many things, but the most important lesson was that love, family and honor, cannot be bought, sold or destroyed. That being poor was not a disgrace, but that being poor of spirit and ill of heart were a disgrace.

To my beautiful beloved grandmother Lucia, whose beauty was only surpassed by her loving heart. To my mother Josephine who has been a source of family information and encouragement. To my niece Suzanne Olszewski, who has now suffered through two books with me, lending me unconditional help, ideas and her love, thank you. To my dear friends Gae and Michael LaSalle who have showered me with love and support. A special thank you to Gae who gave me the name for this my second book. To my friends Douglas Carabe and Ed Graziano who have been a great inspiration and have promoted my work to any poor soul who would listen; a special thank you to Douglas for his brilliant editing. To my daughters, Kelly and Aya, for their technical help, their candor, and their love, thank you for your encouragement.. To my husband that I have left abandoned most nights while I had an affair with my computer. To my son Matt, who spent hours trying to find the perfect image for this book. Thank you all; and to those who have read *Lucia Mistress of Monteforte* and who are here for *The Ruby Heiress*; thank you, thank you, and thank you.

FORWARD

The Ruby Heiress is the second book in the Lucia Mistress of Monteforte series. In this book, we find our intrepid heiress, who has now been bestowed with the title and responsibility of heading the Rizzo family fortune, embarking on adventures across Europe. We share her dreams and desires; her love and her lust. Lucia's travels will take us to the Court of Louis and Marie Antoinette and the magnificent Versailles. We become voyeurs to Lucia's first introduction to Parisian high society haute couture and sexual intimacy. We embark on a sailing from Le Havre, across the English Chanel to England, where Lucia is transported to the unwelcoming inhabitants of Wallingston Castle.

For the first time in her life, Lucia finds both misery and ecstasy in a foreign land that will never accept her. She is an unwitting partner and victim to the evils that lurk in the dark dungeons of an ancient castle. Evil has cast its wicked shadow upon our beautiful young heiress. It is with great self-sacrifice that Lucia returns to her beloved Monteforte with renewed determination but with a broken heart.

Lucia has grown in endless ways on this journey. She has loved and lost; and found an inner courage she did not know she possessed.

Come; follow the red haired Enchantress as she discovers a world beyond the stone walls of Monteforte.

Table of Contents

BOOK TWO

BOOK THREE

BOOK ONE

CHAPTER ONE

FAREWELL

Monteforte

Looking back over the evening, Lucia was awed by the precision with which her servants had executed the event of the decade. The gala had brought together some of the most prestigious members of European society. The occasion marked a transition of power that had been set in place for the past forty years. Marchesa Maria Sucretti, the present reigning heiress of the vast fortune of the Rizzo family, whose estate, Monteforte, was nestled on a high cliff overlooking the Mediterranean Sea, had been the seat of this ruling gentry for generations. With controlling interest in some of the largest and most prestigious companies in the world, Maria Sucretti had called a summit of the ruling class throughout Europe and they came.

This was no frivolous social gala. Tonight was the witnessing of the transition of power from Maria Rizzo Sucretti to her sole heir and niece Lucia Banfi.

The official title bestowed on the red haired beauty was Marchesa Lucia Banfi, Mistress of Monteforte.

Lucia thought it strange to think of herself as the Marchesa Banfi. She stood in the middle of this magnificent grand ballroom as if in a dream. Although she had been in this room many times tonight, it was no longer a room in her aunt's castle but a room in her castle. The magnitude of it was daunting. Could she, Lucia Banfi, truly become the Marchesa Banfi? For years, her aunt had been priming her to assume this position of power. The endless tutoring, the explanation of how business is conducted, and the extensive holdings throughout the world; even the collection of priceless art and antiquities would come under her control. Lucia was chosen because she was equal to the honor that had been bestowed upon her.

It was very late by the time Lucia said her final farewell to her guests, many of whom would be staying at the castle for the next day or two. She was both overwhelmed yet fearful. Giovanni Romano, whose knowledge of hired assassins was extensive, demanded that she bolt her bedchamber doors and that her personal maid Sophia should sleep in her room. Lucia had encountered her first glimpse of what being one of the most powerful people in the world would mean. A man, whom she had never met, came into her home and her life, without warning or invitation. A man she knew would try to kill her. Of that fact, she was sure. The question was 'why'?

"Mistress Lucia, may I walk you to your room? Your brothers Genaro and Antonio are sharing a room with me which I believe is across the hall from your suite." Lucia was only too happy to have the dashing young composer, Giancarlo Marzoni, escort her to her room. "That would be very nice. I will come to meet you but first I must say good night to my remaining guests as well as my aunt." Lucia watched the retreating silhouette of Giancarlo glide across the ballroom floor. She was definitely aroused. The man was charming and almost boyish. He was very tall but solidly built. His broad shoulders sat atop a narrow waist and a high tight ass, with long slender legs like a stallion. His tousled mass of blonde curls, which refused to be contained within his leather thong, was in stark contrast to his tawny complexion. She felt her womb tingle with excitement.

Lucia, making her way toward where her Aunt Maria was sitting, bid everyone she passed a wonderful good night but before she left she went over to her Aunt Maria "Zia, this was a gala fit for a queen. I can never say thank you enough to express my deepest gratitude for what you have given to me." "Bella, I have told you often that it is you who have breathed life into this old, miserable, soul. For the first time in so many years, I am alive. I am happy. I wish to spend the rest of my days in the quite solitude of loving your Zio." Her expression changed and she became serious "Be careful, I feel the presence of an evil spirit. Be wary of everyone except the few you will keep close to you. Tomorrow, midday, we shall have a meeting with the heads of several of the companies you now own and control. I want you to be prepared to ask questions and let each one of them know that you, Lucia Banfi, are not just a pretty face but also a woman they must respect. Do you understand what I am saying?" Maria waited for her niece to respond. Lucia with those penetrating azure blue eyes hooded by her long thick strawberry lashes nodded her acceptance of what she had been told. "As you instruct Zia I shall be prepared. For now, I am going to retire. I am going for an early ride with Lord Marzoni." She was about to take her leave when Maria Sucretti grabbed her hand and pulled her down to speak directly to her. "Lucia he is a very handsome young man and I see how he looks at you, but, be cautious, he is coming into the prime of his career and views his fame and fortune as a right not a gift. He will eat you up and then spit you out." "Do not concern yourself Zia. I know exactly what our handsome young composer is but I am enjoying the attention." Lucia squeezed her aunt's hand and kissed her on each cheek. "Maybe it is I who shall eat him up and then spit him out." They laughed and Lucia left in a swirl of royal blue silk.

Maria Sucretti looked after her heir with great admiration and love. The child she had fallen deeply in love with was surely now a woman. She watched as the dashing young composer waited with lustful eyes at the end of the grand ballroom as Lucia, making her way through the haze of endless guests, finally met up with him. Giancarlo, thought Maria, was certainly an attractive and talented young man but this was his own time to shine, much as it was Lucia's time to shine. Perhaps, someday, when they had each reached the height of their respective careers they might find love for each other. Maria's thoughts were interrupted by her beloved husband, Giovanni Romano, "Cara, it is late, shall we retire? Tomorrow will come soon and we will have much to do for our remaining guests." " Yes, Giovanni I am very tired and you can be sure that we will be busy for the next couple of days. Tomorrow, midday, I have informed several of the Lords that they shall have a formal introduction with Lucia in attendance. My darling, take me to bed and let us seal the transition of power with passionate lovemaking." "That my Love is a most wonderful idea. You are so wise Cara." He, the gallant Lord of Monteforte, gave his wife his arm and together, tall and lean, with dignity and love, they strode through the grand ballroom biding their guest's a safe journey, or, to those who would be staying the promise of their company the next day.

For the first time in her life, the Marchesa Maria Rizzo Sucretti was free. She looked around the room and realized its beauty. The architecture, the murals that graced its massive walls even the frescos that formed the canopy over her head were simply magnificent. Maria thought to herself that she had never really noticed the splendor of this room.

She leaned in to Giovanni Romano's thin but muscular body and felt the pangs of desire course through her body. She had waited more than twenty years for his return and now would spend the rest of her life making each day count.

Lucia was happy to be on Giancarlo's arm. He was fun and interesting and she knew that every woman, regardless of age, was admiring the young composer. He was striking. Tall and muscular, he and built like a gladiator rather than a man who created beautiful music. His looks were so different from the other men she knew. While many of them were handsome, they bore the same resemblance to their Roman roots. Giancarlo was the perfect blend of swarthy Italian and fair Austrian features. His blonde curly hair stood out among the countless dark haired men. I His eyes, while dark, were the color of polished wood, warm, rich, and glistening. Yes, Lucia thought to herself, she could like this one but could not love him, at least not now.

"This was a fabulous gala Mistress Lucia. Did you have a good time at your own party?" Lucia was smiling but inside she flashed back to her encounter in the garden. "Yes it was wonderful and quite interesting. Again, Lord Marzoni, thank you for the grand piece you played, everyone was talking about it. Ah, here we are, these are my rooms. I shall say good night. Remember, we have our meeting tomorrow at dawn." The young man who stood a few inches taller than Lucia let go of her arm and turned to face her. "Mistress Lucia, you have captured my heart. Your beauty and charm are intoxicating. I will count every second until I see you at dawn." He bent his head down and kissed each cheek, his lips brushed hers, and she felt a hot blush cruise through her body. He lingered for a little longer than was necessary and she could smell his scent, which was a mixture of manly sweat and cologne. Lucia, her pulse racing, looked at Giancarlo with desire but quickly caught herself. "Buonanotte. Si vedrà all'alba." The composer bowed deeply and turned toward his own room but before he advanced, he turned sharply and said "Lucia you have cast a spell on me." He then turned again, with his long legs made a few steps, and entered his room the heavy carved door closing with a thud.

Lucia was stunned at his words as she stood there in the dim hall starring at the closed door. She turned as if in slow motion and out of the corner of her eye, she saw a dark silhouette at the end of the hall. Her heart still racing from her intimate contact with Giancarlo she tried to see who it was, the thumping in her throat was so strong she could barely catch her breath. She was just about to scream out for help when out of the shadow stepped Nicko. He came quickly to her "Mistress you must not be roaming around alone. Master Giovanni has forbidden it. I will be out here for the rest of the night on guard. Now please get inside." Nicko opened the door and walked her in. Sophia was lying on the settee, apparently she had been sleeping, and woke with a start at the sound of their entry.

"Mistress, Master Giovanni has given me strict instructions that I am to sleep here with you and to bolt all the doors. What has happened?" Lucia now suddenly wary from the excitement of the day simply said, "There is a man, who looks exactly like my Grandfather Mateo Rizzo, who wants to kill me." The young maid's face froze with horror and her eyes opened so wide she almost looked comical. "What are you saying?" Nicko grabbed the maid and pulled her aside while Lucia took that moment to walk to her dressing room.

"Sophia, Mistress Lucia is in grave danger. You must be careful and observe everything. If you find there is something suspicious call out for help. I shall be on guard right outside the door. Do you understand?" " Yes, but..." Nicko was annoyed "There is nothing else to know. Someone is trying to harm your Mistress that enough? Now, good night and be alert." With that, Nicko turned on his heels and went to the door. At the doorway he said, "Now come bolt the door and do not open it for anyone unless you recognize their voice. Yes?" Sophia was so terrified she just nodded and did as she was told.

Lucia was exhausted. She asked Sophia to help her out of her gown. "I am so happy to be out of those stays I believe my ribs have broken all over again." Lucia rubbed her aching side remembering only too well the day she was nearly killed by a man who beat her so severely she was injured for weeks. The thought of him and that day gave her a cold chill up her spine. She shrugged it off to being tired.

"Sophia, will you wake me before dawn and have my riding clothes ready. I am going riding early with Lord Marzoni." "Oh of course Mistress, I heard him play this evening, he is not only so handsome, but, he plays like an angel." The two girls were giggling which momentarily distracted Lucia's thoughts from the man in the garden.

Morning came after a restless sleep but Lucia was wide-awake and anxious to get down to the stables. Gandolfo, Master of Horse, was already up and helped with Apollo. "You are up early Mistress even after that long night of dancing?" He smiled shrewdly. "Have you seen Lord Marzoni? He was supposed to meet me for a ride." Just as he was about to say that he had not seen the young composer he walked into the stable. "Good morning Mistress Lucia. My you look bright and well rested." "Thank you Lord Marzoni, I am sorry but I cannot say the same for you? What happened?" "Your brothers are what happened. They coaxed me into playing cards and a few glasses of wine. Sadly, I lost all my money and now my head is ten times too big." " I will speak with them on your behalf and perhaps they will give you another chance to regain your money. As for your head, I do believe it is as big as it was when last I saw you."

Gandolfo who was witness to this banter tried very hard to refrain from laughing aloud at the wit of his mistress. "Shall I get your horse Lord Marzoni?" "Yes, please do." He turned to look at Lucia who was smiling broadly, "As for you Mistress, it is a great wit you possess. We shall see if your riding is as sharp as your tongue." Lucia who looked wounded lowered her head and shrouded her eyes in an expression of contrition. "As you wish Lord Marzoni."

They mounted their horses and casually cantered toward the cliffs. Lucia purposefully did not mention to Giancarlo that the ground could be slick from the overnight dew. Once they were past the herb garden Lucia leaned over and spoke in Apollo's ear "Apollo, we must ride very well today, our friend thinks that I am just a woman. You will show him who is in power." She reached into her gown, took out a chunk of sugar, and slipped it into Apollo's mouth. As if to acknowledge what his mistress had just said the massive animal nodded and whinnied. As soon as she straightened herself back into her saddle, Apollo took off with a start.

Lucia, a fine rider, with her faithful Apollo, glided over the steep cliffs and left Lord Marzoni in their dust. He called after her but she feigned deafness. Suddenly, she heard a loud moan and the bellowing of a startled horse. Lucia took up Apollo's reins and halted. Turning in her saddle, she saw Lord Marzoni lying on the ground. She hurried to him and quickly dismounted. "Giancarlo are you injured?" It was the first time she had called him by his given name.

The brash young man looked embarrassed but was slightly hurt. "I will manage I think. My horse slid on the incline and I lost hold of him." "Is anything broken? Can you get up?" Lucia knelt down by his side to see if he was badly injured. "My head hurts." She came very close to examine his head putting her hands through the thick mass of curls. It felt so good. Without warning, he pulled her to himself and kissed her hard on the mouth. Lucia was stunned. She pulled free and slapped his face with all her might. "How dare you dishonor me sir? I am not one of your whores to have as you please."

With remarkable speed, Lucia got to her feet. Giancarlo rose quickly but with a noticeable stumble. He fell back down on his knees, his hands breaking the fall and rescuing him from hitting his face. "I am truly sorry Mistress Lucia; I don't know what made me do that. I am so sorry." Lucia was angry but realized that perhaps he was actually injured. Again, she tried to help him to his feet. This time he managed to stay upright but all the color had drained from his face. "Here let us sit a while until you regain your strength."

They found a grassy spot and sat down. "Are you ill? Shall I go and get help?" Giancarlo was now truly embarrassed "I'm fine. It must have been the combination of lack of sleep and no lack of wine." They smiled amicably. The two of them sat there in silence for what seemed a long time.

The sun, now just peeking over the mountain, cast a shimmering light upon the sea and it looked like millions of tiny crystals had descended on the water. It was a beautiful moment of peace with nature. They both sat there and absorbed the splendor of the artistry of God. Giancarlo broke the silence "It is so beautiful here I could stay forever. Mistress Lucia, I am very sorry if I offended you. I told you that I am under your spell. I have been thinking of you every minute."

"Giancarlo, Lord Marzoni, I too find you very attractive, to say otherwise would be a lie, yet, I cannot find myself in a relationship with a man at this point in my life. It is different for you a man, it is acceptable for you to have multiple affairs with women. I, a woman, must maintain my dignity and good name, until I choose to wed. I am sure you understand my position." " Yes, I do understand but it does not diminish my desire for you. You are perfect in every way. You are what every man dreams for in a woman and in a wife."

"If I were not so committed to my career I would ask you to marry me, but, regrettably, right now I am too in love with my music. Please, I beg you to forgive my transgression. I would be so dishonored if you did not forgive me." The young composer was now on his knees holding both her hands in his and kissing them with sincerity. "I do forgive you Lord Marzoni and I wish to continue our relationship with the hopes that one day we both may find ourselves in different circumstances in life."

He stood "I want you more than I have ever wanted any woman. When I look at you, I am ashamed for my own lust. I will be leaving

Monteforte today before I say or do something I shall regret. Dear Lady, it is with a heavy heart that I must say farewell. You have taken my heart."

Lucia was sad but knew only too well that she could not let this dangerous young man too close to her for at this very moment she would have ripped off her clothes and abandoned her virginity to him. She was panting with desire her pulse racing and the sweat of passion cruising down her body. "Come let us ride back together in friendship. I will bid you farewell when we arrive at the stables."

They rode in silence side by side each to their own thoughts. When they reached the stables, Giancarlo quickly got off his horse and then came around to assist Lucia from Apollo. "I have enjoyed the time we have shared Giancarlo, but, I do believe it would be wise for you to leave, I find that I too am fighting my desires. For now we must find consolation for our passion in our careers, perhaps, someday we can rekindle these feelings."

Again, he knelt down and taking her hands looked up into that face of pure beauty and "Addio. Io penso sempre a te e ricorda con rammarico che dobbiamo mettere da parte nostra sentimenti per l'altro." Lucia, hearing his words of regret for their lost love with her eyes filled with tears just stood there for a moment then said "Goodbye". He released her hands and she turned to go back to the castle and never looked back.

CHAPTER TWO

HOLDING COURT

Monteforte

Lucia, who was visibly upset, was trying to conceal her feelings. Rushing into the castle and was making her way to her room to compose herself before the household awoke. Almost running with her head down and her thoughts on her passion Lucia found herself face to face with Giovanni Romano who took one look at her and immediately came to her "Bella, what is wrong? Did you see him again?" Lucia on the verge of crying just shook her head. Her Zio took hold of her arm and led her to the solar, which was close by. He directed her to a settee and she sat with a plop he then joined her.

"What is the matter?" he said in a concerned but stern voice. She looked at him with the wide-eyed honesty of a child then answered, "I wanted to make love to Lord Marzoni, but, because I am a woman I cannot find pleasure in the company of a man." There, she had said exactly what was on her mind. Giovanni Romano had all to do to control himself from laughing at her childish outburst but knew better.

"Bella, we all have been young with desire for intimacy with someone. When I first came to Monteforte under the employ of your late uncle Salvatore Sucretti, I dreamt of making love to your Zia Maria every day. Therefore, you see I do understand your frustration of I was burning with desire for her, yet I could not satisfy that need for we both would have been killed. wanting someone but not being able to consummate that relationship. It would be easy to see how a young woman would desire the handsome musician. I am proud that you think enough of yourself to have put your personal needs in their proper place." Lucia, her cheeks ablaze with fury and frustration blurted out "It is not fair. It is only because I am a woman."

He then brought her to himself and hugged her tight giving her forehead a gentle kiss. "Don't worry Bella there will be many handsome men for you to choose when the time is right." She threw her arms around his neck and started to weep out of unspent frustration. He let her cry until she felt cleansed of her anxiety. He removed a silk scarf from his coat pocket and wiped her face. "Now do you feel better?" Lucia actually did feel relieved and nodded "Yes Zio thank you. I always feel better when I talk to you."

"Now after I tell you about the letter that arrived the day of the gala you may not be so pleased." Lucia could see the concern on his face "Zio what did it say and who was it from." Deciding not to hold back any information from her, Giovanni

Romano took a deep breath and continued. Her life might depend on knowing all the facts.

"Here read it for yourself. It is from Don Zingaro a man of great power in the criminal world. I went to visit him, as you know after our meeting with the Abbot. I asked him about Professor Fragoli and who would be the person that he could sell the manuscripts to."

Lucia's hands were shaking as she held the letter. The note, which, had been written on fine velum paper, in a bold, steady hand.

Giovanni,

The information you seek regarding Professor Fragoli is not good. The body of this man was found a few days after we met. It appears that he had been tortured then killed and the body was left near an old abandoned road. After making certain inquiries, I found out that this man had hired a local assassin and thief to kill Mistress Lucia.

The word is that Antonio Sanfranco of Milan has the manuscripts you lost. I would surmise that he killed the professor. He is a highly regarded expert in antique books and manuscripts and his clients are among some of the wealthiest men in the world. It is said that he is ruthless and would do anything to possess a priceless antique.

Be careful old friend he is a dangerous man, very intelligent and well connected.

Don Zingaro

Lucia was stunned. "You mean it was Professor Fragoli who sent that animal to kill me?" Giovanni Romano could see the fire burning in those beautiful blue eyes. "Yes it was him and now he is dead. I would make the connection between his manner of death and the missing manuscript that Antonio Sanfranco, the man who introduced himself to you in the garden the night of the gala, is the cause of his execution. Don Zingaro is not one to over tell a story so that makes me very afraid of this man Sanfranco."

"I tell you Zio that when I saw him standing there under the picture of my grandfather I felt as if by some evil device he had come to life. His resemblance to Mateo Rizzo was shocking." Now for the first time Giovanni Romano felt a wave of fear cruise through his body. "I too saw the remarkable resemblance and felt an uneasy feeling. I have shared this letter with you in the hopes that you will be very cautious for this man could be anywhere. I am afraid for your safety Bella."

"Zio I will not live my life in fear. Yes, I shall be cautious but I will not spend every minute of my life cowering in a corner waiting for this Devil or someone he sends to kill me, if that is to be my life I will kill myself rather than live in fear. That is why I want you to train me to use a sword and a bow. I will learn to protect myself as best I can. If he, or someone else, tries to attack me, at least I will have a fighting chance to defend myself. Will you teach me the way to protect myself?"

Giovanni Romano was so proud of this young woman whom he loved like his own beloved Rosalie who died many years before along with his wife Natalie of the plague. "Yes I will teach you to defend yourself."

Lucia now recovered and with a fire in her belly instantly got up off the settee and straightened her riding outfit. She extended her hand to her seated Zio who reached for her outstretched hand to rise and said, "Tomorrow we begin my training. Yes?" "As you wish Bella, as you wish." They were standing facing each other he was but a few inches taller than she was, "I love you Bella. Tomorrow we begin." "Very good Zio now I must go wash and dress to meet the heads of the various companies we own." "The companies you now own Bella. I know you have the knowledge of running these companies, but step lightly on the toes of the Lords who run them for you. They will view you as a mere child and a female child at that. Be strong but be wise and use your beauty and charm to your best advantage." "Yes Zio, Zia Maria has told me all the things I need to know about each one of them. I shall heed your advice." "Very good Bella, now run along and get ready." He kissed her on each cheek and sent her on her way.

Giovanni Romano felt sorry for his darling Lucia. Her beauty would be both a gift and a curse. Men would desire her but would she trust that they wanted her body or her fortune. She was certainly coming of age with her physical desires and he smiled to himself at her candor in telling him of her feelings. Lucia was so honest she could never lie the truth was always written on that beautiful face. God help her and keep her safe he prayed.

Lucia, with the aid of her personal maid, washed and dressed in an elegant indigo blue dress, which accented her tiny waist and full breasts, but had a bateau neckline trimmed in ivory lace. She wore her waist length strawberry tresses in a simple style with ivory combs encrusted with sapphires to match her earrings and gown. Overall, it was an appropriate costume to wear for her first meeting with the heads of her various companies. "What do you think Sophia? Do I look mature and intelligent?" Sophia circled her mistress with an appraising eye then said, "I think you look confident and wise." "Thank you Sophia let us hope that my Lords agree."

Lucia left her suite of rooms to make her way to her aunt's rooms. She knocked gently on the massive cypress door and waited for a response. "Enter." Upon entering the room Lucia saw that her aunt was not dressed and became concerned. "Zia, what troubles you? Why are you not dressed? Did you forget we are to meet with the Lords for our meeting?"

Maria Sucretti sat in her dressing gown by the open door to her balcony. Her expression was one of calm reserve. "Bella, it is not I they wish to meet, it is you who must lead them now. My absence will send the message that you are now in charge and that they must answer to you alone. Remember all that I have told you. Stand your ground but be respectful. You want them to respect you. The last thing you want them to do is resent you. Do you understand Bella?"

Lucia realized how wise her aunt really was and she relaxed. "Yes Zia I do understand and I remember all that you have told me about each and every one of the Lords." Maria smiled broadly "Now go outside for a walk to clear your head. I will join you later in the day. Tonight we will have supper with a few special friends. Come here Lucia." Lucia went to her aunt's side. "Give me your hand Bella." Lucia extended her alabaster hand with its long elegant fingers. Maria Sucretti slipped off the ring she always wore. Mounted on a base of pink gold it had an interesting design. Lucia knew that her aunt always wore this particular ring as a matter of fact she had never seen her aunt without it. It was not a ring of great beauty but it must have special meaning since her aunt never took it off.

"Bella, I want you to wear this ring always." Maria Sucretti pushed the ring, which was still warm from her own hand, onto her niece's finger. It fit perfectly and felt very heavy on her finger. "Never take this ring off. It may save your life one day." Lucia looked at the ring, which was nothing special, and to be truthful, she thought it was ugly. "What is so special about this ring Zia? I have seen you with it my whole life but never thought to question you." "Here let me show you why this is to be worn at all times." Maria Sucretti took hold of the ring and manipulated it in such a way that the top slid open to reveal a hidden chamber. Inside the tiny chamber was a powdery substance. "This, my dear niece is a very lethal poison. A few grains mixed with liquid and it can kill a person within minutes. You would be wise to use it only in extreme circumstances, but if your life is in danger, you will find it a comfort to have with you. This was my mother's ring and her mother before her, each of us had the occasion to use it. I pray you never need to use it, but I feel more secure that you have it with you at all times." Lucia was shocked and amazed but did not question her aunt, she knew better than to ask why she needed to kill someone. Lucia reassured herself that when the time was right her aunt would share the story of how she came to use the deadly powder. Lucia said nothing but slid the top back into place. "I pray also that I may never have a need to use it, but it is good to know it is there if I need it. Thank you Zia; as always you have given me new confidence." "Go Bella; refresh yourself before you must face your Lords."

Lucia gave her aunt kisses on each cheek and left her rooms. While she was walking down the long hall, she fingered the ring. It felt odd on her usually naked hand. It was warm on her cool skin and it made her feel safe. She silently prayed that Jesus would protect her against her enemies and that she would never have to use the poison. She was passing the room where her brothers and Giancarlo Marzoni were sleeping. The door was wide open and it appeared as if the room was empty then she spotted her brother Genaro on the balcony and he was painting.

"Good morning dear brother. How are you today? I see that everyone has abandoned you for food." He got up at her voice and came over to embrace her. "Good morning dear sister. I am fine and yes, they have gone to stuff their faces with food. I must confess that I have not eaten or drunk this much food in years. I am still bloated from last night. It was a splendid party and you were perfect. I love you Lucia." Lucia felt herself blushing even though it was her brother who was speaking. "Thank you Genaro. What is that you are working on?" Lucia walked over to the easel that her brother had been working on.

It was a portrait of Giancarlo Marzoni. This was not strange, since her brother Genaro was a renowned artist commissioned by many people to paint their portrait. However, this painting was different. Lucia came over to where it stood with the sunlight dappling golden rays upon the canvas. It was the portrait of a lover. Lucia turned to look upon her brother's face. Genaro's expression was one of admiration and desire. It was not a look of lust but a look of love. "You love him don't you dear brother?" "Why do you say that Lucia?"

Lucia sat down in the chair next to where her brother had been painting. "Look at the pose, the language of the body, the expression of the eyes and mouth. This is not the portrait of a patron who has commissioned their likeness to canvas. This is the rendering of love for someone that has been transferred to canvas."

Genaro came to sit down in his chair facing the painting. "How did you know? I have never or would never, express such deep feelings to Giancarlo, nor, to anyone. I am shocked that you could see all that in this painting. You have never ceased to amaze me little sister. Your wisdom and understanding reaches far beyond your years." Lucia looked her brother in the eyes and boldly asked "Genaro have you ever lain with another man?" Her brother was stunned that she would ask so forward of a question. "How do you come to ask me such a personal question? Do you not know for a man to lay with another man is a sin?" "Dear brother I have not asked to embarrass or accuse you. I have asked simply because I want to know what it is like to lay with someone. I have so many desires of late and do not know how I am to feel."

Even though Genaro was annoyed that his younger sister was asking such personal questions he did not feel awkward about sharing his intimate secrets with her. "Yes Lucia I have laid with another man. I have lain with a number of men. The intimacy between two adults can be most enjoyable, however, sometimes if you really care about that person, but they on the other hand only wish to have your body for their own gratification, you can get hurt. I need not tell you that I must exercise much discretion in my personal life if I were discovered it would be my ruin. Sadly, my predisposition toward men rather than women has left me to be alone. I long for a meaningful relationship with someone who would love me and me alone." Lucia felt the heavy sorrow her beloved brother was carrying within himself and the conflict he must be facing.

"I too have a great attraction for our young composer but I know that he would not be a suitable match for anyone right now. Giancarlo is in love with himself and his music. He must pursue his fame and fortune before he can find love in that one special person. Do yourself a favor dear brother and put him aside he is not deserving of such love and devotion. He will break your heart. I am told that in France such relationships are widely accepted and perhaps it would be wise for you to take up residence there."

Genaro looked at the woman who was sitting next to him with deep admiration. "Lucia, you are perhaps the only woman I could love if only you were not my sister." They laughed and Lucia came to him, sat on his lap, and hugged him tightly. "I love you Genaro and I want you to find happiness. I hope that someday I will find happiness as well." "Don't despair you are so perfect in every way someone will make your heart sing with joy."

Giorgio broke up their special moment of bonding. "Mistress Lucia the Lords have been waiting for you in the library. Upon your arrival shall I begin the meal service?" "No Giorgio they will wait for their food until I have had a chance to speak with them. I do not want them distracted by Marcello's delicious food but bring them some wine, just a glass of our best vintage. Too much good wine will go to their heads without the accompaniment of food. Please be ready to serve the food when I ring the bell. Thank you for all your hard work I know how much all of you have been working to make these past days so special. Oh, would you please bring my brother some espresso and a light tray of food. I shall leave now." Giorgio bowed deeply with a smile on his face "As you have instructed Mistress."

"Dear brother will you stay a few more days I long to spend some private time with you, please stay?" He nodded "Yes I will be alone since Antonio is leaving this afternoon as is Giancarlo. We shall talk some more. Good luck with your first meeting."

Lucia was very anxious to enter the library. Nicko was in the hallway waiting for her arrival. "Mistress Lucia" he bowed "Good morning. All the Lords are present and waiting for you. If you need anything I shall be right here." Again he bowed and Lucia said "Thank you Nicko, I shall be fine especially knowing that you are ever present watching over me." He grabbed her hand, bowed, and kissed it with great affection. He then opened the massive carved cypress doors and announced "The Marchesa Lucia Banfi, Mistress of Monteforte." There were eight Lords seated around a long wooden table. They rose and started to clap. Shouts of "Salute" "Bravo" "Bona Fortuna" resonated throughout the room. Lucia felt the heat rise to her cheeks and the moisture form under her arms, yet, she remembered what her aunt had told her and nodded acknowledgement to each Lord as she made her way to the head of the table.

"Lord Russo, thank you for coming" the older stout man with powdered wig bowed and kissed her hand. "I am sorry to hear of the ill health of your wife please send her the best wishes from all at Monteforte. Mistress Sucretti has spoken highly of her over these many years." Lucia could see that the old man was pleased that she should mention his wife. "Thank you Mistress Lucia I shall bring your wishes to her."

Next Lucia stood in front of the Marquis de Fauntil of France. "Lord de Fauntil you have had a long journey and I thank you. I understand from my Master of Horse, that the young man Piro whom we sent to you for apprenticeship is doing well." Lord de Fauntil was a distinguished looking older man, who must have been quite handsome in his younger years. His eyes were still sharp and a light brown color that seemed to light up when he spoke. "Oh yes My Lady he has been a most efficient student and is progressing nicely. I am honored to be his sponsor, just as I am honored to be here with you and your family. I wish you all the success in life." He bowed deeply and kissed her hand.

Sitting just to his right was a short round man whose powdered wig was slightly askew upon his ball of a head. He was so stout that he was devoid of a neck and his head sat upon a massive ball for a body. He was quite comical but he had the most pleasant face and jovial smile. "Lord Sposa, you too have come a long way to join us and I thank you. I have been informed that you are in great distress with some pain you are harboring in your foot. Shall I have my physician call upon you in your suite later today?" The round ball of a head bobbed up and down and thus setting his wig even more off to one side "No, no, that will not be necessary my dear Mistress. It is a familiar ailment, I must confess it comes of my over indulgence in such magnificent cuisine. Your chef, Marcello, would be the death of me if he were in my service." With that statement, the whole table laughed but they all agreed that Marcello was a culinary genius.

Lucia continued around the table entreating each Lord with a personal greeting. The atmosphere in the room was relaxing as was Lucia. "Lord Bianchi you have also journeyed a considerable distance to be with us and for that I thank you. I hope your voyage was not too disagreeable, I understand that your vessel encountered some unwanted visitors." The middle-aged man raked his rather thick mustache with his fingers and replied, "I would not exactly address them as visitors Mistress, more like pirates, but, fortunately for us, our captain and crew were well equipped to exercise enough force to settle the matter." This statement had the table buzzing with hushed conversation. "Let us be grateful for your safety." Lord Bianchi a thin man of average height bowed his head in appreciation.

"Lord Esposito, I have often dreamt of seeing your beautiful Spain, I shall have to find time to visit. I thank you for coming to Monteforte for the celebration of my transition to Marchesa." Edgardo Esposito looked at her directly, he was a handsome man, perhaps in his early thirties, and "It would be my sincere honor for you to come to Spain. I shall take you everywhere and you would enjoy my hospitality. I will look forward to your arrival." Lucia blushed at the invitation "I shall make my plans and send you word. Thank you for your gracious invitation."

"I believe I speak for all of us Mistress Lucia when I say it would be our honor to host a visit from you. You must, I insist, come to England, and I promise you a grand tour of my beautiful country." Lucia was smiling broadly, "Why Lord Brunswick, how kind of you to say that I would be welcomed to your country. I will be so pleased to tour the grand country of England." Brunswick was a feisty man with a robust physique and a shock of thick white hair and beard and red rosy nose and cheeks. Lucia thought he looked like a happy man and one who would certainly show her a good time.

Her next stop was at the side of Lord La Piazza. He was a small man, wiry and fragile, with dark beady eyes and a long sharp nose. Lucia did not like the looks of this man. "Lord La Piazza how do you find things in the northern regions of the country?" "Fine; just fine." He answered curtly. Lucia could sense that the old boar did not like women in charge of men's affairs. She would deal with him in her own manner but for now, she would make light of his rudeness. "That is good news I would be alarmed if the situation was not fine."

Lucia noticed that the others were smirking at La Piazza; she surmised that he was not well liked.

Finally, Lucia came to her own place at the table, but before she sat, she reached for her glass, which was filled, with her finest vintage. "My Lords I would like to propose a toast." Each man took up his glass and stood. "Let us raise our glasses to the continuation of past and future success. I promise to be a good learner and pray that you all will help me discharge my duties to the best of my ability. Salute!" They all raised their glasses and cheered "Salute!"

Lucia sat and the lords followed. "I have for quite some time been preparing for my role as Marchesa of Monteforte. I have learned many things from my Aunt, and been educated by some of the finest minds in Europe. From time to time, I will meet with each one of you individually to discuss ways to improve our production or sale of our goods. I am always willing to hear what you may think will benefit all of us. I know you will not trust me, at least not yet, for you believe that I am too young. I beg you to trust in my knowledge and judgment and help me when I falter. We shall communicate often and I will be personally coming to each of you to see how we function. I hope that I will be received with an open mind and with all the same respect that you previously held with Marchesa Maria Sucretti."

Lucia picked up the servant's bell and rang it softly and Giorgio appeared within seconds. "Giorgio please let us feed our guests." Giorgio bowed deeply and turned sharply on his heels to alert the staff. Just as her aunt had instructed Marquis de Fauntil was on her right and Lord Esposito was on her left. She was making small talk with both of them but not ignoring any of them. After a few minutes, a compliment of serving maids came bearing tray upon tray of fragrant delights for their enjoyment. Lucia was watching their faces especially Lord Sposa who was salivating.

The rest of the time was spent amicably eating, drinking, and pledging their loyalty to this child turned woman. Lucia thought that they would test her at every turn but that she would be ready for the challenge. God help me she thought to herself. After they had exhausted themselves and were satisfied Lucia stood to leave. Lord Esposito who reached for her hand, "I pledge my loyalty to you Mistress Lucia. I am smitten by your grace, wit, and beauty. Please, you must come to visit me."

Lucia was surprised at his forward invitation but pleased. She looked him in the eye and said "Lord Esposito, I am grateful for your pledge and look forward to our meeting in Spain. I will come as soon as I can." He was still holding her hand and brushing his thumb across it. For a moment, Lucia felt uncomfortable and felt the crimson blush rush to her face. He saw it too and smiled broadly. He won the first round by catching her off guard. They both knew it but Lucia was displeased with her lack of self-control and gently pulled her hand from his grasp.

Lucia wanted to speak privately to Marquis de Fauntil. He came to her and she asked "Lord de Fauntil would you find some time before supper to meet with me privately?" The handsome older man seemed interested "Yes of course. Where and when?" "Shall we say at seven o'clock in the solar, if that is convenient for you?" He bowed deeply and replied, "I shall we waiting."

Lucia was the last to leave. She was both pleased and displeased with herself. She must learn to control her emotions. It was stupid and childish that she let Esposito get the better of her. Now he would think of her as a simple girl who cannot control her emotions. Stupid, stupid, stupid, she chastised herself.

Just as she expected the Marquis was waiting for her in the solar. Upon seeing her, he immediately rose and bowed deeply. "Good evening Mistress Lucia you look lovely this evening." Lucia just nodded and gave a slight curtsey and moved over to the chair next to where he was seated. "Please join me Lord de Fauntil." Once he was comfortably settled Lucia leaned forwards as if to make their conversation that much more intimate. "Lord de Fauntil it has come to my attention that most of the items we produce, such as olive oil and wine, are shipped to other parts of Europe and even America. I would, with your assistance, like to start our own shipping company. We could build our own ships and not only export our own goods but also sell space to others. What are your thoughts on such a venture?"

The Marquis de Fauntil, sat back in his chair, reached for the glass of wine that was on the table, and took a long swallow. He then leaned forward once again to respond, "I believe that would be a brilliant idea. We spend a considerable amount of money paid out to shipping companies when we could harvest that portion of the profits directly and open our cargo holds to others making the trip paid for by our customers." He sat back once again and looked deeply into Lucia's face, "How did you come to this idea Mistress?"

Lucia then sat herself back in contemplation of the answer. "After I had reviewed the ledgers for our shipping costs it seemed to me that even if it cost us a great deal of money to start our own ship line in the end we would profit from it." The marquis was smiling and nodding his head in support of this argument. "There is just one provision that I would make. I want Piro to be in charge of this new company. In your estimation is he ready?"

It took several moments of thought before the man responded, "I will oversee his management yet he will not even be aware that I have done so. I have faith in his abilities and he has proven to me his loyalty and intelligence. Why do you insist upon this particular young man?" Lucia looked down at her hands, which were on her lap she was not going to tell him the truth but felt that to lie would serve no purpose. "Piro almost died because of me and yet in his pain and sorrow he rescued me from near death. I feel that I must repay him in a way that will make him feel that he has become the man he promised me he would make of himself."

She knew that the man understood what she had said. "I respect your integrity and I thank you for your honesty. I do believe that such honesty will be difficult for you when you are faced against an enemy. Be cautious, there will be many who will try to harm you or deceive you. I have served your aunt for many, many, years, but, she is of a different cloth than yourself."

Lucia, touched by his concern replied, "I do not have the ability to lie, the truth is always written upon my face, but, I have found that the truth will ultimately always serve me well. I thank you for your concern and I would like to count you as my confidant and friend. May I do so?" The older man stood, came to stand in front of her, and bent his knee, "It would be my honor to serve you Marchesa. Call upon me at any time and I shall flee to your side." The Marquis de Fauntil took her hands in his and kissed them tenderly. Lucia knew she had an ally in this man.

"It is settled then. As soon as you can please make whatever inquiries are necessary for us to embark upon this new venture. I want you to be discreet and not announce our plans until we are sure of the profitability of doing so. I shall trust your judgment, just as my aunt has, to secure the best location and finest craftsmen. We shall build the best vessels afloat on the sea." By now, Lucia was standing directly facing the Marquis. "You may be confident in my discretion. I will gather all that is needed and send word to you as early as possible. I will bring Piro, with me so he may learn from the start."

"Shall we join the others for supper, suddenly I am famished." The handsome gentleman put out his arm for her and they walked companionably making small talk to the dining hall. Upon entering, all eyes were fixed to the elegant couple, and Lucia was beaming with pleasure. The Marquis walked her to her seat at the head of the table, bowed and retreated to his own place. At the far end of the table sat her Aunt Maria and Zio Giovanni, both of whom were flushed with delight at her appearance. Lucia, in a resounding voice, lifted her glass, and with a flourish said, "To my Zia and Zio, and to my Lords, may we all find our happiness. Salute!"

CHAPTER THREE

THE ABBEY

Montecassino

Lucia knew she needed to share the latest information with Abbot Vittorio from the Abbey at Montecassino. She also knew she needed to free herself of her guests. It was already day three and most of the guests had departed. Lucia wanted to spend some time with her dear brother Genaro as well.

"Genaro will you come with me to the Abbey de Montecassino, I need to visit with the good monks and bring them money for the poor. It will be on your way to Naples." Lucia's older brother was only too happy to accompany his beloved sister. "I have always wanted to see the great Abbey will you show me around when we arrive?" They were walking in the garden, it was a clear day, and the breeze off the sea carried the sweet scent of lemons. "This is such a peaceful place I could stay here forever." Lucia looked at her brother and said, "Dear brother, you cannot hide here in this remote place seeking refuse for your loneliness. I know how it feels to be isolated from the world. I have promised myself that I shall see all the great cities of Europe and maybe even someday to venture to America."

"Why do you think I want to hide?" Lucia stopped walking and turned to face her brother, "You want to hide your desires from the rest of the world. You have needs but are ashamed to show how you feel. You fear that you will be mocked and persecuted for your tastes. I do not blame you. I understand how you feel. I want to know what it is like to share intimate feelings with a man but I cannot for fear of what others will say or think. I am a woman, and no matter how much power and wealth I possess, I can only be the property of a man. The thought of being a wife chained to a husband is so painful. I am sick of the thought of it but there is no hope for either of us. You my dear brother can come and go as you please; if you find the right place in which to expose your true self."

"Lucia you will never be just another woman. You will never be just someone's wife. Already you are one of the most powerful women in all of Europe. You must marry some fool who will let you seek adventure." "Genaro, can you find me such a fool?" The mood had changed to lightheartedness and they were both grateful for it.

The small caravan that consisted of Lucia, Genaro, Nicko, and two armed guards, made their way to the Abbey de Montecassino. It was an excellent day to make the journey with the weather so fair. They chatted of simple things along the way. Genaro asked his sister, "Lucia, will you always have to travel under armed guard?" The expression on her face told her brother more than the words she answered him "Sadly, at least for now, I have but little choice for someone wishes me dead." She saw the shocked look on her brother's face "Why would anyone want you dead?" Lucia was hesitant to share with her sibling the man who had addressed himself as Antonio Sanfranco of Milan, but felt there would be no harm in his knowing. "The night of the gala I had secretly escaped to the garden to find a moment's solace in the fresh air and quiet to enjoy Zio's magnificent work, when I was suddenly interrupted by a man. He was tall and strikingly handsome. He spoke in a confident and educated manner. I believed he was one of the guests, most of whom I did not know. He seemed to have known a great deal about me. When I told him that I was at a loss for who is was he gallantly introduced himself with a bow and a flourish as Antonio Sanfranco of Milan."

Genero had a quizzical look of askance "But who dear sister is this man from Milan?" "Well, that was the point, when I asked Giorgio to check the guest list his name did not appear so I then inquired from Zio if he knew such a name. He did not know this man either. We reasoned it was someone, who out of curiosity had come uninvited to sneak a look at the grand affair. Then at the end of the evening I was saying my farewells to my guests and I looked up to the second floor balcony and right there under the life size painting of our grandfather, Mateo Rizzo, stood the mysterious man and he was the living image of the man in the painting."

Lucia paused in her story to watch the reaction of her brother. It was a look of confused horror. "Dear sister do you mean to tell me that this intruder came to be in the castle uninvited and was standing in the second floor balcony in front of our grandfather's portrait and was his image incarnate? How is that possible?" Lucia sighed deeply "That is the question for which neither I nor Zio has any answer, however, after making some inquiry it was found out that the man claiming to be Antonio Sanfranco of Milan is in fact a real person. He is known as a purveyor of the highest quality antiques, books, and manuscripts. He is very wealthy and highly regarded for his expertise of ancient items. His patrons are some of the wealthiest in the world. Unfortunately, he is also known to have ties to some of the worse criminals and is reputed to be ruthless and cunning."

"Yes, but, be that as it will, what is this connection to our grandfather and why would he want you killed?" "That is what we must ascertain." They continued in silence but kept to their thoughts. It was Genaro who said "I will be going to Milan very soon for I have a commission to work on the Basilica. While I am there I shall seek information regarding this man." Now Lucia was anxious "Genaro, please do not do this, from what Zio tells me this man is very dangerous, if he thinks you are a spy or a threat he might try to hurt you as well. Please promise me you will not do anything that would compromise your safety. Promise me." Her brother, his head bowed said, "I will do nothing to endanger myself. I promise."

By now, they were up to the main gate of the monastery. Its sprawling design and austere appearance did much to conceal its interior beauty. It was already midday and time for rest and food. Nicko had gone ahead to announce their arrival and seek their audience with the Abbot. Nicko was waiting for them at the main entrance to the grand building. The sight of the three intricately carved doors always struck Lucia. From the right side door emerged the toothless lay brother that had greeted Lucia so many times before. She had found that his name was Bruno. The scrawny lay brother with his perpetually soiled robe, beady eyes and toothless smile greeted her with his usual flair for drama.

"Ah, Mistress Lucia, it is always a welcomed pleasure to see you. You bring the sea and sun with you. Abbot Vittorio was happy to hear of your arrival. I shall have them prepare supper for you and your party." "It is I who is filled with joy to be back with such good friends and this holy place. Thank you as always Bruno for your warm welcome. I look forward to seeing the dear brothers. Come here by me." Lucia reached into her riding gown, pulled out a small purse, and handed it to the lay brother. "This is a small token for your help. Please do with it as you would like." The man, a little more than a scarecrow, hefted the purse, bowed his head, and said, "You are most generous My Lady, I am but your lowly servant, and a servant of the Lord, and I have no need for such a gift." Lucia pleased with his piety said "Bruno, you have earned this small token of my appreciation, if you cannot keep it then put it to use in the abbey coffers or give it to your kin. It is but a tiny reward." The man, who seemed never to have received a gift before, picked up his head and tears were running from his eyes. He knelt down, reached for her hand, and kissed it with much sincerity. "I shall share this with those in much greater need than myself. Thank you for your kindness My Lady."

This little scene was interrupted by a gentle cough from Nicko. The lay brother rose, bowed deeply, grabbed the reins of Apollo, and was heading for the stables. "Abbot Vittorio will see you now Mistress." "Thank you Nicko, please see to the horses and Bruno has said that a meal will be prepared for you and the men. I shall be here for as long as the Abbot will have time to speak with me." Nicko, the handsome and dutiful servant, bowed, turned on his heels and set off after the thin monk with his men and the horses.

"Come brother; let us visit with my old friend." Genaro followed his sister into the grand hall of the monastery. His eyes, once accustomed to the dimness within, could not hide his appreciation of the beauty and splendor of the place.

"Lucia, dear sister, this is a magnificent structure. These frescoes and mosaics must be hundreds, maybe thousands of years old. Do you think the Abbot will let me look around? I have on chance brought my book of sketches and would jump at the opportunity to make some drawings."

Lucia did not have to respond for coming from the east wing of the abbey was Abbot Vittorio who had heard the conversation. "Dear Mistress Lucia, my heart is filled with joy at the sight of you. This young man must be your brother; I can see the Banfi blood in his handsome face."

Bowing deeply, Lucia came to embrace the abbot. "Dear Abbot, it is always with great love and joy that I come to this grand place and to visit with you and your brothers. Yes, this is my beloved brother Genaro." Genaro bowed deeply, "Your Eminence, what an honor to meet you, my little sister speaks so highly of you and your brothers. This is an astounding place; I would love to see it." The abbot removed a small object from his robe pocket and with a click; there appeared a young boy clad in a white robe, its waist rope drooping from lack of hips to keep it in place. His face was flushed, and his thick black curly hair did not yet sport the customary tonsure. "Yes Abbot." "Marino, please see to the needs of Master Banfi. He would like a tour of our great monastery. First, see that he is well fed and has our best wine. You may dine with him if he so chooses." The young boy's face lit up like a pyre set to flame. "Yes Abbot." He bowed deeply then turned to Genaro "Master, please follow me, I shall be honored to see you around."

The Abbot and Lucia watched as her brother and the boy strolled leisurely away from them while Genaro with his head looking all around. She heard him say to the boy "Please call me Genaro." The two of them smiled in the easy way that old friends make their comfort. "Shall we have our supper in my private dining room? I presume that you have news I would want to hear shielded from public notice."
"That would be very good. Yes, I have news to share."

They retreated to the private rooms of the Abbot. Lucia who had never been in this part of the grand building found it to be comfortable but austere. They were greeted by another young boy, this one slightly older that Marino, and he wore the customary brown robe of the order and he had his shaven tonsure. "Brother Ambrose, this is Marchesa Banfi, she is an old friend and great patron to our monastery, and she and I will dine here in my room. Please bring food and wine, and then you may be dismissed until I call for you. Thank you."

"It is always a pleasure for me to come to Montecassino which fills me with peace and hope. I apologize for coming unannounced but time is of the essence." The abbot gestured to a chair by the fire. Lucia took it and waited until he had sat before speaking. "I come with news of Professor Fragoli and our missing manuscripts." The abbot sat in silence for a moment then said, "I can only guess it is not good news you bring since you come under armed guard." Lucia, her face pale, looked him in the eyes and said, "No it is not good news that I bring. I shall share with you a letter received by my Zio Giovanni Romano."

Lucia extracted the letter from her pocket and handed it to the monk. He felt the fine vellum and looked at the seal. He opened the letter with great care and began to read. Lucia watched his face to see what he would make of this news. When he was done but before he could comment there was a soft knock at the door. "Enter." Brother Ambrose was carrying a heavy tray, and in his shadow was a small kitchen maid also burdened by another heavy tray. They hurried to place the trays on the rough wooden table, gather the dishes and glasses from a sideboard and laid everything out for the feast, and when they were done, they both bowed deeply. "Thank you. Brother Ambrose, see that Marino has taken proper care of Master Genaro the Marchesa's brother." Again, the young monk bowed deeply, said nothing, and quietly closed the door upon existing.

They removed themselves to the table and partook of the simple but tasty food that was laid before them. The abbot reached for the wine and filled their glasses. They did not speak of the letter until they had finished their meal.

"This is a troubling letter that Lord Giovanni has received, it portends that the manuscripts have been discovered. It does not answer to the question of how many others are aware of their existence. Most unfortunate about Professor Fragoli, but, if it is true that he plotted your murder then he received God's punishment. I am most curious about this man, this Sanfranco. What do you make of him?"

Lucia related the whole story of the evening of the gala, of his uncanny resemblance to her grandfather and of the concerns of her Zio. "That my dear Lucia is a most fascinating story. It is intriguing, how he came to be in your castle? Moreover, how is it that he looks like your grandfather? If he had the professor killed, then he is a dangerous man. The fact that he is known to a man like Don Zingaro gives me pause for concern." "My Zio and I share the same concern that is why I must now live under the watchful eye of my personal bodyguard and armed men. He will be coming for the rest of the manuscripts that I am sure Professor Fragoli told him about. I pray that he does not make the connection between the manuscripts and this abbey."

Abbot Vittorio stood and walked over to her side and took her hand. "Lucia do not concern yourself with our safety. We may be simple monks but we have fought off many who would try to rob what treasures we have, I must pray for you. If he finds that we have replaced the originals with false copies, he surely will not be pleased. Yet I am troubled that this is not an ordinary thief, for he showed you his face and gave you his identity. This man seeks more than the manuscripts. I implore you to have your Zio find out who this man is and how he came to have the face of your grandfather." Lucia still pale at the thought of her would be assassin, held tight to the monk's hand "He is doing so as we speak but I must confess that I fear for his life as well as my own. I feel that if we get too close we shall get hurt."

"We are progressing, Brother Angelo, and I, in finally interpreting the ancient language of these Byzantine monks. It appears as though there was a secret place within which was contained something that Holy Mother Church had forbidden anyone to see. It refers to some evil knowledge. This object is said to be surrounded by the souls of the dead. We have been struggling with a particular passage for some time and cannot find meaning in its rendering. Perhaps you can find some ancient papers at Monteforte that ascribe to this unholy object that lies hidden among the souls of the dead. For now, we must content ourselves with what we can uncover from the remaining manuscripts. At least for now we have established a timeline which seems to start around 650 AD." Lucia was captivated with the information "I will do all that I can to find out anything that will be of help in solving this mystery. In a few weeks, I will be leaving on a year's journey to each location where I have companies. If you need to reach me, please do so through my Zio Giovanni. For now I must satisfy myself with knowing that the manuscripts are in good hands and soon enough we shall find all the missing answers."

"Dear Lucia, do you think it wise to travel so far from Monteforte and the protection of your family at this time?" She saw the depth of his fear in his eyes and responded, "I have vowed that whatever shall be the will of Jesus will be my fate. I shall not live my life cowering in a dark corner waiting for the face of my killer. I will live my life in the open. I will fight until I have no more breath but I will not live in fear, for if I did, then I would pray that Our Lord would take me to Himself and put me out of my misery." The monk nodded and said, "Lucia you are brave and beautiful and your faith in Jesus Christ will always keep you on the road to righteousness. Trust few and be cautious. I shall forever keep you in my heart and my prayers. As soon as I discover anything new, I shall call upon Master Romano and give him word. Be wary of those who would befriend you for you are too precious and honest and would not see the face of the Devil even if he were standing in your midst." He said "Marchesa Lucia Banfi, come and knee before the altar so that I may impart a special blessing upon you."

Lucia rose and followed the monk to the far side of the room where stood a small but impressive altar. He took a sacred shawl from the table that held the ewer and pitcher. He kissed the shawl, placed it around his neck, put his hands into the pockets at the end of the shawl, went to the tabernacle, and removed the monstrance, which housed the body of Christ from its holy place. Without touching the golden vessel with his hand and only using the cloth of the shawl, he placed it on the altar facing Lucia. He kneeled down and prostrated himself before it. Lucia dropped to her knees, closed her eyes, and prayed for God's blessings. Standing, the Abbot took hold of the golden monstrance and faced the kneeing Lucia. "In the name of the Father, the Son, and the Holy Spirit" he intoned while making the sign of the cross with the vessel in his hands. Turning, he returned it to the altar, opened its face and removed a white round wafer, which he laid upon a golden dish.

"Lucia Banfi, Marchesa of Monteforte, do you renounce the Devil and all his works?" "I do." "Do you swear before God that you will strive to follow the voice of our Lord Jesus Christ?" "I do." He then walked over to her and stood in front of her with the wafer in his hand; he then came to her. "Lucia have you confessed your sins before the Lord your God?" "I have." "Then take this body and blood of our Lord and fall under his protection." Lucia lifted her head and stuck out her tongue to receive the wafer. She then prostrated herself before the altar and stayed that way for a few minutes. When the abbot had replaced the golden monstrance back into the tabernacle and removed his shawl, she came back to her knees and waited for him to come to her. "Mi benedica Lucia Banfi e può lo spirito di Saint Michael guarda e proteggere dalla malvagità e sneers del diavolo." Lucia relished in the blessing for protection from Saint Michael the Archangel who was a great warrior against the Devil. The abbot then anointed the sign of the cross upon her forehead and lifted her to her feet. He held her face in his hands and kissed each cheek. "I love you Lucia and will pray for your safety."

"Let us go and search for my dear brother who is just now so excited to see the treasures of this beautiful place. Dear Abbot, before I go can we go to the Chapel of Relics so that I may prostrate myself in their honor." "Of course, I am only too happy for your faith Lucia." They made their way to the Chapel of Relics and he left her there to find Genaro. When she was done, she met them in the grand hall waiting for her to arrive. "Beloved sister I am filled with joy for having come. Thank you for bringing me to this wonderful place." Genaro then turned to the Abbot "Dear Abbot, my sister is of great faith, I only wish that I had such strength of character, it has renewed my soul to come to this holy place. Thank you and young Marino for a wonderful day filled with peace."

"Genaro, were you satisfied with our art. I know you are a great artist and have been commissioned even by the Holy Father himself for work at the Vatican. Did you make many drawings?" "I am but a simple artist who by the luck of God have found some favor among those who can further my little talents. Here see for yourself what has inspired me from your grand monastery. You can be the judge of what I have done."

Abbot Vittorio took the book that Genaro handed him and leafed through the pages. He was awe struck by the raw beauty of what the artist had rendered onto paper. "I am astounded at how you have captured the essence of this place. The beauty of your interpretation is a true gift from God. You are blessed with this natural talent." Genaro felt himself blush with pride "Thank you Abbot for your kindness and generosity." Lucia leaned over to the monk and asked him to bless her brother. "Kneel down Genaro." He reached for the young man's hands and holding them said "May Our Lord in his infinite mercy continue to make these hands create beauty in His image. May He love and protect you all the days of your life. Amen." He then made the sign of the cross on each hand and on his forehead. Helping him up he gave Genaro a manly embrace and to both of them said "May the peace of Christ be with you."

They went outside and waiting for them were their horses as well as Nicko and the two guards. While Genaro mounted his horse, Lucia embraced the Abbot and kissed both cheeks. "I will hear from you soon. I shall pray for you dear Abbot. Until we again find ourselves in each other's company be safe and farewell." She turned to Nicko who gave her his hands to boast her into her saddle. "Are we ready Mistress?" "Yes Nicko, let us go home." They left the monastery and they rode for a long way in silence each savoring the solace that is Montecassino.

"So dear brother did you enjoy your day at the abbey?" Genaro's face broke into a wide smile "I did. I was speechless at the artistry of its treasures. I felt a peace that descended upon me the moment I stepped foot into the place. It is hard to describe such a feeling." "There is no need to describe it for I feel that way every time I am there. I am so happy you came." "As am I; as am I."

CHAPTER FOUR

THRUST AND STEP

Monteforte

Lucia was unhappy that Genaro had to leave she truly enjoyed her brother's company. "Genaro when will I see you again?" She stood there, nearly as tall as her brother, yet like a little girl, with her eyes filled with tears and her lips pouting. He came to her and embraced her with great affection "Ah, little sister I must be about my work. I shall come for Antoinetta's wedding in three months. I understand from Zio Luigi that he is to receive his appointment as Bishop shortly before the wedding and so I shall see you twice within the next three months. Do not despair I shall write to you." He hugged her and brushing back an errant curl from her alabaster skin said, "I love you sister and I am so proud of you. I do believe you are perhaps the only person in the world who understands me. Thank you Lucia. Be careful. I will look forward to our next meeting." He kissed her on each cheek.

"Please be well my sweet brother. I will pray for you every day that you may find happiness. We shall talk some more the next time we meet. I love you Genaro." The young artist fixed himself on his horse and started off. Lucia stood in the shadow of the front loggia and watched as her brother rode off to begin his next commission in Milan. Suddenly, she remembered something and started to run after him. She caught up with him after shouting his name and he pulled up his horse and waited for her to reach him. Winded from the strain she managed to catch her breath. "What is so important that you are running like a deer at the sight of a hunter?" Having composed herself, she said, "Do not confront Antonio Sanfranco when you reach Milan. Make some careful inquiries, but do not go directly to him. Zio says he is very dangerous. Promise me Genaro." "Lucia do you take me for a fool or know me to be a warrior? I will not confront this man but will only observe him. I promise to keep myself safe." "That is good because if anything should happen to you on my account I will kill myself." They laughed in that easy way that siblings know the limits of their own humor. "May I go now Marchesa Banfi?" Lucia did not answer but gave his horse a smart slap on the ass and he took off with a start, which took Genaro by surprise. "I will get you for that little sister," he shouted over his shoulder as his horse galloped away. Lucia shouted back "I love you." He waved and yelled back, "I love you Lucia." He was too far already and she started back to the castle.

Giovanni Romano greeted her at the front steps of the castle. "Ah, there you are. I have been searching for you and Giorgio told me you were out saying farewell to Genaro. Are you ready for your first lesson?" Lucia was excited "Yes dear Zio I am ready." "Very well then we shall go to the stables and get started."

The day was warm but clear and bright. Lucia had her riding gown on and felt comfortable. Giovanni Romano had removed his waistcoat and only had on his tunic. His lean muscular body was that of a man who was years younger. He wore his customary patch over his damaged eye and caught his greying hair in a leather thong. "Lucia I want to teach you how to defend yourself if someone comes from behind." Lucia was intent on learning how to protect herself and was an eager student. Her Zio had selected a beautifully balanced honed dagger much like the one she always carried but this one had belonged to her grandfather. It was inlaid with precious stones and ivory. The hilt was of a good proportion to the length and weight of the shaft so the instrument held its balance.

Lucia at the instruction of her Zio held the dagger in the palm of her hand. "How does it feel?" The sun had caught hold of the polished steel and a ray of light glinted off its shaft. "I like the way it feels. It is comfortable in my hand." "Good. Now I shall pretend that I am an attacker and approach you from behind. I will have your seamstress design a pocket for the weapon that will be concealed in all your garments. It will be of my own design but for now you are to tuck it into the sash of your waist." Obediently Lucia slipped the beautiful dagger into her sash. Giovanni Romano came to face her. His face, which bore the scars of years of living hard, were now softened by his love for this young woman. "Listen to me Cara; you will always react the same way if someone surprises you from behind. Your first reaction is to struggle, that is natural. What you must discipline your mind to do is not to struggle but to keep a level head. How is this possible you ask?"

"When I grab for you it will be around the throat. I will want to cut off your breath before I finish you off with the weapon. If you do not panic, you will have a second or two to reach for your weapon. More than likely it will be a man who comes for you. With the heel of your shoe grind it into his foot and with your free hand reach for his groin and with all the strength you have squeeze until he loosens his grip on you. Turn as quickly as you can and set your stance. He will try to throw you off balance. Here look at me. I have set my feet in such a manner that it would be difficult to knock me down." Lucia observed his stance and copied his form. He nodded his approval. "Very good, and now that you are facing your assailant stay at arm's length with both your hands wound tightly around your weapon. Shove the blade as forcefully and as deeply as you can into the heart, then, with all your strength bring the blade down through the stomach. Again, watch the movement I am making." While they were, talking and making moves Gandolfo appeared with a pike upon which was the effigy of a man dressed with a mask over his face. He drove the pike into the ground and said, "This is a very bad man. You should practice upon his wicked body." They all laughed but it was not a joyous laugh for they knew only too well that these lessons were meant to save Lucia's life. The two older men, not to instill fear in her were trying to make light of the situation.

Their practice went on for hours and while she was exhausted and hot, Lucia did not complain. She wanted to learn how to defend herself. Finally, at midday with the sun raining down upon them the three decided to quit for the day. "Tomorrow we shall handle a sword." Giovanni Romano who was visibly tired came over to her and put his arm around her "This is hard work Bella but you have done well and have made no complaints. I am very proud of you." Gandolfo said, "I have taught many a young man how to use a dagger and none did as well as you." Lucia looked at her Master of the Horse and said "Gandolfo that is very sweet for you to say but don't lie to me." "Mistress I swear to you on all that is holy. Young men try to be too rough or act too much with their back not their head. You have proven that patience and intelligence is a far greater weapon. Well done." Giovanni Romano was standing with his hands on his hips smiling and nodding "Lucia you know Gandolfo is right in what he says. You are a good student. Come let us get you some nourishment or you will die from lack of food and drink." "Thank you both for training me. I will try hard." Lucia then bowed to both men and went off to wash the dirt and sweat from her face and hands. "Zio I shall catch up with you after I wash."

The next day the training commenced once again. Lucia had just completed her daily ride on Apollo. Both rider and horse pulled into the stables anxious to get started on the days training. This time it was the sword.

Giovanni Romano was waiting for her to dismount. "Good morning Bella. Did you have a nice ride?" "Good morning dear Zio; Apollo and I always love to ride and watch the sun come up over the mountains." Her Zio watched her dismount and she approached him and gave him a kiss on each cheek. "Shall we begin before the sun gets too high?" Lucia was excited she enjoyed the physical exertion and the feeling of being in control. "I am ready." With that, her Zio handed her a long sword. Never having held a sword Lucia was amazed at its weight. "Wielding a sword is all about stance. As with the dagger or any weapon if your opponent can knock you down then they hold a better chance at overpowering you. You are a woman but you are strong and tall so use those to your credit. I want you to stand with your feet spread apart but not side by side. Put the right foot in an open position and left slightly behind it. Try it." Lucia felt like she could spring into action if she had to.

From the stable door, she could see Gandolfo heading over to lend a hand in her instruction. Lucia could also see that a small audience of grooms and

kitchen maids had also gathered. She felt a slight embarrassment but continued with her lesson. "Ah Gandolfo I see we have an audience of spectators this morning. Well perhaps we should give them a show. Will you be the worthy opponent for the Mistress?" " With pleasure." Gandolfo armed himself with one of the three swords that were on display. He took up his position. "Lucia now I want you to visually mark your opponent. Check his height, look at his arms." Lucia interrupted "Arms?"
"Yes his arms and legs to see what his reach could be. Now Gandolfo is of a fair height for a man so he will be a good marker. However, the most important thing to be sure is to hold contact with your opponent's eyes. His eyes will help you determine his next move. You must block out all distractions and concentrate on his movement. Do you understand?"

Lucia was sizing Gandolfo up and down, and determined that he would have a substantial reach, due based on the length of his arms and legs. "Yes Zio I understand. I am ready." Gandolfo came circling around her and pretended to lunge at her but she backed away. Lucia made the initial thrust and nearly caught him in the neck. The two men were stunned and the crowd cheered. Gandolfo decided to be more aggressive and swung his sword high and Lucia blocked it, the sound of steel on steel resounded in the air. There was much tension and the game was getting heated. Giovanni Romano was circling giving Lucia instructions. Lucia thrust once more and Gandolfo managed to overpower her with his free hand. She remained locked in his grasp but then swept her leg behind his and the Master of Horse hit the ground with a thud. The small crowd went wild with excitement. Lucia went over to him and extended her hand to help him to his feet. Gandolfo was red faced but grabbed for her hand and in one swift movement brought her to the ground as well.

"Never feel sorry for your opponent. Never trust that your opponent is critically injured and never, ever, turn your back on your opponent unless you know for sure he is dead." There was much yelling and clapping for both opponents. At first Lucia was angry but then realized that Gandolfo was absolutely right and it was a lesson she would not forget. They both laughed and he said seriously "I am sorry Mistress but someday you will remember this small affront and thank me." "I know Gandolfo, better to lose my pride than my head." With that, he rose and graciously helped his mistress to her feet with a deep bow.

Giovanni Romano was laughing as well and the three bowed to the standing crowd who repaid them with cheers and shouts. "Now get back to work," shouted Gandolfo and the small crowd scattered instantly.

"You see how easily one can be disarmed. Today we can laugh at the situation but if Gandolfo were an assassin, you would be dead. Do not pity your opponent, you are there to kill, or be killed. Do you now understand exactly what is at stake Bella?" Lucia saw no humor in her Zio's eye, he was fearful for her safety and she did understand that this was not any plaything but a deadly weapon. "I do understand the importance of everything you have both told me."

"Thank you Zio and you too Gandolfo for your love and support. I will remember all that I have been taught." Gandolfo came to her and embraced her in a fatherly hold. "Please Mistress we wary. I have seen many things in my time here at Monteforte. There will be those who will hate you, not only for your power, but also for your beauty. I will pray for you every day." She was touched by his kindness, and kissed each cheek. "Thank you dear Gandolfo."

Giovanni Romano and his prize student made their way back to the castle. "Bella, if you remain calm and use your wits you will be a formidable opponent to anyone. Remember that size and strength cannot overcome intelligence and cunning. You are a brilliant woman use that always as your most important weapon." Lucia felt a sense of pride at his words. "Oh one more thing, assassins come in all forms." "What do you mean Zio?" "Someone disguised as a priest for instance, or a child, a mother with children, an old beggar, you never know. An assassin can wear the face of a friend; even a lover.

Your gut will tell you when, and who, not to trust and you must listen to that inner voice. I have survived all these years because I was cautious and trusted only myself, if not I would be long dead."

CHAPTER FIVE

THE ORDINATION

Naples

The next few weeks were hectic for the whole family. Rafaela and Donato were both staying at Monteforte in preparation of Antoinetta's wedding to the dashing Tomaso Catalano. They seemed perfectly matched and very much in love. They all agreed that the wedding ceremony would take place at the Abbey de Montecassino, and concelebrated by both their Zio Luigi and Abbot Vittorio. The wedding feast would be held at Monteforte. Between the two families and invited guests there were two hundred people coming to help celebrate the union of two powerful families.

Antoinetta was fortunate that the castle and its magnificent gardens had all been refurbished for the gala only six months prior. Antoinetta was like a queen bee buzzing all over the castle. Rafaela had outdone herself with the creation of the most extravagant wedding gown. Antoinetta looked like a tiny doll all dressed up in yards and yards of the finest silk money could buy. The crown she would wear was a family heirloom of cut diamonds. Rafaela was sewing tiny pearls on the veil and lace trim. Even the dress that Antoinetta chose for her sister as well as the two attendants was lovely. Lucia held the tiniest bit of jealousy for her sister's happiness yet knew she could not be like her sister in wishing to be married.

With most of the family gathered in anticipation of the wedding the first order of business would be their attendance at the ordination of Luigi Rizzo to the office of Bishop of Naples. The Rizzo and Banfi families were filled with so much joy at these two blessed events.

It was early in the morning when Lucia arrived at the Basilica of The Immaculate Conception. She wanted to see her Zio before the ceremony for his ordination to Bishop and before all the others arrived. Between family and his faithful flock, more than five hundred people would be present. She had instructed Nicko that she would see her Zio alone and that her two armed guards were to wait outside of the Church until after the services. Lucia made her way to the sacristy. Since it was more than two hours before Luigi Rizzo would be ordained, she knew she had time to talk to him. Upon entering the sacristy, she saw the powerful figure of her Zio kneeling at his prie dieu. Lucia did not want to disturb him and was about to turn and leave when he addressed her "Dear Lucia what brings you to me?" Lucia was pleased that he had called her back.

"Oh Zio Luigi, I did not mean to disturb your prayers, this is such an important day for all of us. I have come early to make my confession. Will you find time for me?" "For you Bella Lucia I will always have time. Come let us make our way to my private confessional." They walked companionably towards the back of the old sacristy until they came to a curtained recess in an alcove. "Go in and I shall hear your confession."

"Bless me father for I have sinned, it has been two months since my last confession. I need to know if it is a sin to withhold a secret but will tell it later on?"

"Lucia I am confused. You have a secret but cannot tell it at this time?" "Yes." "But it is your intention to share it with someone who is affected by it later on?" "Yes." There was a brief moment of silence then the deep voice of her Zio came back through the latticed partition. "If by not telling your secret does not harm anyone, than I cannot believe it to be a sin, however, if withholding the information contained in that secret can cause harm and you, for selfish reasons, have not shared the secret then that is a sin. Do you understand?" "I do understand Zio and I do not believe at this time my secret will cause harm to anyone but me."

Upon hearing the last remarks, her Zio slid back the wooden lattice and looked directly upon her face. They were so close she could feel the warmth of his breath on her cheek. "Lucia, are you in any trouble? If so you can tell me, and I will help you." "No, well not exactly. There is reason to believe that someone is trying to kill me. Zia Maria and Zio Giovanni are aware of it and so I go everywhere with

Nicko and two armed guards." "Who is this person who wants you killed and why?" There was now genuine concern in the priest's voice. "A man named Antonio Sanfranco of Milan. Zio he looks exactly like your father." There was complete silence. "I remember that my father used to take trips to Milan all the time. One day I wanted to go with him but he refused. I followed him and was sure that he did not discover that I had done so. He went to stay in this beautiful house right in the heart of Milan. I remember because a most elegant woman answered the door and gave my father a loving embrace. I wonder if that has anything to do with this mysterious man from Milan." Lucia felt as if her uncle who was now making his own confession. "Did you ever question him about the woman?" "No of course not he would have beaten me to within an inch of my life. My father was not a very pleasant man." Lucia went on to confess some minor infractions but silently asked God to forgive her for not mentioning her lustful feelings. She would have been too embarrassed to tell her Zio that she wanted to lay with a man. She would speak directly and privately to God about that problem. She finished her confession and her Zio gave her absolution and a decade of the rosary for her penance. They emerged from the confessional and Zio Luigi did not say another word regarding what had just transpired. She knew he would tell no one of her confession.

"I will leave you now dear Zio to find your thoughts before the ceremony begins." He embraced her with a powerful hold and whispered in her ear "May the Blessed Mother watch over you Lucia. Be careful and know that I will also be here for you." He then pushed her to arm's length and looked at her appraisingly "You are the image of my mother whom I loved so much." He then gave her a kiss on each cheek and made the sign of the cross on her forehead. "Now go and get the best seat in the church. I will keep you always in my heart and my prayers."

Lucia scurried off to get a first row seat. You could feel the excitement, seeing the faithful filing into the enormous church. There was a hushed buzz throughout, with young boys running here and there lighting candles, polishing chalices, filing bottles with wine or water and preparing the incense. The altar had been arranged with two magnificently carved Rococo chairs upholstered in a deep red velvet, a third chair, which was smaller and not as elaborately ornamented was placed directly in front of the other two but centered between them.

There was a table set to one side of the altar laid with a white vestment, the liturgical headdress of two pieces of stiffened silk, which was tall and pointed, two gold lappets hanging from the back, with precious jewels on the simple white hat, called the Helmet of Salvation. There was a gleaming gold shepherd's staff lying there as well. Lucia had read about these symbols of the Office of Bishop.

Her attention was drawn to the choir loft, where the massive organ filled the space with a resounding sound. A choir of young priests filled the overhead loft. Their bright young faces glistened with excitement. The older priest worked feverishly to tune the organ before the ceremony began.

Lucia's family was beginning to arrive. She was happy to see her Zia and Zio, her parents and her siblings as well as many other extended family members. Each one came to her in an expression of respect even though she was the youngest member of the family. Lucia felt slightly awkward but accepted her position with great humility. The Basilica was filled to capacity with those arriving late having to make do with standing in every free inch of space spilling to the outside. There was a controlled volume of respectful speaking.

Young nuns clad in black robes the only portion of their flesh showing was a small opening for their faces. The headdresses were stiff white and looked very uncomfortable. They moved in silent precision about the naïve of the church directing local dignitaries and their families to reserved pews. The mother superior was overseeing their operation with a stern expression having taken up a position of some authority at the back of the altar.

The sun played upon the stained glass windows casting prisms of jewel toned rays down into the pews. This was truly a grand structure with its soaring groin vaulted ceiling in the Gothic style architecture. Lucia was soaking in all the sights, sounds and smells and was vibrating with anticipation. It was a great honor to have a Bishop, her dear Zio Luigi, conferred with this position of importance within the Roman Catholic Church.

From up high the resounding bellows of the organ began filling the air with music. The young priests and other members of the choir began their mournful chanting. All eyes focused toward the rear of the Basilica and then the procession commenced. Two dozen altar boys in their black robes topped with white smocks carried lit candles, followed by little girls dressed in nuns' habits with only their rose-colored tiny faces beaming from under their headdresses. Yet another dozen young priests, a dozen brown robed monks, a column of nuns and finally two priests robed in magnificent vestments, followed them. Lucia was shocked to see that one of them was none other than Abbot Vittorio. For some unexplainable reason she felt such a sense of pride upon seeing him. She had never seen him in any other garment but his brown robe. He walked with an air of humble dignity.

The last person to bring up the rear of this impressive procession was Luigi Angelo Rizzo. The imposing figure of her uncle, who was so simply dressed in the basic white cassock he wore. Upon his thick black hair sat the zucchetto, the round skullcap, symbol of his new office. As the players in this long line found their places, the two richly vested men took up their seats on the altar. For one second Abbot Vittorio caught the eye of Lucia and sent her a broad smile and a nod of his head. She acknowledged it with her own warm smile and slight bow. Everyone's attention was focused on the person of Luigi Rizzo.

Approaching the altar, he suddenly dropped to the stone floor and prostrated himself before the two figures that were now standing in front of the altar. After a few minutes of complete silence with his body prostrated and his face pressed to the stone a small group of young priests began surrounding the inert body incanting him with clouds of incense which engulfed his body. The Bishop of Florence and Abbot Vittorio came down from the altar and circled the body chanting prayers in ancient Latin. Each man dipped into a golden bucket filled with holy water and sprinkled Luigi Rizzo with its healing droplets. The whole ceremony took about twenty minutes. Finally, with two of the young priests to assist, Luigi Rizzo arose.

Abbot Vittorio came forward and speaking only to her uncle, placed his hands upon his head, and chanted some prayers. Without calling for him, a young priest appeared at the Abbot's side with a large book. The Abbot's usually soft voice now resounded in the confines of the church. After he had said the prayers in Latin, the music resumed. A monk and a priest came forward carrying the vestments of the office of Bishop. Now for the first time she saw that the priest was her brother Francesco. Lucia was thrilled that her own brother was there to be part of her Zio's ordination. Together they carefully dressed the newly anointed bishop from head to toe. Placing the Bishops Miter, which is the liturgical headdress of the office upon his head, and handing him a golden staff encrusted with jewels. The other Bishop had been watching alongside Abbot Vittorio and now the three men all came upon the altar. In a deep baritone, the Bishop of Florence addressed the gathered faithful.

"Dear Brothers and Sisters in Christ, today you have witnessed the ordination of Luigi Angelo Rizzo who has been elevated to the Office of Bishop of Naples. We must keep Bishop Rizzo in our prayers for he has much responsibility now as the shepherd of so many faithful souls. It is with joy and a prayerful heart that I would like to introduce Bishop Luigi Angelo Rizzo of Naples." Everyone stood and shouts of good blessings were echoed throughout the massive church. Tears were streaming down Lucia's face and she silently prayed for his protection. Lucia saw that her Aunt Maria was also crying as was her mother and grandmother, actually all the family even the men were in tears. Her Zio graciously waved and nodded to the crowd his own eyes filled with tears.

This was such an honor to be bestowed on the Rizzo family. The joyous chatter slowly diminished as the organ began once more to spew out the mournful sounds that infused the church with its music. The monks and priests were singing beautiful chants from high up in the choir loft, their rich voices filling the space with soothing melody. Lucia was filled with love and faith. It was time for receiving the Holy Eucharist and the lines were forming to come to the altar. Zio Luigi was in the center with Abbot Vittorio and the Bishop of Florence on either side. It was an astounding sight and its importance was not lost on those gathered.

Lucia and her family were the last to receive the sacred host, which was served to them by their Zio. She knelt down at the altar rail, her hands clasped together, her head tilted back with her eyes fixed on the massive crucifix with the corpus of Jesus nailed to it. So entranced in her thoughts Lucia did not see the person next to her; she was so anxious for her turn to receive she put out her tongue and was waiting for the wafer to touch it. She saw the smiling face of her Zio Luigi as he reached into the golden chalice to retrieve the host, which he laid upon her tongue, and then he made the sign of the cross on her forehead. As he stepped to the man next to Lucia, his face froze in surprise. Kneeling next to her was Antonio Sanfranco hands folded upon the altar rail and smiling. It was only then that she realized that these two men could be twins were it not for the age difference. Luigi saw the resemblance and was stunned. Antonio was not troubled, tilted his head back, and extended his tongue to receive the sacred host. Luigi went through the motions of laying the host upon his tongue but could not believe his eyes that he was seeing his own image in this man's face. Upon receiving the host, Antonio stood, made the sign of the cross, nodded to both Luigi and Lucia, and casually walked away.

By this time, the rest of the family were now settled into their pews, caught a glimpse of what had happened and looked on in shock. Their heads looking from Luigi to Antonio and their expressions were that of amazed disbelief. It was her grandmother, Helena, who seemed the most affected by the sight of this intruder. Even though this scene only took a few moments, it seemed like time had stood still around them. Lucia was transfixed with watching the man who looked like her grandfather and Zio walk out of the church as if it were all normal. As he reached, the outer door of the church he turned and his eyes met Lucia's and he smiled broadly bowed then left. Lucia felt a spark of excitement and instinctively fingered the dagger in her pocket. A hot flush had come to her and she was annoyed with herself.

Giovanni Romano who caught sight of him and wanted to follow in pursuit but Maria held him back. She whispered in his ear "We will do nothing to bring dishonor to Luigi. This is his day and a proud day for my family. You will need to explain all this to me later." Giovanni knew that Maria was upset and that he would have to tell her the whole story from the beginning. He also knew that she would be angry with him for not sharing it sooner but he would deal with that later. He bent he head and replied, "Of course Cara, I would never do anything to bring stain on the family especially on Luigi. We will talk. I love you." He grabbed her hand and gave her a loving squeeze. She nodded.

After Mass, invited guests were received in the new residence of the Bishop of Naples where a lavish reception was held to celebrate this important day. Many people were invited and there was much joy. Maria Sucretti had sent her chef, Marcello, and his staff, to assist in the preparation of a sumptuous feast. Casks of the finest vintage from the Rizzo vineyards had been sent for this occasion. Everything was perfect, at least on the surface. While the presence of Antonio Sanfranco was not mentioned in public, the immediate family knew something was wrong.

Lucia made her way over to Abbot Vittorio "I am so pleased that you are here for my Zio. It was such a pleasant surprise to see you." The Abbot smiled "I am sure you did not recognize me at first in my lavish vestments." He joked with her but he knew she was troubled for he too had seen the man who looked like her Zio. "Lucia, was that the man who was at the gala?" Lucia's expression instantly changed "Yes it is. Do you see how he is the image of my Zio? He also looks exactly like my grandfather Mateo. What is this man trying to do?" Abbot Vittorio took her by the arm and walked to a quiet corner of the grand room. "Dear Sweet Lucia, do you not realize that this man is trying to instill fear in you. He knows of the manuscripts and their worth. Yet I am troubled as to his appearance. Could he be a child of Mateo Rizzo? The resemblance to both your grandfather and your Zio is not just a coincidence." She was about to answer when they were joined by Giovanni Romano "We all saw him. Now what do we do? This man is a ghost and shows up everywhere. We must find him and find out what he wants." The monk spoke "Giovanni I do believe we know that he wants the manuscripts. Yet there is more to this than basic greed. The fact that he is a mirror image of Mateo and Luigi Rizzo is very unsettling. At some point we must talk with Helena and Luigi to see if they can account for this man." "I too was thinking along those thoughts. The time has come to make the family aware of what has happened. Do you agree Lucia?"

During this conversation between Giovanni Romano and the Abbot, Lucia was deep in her own thoughts. "Lucia?" "Ah, yes, it is necessary for now we are all in danger and I fear that you too Abbot have been compromised. This man I sense will stop at nothing to achieve his ends." A look of sadness fell upon her beautiful face. Giovanni Romano spoke, "I will make arrangements for all of us to have a meeting at Monteforte. We will all be gathered for Antoinetta's wedding next week so that will give us time to make a plan." The Abbot had been asked to join some other priests and dignitaries, which left Giovanni and Lucia standing alone. "Your Zia Maria is quite upset as you might imagine. She wants me to give her a full accounting of what this is all about." "I am so sorry Zio for placing you in this position. I shall ride back to Monteforte with you and Zia and together we can explain the situation." Giovanni seemed relieved at the suggestion and nodded. Secretly, Lucia was not at all pleased with the situation. She dreaded the thought that her Aunt Maria felt that she had been deceived. It would not be a pleasant ride back to the castle.

CHAPTER SIX

PROOF

Milan

Antonio Sanfranco laid his beloved mother Felisa to rest in the churchyard of Our Lady of Sorrows. Every day for as long as he could remember Felisa Sanfranco would look out her bedchamber window into that churchyard which was simple but beautiful and say to her son "Antonio, someday I will be buried there." Little did she, or her son, know that it was reserved for members of the religious order and not for laypersons. Besides, it was a known fact that Felisa had been a prostitute and therefore in a state of mortal sin. After much pleading and an ample donation to the church coffers, Father Peter was persuaded to make an exception for this penitent woman. After all, Jesus himself forgave Maria Magdalene who was a prostitute. It was only fitting that Felisa should be buried there.

After all arrangements had been satisfied, the exquisite casket was carried on the shoulders of six young men clad in black waistcoats. After the Mass of the Resurrection, the priest, followed by Antonio and the small gathering of mourners, were led down the church steps and into the churchyard. The grave, which Antonio had selected, was directly facing the villa his mother had lived in until her death. He turned from the casket and looked up to the window where she would have stood. He squinted against the brilliant sun yet could not see her. There was a small procession of friends and neighbors, several of Antonio's acquaintances but a rather tiny group in all. When they reached the grave, the casket was lowered to the wooden boards that were placed over the gaping hole. The smell of freshly turned earth filled Antonio's nostrils. He could not weep.

It was a warm day and the sun was already high in the sky. The pallbearers were sweating under the burden of the heavy casket. It was as if Antonio was watching from up in his mother's window. The whole scene was so unreal to him. The priest was speaking in a low monotone; the altar boy was holding the vessel with the holy water. When he had finished his prayers, the priest nodded to the altar boy who brought forth the vessel of water and the scepter, which he now handed to the priest who began sprinkling the liquid on top of the casket while chanting in the same dull monotone. "Riposo eterno concedere a lei e lasciate che perpetua luce splendere su di lei. Lei può riposare in pace. Nel nome del padre, del figlio e dello Spirito Santo. Amen." It was done. The gravediggers, who had been discreetly standing in the shade of a nearby tree, now emerged with their shovels in hand. They bowed deeply to the priest then to Antonio and proceeded to their task. The planks holding the casket over the hole were slid out and the once pristine box, which held the remains of his mother, immediately fell into the hole with a loud crack and a thud. Those gathered came forward and threw roses into the open hole then turned to Antonio with their condolences. He thanked them for coming and then they were gone. He stayed and watched as each man filled his shovel from the pile of earth that had been lying to the side. With every rock that struck the ornately carved box, Antonio's heart ached. Finally, when they had completed their task the men moved silently away from the sodden grave. He stood there in the brilliant sunlight and now for the first time he began to cry. Antonio was struck by the realization that he was truly alone in the world. He was scared. He found himself back in his mother's room but could not remember how he got there. It was already dark. He had not eaten or drank anything in two days and he was starting to feel the effects of this fast. He had been sitting at the foot of his mother's bed. It was a perfect reproduction of King Louis XV's bed at Versailles. He had been so excited to give it to his mother. It was the first purchase he had ever made as a young man. The thought of it warmed him.

He stood but felt the blood rush to his head. He felt weak and his stomach was watery. He spied the little servant's bell on the night table and rang gently. His mother's maid, Alba, appeared in the doorway. "Master Antonio I tried to wake you several times but you were very tired. I shall prepare some food and wine for you. You do not have good color." He saw the old woman, who had been with him and his mother for twenty years, "Thank you Alba I think I am hungry. Call for me when it is ready." The old woman bowed and left him in the darkness of the receding light.

Antonio was thinking of where he would begin to unravel his life. Upon her deathbed, his mother had revealed some startling information. For the first time in his life, he felt that he had a pedigree. He was determined to find out more about himself. In the box that his mother had kept hidden, he discovered letters of transfer to the Bank of Milan. Tomorrow he would go there and find the documents that she told him he would find. For now, he would nourish his body and then he would feed his soul.

When morning came, Antonio who had slept in his mother's bed felt renewed and comforted by the scent of her, which still lingered in the room. He got up and looked out the window down into the churchyard and there was the bare grave, which stood out among those that were covered in grass and decorated with headstones. Yet, even though, it was raw and standing alone he felt good that she could look up into her window and see him looking at her. He made a mental note to visit the stonecutter later in the day. He vowed to give her the most beautiful headstone that anyone ever had.

Alba had his breakfast ready "Good morning Master Antonio. Praise Jesus that you have regained your color. You must take care of yourself. Master I am sorry to ask but now that Mistress Felisa is gone will you be dismissing me? Please forgive me for asking but I would need to find somewhere to live." Antonio had not thought about what he would do with his mother's villa. "No Alba, I will keep this place and would ask that you stay on here. Is that acceptable to you?" He could see the relief in her face "Oh Master Antonio you have been like a son to me. I have loved you since I first came to serve your Momma. She was a good woman and very kind. I shall truly miss her." The old woman did not cover the tears that were falling down her cheeks. He went to her side and embraced her and they wept together for Felisa Sanfranco and for themselves.

The Bank of Milan was an impressive edifice. It had once served as the castle to a very wealthy merchant. Its façade was imported limestone and granite with a carved frieze that wrapped around the entire building. Massive doors with the original family crest looked imposing to would be clients. Two armed guards stood on either side of the doors and bowed upon his approach. Antonio was a known client and was cordially greeted and escorted in. Once inside, he was greeted by a young man in a neat but tired waistcoat. He recognized Antonio "Signore Sanfranco, always a pleasure to see you.

Please come with me I am sure Signore Dalamagio will be happy to assist you" and led him directly to the back of the reception area. He followed him to a well-appointed office at the rear even though he had been in the bank many times before for some reason today it seemed oddly different to him.

The young clerk knocked softly on the door and a gravel voiced reply answered instantly "Enter." "Signore Dalamagio it is Signore Sanfranco to see you." Antonio waited until the elder banker rose and came from around his big desk. "Signore Sanfranco it is always a pleasure to see you. How may I assist you today?" Antonio turned to the young clerk who was still standing there and the mere look on his face was enough for the younger man to bow deeply and excuse himself, closing the door with a soft thud as he exited.

"Please Signore have a seat. May I offer you some wine?" Antonio who knew Dalamagio and the fact that he liked to talk, yet Antonio did not want to make any pleasantries, he wanted to be about his business. In the past, the two men had contrived mutually agreeable arrangements for some of Antonio's rather sizeable deposits. Today it was different. He felt an urgency that he had not experienced before. "I am so sorry Signore that I did not acknowledge the passing of your beloved mother. I only heard today of the sad news." Antonio was somewhat relieved by this statement and used it as the opening for his purpose in being there. "Thank you. That is precisely why I have come. I must clear up some unfinished business that my Mother had instructed me to do. I have in my possession a receipt for a certain box that I understand from her that your bank has been holding in security for some many years. Is this correct?" The elder man advanced around the desk once more and walking to the door called out to the young clerk who hurried over. "Go to the older vaults and bring back the cask with the name Sanfranco on it. Quickly. Thank you." He closed the door and came to reseat himself. "I had a feeling that you would be in soon to collect your Mother's things. Before she became so ill she came to see me and instructed me that upon her death you were to be notified of the existence of this cask."

The young clerk knocked once again and without waiting for a reply opened the door. He was carrying a plain wooden box and on one end was burnished the name *Sanfranco.* He placed the box reverently on the desk bowed and waited for further instruction. "Escort Signore Sanfranco to one of our viewing salons and, Signore, take as long as you need. If you have any need for my assistance do not hesitate to have someone come and get me." Antonio nodded and followed the young man to a comfortable but small room at the far end of the building.

"If you need anything Signore just ring this little bell and I shall come. Before I leave would you like some wine?" "No thank you. Just close the door on your way out. I will only be a short while." The room felt confining and musty. He ran his hands gently over the polished wood of the simple box his fingers outlining the letters of his name. Antonio turned the box's clasp to face him and reached in his pocket for the tiny key he had found amongst his mother's last notes. Fumbling with the lock for his hand was shaking he managed to unlatch the box. He was trembling with fear and anticipation. What would he find in this box? What had been so important that his mother had found the need to save it for so many years? Antonio licked his lips, suddenly finding himself dry. He thought of ringing for the young man to bring him some wine but selfishly did not want to share any part of this moment with anyone else.

Taking a deep breath, he closed his eyes and opened the box. Drawing the silver candelabra closer to himself to cast a better light on its contents while the movement of it made shadows dance on the walls. There were little books, each one marked with a name, some of those names Antonio recognized. He shuffled through the assortment of small journals, all written in the same hand, his mother's hand. He opened one randomly and saw the neat careful penmanship of his beloved mother. She would always say, "Antonio my darling, you must write with a strong and neat hand. People will judge you on the care you take when putting ink to paper." He smiled at the thought, recalling the sound of her voice. What were these journals? He would spend time reading each one but for now, he must conserve his energy for matters that are more important.

At the bottom of the box, lay letters that were worn and discolored. They appeared to be official documents and so he handled them with great care. In spite of the dampness in the room, he was soaked with perspiration. Before he picked up the document that had caught his attention, he wiped his sweating hands on his breeches. With great attention to what he was doing, Antonio picked up the document that bore the seal of the Kingdom of Milan. It was a beautiful seal and one he had seen many times. It was a certificato *maschile* di nascita for Antonio Sanfranco. On this document was listed the name of the child's mother which read Felisa Sanfranco and the father which read Mateo Rizzo. There it was on paper signed by an official for the Kingdom of Milan. Father, his father, for the first time Antonio felt a tremendous sense of anger, anger at his mother for not telling him sooner. He had spent his whole life not knowing who his father was and now it was true what she had told him as she had lain there waiting for death to release her from her earthly sufferings. Tears had been cascading down his handsome face but he did not even realize that a small puddle was soaking some of the papers in the box. Why had she not told him sooner? He suddenly felt such overwhelming tiredness that he could not keep his eyes open. "I shall lay my head down for a moment to clear my thoughts" he told himself and then drifted off to sleep.

He was dreaming of the man called Mateo Rizzo. He only remembered looking at him as a small child. Mateo was a large man and the one thing he recalled very distinctly were his hands. They were massive hands and he was thinking that they did not have calluses but were smooth and soft like his mother's hands.

Antonio who had spent a lifetime enduring the taunts of those who called him a bastard, the child of a whore and some nameless patron, savored this moment. If only he had known who his real father was, he could have defended himself.

He had not yet read several of the documents. He wanted to savor each one individually. There came a soft knock at the door of the salon. He paused for a moment, when he tried to respond, his voice so choked with emotion he could not speak. Antonio cleared his throat and was able to send out a weak "Come." The door opened and Signore Dalamagio came in "Signore I do not wish to disturb you but the bank will be closing. Shall I make arrangements to stay late with you?" Antonio had not realized how long he had been at his task. "No I was just about ready to leave. Please give me something to place all this in so that I may take it home and review it at my leisure." "Yes of course. I shall be back in just a moment. Signore, if you will excuse my bluntness but there is the matter of the monies your mother had on account, as well as the trust in your name. These are substantial sums. How do you want us to distribute them?"

"There is no need just yet to move any of the money. I presently do not require more money than I have. Leave it exactly where it is and when I am ready for it I shall give you advance notice. Is that acceptable?" "Yes certainly Signore we will keep it just as it has been all these years. I shall return with a pouch for your papers."

While he was waiting, Antonio rummaged to the bottom of the pile of papers and found a ring. It was clearly a man's ring with a star sapphire gem set in the middle and around the faceted stone, the name *Mateo Rizzo* was inscribed. In his shock, he

dropped the ring back into the box and pushed it away as if it held some force too powerful to hold. He was so engrossed in his thoughts he did not hear Signore Dalamagio return and jumped slightly at his approach. "I am so sorry I did not mean to startle you. I have seen this reaction many times when someone faces the past secrets of their loved one. Sometimes it is too painful for the survivor to bear. Here let me help you with these things." The man quickly placed all the contents of the box in the leather pouch and handed it to Antonio. "Thank you, I shall contact you when I am ready for any of the monies you are holding." He was now holding the pouch tightly under his arm and was walking to the door. "Ah, Signore Dalamagio just for curiosity how much is in those accounts?" The older banker stood up straight and with a broad smile replied in a professional voice "Currently there is a little over ten million lira in your mother's account" and here he paused for effect then continued "and forty million in your trust." Antonio was astounded but did not want to act foolish. "Well that is a tidy sum of money."
"That it is Signore. That it is."

CHAPTER SEVEN

A CHANCE ENCOUNTER

Milan

Antonio decided to stay at his mother's villa at least for now; he found solace in being around her things. Her scent still filled the air with the familiar perfume of gardenias. Alba who had always been like a mother to him, wasted no time in keeping him well fed. He would look out the window of his mother's room into the churchyard. He spied her grave, which was growing a soft down of green covering. Antonio was pleased that he had selected a most beautiful sculpture for her headstone. It was such a pleasant day he decided that he would take a walk down to the churchyard and lay some flowers on the grave.

The doors of the Basilica of Our Lady of Sorrows were wide open which for this time of day was unusual. There seemed to be some excitement and voices coming from inside. Antonio could not restrain his curiosity at the disturbance and stepped in. An enormous scaffold had been erected. Atop the structure were two men. At the bottom was a young boy who seemed to be filling buckets with some kind of liquid and hoisting them to the two on the top from a pulley. One of the men was calling down instructions "Franco I need the vermillion not the burnt sienna. Do you not yet recognize the difference in hue? You stupid boy I should beat you within an inch of your life." The boy was clearly wounded by this "Yes Master Banfi I am sorry for my ignorance. I shall mix it up with haste." "Do not bother yourself I am coming down to mix it myself."

Antonio was amused when he heard the name Banfi, knowing very well that the man coming down the scaffold was none other than Genaro Banfi the famous artist, and brother of Marchesa Lucia Banfi of Monteforte. He sat down in the last pew of the church and silently watched and listened as the artist climbed down from his perch atop the high structure. "Franco, I am sorry for getting angry with you but it is very important that the colors I ask for come up when I need them while the under layer is still wet. If you are to grow in knowledge, you must learn and understand fully the process of the work. Understand?" The young would be artist was hurt but did understand the necessity of getting the correct mixture of colors. "It is I who am sorry for failing in my duties. I will try harder Master please forgive my ignorance." Genaro, who had a kind and handsome face albeit smudged with paint, tousled the youngster's thick mop of hair and reaching in his pocket drew out a few coins. "It is very warm in here and I am dry to the bone. Here, go fetch some refreshments and treat yourself to some dolce. We are all tired from working so hard. Go and hurry back." The boy was beaming at the thought of a treat and from up high came a high-pitched voice "I want some dolce as well." Genaro and Franco shook their heads and laughed. The boy was gone in a second.

Genaro now spotted Antonio sitting in the far corner of the back of the church. The bright sunlight that was filtering from the open doors cast the man's face in shadow. Genaro gingerly approached the seated man and implored, "Signore, I apologize for our rude outburst in this sacred place." Genaro bowed deeply to the stranger in the hopes of squelching any negative response.

"There is no trouble Master Banfi your artistry in restoring the church that I grew up in is most appreciated. I have seen your many accomplishments and have always marveled at the splendor of your work. Truly you are a gifted artist." Genaro, who never accepted that he was so famous, was flushed by the compliment from this lone stranger. "You are too kind Signore, I am but a tool used by Our Lord to embellish His holy dwellings. Thank you for your understanding. We shall strive to be as quiet as we can." Antonio felt himself drawn to the artist there was something about him that was genuine and exciting. Antonio vowed that he would get to know Genaro Banfi better but for now, he would quietly watch and wait.

"Please do not let my presence disturb your work. I am very happy to watch you create such beauty. These images are so different than the usual church art; where did you find your inspiration?" Genaro was enjoying this little conversation for clearly the man was well educated and had a keen sense of art. "I have recently returned from a trip to the Abbazia de Montecassino in Naples. The art is amazing and has inspired my interpretation of what was created hundreds of years ago. I am pleased that you approve, I am not sure Father Peter is so happy with it." " Ah, Father Peter is a blessed priest but not much of an art lover. Do not concern yourself with his opinion. If you wish I shall have a talk with him regarding the matter we are old friends." Genaro was pleased at the thought that this stranger would intercede on his behalf and replied, "You are very generous Signore that would ease my worry for his opinion."

By now, Franco had returned winded from running with a sack filled with jugs of wine and another bag stuffed with fresh baked cakes. The aroma filled the church and made Antonio's mouth water. Genaro called up to the man left on the scaffold "Carmelo, come have some refreshment, maybe your work will improve." This obviously was a common theme because Franco started to laugh aloud as did Genaro. Carmelo climbed down the shaky scaffold and partook of the tiny feast. Genaro came to sit by the stranger and offered him some of their bounty. "I cannot resist the taste of fresh baked cakes. Thank you." He broke off a corner of the cake and sinking his teeth in the warm moist pastry, it was delicious. They sat there in the nave of

Our Lady of Sorrows and shared the pleasantries of a simple respite. Antonio thought to himself, this was a man that one day I shall claim as a friend. However, what would be his reaction once he revealed who he really was, but for now, while it lasted, he would enjoy this moment of genteel companionship.

Antonio came to watch Genaro work every day. On the third day, he brought a basket filled with prosciutto, provolone cheese, figs, wine, and pastry. Alba had prepared the basket for him and looked questioningly at him but he did not render any information. For now, right now, he needed a friend and this man seemed a good fit. When Genaro, Carmelo and Franco saw what the stranger had brought they were thrilled. "This, my friend, is a treat we don't usually have during our work days. How will we repay you?" Antonio was beaming with satisfaction "There is no need to repay me I have found comfort in your company. You see, recently, my dear Mother died and I was feeling very sad. Coming here to find solace in this sanctuary was my only escape from my sorrow and then I came upon the three of you working on my church. To watch the artistry of your work has filled my heart with the void from my loss. Can you understand what I am saying?"

Genaro lowered his head and spoke so softly directing himself to Antonio "Yes, I understand what it feels like to be alone and grieve for a lost loved one. Sometimes we mourn even when the person we love is not dead. Please, find comfort in knowing you are among friends." Antonio had to choke back his tears and whispered "Thank you." After an enjoyable meal, the trio set about their work once again. From time to time, the faithful would stop in not only to say a prayer but also to spy on the progress of the work. Antonio, who had practically abandoned his shop watched them come and go and when someone lingered too long or caught the attention of Genaro he would become jealous and protective.

Every day for weeks, Antonio would take up his spot in the shadows. The work was progressing in such a splendid manner. He could see that Genaro's commission was almost complete. It was during this time that the two men shared personal information. They talked about the places they had been, the foods they enjoyed, and even their political and religious thoughts. They were both very comfortable with each other.

Genaro wanted to ask the stranger his name but thought the man was too grief stricken from the loss of his mother. He did learn that the man was an only child; he was not married, and had no children. The artist knew that when he was truly comfortable he would come from the shadows and announce himself, but, for now, he was content to share some time with this mysterious stranger.

For four days, Genaro did not see the mysterious man and found that he missed his presence. He would come every day and look about the dark recesses of the naïve to see if he spotted him but after the fourth day had passed Genaro was sure that the man had moved on or was perhaps tired of watching them work.

Genaro was putting the final brush strokes to the ceiling of the church. Carmelo had climbed down from the scaffold and Franco was packing their pots and buckets, cleaning the brushes and folding their canvas. It was always sad when he had completed his work. It was like leaving a bit of himself wherever he worked. Genaro now joined his companions and was stepping back to look at the finished work. He was so engrossed in seeing it from all angles he almost missed his friend lurking in the back.

It was already late in the afternoon when Genaro spied the lone stranger sitting in the back pew with the shadows that hid him. Genaro was so excited to see his return he came over to seek some small conversation with the man. "Signore, I have missed you these days past, I was worried that perhaps you might have been taken ill. I would have asked after you in town but sadly you have not shared your name with me." Genaro let the last statement hang in the air between them waiting for a simple reply. Genaro noticed that the man seemed anxious and suddenly uncomfortable. He did not want to intrude on the man's privacy but did want to befriend this interesting stranger. "There is no problem Signore, I will respect your privacy. I apologize for making you feel uncomfortable."

Antonio had been dreading this moment. He had grown fond of the artist and even while he was away on business thought of him constantly. Never one to delay the inevitable Antonio set his shoulders and came away from the shadows. The second Genaro saw him in full light he gasped his eyes burned into the face of the man he had shared so much time with over these past weeks, a man whom he wanted to call his friend. "It is you. You are the one who is trying to kill my sister. How do you dare to come to me every day and falsely pretend to be my friend? Have you no shame Signore?" Antonio expected this reaction and was somewhat prepared to address the situation. "I have done nothing wrong Genaro. I swear to you on the eternal soul of my beloved Mother that I had nothing to do with that animal who tried to kill Lucia. I came just by chance to find you in the church of my birth and knew who you were before I knew of your sister for I am an arts dealer after all. I was as surprised to find you here working as you are to find me here admiring your work. Please I beg you to give me the opportunity to explain. Please?"

Genaro was outraged but somehow there was something so oddly sincere in the man's voice, in the depth of his eyes, that he felt compelled to hear his explanation. "What can you say for yourself? I have heard stories that you are a ruthless man, who will stop at nothing to get what he wants. Is it true?" Antonio would have laughed aloud but did not want to antagonize the artist. "Yes Genaro it is true but that is in matters of business. I am successful where others have failed because I have educated myself in the history of fine antiquities. I acquire priceless works of art or ancient manuscripts for the most discerning of men. I have earned a reputation for excellence and accuracy of authenticity. It is also true that I have sometimes achieved my prize at the expense of others stupidity. It helps my business to encourage the reputation of being ruthless and cunning. Wealthy people like to deal with people of like minds, it makes them feel comfortable."

By this time, Carmelo and Franco had gathered to hear what was going on. They saw that the usually mild mannered artist was furious with the soft-spoken stranger and came over to investigate the situation. Carmelo asked "Genaro what is the matter?" At this point Genaro did not know if he should come out with the whole story of how he came to know this man and why. He decided he would maintain his privacy, at least for now, and would let time be the storyteller. "It is nothing Carmelo just a difference of opinion with the Signore. We must get the scaffold down and all our tools packed." Genaro was starting to walk back toward the scaffold then turned to Antonio "We need to talk in private. I must find out the truth." Antonio was only too happy to suggest "My villa is but across the road. When you are finished, we can meet there and I will reveal all you want to know. Will you come?" For a moment Genaro was going to refuse but knew in his heart he needed to get to the bottom of this not only for himself but more importantly for Lucia. "Yes I will come."

Genaro finished for the day as the light was drawing shadows over this work. He gave Carmelo and Franco some money for their supper and told them he would meet up with them later. "Where are you going?" asked Carmelo. "I'm going to the house of the stranger from church, I have discovered from speaking with him that he is an old friend of my family. He knew my grandfather and I am most curious to learn more about the man. Don't worry I will be fine, go ahead and enjoy your supper and I shall see you both when I return."

Upon arriving at the villa, Genaro was surprised at the apparent wealth of the place. He knocked at the door and an elderly woman servant answered, "Yes Signore please come in my Master is waiting for you on the terrace." The artist followed her to the rear of the house but his finely tuned eye did not escape the rich tapestries and exquisite furnishings of the place. As soon as he saw him, Antonio got to his feet and swept his hand to the empty seat. There was a decanter of wine and crystal glasses on the table, which was sheltered under an arbor of fragrant gardenias. "I am so happy that you have come. To be honest I was not sure if you were going to actually join me." Genaro just nodded as if in his own thoughts acknowledging that he felt the same.

The old servant appeared with a rolling table filled to the breaking point with dishes of olives, cheeses, figs, dates, hazelnuts, and breads. She proceeded to place the bounty on the table and said to her master "Master Antonio shall I wait until you ring to serve the main course?" "Yes Alba, give us some time to enjoy what you have brought and I will ring when we are ready. Thank you." She bowed and went off dragging the rolling table with her. "Wonderful woman she practically raised me and she is now lost without my Mother to care for." Genaro could see that Antonio was in no hurry to dive into the dark waters of how he came to look like Mateo Rizzo and strangely, he too was comfortable with the arrangement. They ate, drank, and talked of art and travel. Antonio finally rang for the servant to bring the next course, which she did promptly. A delicious zuppa di pesce in a rich tomato broth, a salad of tomatoes, olives, and arugula leaves on fine china plates. The food and wine was of the highest quality. Genaro enjoyed the meal as well as the company.

It was during dessert that they knew it was time to face what was standing within them. Antonio decided that he would pose the question for he knew that Genaro was too much of a gentleman to insult his host. "It is now time for us to discuss our present situation. Yes?" Genaro nosed the delicate bouquet from the glass of cognac he had in his hand and admired the depth of the amber liquid. "Yes Antonio it is time."

"I shall start at the beginning. My beloved Mother Felisa Sanfranco was a beautiful, intelligent, and cunning woman. She had been the companion of many wealthy and influential men for years. Among her list of clients was Mateo Rizzo. He came to visit my Mother several times a year. Some years more, and some years less, but he always came. My Mother kept a book for each of her clients and in Mateo's book, perhaps without even realizing it herself, she wrote about her feelings rather than his particular needs. It is hard to explain but the way she described him in such detail it was as if I were seeing myself in a looking glass." Antonio paused, and Genaro could see the emotion in his face, and heard the raw sorrow in his voice.

"One day my Mother found that she was with child, Mateo's child. You might ask how could such a woman know whose child she was carrying in her womb? Whenever she was intimate with Mateo, she never used the special potion that had prevented her from becoming pregnant. Then after I was born and started to grow my parentage was too obvious to ignore. She wanted a child and she especially wanted his child. She loved him. Even after I was already four or five years old and he still came to my Mother, she made sure that I was always with my nursemaid. She told me there were two reasons for this. First, she feared that he would try to take me away and secondly because she did not seek to burden him for any help or support. I was hers and hers alone."

"You did not know who your father was? Your mother did not tell you that you were the son of Mateo Rizzo the Marquis of Monteforte? How is that

possible? What did Mateo do when he found out?"
"These are the questions I have been asking myself all my life. I grew up enduring the taunts and wicked tongues of all those who live in this town. I was called the son of the whore. I was the bastard child of that prostitute."

It was not until my Mother was on her deathbed that she revealed who my father was. I did not believe her at first, thinking perhaps the pain that was making her delirious. It was only after I followed her dying instructions that I came to believe the truth of my parentage. I was so angry with her for not telling me and for letting me grow up thinking that I was just the wasted and unwanted seed of some lustful pig."

Genaro was enthralled with the story. Antonio was now on his feet and pacing back and forth. He poured himself a full glass of cognac and refilled Genaro's glass. He was agitated, hurt, sorrowful, an avalanche of emotions all gaining momentum as he revealed his history. Genaro could see that Antonio needed to tell him and he needed to understand this man not only for himself but also for his sister and for that matter his whole family. Gently Genaro said, "Continue Antonio this is a fascinating story and I am much intrigued."

Antonio took a deep swallow from the glass then laid it on the table. It was already late and the temperature had dropped. They were almost in darkness now but Antonio did not move to light a torch. He resumed his tale "It was on one of his trips that my nursemaid had been taken suddenly ill. I had no one to watch over me except my Mother. She did not know that Mateo would come to her that day and when she opened the door, she forgot that I was playing quietly in the other room. I remember that day so clearly even though I was but a small boy. The big man came into the front salon and sat on the settee. My Mother was busy getting him a glass of wine and fussing over him. I wanted my Mother to play with me and so I came into the room. All of a sudden, the whole world stopped for my Mother and the big man. He looked at her then he looked at me and he stared at me with his eyes wide and his mouth open. At first, the big man frightened me and then I caught my Mother's expression of horror. She dropped the glass of wine and it shattered spreading the deep red liquid like rain.

I started to cry because I was afraid. The big man came over to me and picked me up by my arms and my face was in front of his. He was staring at me with such intensity that I was paralyzed with fear. I just hung there in midair, looking into those eyes the color of black olives. I could hear my Mother yelling to him 'Mateo please do not hurt the boy. Put him down, please I beg you.' My Mother came over began pulling at his arm to let me down. Carefully, as if in slow motion, he set me down on the floor. I ran to hide behind my Mother. It was like a dream but it happened so fast.

She grabbed my arm, picked me up, ran upstairs to the nurse's room, and told her to keep me in the room and to bolt the door. That was the last time I ever saw the big man named Mateo. For a long time after that day, I would have nightmares and wake up screaming that the big man was going to hurt my Mother and me. After a while, I stopped having the dreams and never saw the big man again. I had completely forgotten about Mateo Rizzo until just recently when a childhood friend had contacted me to help him sell an ancient manuscript of considerable worth. Unfortunately, the gentleman of whom I speak is now dead and the whereabouts of those priceless manuscripts was told to me to be held at Monteforte."

The story was up until now very surprising. Antonio was keenly observing the face of his guest and watching his reaction to the story. He now detected a note of cautious weariness. He poured them each another glass of the exquisite cognac and Genaro took it into his mouth and felt the warmth of the smooth liquid coat his throat. "When did you come to realize the full extent of your relationship to my grandfather?" By now, Antonio knew he had baited the hook with expert precision and was going to reel in his catch. He had gotten up, walked into the adjoining study, and beckoned Genaro to join him. It was a most impressive room with walls lined with burl wood, a Persian rug of extreme quality, and a desk that sat in the middle of the room that was fashioned in the Rocco style. Everything about this room spoke of the poise and breeding of its owner.

Antonio went over to a massive cabinet and withdrew two boxes. One box ornately adorned with silver inlay, and the other was a simple wood box with the name Sanfranco burnished on the cover. He laid down the two boxes side by side. He opened the ornate one and retrieved two cigars, handing one to Genaro who could already smell the sweet pungent aroma of the tobacco. While he did not customarily, smoke the smell of the cigar was too enticing. They each lit their own cigar and sat back watching the smoke waft all around them. If it were not for the matter at hand, a casual observer would have taken this scene for two old friends, gentlemen, having a companionable smoke. The tension was hanging in the air much the same as the smoke. It was getting late and Genaro could hardly contain his anxiety to conclude this story.

No fool to the art of negotiation, Antonio had made it his life's work to be able to read the mood of a potential buyer. It was time to reveal all that he himself knew to his new found friend. "Genaro, this is the box that was given to me at the Bank of Milan. The bank informed me they had been holding it for the past thirty years with specific instruction that upon the death of my beloved Mother they were to contact me and divulge the contents held therein. I am going to share with you what I found." Now Genaro was totally absorbed in the outcome of this evening. He waited intently while Antonio fished out the contents of the box. He produced the official Certificate of Birth that listed Mateo Rizzo as father and Felisa Sanfranco as mother of Antonio Sanfranco. He handed it to Genaro with great care and ceremony. He then extracted a ring which had been inscribed with the name Mateo Rizzo.

"As you can see I am the son of Mateo Rizzo. My Mother, God rest her soul, knew that Mateo would never leave his wife Lucia and his children to marry her. He wanted to keep this affair, and my birth, from his wife and family to avoid scandal. It was shortly after I was born that Mateo's parents, my grandparents, died of the plague while in France. I do not know when he died but I was still young. I have journals that my Mother had kept on some of her clients and there is one here for Mateo as well. Once he found out about me he gave my Mother this villa and provided financial support through the Bank of Milan for her and I with some conditions attached to this gift. One: that my father's identity never be revealed to me and, second that my Mother would never entertain other men. And so it was arranged that upon her death I would receive the contents of this box and all the monies that they had been holding in my name." Genaro was holding the small leather bound journal in his hands and tenderly stroking the design that had been inlaid with gold. The name Mateo Rizzo was branded into the leather with great care. He opened it and admired the beautiful hand that had once lovingly written on its pages. The stroke of each letter precisely made the robust curve forming words that looked like brush strokes on the aged parchment. "May I read it?" he asked with genteel manners.

"Please do, this is as much a part of your history as it is mine. I will excuse myself for a little while as there is something I need to attend to and I shall return shortly." Genaro was already engrossed in the script that he was holding. It was a love story told by a woman who would forsake her own honor to protect the man she loved. Each page chronicled her time with Mateo in such depth of emotion.

He came again today and I was watching him while he rested. Our lovemaking is so different from the other men I know. He has taught me to enjoy my own pleasure. He gives of himself with great generosity. He worships my body and caresses my soul with his passion.

His body is strong and beautiful. He looks like a Roman God. I can see with every movement the tightness of his muscles. His hair is the color of coal and those eyes that bear down into my soul are as black as the darkest night.

Why does he come to me? He speaks with such affection of his wife Lucia. He tells me of her beauty and her goodness. He loves her and his children yet he comes to me. Why? Because he is a troubled soul who fears that, he will not live up to the expectations that are required to be the Marquis of Monteforte. Fear drives him to abandon his family, to drink and gamble.

I fear that he will soon either kill or be killed at the hand of his own making. I feel safe and whole when I lay in his arms and his touch makes me shutter with desire. I have never loved a man such as I love this man; yet, I know that our love will never be.

I have made a very serious decision. I will have the seed of Mateo fill my barren womb. This man that I love so much will be the father of my child. It will be from this union that I will hold on to his love forever.

Genaro felt the tears welling in his eyes and the lump that formed in his throat. The love and passion between these two people was so profound but never to be realized. It was such a sad story. He wished to continue reading and hoped that Antonio would stay away for a little longer. Brushing the wetness from his cheek, he wiped his eyes on his sleeve and continued.

After a few years, Antonio had evolved into the mirror image of his father. The tall lean body, with broad shoulders and tight narrow hips, the thick black hair and skin the color of hazelnuts. However, it was the eyes that held the pedigree of his father, those deep, bottomless eyes that were the color of the darkest night. His eyes could penetrate your very soul and capture your heart.

Every time I look at my son, I thank Jesus and all the Saints for having given me this gift of my son, a son that was born between two lovers. Antonio is the child of a great and wonderful man who gave me so much love and respect.

My only regret is that I could not share with my beloved Antonio the memory of his father. I would have told him of his kindness and honor. We may have sinned, for I am a sinner, but our love, and the birth of our child was not a sin, it was an act of mercy. If I had not met Mateo and had my son, surely I would be dead long before my son will have read this journal.

Antonio, I beg you to forgive your father and me. You were conceived then born into this world as an act of love. I have love d you my whole life . I have tried to show you all that was good in the world. Forgive me. I love you.

Genaro was weeping and did not attempt to hide his emotions. A sad Antonio came back into the room that was now filled with emotion so dense that it hung like fog in the forest. The two men, similar in age and appearance, sat in morose silence each to their own thoughts.

"What is it that you want Antonio?" It was a simple but direct question. Genaro, trying to understand what could be going through his mind, looked deeply at the man across from him. Finally, after a long while, Antonio answered, "I want to be part of a family. I have lived my whole life in exile. I was the bastard son of a whore with no one to call family. I loved my Mother beyond all understanding, she was pure of heart, but now that she is gone and I know who my family is, I want to be part of that. I was a lonely boy who grew up to be a bitter lonely man. I do not want to die with no one to shed a tear at my grave. Can you understand?"

Genaro was stunned by his admission. Antonio seemed to possess all that one requires to live a comfortable life. Sadly, Genaro knew all too well what it was like to be lonely, to be different from the rest, to stand out in a crowd of people. He loved his family but the only one who understood him was his baby sister Lucia. Would she accept this man into our family? Was it on her authority that he would be granted permission to join our family? So many things were running like a raging bull in his head and in his heart. He so desperately wanted to embrace this man and let him know that he understood completely how he felt.

"Yes I understand more than you can believe. I too feel lonely even though I have a loving family. Being part of a family is not a cure for being alone.

Loneliness comes from within. There is only one person in my life that I can truly feel free to speak my mind and that is Lucia. She understands me better than I know myself. I am hungry for a relationship where I am not the only giver and it is with my sister that I receive more than I give." Antonio looked desperate and wary "I too long for a relationship built on trust and love."

"Genaro will you become my friend?" it was the small voice of a child asking a playmate to befriend him. By this time, Antonio was standing right next to the artist. Two strikingly handsome men, the bloodline would not be denied. Both were tall and slender with broad shoulders, chiseled features, their tawny complexion offset by thick wavy black hair, and eyes the color of the darkest night. Antonio was so close that Genaro could smell his scent, which was aromatic sandalwood. Genaro was aroused by the urgency of the other man's needs. Antonio came to him and embraced him with such passion and strength.

Antonio kissed Genaro's neck, which sent a reverberating thrill down his spine. He drank in the musky male odor of this man whom just hours earlier he wanted to harm. There was an instant connection between the two men. Genaro felt lost and confused by this sudden and unexpected display of emotion. Was this the embrace of a brother or very close friend, or, was the embrace of a man who wanted a lover? How would he know? While Genaro was trying to sort his feelings, Antonio was becoming more aggressive, stroking his back, and kissing his ear. Genaro pulled away not sure of himself.

Antonio, seeing the look of surprise on Genaro's face was not wounded by his action. "I thought you would like that?" he said almost coquettishly to the artist. "You think that it is men that I prefer?" Genaro questioned trying to act offended. "Yes." Now he was baffled that this stranger should have read him so completely. "You seem so sure that is my preference. What has led you to this conclusion?" Antonio knew that he was a great reader of men, which was a gift that he had inherited from his mother. She desired by wealthy, intelligent men because she had the ability to know and accommodate their desires. He stepped back away from the artist and studied him carefully. Finally, he spoke while looking directly at the artist, his onyx eyes penetrating.

Genaro was restless and a bead of sweat had crept to his upper lip. He could feel the fire growing inside of him, in another moment his feelings would be more than obvious to anyone. He tried desperately to distract his mind from the man before him. The exquisite cut of his waistcoat, how it draped across his broad shoulders, and the silk of his breeches caressed his long muscular legs and high tight ass. Yet it was his eyes; those soulful black orbs of beauty that cut into his heart's desire.

"I do not wish to hurt or offend you Genaro. I am very fond of you and have for many weeks since our first encounter, been observing you. I see how you have a natural ease with Carmelo. How from time to time you stroke his arm or rub the back of his neck when he has been on the scaffold too long. I do not believe that this man is your lover but you would use him for your needs if he presented himself to you. I have studied the art of understanding people; it is that ability that has kept me alive and made me prosperous. However, there is something so unique about you dear friend. Because you are kind and true, you would never press yourself upon someone. You long for intimacy but fear its pain."

"How do you dare to know my fears and desires? How; I demand to know?" Now Antonio came back to be standing directly in front of Genaro their toes were touching he was so close, his eyes burning with desire. "I know because it is my own desire that I speak of. I have dreamt of you since the day I laid eyes on you. I can imitate your walk, the way you tilt your head after each brushstroke to see how the light catches what you have just painted. I enjoy hearing the sound of your voice as you hum songs while you are concentrating on your work. I breathe in the smell of your sweat soaked manliness after hours of laboring on the scaffold. These are my desires not yours."

Like a striking snake, Antonio reached his hand behind Genaro's head and brought him hard and fast to himself, their mouths clenched in a passionate kiss, their tongues exploring each other's mouth. It happened in the blink of an eye. They held their embrace for a long time, or at least it seemed that way to Genaro who was stunned by the action but did not pull away. It was clear that Antonio was the aggressor and as such would control the next move.

Antonio's hands were roaming over the slender frame of the artist. As fast as the initial strike had been, Antonio now took his time, to size up his prey. He pulled himself back and looked Genaro in the eyes. "Do we continue?" Genaro's heart was pounding, his body so feverish with lustful desire he could not speak but meekly nodded his head. Antonio did not speak but started to walk into the villa. As he approached the doorway, he looked back and nodded and Genaro came up behind him. He followed him down a dimly lit hallway to what he assumed was his bedchamber. They entered a beautifully decorated room in the middle of which sat a massive canopy bed of carved mahogany wood and covered in ivory silk. When Antonio reached the bed, he extended his hand to Genaro who was shaken and excited. It was not that he had never lain with another man but this man was different, he was powerful, not in body, but in mind. Genaro was excited and fearful of the man who was now beckoning him, but he could not resist the lure of this man.

"Come here I want you to remove your tunic." Genaro did as he requested and pulled the threadbare garment over his head. He stood there bare chested and felt a moment of embarrassment. Antonio pulled him closer and placed his soft warm hands on the artist's chest. He toyed with the patch of curly black hair that covered his chest and tapered V shaped to his navel. The pants that Genaro was wearing had grown loose and they hung from his hips exposing the area just above his groin. Antonio was breathing hard as his fingers were making circles around Genaro rock hard nipples. He grabbed one in each hand and pinched, letting go then pinching them again, he did that several times until his mouth came down on the one while his hand worked the other and he sucked and nibbled each one in turn. Genaro was going out of his mind with desire. He had never experienced such seduction. All his sexual encounters had been fast, impersonal and meaningless.

Antonio stood back to admire the taut abdomen of the young artist. He began to remove his own clothing, removing each layer slowly until he too was bare-chested. It was now Genaro's turn and he did what Antonio had done to him. His hands reached down to untie the silk cords of Antonio's breeches. When he had gotten the tie undone, he put his hands on either side of his hips and pried the silk down. It slipped easily. Antonio was now fully exposed. The tight clutch of pure black curls encircled the erect penis. Genaro's hands were shaking slightly and his eyes caressed the organ with their wonton anticipation. He fell to his knees and touched Antonio savoring the moment, the feel of the silken skin, and the scent of his musky seed and licking the drop that threatened to escape.

"You are truly beautiful Antonio. I have never seen a man so exquisite in all my life." He had barely finished the sentence when he gently and reverently brought his mouth to the engorged phalanx and tasted the sweetness of the man before him. His mouth was moving slowly for he did not want to rush. Antonio pulled himself away. "I want to make it last. It is my turn to partake." He helped Genaro to his feet and undid the cord that held up the battered and paint encrusted linen pants that flopped to his ankles. Antonio gave his hand and Genaro stepped away from the puddle of fabric. Antonio was admiring the younger man's body. It was thin but well built. The crown of fur that cradled Genaro's penis was a deep rust red, which was in stark contrast to the deep black on his chest. The sight of the red hair delighted Antonio who dropped to his knees and snuggled his nose and mouth in the mound of fire. He reached for the artist's testicles, drew one into his mouth, and rolled the ball within around his tongue. Genaro was now desperate with need for this man. With his other hand, he pulled gently on the tip of his penis.

It had been a long time since Genaro had been with a man. He knew he would be sore for a few days but the thought of Antonio inside of him was beyond any pain he might experience. When he got up Antonio knew Genaro could not hold on much longer and neither could he. "Lean over the bed I will have you that way." The artist obeyed. Antonio came up behind him, he felt his fingers working an oil into his anus, and he was grateful. "We shall go slowly." Genaro winced slightly as Antonio eased his well-endowed organ into his tight hole. Antonio was stroking the artist's penis while he slowly drove himself deeper and deeper inside. The pain was exquisite and excruciating all at once.

Genaro burned from desire and pain but he was panting as Antonio thrust and then eased, then thrust and continued until he had spilled his seed all over him. As he pulled out of Genaro, he slapped him hard on his bottom "That my friend was wonderful. Did you enjoy yourself?" Genaro wanted to recoil from the sting to his ass but rather enjoyed it. "May I come in you?" he asked gingerly. That simple question established that Antonio would be the dominant lover. "Why of course, I wish to have my pleasure as well." Genaro came behind him, found the jar with the oil, and similarly worked it into the other's backside. He then eased himself into Antonio pushing the full range of his erection as deep as he could, thrusting, and pulling back until Antonio was moaning with pleasure. Suddenly, Genaro smacked the other's ass with such force his hand stung. "Ah we shall have to establish some rules my friend, but for now we will bask in the luxury of our forbidden pleasure."

When they had satisfied their lust for each other, they curled upon the big bed and held each other. They did not speak, no words were necessary, but they held each other tenderly and wept. Their love so deep and their passion so intense yet so forbidden. Emotionally and physically spent, they fell off to sleep in moments. Before he succumbed to the clutches of deep sleep, Genaro gave up a prayer of thanksgiving to the Lord. He had found the man be had been searching for his whole life.

Antonio fell asleep knowing he finally found someone to love.

CHAPTER EIGHT

MARIA'S SECRETS

Monteforte

Lucia did not know who looked more miserable, herself, or her Zio Giovanni, at the prospect of riding home with Maria Sucretti. There was a lot that had to be explained and sadly, they would have the time to retell the story on their long journey home.

The beautiful carriage pulled up to the Bishop's residence. Waiting just inside the threshold of the residence in the grand foyer was the newly appointed Bishop of Naples, Luigi Rizzo, who looked tired and anxious. He had spoken with Giovanni Romano and Lucia earlier in the evening before the reception regarding the man who looked like his father Mateo Rizzo. Lucia knew there were so many unanswered questions but this was not the time or place. She and her Zio Giovanni gave the Bishop a brief accounting of the events that preceded Antonio Sanfranco's appearance in the Basilica today. The worse of the day lay before her and Giovanni Romano, as they would have to explain everything to the former Marchesa Maria Sucretti of Monteforte. There were kisses and promises to come visit and before she descended, the step to the carriage Zio Luigi grabbed Lucia's arm and whispered in her ear "Be wary Bella this man is either a devil or an angel I have not yet determined which. I will see you in one week at the wedding. Be safe and God's speed. Oh, and good luck on the ride home, I would not want to be in your seat." "Pray for me Zio" they each gave a nervous laugh and he kissed her gently on each cheek "Ti amo mia madre sarebbe stata così orgogliosa di Lucia."

Nicko helped her into the carriage and she sat opposite her aunt and uncle. The door closed with a thud and the carriage shook. It was still light and Lucia could clearly see that the veins in her aunt's forehead were bulging. Maria Sucretti was a seasoned diplomat and knew how to control her temper but there was no denying that she was angry. Giovanni Romano, ever the patient man, sat close enough to his wife without actually touching her, probably thinking it would be best to have some space between them. The carriage lurched forward as it gained its momentum and soon they were on the main road out of the city. It had been a lovely day, the temperature was just warm, not hot, and humid, and the ceremony was humbling and grand at the same time.

Lucia thought it would be best for her to initiate the conversation that she knew her aunt was waiting to have. Even as a little girl, she dreaded when she did something to upset her beloved Zia Maria who generally was easier on her than she was on herself. She prayed that this was one of those times. "Zia I need to tell you a long story. I hope that when I am finished you will come to understand my reason for not telling you sooner." Lucia looked at the impassable expression on her aunt's elegant but aging face her eyes were twitching with agitation. Calmly, Lucia embarked on her tale beginning with the discovery of the illuminated cave and ending with the gala. "You see Zia we were not sure who we were dealing with and what the manuscripts contained. We wanted to spare you any concern." After speaking almost for a solid hour Lucia was parched and troubled that, her aunt had not asked not even one question or changed her expression. Lucia had never seen her in this state before and it troubled her.

The sun was just starting to bend to kiss the sea and the fragrant citrus scent of the lemon grove that skirted the road to Monteforte was drifting its perfume into the stale cabin of the carriage. Maria Sucretti was beside herself but exercised such practiced control on her emotions. Finally, she turned just slightly to face Lucia dead on. "How dare you, or anyone, presume to think that I am incapable of knowing what is going on? I have fought, alone, for my entire adult life, the sole guardian of Monteforte and all its secrets. Have I now become a feeble old fool to be sheltered from the truth?" These words, which she spoke in a whisper, came out with such vehemence that it stunned both Giovanni and Lucia. "I may have relinquished my title, but, I still have my wits. I fear no one, and will fight until my last breath for what I believe. Now I shall tell you both a story."

Giovanni Romano, loved, and, respected Maria Sucretti with his whole being. He knew to keep his mouth shut and bravely Lucia could see that his hand crawled over to hers and he held it in his own. Maria did not attempt to thwart his advance, but clearly, she was still angry; of that, Lucia was most certain. Lucia for her part did not reply and like her Zio sat quietly.

"When I was a young woman and Salvatore was not yet ill with his disease we would take trips to Milan to the music houses or on trips to see how our merchants were doing. I used to love these adventures. Milan was, and still is, such an elegant city with refined tastes so different from Naples. Salvatore would take me all around the city to grand parties. On several occasions, Mateo would accompany us. He would leave Lucia home with the children. It was this one particular trip that Mateo had joined us, it was shortly after the death of our parents, and I thought a trip into the city would do wonders for his temperament. He came and while Salvatore and I were going about our business, Mateo feigned some excuse for not being able to come around with us. Salvatore, who knew what his younger brother-in-law was up to, gave Mateo a pat on the back and sent him away. When he returned that night, he was different, his mood was darker than usual, and he had been drinking heavily. When

I questioned what happened all he said was "I must take care of my son." At the time, I did not make anything of it because he was drunk and acting strangely.

Several weeks later, he announced that he was making another trip to Milan, which was unusual given the fact that it was a distance away. I noticed that Luigi had snuck out after him and was hiding. Upon his return, I confronted Luigi who confessed that he had followed his father to the house of a beautiful woman in Milan. I made the boy give me all the details and location of this house.

It was many months before Salvatore and I traveled once again to Milan. This time with the excuse of seeking out a particular dressmaker, I located the house where Luigi had followed his father. As I was making my way up the walk to the door, I saw a little boy playing in the garden. I would not have thought twice about it but that I thought that once again Luigi had disobeyed my instructions and had followed us. There before my very eyes was a boy who could have been the twin of my nephew Luigi. I was struck dumb by the sight of him. He was a handsome friendly little boy and ran to me as soon as he realized I was looking at him. "Hello I am Antonio. Do you want to see my Mama?" I bent down to get a better look at this child who was a miniature of my brother Mateo. "Yes. Bring me to her."

Felisa Sanfranco was not what I expected. She was beautiful and had an air of intelligence about her. She spoke with great refinement and education. I did not waste any time "I am Maria Sucretti. I am the sister of Mateo Rizzo of Monteforte. Do you know him?" The woman before me started to shake; I could see that she was greatly affected by the question. "Yes. What has happened?" "Nothing has happened but this child that I saw playing in your garden announced himself as Antonio is he my brother's child?" "Yes" she answered with her eyes cast down to the marble floor. "Does he know of this bastard child?" "Yes."

Maria wanted to beat this whore that was standing in front of her but could not find hatred for the woman. There was something so pure about her that she was taken aback by her own reaction. "What do you, or my brother, intend to do? You know he is married with children." "Please Mistress sit down. May I get you something to drink?" Maria did not expect this reception, she would have preferred to have scratched her eyes out, but found herself sitting in the sun-drenched salon with a woman she thought she wanted to hate. "I want nothing from Mateo. I did not tell him of the boy. It is only recently that he found out about him. I love your brother. Yet, because he is too honorable, and would never leave his wife and children. He is a troubled man and since the death of your parents, he has gotten worse. I fear for his life. I have sworn an oath that until the day I draw my last breath I shall not reveal to the boy who is true father is."

Maria was stunned by this admission. "You seek nothing for the child or yourself?" "No. I just want to live without trouble with my son. Every time I look upon his handsome face, I see Mateo. Our love could never be and I knew that when I failed to protect myself after being with your brother. I had never wanted to bring a child into this world but then I met Mateo and knew I needed him to be part of my life. Rest easy Mistress I will not bring shame to the House of Rizzo. Mateo loves his wife very much and his children. He often spoke of you Mistress and his love for you."

Lucia and Giovanni Romano were in rapt attention as she was telling the story. She knew all the while of the mysterious Antonio Sanfranco. Lucia could not hold back her excitement any longer "Zia what ever happened? Did you keep in contact with the boy or his mother?" "When we returned I confronted my brother and told him that he must provide for his son and his mother. He asked me what he should do and we then consulted with our avvocato for advice. It was determined that the woman would sign a legal document never to divulge the parentage of the boy and in payment, monies would be held in trust for both of them until her death. I never saw either of them again, until today when the boy, now a man, showed up at Luigi's ordination. It was shortly after that when Mateo was killed. I thought his secret had died with him."

"What do you think this man wants Zia?" Maria who had settled back into her diplomatic demeanor said, "I am not sure. He cannot by virtue of his illegitimacy claim any rights to the Rizzo fortune or Monteforte. However, I have a feeling that we shall soon discover his intent. Now, do not think you are still not in trouble. I must include you in this misadventure Giovanni." For the first time in the two hours they had been traveling did Giovanni Romano speak "Cara, you have been carrying such heavy burdens all your life I felt that it was my turn to shoulder some of the weight from your yoke. I was there to protect Lucia the moment we knew she was in true danger. I would never do anything to deceive you. Lucia would never disrespect or bring dishonor to herself or the family. You must learn to trust her and me."

Maria, now sat comfortably back into the deep upholstery of the carriage, closed her eyes and drank in the clean, sweet, air of the evening in the mountains. "Now Lucia let us discuss the business of these manuscripts." Lucia relieved by the change of subject threaded cautiously. After telling her all that she knew of the manuscripts and Antonio Sanfranco's involvement she asked her aunt a question. "Zia, Abbot Vittorio, has asked if there are any ancient books here at Monteforte that have been secreted away. Are there?" Maria's expression once again changed but she would not lie or withhold anything from Lucia. "When I was a little girl my father summoned me one day and brought me to his private library. I was very excited to be there because no one was permitted entry. He held the room under lock and key. I shall never forget that day until I take my last breath. He drew me into the salon and sat me down. I was afraid thinking that I had done something wrong. I was about to plead for mercy but he saw that I was frightened and tried to put me at ease.

He took my hand and brought me to the back of the room, which was lined, with racks of books. Many of them were covered with a down coating of dust for no one was permitted within this room. He reached up to a particular book and I thought he was going to show me the book when the wall started to open in front of me. I shook with fear. He once again took up my tiny hand and brought me deep into the room behind the wall. It was dark and musty. He lit a torch and the room became bright enough for me to see that there was nothing in it except a small table in the middle of the floor. Upon this table was a book. We walked up to the table and I was about to reach my hand out to touch the book and my father slapped my hand away. "Do not touch that book. It is a book with the instruction for finding the Light of the Devil." I started to cry both from the sting on my hand and fear. "Papa why have you brought me to this terrible place I am afraid." My father who was a big man scooped me into his arms and held me tight. "Do not fear my sweet girl but you are the oldest and if something should happen to me or your mother you must know of this place. He kissed me, we left, and I have never returned to that room. Actually, after Mateo died, I had it sealed in brick.e He HHe

"Lucia, Bella, I have shared this story with you because of who you now are, the Marchesa of Monteforte. I have never believed in old wives tales and gypsy curses but I believe in that room and in that book. My father never spoke of it again and I never told anyone since that day. Even my mother did not know of its existence." The darkness came upon them. No one spoke another word leaving them to finish their journey entombed in the darkness of the night and their thoughts.

CHAPTER NINE

FINAL PREPARATIONS

Monteforte

Monteforte was in a state of high anxiety. In two days, the marriage of Antoinetta Banfi and Tomaso Catalano would take place. The Sacrament of Marriage would take place at the Abbazia de Montecassino officiated by both Bishop Luigi Rizzo and Abbot Vittorio, what an honor for this young couple. The wedding gala would be held at Monteforte with over two hundred guests in attendance. Poor Giorgio and Marcello who were still recovering from Lucia's gala several months earlier were being put to the test once more. Lucia was so proud of her staff.

Lucia found any excuse to be out of the castle. She was not one for fussing over every detail that was someone else's job. It was the morning of day two before the wedding and she left early, before dawn, to ride Apollo, and relieve herself of the chaos. It was a cool morning and she prayed that it would stay that way for the day of the wedding. The gown her mother had made for her surely must weight five stones. She did admit to herself that it flattered her nicely but if it was a hot day she would faint from the heat.

The endless procession of guests arriving with their equally endless array of servants was maddening. Lucia was desperate for escape. "Good morning Gandolfo I am going for a long, long, ride today." The Master of the Horse was smiling broadly "Too much comings and goings for you Mistress?" "Dear Gandolfo, I feel sorry for you, Giorgio and Marcello, but, I feel sorry for me as well. If I hear one more thing about my sister's gown, or her hair or her veil, I will stab myself in the foot. The pain would be far less than that mindless chatter." By now, Gandolfo was laughing, "But Mistress wait until it is your turn to wed we will have to go through all this again." "Have no fear my dear old friend, I will never wed." The old man looked at her with a frown on his face "What are you saying there are worthy men lining up all around the world to wed you Mistress?" Lucia just shook her head and replied, "I would not be a good wife, and then I would be some man's property to order around as he pleased. At least for now I shall stay in command of my own destiny. That is unless you want to marry me?" The old man laughed heartily "Ah, to have such a dream, if only I were forty years younger I would sweep you off your feet." "Well, you see that is my problem, all the good men are unavailable."

The pleasantness of the weather was not lost on Apollo who enjoyed riding on cooler days. Lucia was enjoying the peace and quiet of the early morning. "Lucia, Lucia. Wait up." Lucia turned in her saddle and caught sight of her beloved brother

Genaro riding to catch up with her. She immediately reined in Apollo and waited anxiously for her brother to close the gap.

"Dear Brother, come help me down. It is so wonderful to see you. How did you know where I was?" Genaro dismounted his own horse and came around to give his sister a hand down "Gandolfo told me where he thought you might be by now." The artist embraced his sister with deep affection and brushed an errant curl from her cheek. "I have missed you so much dear brother. Let us sit for a moment; I am dreading the prospect of going back to the madness that has spawned back there." Genaro was laughing but shook his head in acknowledgement "Yes, I had stopped there first to seek you out the place is afoot with far too many people running here and there. Are all weddings such causes of anxiety?" "Truly I am not the one to ask such a question but I am quite disheartened by the whole process. Well, enough of that, how have you been? I am thinking you are well since you look happy and amazingly light of heart."

It was now that Genaro's demeanor had changed so noticeably that Lucia was concerned that she may have said something to offend him. "Genaro, have I said something to offend you?" she gathered his hand in hers and looked at him with deep feelings. Genaro sought the assurance of her love in those penetrating azure blue eyes "Beloved Lucia, I am happy as you have evidenced by my appearance. I have met the most wonderful man, not just a lover, but a friend, someone who shares all my dreams and desires." Lucia was filled with joy. She put her arms around her brother hugged and kissed him "I have prayed for your happiness and God has answered me. Where is he? Has he come with you? Tell me about him?"

Genaro's face lit up by his sister's enthusiasm for answers. "He is tall and slender much like myself with thick black wavy hair and deep set eyes the color of night. He is very handsome, talented, and educated. You will love him as much as I do." Lucia was all giggles, "So, when shall I meet this wonderful creature, who remarkably sounds like he could be your twin." Now Genaro became serious once again and this time he reached for her hand. "Lucia let us walk for a bit, I have a story to share with you, a story that you shall find very interesting."

The artist stood, and for the first time Lucia noticed that, he was well dressed, having forsaken his usual peasant garments for a properly fitted waistcoat in a fine woven fabric and silk breeches, so different from his customary attire. He looked so handsomely groomed, his hair trimmed and the addition of a few ounces on those lean bones gave him a most striking appearance.

They were strolling along by the edge of the cliffs, the sea roiling a rhythmic tune in the background. A soft breeze blew the clean scent of citrus cleansing the air. "I was working on a commission at the Basilica of Our Lady of Sorrows in Milan, a beautiful church but much lacking in artistic decoration. The Bishop asked me to embellish the ceiling of the nave with a fresco. After seeing the church, I was only too happy to accommodate his request. We, you know Carmelo and Franco, had just started sketching out the design, when I saw this man sitting in the shadows at the rear of the church. I had just minutes before spoken loudly and rudely to Franco for not mixing the right color paint so I went over to apologize for disrespecting the holiness of the church and for disturbing him.

As it turned out, he was an art dealer who had just buried his mother in the churchyard and was there to bring flowers to her grave. He knew who I was and we spoke for a few minutes. Well, every day the man would come for hours to see us work. He would bring sumptuous baskets filled with food and wine. We would talk, about everything, but especially about art. He is very knowledgeable and loves art as I do. This went on every day for weeks. We grew quite fond of our daily chats. Then one day the man did not come. The second day he was also missing. I felt sad and wondered why he was not there. It was a week later that the man once more took up his place in the darkest shadows of the church. My heart leapt with joy at the sight of him. When I ventured over to ask of his health thinking he might have been taken ill, I told him that I would have asked after him in the village but sadly, even after all this time, I did not know his name. He seemed agitated by my inquiry and since it was my last day of work at the church I was sorry that I would never see him again." Genaro stopped walking and motioned for Lucia to join him on the grass. She did but did not want to interrupt his story.

With a deep breath, Genaro resumed his story, which Lucia could see was weighing heavy on his heart. "I told the man that I cared for him and was only asking for his identity so that we could continue to be friends. It was then to my horror that the man with whom I had been sharing my daily meals came into the light. At first sight, I was struck with such shock and vehemence that I was sure he was the ghost of the man I had grown to know and care for. He needed no introduction for I knew who he was. To my dismay he was Antonio Sanfranco." The artist stopped speaking to let his words sink into his sister's brain. He looked her straight in the eyes and watched as her mind worked out the words her ears had just heard. "What are you telling me Genaro that the man in the church was none other than Antonio Sanfranco?" A deep flush now colored her alabaster skin and the blue of her eyes grew darker. Genaro waited then slowly resumed the story.

"I confronted him right there in the church. How dare you deceive me?' I asked him. 'You who have attempted to have my beloved sister killed, you who has intruded on my family and have tried to trick me, will you kill me next?' I asked him with such earnest he was taken aback. Even as I was asking him these questions and making these accusations, I knew in my heart that the man whom I had come to know over these many weeks could not be the man I thought him to be. He then invited me to the home where his mother had lived and would tell me the entire truth. At first, I feared that he would kill me but I knew he would not and so I went. He shared with me his whole life story, showed me official documents of his birth, attesting to the fact that our grandfather was in fact his very own father. He showed me a book written in his own mother's hand about Mateo Rizzo. I was awed by what I had seen." He suddenly and with great urgency held Lucia's arm and pleaded "Lucia, my beloved sister, I love this man, like I have never loved anyone else except for you. He has changed my life. He told me that his whole life he believed that he was a bastard child. He had endured great suffering at the hands of everyone who mocked and ridiculed him and his whore mother. Out of her love for Mateo, she promised that she would never reveal who his true father was. After her death, Antonio realized that he was truly alone in this world, a bastard with no father, a dead mother, and no family. He is desperately lonely and his only wish is to be part of a family." Tears were falling down Genaro's face he was sobbing. Lucia seized him in an embrace and she too joined in his sorrow.

"Genaro you love this man?" "I do." "Does he share your preference for male companionship?" Genaro flushed but answered her truthfully, "He does. Sister I have never laid with a man who shared himself so completely with me. It was not just the pleasure of the flesh but also the sharing of heart and soul. He loves me too. We are very much alike. Please Lucia, I know you are now the head of this family, I need for you to give our union your blessing and to make the rest of the family agree to accept Antonio. Please dear sister I beg you. I love him and so will you."

Lucia was both happy and sad for her brother. "Genaro are you sure of who this man is and if his heart is pure? Has he poisoned your heart with false affection only to gain access to our family?" Genaro got to his knees and pleaded with her "I pledge to you and all the Saints that he is not the man we had believed him to be. He has been much maligned. Yes, he is cunning and ruthless but that is only in the course of his business, which is cutthroat and devious. He encourages that reputation because his clients have come to trust him because of it. Please believe me and find out for yourself for he has come with me here. He is anxious to meet you and all the family. He is, let us not forget, our kin, blood of our blood."

Lucia was silent for a long time looking at her brother on his knees before her pleading for the man he loved. Finally, she answered, "Genaro, I love and trust you above all others, if this is the man you love I shall love him also. Yet I warn you dear brother I shall watch him like a hawk looking for his prey, if he gives me one moment of doubt I will destroy him. Do you understand?" " Yes I do. Thank you dear sister, thank you. I love you. Trust me you will love him as I do. I will go and get him and bring him to you. Will that be good?" Lucia was smiling to see the joy return to her brother's handsome face "Yes dear brother, bring him to me so that I may welcome a new brother into my heart. Genaro, I am so happy for you and I am jealous for I too wish to find someone to love. Will you tell of your new found lovemaking so that I may learn?" Now a deep blush painted across the artist's face "Lucia you are too hungry for knowledge of such matters, but, I will share with you things that I would never tell anyone else." "Go get him I am anxious to meet him finally."

Lucia sat waiting for them to return, her mind filled with questions, her heart heavy with emotion. Her brother was happy, it was not just empty words, and she could see the transformation written all over him. She went to her knees and looking out over the cliffs down to the sea with all its beauty and splendor and she prayed that God in his infinite wisdom and mercy would let her see the same Antonio that her brother saw. She prayed that she too would one day find such a love. She waited for their return.

CHAPTER TEN

A TRUST

Monteforte

Genaro returned with the excitement of a young child bringing a stray puppy home praying it would be accepted. Lucia was pacing and did not hear their approach and only turned after she heard Apollo whinny. Out of the corner of her eye, she saw him, the man who had been mysteriously appearing at their family gatherings. She turned to face him straight on and set her shoulders her eyes drank in his appearance.

Very formally and with a great deal of reserve Genaro and Antonio approached. "Dear sister, I would like to introduce Antonio Sanfranco" he made a courtly bow and stepped aside as the other man stepped forward. With great flourish, Antonio bowed deeply and reached for Lucia's hand, which she gave. He bent forward and kissed her hand with much reverence, while his eyes never left her face. She stood there tall and elegant and was not sure exactly what to say. Antonio broke the silence and said "Dear Marchesa Lucia I have admired you now for quite some time from afar. Your beauty and elegance is only surpassed by your intelligence and purity of heart. By now, your brother has confessed our secret and I am told that you are not appalled by our relationship and for that, alone I treasure your kindness. I beseech you to grant me the privilege to become part of your family."

Lucia had said nothing while he had spoken but took in his manner and looks from head to toe. The resemblance not only to the man who had sired him was remarkable, but to the man next to him, her very own brother Genaro, especially now that he was properly groomed, was nothing short of amazing. There was no need to deny his birth, even her Aunt Maria had known of his existence. As she absorbed his essence Lucia was struck by his elegance and sophistication, it was apparent that this man had been properly educated. He and the reputation that now preceded him intrigued her. None of the three spoke for what seemed a long time.

Lucia spoke, taking her time and choosing her words carefully. "I welcome you to my ancestral home, my home, and invite you to join our family. While I, like you, did not know my grandfather, Mateo Rizzo, I have heard many stories. My brother tells me that your Mother, whom I understand you have recently lost, may God rest her soul, was in love with him and has left a written account of the man. I would, with your permission, wish to read it. I am saddened by the fact that your reputation has done much to malign our thoughts of you, however, I am sure you will work hard to let us learn the true nature of who you really are. Only for the fact that my most beloved brother calls you friend and loves you that I will open my heart, and shelter whatever reservations I presently harbor. I must warn you that the trust I give you, and the love I hope to share with you, must be earned, and that I will watch you to be sure your intentions are honorable. Do not bring dishonor to me, my brother or our family, for the consequences of such deeds will result in your demise."

"I accept and understand your feelings. I have lived so long in this world like a ship with no sail I will now have a compass to find my way. I am so impressed with the wisdom and diplomacy a young woman such as yourself possesses; truly, you are everything Genaro has claimed you to be. Someday I wish to call you sister."

Genaro came forward his expression was one of pure gratitude and admiration for his sister. "Lucia, will you tell the others about Antonio before we come up to the castle?" "I think that would be most wise since there are those who do not have my particular sense of forgiveness. After all, we all thought you were my assassin. Of course, I hope we were wrong. Were we?" Genaro looked astonished for such a question then began to laugh. "Sister your wit is wicked but that is one of the many things I love about you." He came to her, embraced her with a solid hug, and kissed her forehead. "Thank you. Once again, you have demonstrated a wisdom that is so far beyond your years, and a love that finds a home in everyone's heart. I am so proud of you. Now you must convey those feelings of trust and acceptance to the rest of the family; this will be no small task, yet I have complete confidence in you. We will remain in the guest villa until you send word for us to come up."

"Genaro, I need not tell you to remind Antonio that none of our family is aware of your preference for men. That bit of information would not sit well for either of you to divulge." "I so agree dear sister."

Lucia was about to leave when Antonio came up to her. His deep set black eyes, as penetrating as her own blue orbs met his, and it was as if they were looking into each other's souls "Mistress I love your brother and have found within him the man I have so longed to be. He loves and adores you and I now know why. I find that I who do not even know you, yet already love you. I hope that someday you will come to possess the same feeling toward me." Lucia was stunned by this display of such raw and unguarded emotion the man had tears welling in his eyes. She placed her hands on either side of his face and said "I do not find love hard Antonio, it is disloyalty and betrayal that I hate. You will be my brother and I will love you." She kissed him tenderly on each cheek. "Now I am your baby sister." Antonio held her with great affection and wept. She too had tears, as did Genaro. They were family.

CHAPTER ELEVEN

BLOOD BROTHER

Monteforte

As much as she dreaded returning to the castle, Lucia sucked in the fresh air before entering. The mayhem was now in full progress since it was time for breakfast. She was greeted by Giorgio who was at high alert for the most obscure need of one of the myriad of guests who had descended on the bucolic estate. "Ah good morning Mistress back from your ride and ready for another round?" "Dear Giorgio, I do apologize for all this madness. Now, however, I must add to your dismay. Come let us walk while I give you some instruction." While they were walking toward her rooms, Lucia shared many of the details of Antonio Sanfranco's pedigree with the head of her household. It was important that this man know and understand Antonio's future position within the family.

Lucia explained about Antonio and Genaro's arrival, and what she hoped would be her next move. "I am hoping that all the confusion of the wedding plans will be enough of a distraction to save the poor man from being drawn and quartered. You need to find Nicko and my guards and advise them of what I have told you. They are to discretely watch him but in no way to disrespect or harm him. I want that to be perfectly understood. Now, do you know where Zia and Zio are?" Giorgio was patiently receiving this information "They are in their bedchamber and have decided to take their breakfast in the peace of their own rooms." "That I believe is a very wise decision, but I am going to join them as soon as I take my leave from you. I want you to give me some time then I would ask that you send word to the guest villa to retrieve Genaro and Antonio and escort them to Zia's room where I shall be waiting. Oh, and have Marcello send up breakfast for three. Thank you Giorgio, oh, one last thing, please instruct all staff that they are to treat Antonio with the same respect as my brother, he shall be addressed as Master Antonio or Lord Sanfranco."

"Of course Mistress I will see to all details. Mistress, if I may be so bold, is this not the man who tried to have you killed?" Lucia smiled "It is, or, at least we thought it was. I have been assured that it was not he who sent the assassin but Professor Fragoli. For now dear Giorgio we shall open our arms and hearts to him for my brother's sake, but wisely, we shall also keep our eyes closely upon him. Yes?" "As always you are too kind and very shrewd." The servant bowed and went about his assignment.

Lucia quickly went to her own rooms and refreshed herself, washing the dust of riding off. She slipped out of her riding gown and had Sophia bring her a simple saffron colored gown. Sophia expertly braided her hair, which was wild with curls, and she dusted on some talc. The whole process had taken only a few minutes.

Making her way to her Aunt's rooms Lucia knocked then opened the door. Both her aunt and uncle were seated on the terrace. She made her way across the room and was spotted by Isabella her aunt's personal servant. "Good morning Mistress shall I serve you breakfast." "Thank you Isabella, I have asked Giorgio to have something sent up. I would like to speak with my aunt privately. Please let me know when Giorgio arrives. That is all." Isabella bowed and silently left the room closing the door behind her.

"Good morning." Lucia rushed over to her aunt and uncle planting kisses upon them. "I see the two of you have hidden from the turmoil that is now the custom of Monteforte. Shall we survive this wedding?" The older couple just laughed and Maria replied "It is quite a spectacle that has evolved, yet on some strange emotion I am enjoying the process, but, grateful for some place to seek refuge." They all laughed. "So Bella, what brings you to our hiding place?" asked her Zio Giovanni. It was now that Lucia would have to discuss her new and potentially most interesting guest.

"I have come to tell you of a special guest that I have invited to join us." Giovanni who was always so keen "Oh, and who might that be Bella?" "I have asked Antonio Sanfranco to become part of our family as is his birthright." Maria Sucretti's eyes grew large and intense "Have you gone mad? Is this not the man who tried to have you killed?" Now, Giovanni Romano stepped in, "No Cara, it was not Antonio who hired the assassin it was Professor Fragoli. I am surprised that you have come to such a decision Lucia. What has caused this decision?" Lucia understood their concern and secretly held those same concerns herself. She told them of Genaro's story and they absorbed all that she had said.

"Zia you knew of this man's birth long before he came to be known to the rest of us. Surely, we cannot deny him his birthright. He has endured much for the sake of your brother Mateo's infidelity. It is only right that we accept him into our lives and hopefully in time into our hearts. For now, he has befriended Genaro and they are happy. For my brother's sake I will have him sit at our table."

Maria Sucretti bowed her head and after of moment of internal conflict did reply "Lucia I must say that I do agree and accept your decision. Toward the end of his life my brother did regret that he had left the boy fatherless yet he tried to make sure he was always cared for financially. I know what Mateo did was wrong, but he was a troubled man and Felisa Sanfranco gave him the escape he so desperately needed. As you say for Genaro's sake we will welcome him into our family."

At that moment there was a knock at the door. "Enter" called Giovanni Romano. There, standing at the door was Giorgio who came first, bowed, and addressed the trio "Mistress as you asked I have brought your guests, shall I escort them in, and I have servants waiting in the hall with your breakfast." Lucia was beaming "Yes, yes, bring everyone in as well as the food. I am starving."

Suddenly a small procession of servants brought in food, set up chairs, and placed their bounty on the table. It was a whirlwind of people and preparation. Finally, the servants left and Lucia, Genaro, and Antonio were left standing in front of Maria and Giovanni. It was, to say the least, an awkward moment, but Lucia jumped right in "Zia Maria, Zio Giovanni may I present Antonio Rizzo Sanfranco, son of my grandfather and my new brother." It was said with such warmth and flourish that even she was surprised.

As always, Giovanni waited for his wife to speak "Welcome to our family Antonio I have known of you since your birth and I regret that you had to suffer so much for the sake of my brother's honor. I met your mother once when you were but a small boy. I was smitten by her beauty and honesty, much the same qualities that I am sure my brother saw in her. I regret her passing and pray God watch over her soul. Come join us for you must be hungry."

Antonio, a poised and sophisticated man, came to her and knelt down reaching for her hand "Mistress Sucretti you cannot grasp how much this means to me I am grateful for your acceptance." Maria reached her other hand to his face and tears rolled down her cheek "I see my beloved brother in this handsome face. I loved him so much. His death left me with a hole in my heart. Now that I gaze upon you, my heart is filled with the love I had for him. Do not break my heart once again Antonio." He too had tears, as did Lucia and Genaro. Antonio spoke in a choked voice "May I call you Zia?" Maria, a sob escaping from within her said, "Yes, please do." Giovanni Romano came around to help him up, gave him a manly embrace, kissed each cheek, and said, "I am so happy I did not kill you." They each looked to the other with shocked expressions, then slowly realized the humor it was meant to bring, and they all laughed heartily.

The little group sat and enjoyed their breakfast removed from the pandemonium that was growing within the confines of the castle. For now, life was good.

La famiglia.

CHAPTER TWELVE

THE WEDDING

Montecassino

Not a moment too soon the day of Antoinetta and Tomaso's wedding arrived and it was perhaps the hottest day of the year. All the guests who were staying at the castle had embarked in carriage after carriage to take them to the Abbey. The only people left to leave were the immediate family including the bride. As was custom Tomaso was not permitted to see his bride until she met him at the altar.

"Papa, come we will be late" cried Antoinetta who looked like a porcelain doll. Her petite frame wrapped in the finest silk, yards, and yards of imported Belgian lace, which Rafaela had embellished with pearls and semi-precious stones. The overall effect was breathtaking. Donato, the proud father, as well as Rafaela the radiant mother, would ride in a beautifully decorated carriage to the Abbey. After the wedding, the same carriage would be used by the Bride and Groom to take them back to Monteforte and the celebration.

Both parents were already seated in the carriage. Antoinetta was just about to step in when she heard Lucia calling her from behind. "Antoinetta, before you leave I just wanted to tell you how truly beautiful you look. This will be the first day of a life filled with happiness. I wish you every special blessing that God can offer a man and a woman. I love you dear sister." Antoinetta started to cry and embraced Lucia with great emotion. "I would like you to wear this today." Lucia opened a leather case and presented her sister with a magnificent necklace. A cameo had been carved with Antoinetta's image on it. The frame around the cameo was gold inlaid with diamonds and sapphires it was a splendid piece of jewelry. When she saw it, she gasped, "Lucia it is so beautiful. Yes, I would be so honored to wear it. Thank you so much." Lucia removed it from its case and secured it to her sister's neck. It fit perfectly and set off the deep neckline with grand style. "Ah a perfect piece for a perfect bride. Now go before Tomaso changes him mind." They kissed once again and Lucia helped her into the carriage with the assistance of Nicko.

It was time for the rest to be on their way to the abbey. Lucia chose to ride with Genaro and Antonio. "You look so beautiful Lucia," said Antonio as his eyes were drinking her in from head to toe. "I must agree with him. To have two such stunning sisters is more than one family deserves. I suppose I am lucky that Antonio prefers male companionship or I would be jealous for the way he is looking lustfully at you." They laughed and Lucia swatted both of them with her fan. The heat was oppressive. "Antonio, since we already have a dear brother with that name we shall have to invent another name for you. What shall it be? Perhaps we shall call you Mateo to distinguish you from the other Antonio." Genaro jumped on that and said "I think it is a splendid idea so when I am making love to you and call out Antonio I will not be thinking of my handsome brother." This was all in good humor at the expense of Antonio. "I rather like being called Mateo, and so it shall be that I will become Mateo Rizzo Sanfranco."

The wedding looked more like the coronation of a monarch than the sacramental union between a man and a woman. Zio Luigi and Abbot Vittorio with Francesco assisting with the ceremony, administered the actual invocation of the marriage vows. Francesco was truly an extraordinary looking man with delicate features and light tawny skin and a rich chestnut color to his hair. His eyes were a mixture of blue and green with specs of gold. There was always something so angelic about him even as a child it seemed that a holy aurora surrounded him. Even now, standing there in a richly embellished vestment, his sanctity shinned like a beckon from Heaven. Lucia was so proud every time she saw him. She had always known that Francesco would become a servant of the Lord. He was always so good and so kind.

Once the ceremony was concluded, the invited guests were brought back to Monteforte to join in the festivities. It was a dazzling display of food, drink, and musical merriment. Lucia had sent word through Giorgio to have Tomaso's wedding present brought up to the ballroom terrace.

"Tomaso, dear brother, I have something I would like to show you. Will you and Antoinetta join me on the terrace?" It was as if Lucia had made a grand announcement for all to follow. Her beauty and poise were like a magnet and drew men and women to follow her every movement. There being led by the Master of the Horse Gandolfo was a horse. It was no ordinary animal. Lucia, months earlier, had sent Gandolfo to Spain to purchase this horse. It was an Arabian Stallion of such pure breed that it was worth a king's ransom. It was pure black in color, its fetlocks, mane and tail had been expertly braided. A saddle of the finest Cordovan leather had been hand tooled with gold inlay and the Catalano crest had been branded into the leather.

When Tomaso laid eyes on this magnificent animal, he gasped and instantly went to him. He stroked his head and a servant was standing by with carrots and sugar for the animal, which he offered to the Groom. "What say you dear brother, do you like him?" "Of course, he is the finest stead I have ever seen. Is he not an Arabian Stallion?" "Yes he is and of the purest breed. He was sent to me from the farthest reaches of Spain." "What a perfect animal. He looks so regal and well trained. He is massive. I estimate him to be eighteen hands." "That is precisely how tall he is. Why don't you sit him and see how he feels." There was no need to coax the young bridegroom who did not hesitate to climb aboard the well-trained animal.

By this time, the entire assemblage of males was out on the terrace admiring the horse. He was perfect down to the smallest detail. Tomaso, himself a handsome man, sat atop the horse with great bravura. They looked perfect together. "Tomaso, dear brother, what will you name him?" Lucia asked looking up at him. "What shall I name him, but, he is yours." "No he is yours. It is my gift to you for your wedding." Tomaso quickly dismounted and ran to her "I cannot accept such a gift it is too grand." "There is nothing too grand for my sister's husband. Now give this poor animal a name." "I shall call him Nero."

All the gathered men and most of the women who had come to see what was going on cheered and clapped. The men had spilled out to the terrace to inspect the horse that was so grand that he did not even blink at all the fuss. Tomaso came to her, embraced her, and swirled her off her feet "Dear Sister this is the most wonderful gift you could have given me. How will I ever repay you?" Lucia now grounded once again looked him in the eye and said, "Treat my sister with all the love, dignity, and respect she deserves. Bring honor and prosperity to this union. Oh, and one more thing, lots and lots of babies. I am dying to be an aunt." Again all those gathered began to shout and clap until Antoinetta, who was standing by Tomaso's side, engaged in a kiss. Antoinetta came up to Lucia, "Thank you for my beautiful necklace, this grand and very large animal, as well as this fabulous gala. I cannot thank you enough baby sister." Lucia faced the crowd and said,

"Now let us enjoy this gala with much drink and merriment." Maestro she shouted, "Play something that is light hearted."

Abbot Vittorio approached her "Lucia you are so kind and thoughtful I am sure Tomaso is thrilled with his present." "Tomaso dreams of horses, I could not have given him a better gift. I just pray he doesn't expect my sister to get up on that beast." They laughed companionably. They were taking a stroll towards the gardens "I see you have adopted Antonio Sanfranco. How is that working out?" "It is amazing how our impressions of him were so opposite to the nature of the man we have come to know and love. I am really quite fond of him already. I pray, and I ask you to join me in that prayer, that he is truly who he seems to be and does not turn out to be the devil in disguise." "I shall pray for all, especially for you dear Lucia." "When will you marry?" "Ah, dear Abbot, do you not know that I was born with a curse? I shall never find love in marriage." The monk looked at her with a strange expression on his face "Why do you say this?" "When I was born I was imprinted with a certain birthmark. It is said that whoever possesses this mark will never find love or happiness in marriage." The monk grabbed her arm and held her tight "Lucia, do not say such things, of course you will marry and the lucky man he shall be." "Do not concern yourself I am resigned to my fate. Already I am cursed with desires I cannot satisfy." "Your desires are natural for any young woman. Do not punish yourself Lucia."

Their intimate conversation was interrupted by Giancarlo Marzoni. "Marchesa I am so delighted to see you once again, as always, you have enchanted every man here." The gifted musician bowed formally to both Lucia and the Abbot. "Abbot Vittorio, how nice to see you also, it was truly a beautiful ceremony you and Bishop Rizzo performed today." The monk said nothing but just smiled and bowed his head. "Mistress, Lord Marzoni, if you would excuse me I shall be taking my leave to head back to the abbey." "Dear Abbot so soon. Wait, I shall ask Giorgio to prepare some baskets for you to bring back to the Abbey which I promised all the brothers I would do." "That is too kind Mistress I would decline but then I would be fearful to return empty handed." The three of them laughed. "Lord Marzoni, if you would excuse me as well, I shall find Giorgio and seek you out when I am finished." The musician bowed "Of course Mistress" but the frown was etched on his face.

Lucia took the monks arm and they walked across the grand ballroom to find Giorgio who they were told was in the wine cellars. "Abbot must you leave so soon I enjoy your company?" They were walking in the dim light of the hallway that led to the cellars. The monk stopped, turned Lucia to face him, and wrapped his arms around her in a tight embrace. His face so close to hers she felt his breath on her skin. He bent forward and kissed her on the lips with such passionate intensity. Lucia was confused. She did not know if she wanted to push him away or to pull him to herself. He suddenly backed away from her falling to his knees "Lucia forgive me; I am consumed with my desire for you. I dream of you always. I am so ashamed of what I have done. Forgive me." By now, the man before her was weeping. He reached for her hands and kissed them. "I have tried to wipe your image from my heart and my mind but I am too weak of the flesh."

Lucia was speechless. A million thoughts were racing through her mind. What should she say? What should she do? Without thought, she too fell to her knees to face him. "I too am sorry. I have thought of you so often even though I know it is forbidden. We have both sinned. Please, I beg you; do not let this destroy our friendship. You are too precious to me. What we have, our feelings for each other, is more than physical. My love for you goes beyond my body." The man, a man of God, was ashamed of his lustful desires. "I have prayed so hard to control my urges for you. It is not just the beauty you possess but also the purity of heart that drives my desires. I am a broken man that kneels before you, ashamed for my actions. Can you forgive me?" "It is I who have driven you to this for it is the curse that I was born with, you must forgive me, and above all else you must pray for my wicked soul."

They were starting to hear voices coming from down the end of the hall. "Come we cannot be seen in this state by the servants for surly they will be wagging their tongues." Quickly, they picked themselves up, and slipped into a nearby room.

Once they heard the voices pass, they began to speak "Do not let this one moment of affection drive a wedge through our relationship. We know that our love can never be. Promise me that you will always be my friend and confessor?" The monk was visibly shaken "In all my years in the service of Our Lord and His Blessed Mother I have never broken my vow of chastity and thanks to you and your faith I will continue to serve the Lord. Pray for me Lucia. Pray that I remain steadfast in my vows." " Devo pregare per te sempre. Ti amo, ma non della carne. Ti amo della mia anima." With that, they embraced in a deep emotional clutch each knowing that they could never break such a sacred bond.

After he left Lucia, felt a void in her heart. This man, this holy man, had almost broken his vow because of her. She was disgusted with herself and cursed the fate that she had inherited. Lucia found herself walking in the garden, her thoughts overridden by her heart, tears streaming down her beautiful face. She did not see her brother Francesco who was kneeling before a statue of the Blessed Mother, which her Zio Giovanni had set into a faux grotto. Candles had been placed within the grotto to light the statue, which cast shadows against the stone backdrop. She did not approach him right away he seemed so intense in his prayers. After a few moments, Lucia came over to where he was and softly called his name "Francesco I am so happy to see you." Her brother, his face illuminated by the dancing flames of the candlelight, rose and came to her, embracing her with great tenderness. "Dear Lucia I have longed to see you. Come sit here on this bench and we can speak." The priest looked deeply at his beloved sister and knew instantly that she was troubled "What ails you Bella?" Lucia's voice would not come but the tears fell with no restraint. "I am a wicked woman." Francesco frowned "How can you say such a thing? You are by far the noblest, purest, woman I have ever known, except for our beloved Mother." " I am ashamed to speak to you of my thoughts and desires. You will think I am a whore." Now her brother smiled and his voice was low and held a deep intimacy "Oh dear sister we all have dark thoughts and desires, it is the nature of the human animal. Do you think just because I am a servant of the Lord that I do not fight against my human needs for sexual desire? You are without a doubt one of the most beautiful women in the world, men will dream of ravaging that magnificent body, but you my dear sister are more than physically beautiful, you are inwardly beautiful, and that is what makes you so special." "But Francesco I want to experience love and to have intimacy with men but I cannot marry."

Francesco was confused to hear his sister say this "Why can you not marry?" She turned to face him and with sorrow in her voice said, "I was born with a curse." He reached for her hands "There is no curse that cannot be washed clean. Who told you of this curse?" "Our Mother." At this, the priest was truly befuddled "Our Mother believes in curses? How can this be? Surly you must be mistaken. What is the nature of this supposed curse?" Lucia felt herself become very uncomfortable but decided that she needed to relieve herself of this burden "I was born with an extra nipple. The legend tells that the God of Mars copulated with a human woman whom he loved very much. She gave birth to three of his offspring. In order to satisfy the needs of his children he gave the woman a third nipple so that each could suckle. One day the woman grew bored with just being a mother to her three babies and left them unattended and ventured off to the village. In her absence, a wolf came and ate one of the babies. When Mars found out, he was so overcome by pain and anger that he placed a curse upon her. He decreed that she and all her descendants who were born with a third nipple would never find love or happiness in marriage. These women would only experience carnal knowledge and lust."

Lucia was now openly weeping her voice so choked she could barely control herself as she told him the story. Francesco was shocked "You believe this old wives tale? How could a woman who possesses such intelligence and faith fall prey to such nonsense?" Francesco had raised his voice almost in anger. He took her firmly by the arms and shook her "Listen to me Lucia" he said in a tone she had never before heard from him "Only God can control good and evil. You are good dear sister. If by some rare act of fate you were endowed with some kind of birthmark, then it was the will of the Lord. Do not put your faith in faery legends." "But..." Francesco interrupted her words by placing his finger over her lips, "No Bella, there will be no talk of curses. When it is your time, the Lord will guide you, until then enjoy yourself and relish in your youthful beauty. Now, I hear that you will be traveling to visit many of your companies, be careful Bella, there are those who would wish you harm."

Lucia felt better for having spoken to her brother and her burden had been slightly lifted, it was only when she heard Genaro's voice call to her that she found joy in her heart. "Lucia you are a mess, come here and let me wipe that ugly face." The priest drew a silk scarf from his pocket and brought it to her mouth "Spit" he commanded and she obeyed. He gently rubbed the scarf across her face and dabbed at her swollen eyes. "Oh if only you were pretty then the curse would be so much more meaningful," he said in a mocking voice. They laughed and then he kissed her on her forehead, her nose, and each cheek. "I love you Bella, do not fear you will find your way. I promise."

"Oh there you are and with our dear brother." The two brothers embraced pounding each other on the back. "Francesco you have not aged one day since you were about twelve." "Genaro, I can hear your confession now, for surely you have committed the sin of lying." Again, the three siblings laughed in that special way that families share light moments. "Brother have you met the latest addition to our family?" "No can you introduce me?" Antonio, now known as Mateo, was not far behind Genaro, he was sporting an expression of embarrassment for interrupting this little scene. "Mateo, come meet our brother Francesco. He is the second holiest person in our family, after Zio Luigi that is." "It is my pleasure to meet you Father Francesco, Genaro speaks of you all the time, I feel like I know you already" with that he made a deep bow. "There is no need to be formal Mateo, we are family. I am so happy you have come into the family and one day we shall sit and talk of your past so that I too can come to know you better." "It would be my pleasure to share my past with you Father." "Please just call me Francesco when we are alone." Mateo was eyeing the man before him with intense scrutiny. "They have all said that there was something unusual about you and now I can see why. There is a sense of holiness that surrounds you and I can feel your goodness." A deep blush colored Francesco's face "A few more goblets of my sister's fine wine will have me walking on water." They laughed heartily. "Let us join the merriment. Come Lucia everyone is looking for you."

When they made their way back into the grand ballroom Lucia spotted Giancarlo Marzoni playing at the harpsichord, the other musicians were following his lead. It was the music he had played during her gala months before. It was a wonderful piece, Lucia made her way to where he was playing, and when she caught his eye, she curtsied in acknowledgement of the song. Giancarlo was delighted that she remembered and nodded his head toward her. At the conclusion of the piece, the crowd cheered and clapped and the composer stood to respond to their appreciation of his work. "Dear Mistress may I have the honor of this dance?" Lucia felt an instant flush of heat rise within "Yes you may." The music began to play and the handsome couple alighted upon the ballroom floor. Giancarlo was an exceptionally good dancer who held Lucia just a little too close for her comfort, but she would be lying if she denied that she was not captivated by the tall, muscular, composer. As they waltzed, around the room, all eyes were upon them and Lucia felt beautiful and elegant in his arms, which swept her off her feet. When the music stopped, Giancarlo gallantly twirled Lucia around then caught her up in his powerful arms. The crowd went wild with salutes and cheers.

Giancarlo guided her toward the terrace where the sea breezes were filtering through the trees and carrying their fragrant perfume of citrus. "That was wonderful Lord Marzoni." He held out his arm for her to hold on to and they strolled down to the first tier of gardens. Lanterns cast subdued lights along the ground-shelled path. They came to a stone bench and sat down. "Mistress Lucia I have thought of you often since our last encounter which I fear did not go well toward your opinion of me." Lucia smiled and reached over to pick a flower from a nearby bush. "Giancarlo I am quite fond of you as I had told you before, but sadly we are like fish swimming in the same pond. Unfortunately, it is but a small pond and there is room for only one of us." He too smiled at the comparison "You may be right but that does not alter my feelings for you." "Tell me Giancarlo, and you now must be truly honest, is it my body you desire or my mind?" The handsome composer's face twisted into a grimace "You ask the most pointed questions. I am embarrassed to say I lust for your body. The feel of that skin that it as white and pure as polished marble, those breasts that are as ripe as melons, and those lips that taste of honey. What man in his right mind would not want that body?"

By now, Lucia was giggling at his description of her attributes and a warm glow came to her lovely face. "Ah, now you see why we cannot be together. I want a man who desires my mind. When I become old and have lost the tautness of my belly and my breasts sag the man I love will cherish my mind." "There is no man who would not desire a creature as beautiful as you. A man does not choose a woman for her ability to think; actually, they prefer their woman to be simple but willing. It is the desire for full breasts to suckle and wide hips that warm a man's passion. You are right dear Mistress, we could never be together because I fear that I would never be able to outwit you, and alas, when I too am not in my prime and everything has shriveled up you will still be wiser than me." Giancarlo grabbed her hands, brought them to his lips, and kissed her softly. "For now I shall have to content myself with making passionate love to you in my dreams." He turned and kissed her gently on her lips. He stood and extended his hand "Marchesa Banfi shall we join the festivities?" Lucia took his hand, and for the moment was relieved, but a little saddened that, he had resigned himself to end the chase. The huntress had outwitted her prey.

BOOK TWO

CHAPTER ONE

THE JOURNEY BEGINS

Paris, France

Lucia was so excited about her the prospects of her trip across Europe. In speaking with her Aunt Maria and Uncle Giovanni, it was decided that her first stop should be France to visit with the Marquis deFauntil.

"Genaro I would ask a favor of you" she addressed her brother in her most endearing demeanor. "What favor could I deny you my most beloved sister?" Lucia beckoned him to join her on the settee. The sun was slowly setting and the doors from the solar were fully open. A pleasant breeze brought a luxurious breath of citrus infused air into the room. She had been reading after dinner but she found she could not concentrate on the tome in her hand. Her mind was ablaze with thoughts of travel. The artist came to sit by his sister's side.

"What would you have me do for you dear sister?" He had a playful tone to his voice and Lucia delighted in his new found appearance. Gone were the days of paint stained tunics and ill-fitting pants. The new Genaro, handsome and with just a few extra pounds on his tall slender frame was groomed and dressed in finely tailored coat and silk breeches. Lucia knew it was Mateo who had transformed her brother, and he seemed happy for it. "I would like to invite you to join me on my first journey to France?" Genaro looked surprised but pleased at the invitation. "Are you displeased with the invitation brother?" He smiled and she could see one slightly crooked tooth a lasting mark from a fight with their older brother Andrea who threw a book at him after a rather nasty reproach about Andrea's lack of talent for physical sports. She remembered that day very vividly because Andrea got quite a lashing from their father for almost knocking Genaro's tooth out.

"Shall I be one of your footmen or bodyguard? If so I shall fail miserably on both accounts." Lucia slapped his hand "You shall be neither. I thought that it might be entertaining for you to escort me around some of the highlights of Paris. After all, you have told me many stories of your time spent there. Oh, dear brother, please come. We shall have a grand time of it." They had been talking softly between each other and Lucia saw that her brother's gaze had drifted toward Mateo who had been deeply engrossed in a book he had taken from the library. Lucia seeing the connection leaned in close to her brother's ear "Mateo can come with us as well. I am certain he knows some rather interesting places."

"Ah, we presume that he would be willing to trek across Europe as the lap dog to the now famous Marchesa Banfi" he said with a very pompous look and haute voice. "Lap dog or not will you come?"

Genaro had become serious for a moment and said, "I can come for my commission work for His Holiness will not begin for several months but I cannot speak for Mateo. He has a business to run. I would be hard pressed to leave him and run off with you, yet, I would jump at the opportunity to travel once again. Let us ask him, shall we? Come with me and we shall see if he is in agreement."

Lucia and her brother, holding hands, approached Mateo. He picked his head up and smirked at their approach. "What?" he said in a quizzical voice with a smile on his face. "You two are up to mischief. I see it written all over your faces." Lucia could not hold back "Mateo I have asked Genaro to come with me to France. Will you both come with me?" Mateo seemed genuinely surprised. He laid down the book he was reading and looked from one to the other. "Lucia, are you asking me to come with you to France?" "Yes. It will be a grand adventure for all of us. Since you and Genaro have been there before you can take me around to all the wonderful places. Please say yes." Mateo was smiling broadly and shaking his head in disbelief. "Genaro, what say you?" he asked.

"Well I don't know. This one, she is very difficult to control, and gives many orders. We will not have a moment's rest and will have to take her to balls and shopping. It will probably be dreadful." Lucia was stunned by her brother's quips. "I shall not be a burden and will not trouble you all the time. I promise." Mateo was now laughing heartily at the banter between the siblings. "When will we leave?" he said it so matter-of-factly that the significance of the question almost eluded her, but being the quick wit that she was she instantly realized what he had said. "Oh Mateo you will come. You and Genaro will come with me? That's wonderful I am so happy." Lucia went to him, threw her arms around him, and kissed each cheek.

Mateo was visibly pleased that Lucia was so happy. He too was laughing along with Genaro. "I will have to make arrangements to have my shop managed while I am gone and to close up my villa. When shall we leave?" Lucia wanted to go that moment but knew she needed time to make her plans. "I will send word tomorrow to the Marquis deFauntil asking for his hospitality. I must start preparing my wardrobe for this long trip. We shall leave in one month's time. Will that be sufficient for you to conclude your own business Mateo?" He seemed to contemplate the question and finally responded, "Yes I believe I will be able to implement a plan for an extended stay in France." "Excellent, then it is settled we shall leave in one month." Lucia turned and was ready to leave "Where are you off to in such a flurry?" asked Genaro. "I must write to Lord de Fauntil and tell him of our arrival I am sure he will have his own preparations for our stay. I will also notify Edgardo Esposito that I will be coming to Spain when my business in France is concluded. There is much to do." Mateo and Genaro looked at each other and shrugged then the three of them were laughing.

Mateo worked longer hours in his shop preparing for his departure to France. He had to admit to himself that the prospect of again visiting the City of Lights was very appealing. The thought of being able to show Lucia the beauty of this international city was also very pleasing to him. He would send word to some of his more prominent clients of his arrival and perhaps he might be able to secure some high placed invitations. This would be the first time that Mateo had companions to travel with and he was excited by the prospects.

Returning to his mother's villa after two weeks of keeping late hours Mateo found Genaro sitting on the back terrace looking out toward the Basilica of Our Lady of Sorrows. He came to him and sat in the chair next to where he was seated. "Genaro you seem forlorn. What ails you?" Genaro just shook his head and did not answer but it was obvious that there was something troubling him. "Please what is weighing so heavy on your mind?" Genaro took a deep breath and turned to face Mateo directly; his handsome features softened by the dim light from the burning lantern. "We have been together for some time now and I have shared with you all that is within me. I have confided in you all my darkest fears and deepest hopes and I have given you my love unconditionally yet you have kept secrets from me. Why is that Mateo?" Mateo seemed stunned by his accusation "What are you saying I have shared everything with you."

Genaro, usually so mild tempered stood up so quickly he knocked over his chair. "I was curious to know where you lived so I asked Alba where you usually keep your residence and she directed me to your beautiful villa" his voice was strained with anger and pain. "I knocked at the door and was greeted by an exotic looking woman. She led me into the villa where the Master of House then met me. I introduced myself but he already seemed to know who I was. I asked who the woman was and was told that she was your concubine. You can only imagine my surprise when I found out that you were keeping a whore on the side while I was pining for your affections. What say you to these statements?"

Mateo looked troubled but calm. He too rose and came over to embrace Genaro but the other rebuffed him. "I demand to know what your game Mateo is?" Mateo turned so that his back was facing Genaro but he was looking straight out toward the churchyard of Our Lady of Sorrows. From where they were standing, he had a clear view of his mother's grave. The tombstone he had chosen was so magnificent and large it dwarfed all the others. He smiled secretly to himself that he had chosen so well. Genaro waited in silence. Finally, after a few moments, Mateo spoke. "I did not tell you of

Serafina for fear you would not understand. She is a special creature that I have loved in my own way." Genaro so choked he whispered, "You love her?" "Yes"-answered Mateo in the same soft tone. "I love her for what she has given me in terms of sexual gratification. I had not found a man whom I loved or trusted to share my life before I met you. Serafina gave me the fulfillment of my perversions without any guilt or denial." Genaro was speechless but listened to what his lover was telling him.

"Several years ago while traveling through the Ottoman Empire in search of antiquities for a special client with certain tastes I found this girl sleeping in the street. She was half-starved, beaten, and abused. I felt an attraction toward her that I had never known for a woman. She was a little more than a waif when she came with me. I discovered that she had been bought and sold like livestock. Her last owner cut out her tongue and left her for dead. She was ill and suffered from poor nourishment.

I took her with me to get her back to health but after a while, I grew in deep fondness toward her. She on the other hand was so grateful for what I had done to rescue her she opened my appetite to many erotic forms of sexual pleasure, which she had been taught. I am ashamed to say that I have used Serafina in many ways that I am not proud of but I have always treated her with kindness and respect. While I love her for her desire to please my every whim I know that I can never love her for a lasting relationship. I will continue to support her because she is more like a child to me now than a lover. I know this may be difficult for you to understand but I must trust that our relationship has grown so securely that you need not be jealous of this girl."

When he had finished he finally turned around to find Genaro seated with his hands covering his face weeping. Mateo came and knelt before him and reached to take away his hands "Please trust me dear Genaro. You and only you have fulfilled my life's dream of finding someone to spend the rest of my days alongside. I am a fool for not telling you from the beginning but I did not know how you would react. It was wrong." Genaro started to sob and Mateo held him in his arms. With a deep convulsive sigh, Genaro pulled back and said, "I am jealous that this woman has been able to fulfill all your desires and I have not. What has she given you that I have not? Tell me so that I can be as she."

At this Mateo sat on his haunches and was silent. "I don't know that you will understand my needs. She has endured much pain for my pleasure and I don't think that is the relationship I wish to have with you." " What kind of pain have you given this girl that I could not sustain?" Mateo hung his head upon his chest and answered so softly that Genaro was straining to hear him "I have used instruments of pain on her beautiful body to satisfy my depraved desires. I have whipped her until she was bloody and then taken her from behind on all fours like an animal yet she has allowed all this without complaint. Why? Because she knows it pleases me." " Is that what you would like to do to me?" Genaro was both excited and scared by the thought of having his body ravaged in this manner. "I cannot ask that of you Genaro. I do not believe that you share this type of desire. I hate myself for what I have done to Serafina yet she was the one who opened my appetite to such wanton fornication." "Would you love me more if I submitted to these desires?" "Yes, but that is too much to ask. I will love you with or without it."

Genaro stood wiping his running nose upon his sleeve and extended his hand to help Mateo off the floor. They now stood face to face and Genaro touched his face feeling the day old growth of his beard "I will be the lover you have always dreamed of if you teach me how to please you." The two embraced their lips coming together, their tongues exploring each other's willing mouths.

The trip to France was long but enjoyable. The little caravan consisted of Nicko, the two bodyguards, Sophia, Mateo, Genaro, Lucia their servants, footmen, horses, a carriage and several covered carts filled to the brim with trunks of clothing and other assorted items. After two weeks of travel Nicko rode ahead to announce their approach at the home of the Marquis de Fauntil who had been anxiously awaiting their arrival. As the caravan trekked over the long gravel drive toward the residence Lucia was immediately struck by the beauty of the place. Flanking the roadway were perfectly trimmed tress pruned to grow round like giant powder puffs. The lawn was a lush green and neatly trimmed. However, it was the sight of his residence that captured her interest. Built in the classical French Mansard style with its deep slate tiled roofs and arched windows. The symmetry of design was a perfectly balanced structure of pale rose limestone accented by the contrasting black slate roof. It was a massive edifice with a main portico dressed on either side by matching wings. For some reason she knew that, the home of this handsome, gentile man would be as perfect as he was.

Standing in the shade of the portico was the Marquis de Fauntil in all his splendor. The man was the picture of aristocratic civility. When the carriage came to a halt, Nicko opened the door and Mateo and Genaro bounded out happy to stretch their long legs. Nicko made a grand bow and extended his hand for her exit from the carriage. Lucia too was grateful for her release from the tight quarters of the carriage and felt the sun upon her face. She closed her eyes and drank in the warmth of the day and the scent of lavender and jasmine for there were clay pots the size of giant caldrons, which were intricately carved with playful nymphs overflowing with the lovely plants. The Marquis did not wait for her to walk to where he was standing but hurried over with great enthusiasm to greet her "My dear Marchesa Lucia, it is with a happy heart that I find you in my company. I have been excited since I received your letter last month. Please find my humble home your own for as long as you will grace me with your presence." Lucia was delighted by his invitation and show of hospitality. The debonair lord bowed gallantly and then kissed her on both cheeks. "You are as always a ray of beauty to these old eyes." "Dear Marquis de Fauntil I am so delighted to be here in your beautiful country. Since I was a young child, I have dreamed of coming to France. I am sure I will not be disappointed. You are looking fit and handsome the years have been kind to you My Lord."

"I see you have brought your brother with you. Lord Genaro Banfi we have met before welcome to my humble home" and the two men bowed formally to each other with the Marquis giving him a manly embrace "Welcome to Chateau la Rose." "Thank you for your generous hospitality. May I introduce our brother Mateo Sanfranco Rizzo." Being no fool the Marquis was aware of the story of the former Antonio Sanfranco whom he had been told was the illegitimate son of Mateo Rizzo. He knew because Maria Sucretti had written to her old friend to ask him to watch over Lucia. Maria was not totally convinced that her new found nephew was as trustworthy as Lucia and Genaro thought him to be.

Mateo made a formal footed bow "My Lord thank you for your kind hospitality you have a magnificent estate. Lucia has spoken so fondly of you it is as if we are already acquainted." The Marquis for the first time realized the resemblance he had to Genaro, but for the age difference, they could have been twins. The older man was highly sophisticated and well-bred it was no wonder why he would have slid right into their lives. "Lord Rizzo I am charmed to meet you and wish you a pleasant stay. If there is, anything you need my staff will be more than happy to assist you. But come let us have some refreshments and dust the road from your weary bones."

The Marquis extended his arm to the beautiful Lucia whose cheeks blushed at the gesture. They walked into the chateau and were greeted by a staff of ten servants all lined up ready for their commands. The Marquis, like a general to his troops, "These are my most loyal servants they are at your disposal. They have shown your own servants to their quarters and helped with the trunks." Lucia smiled radiantly at their willing faces and said in perfect French "Thank you all and we hope not to be too troublesome." They all smiled back and bowed. The Marquis turned to her and was smirking, "I was not aware that you held such a command of my native tongue and I am very pleased for it. Tres bien!" "I hope to perfect my skills while I am here perhaps you will help me." It was now the older man who felt the heat upon his own cheeks "My pleasure."

"This is truly a remarkable chateau. I fancy myself a bit of an expert in the area of antiquities. Some of your pieces are so rare that I have only read of their existence. I commend you on your fine taste and excellent eye." Lucia could see that Mateo was truly impressed with the tasteful array of statues, one of which was displayed in a niche flanked by two lanterns. "This piece" Mateo pointed to the one in the niche "It is from the Greco-Roman era and its condition is of museum quality, but I am sure you are knowledgeable of this fact."

The Marquis was visibly proud and said "All these pieces I cannot accept credit for acquiring, their purchase was the joy of my late wife Auriella. She was a woman of such high intellect and refinement. We traveled all over the world to find the pieces you see here assembled. The chateau is a tribute to her memory. We never were blessed with children, and so, upon my death, these priceless treasures shall be bequeathed to the Academia de Arts. "That is such a generous legacy to leave to the people of France," said Mateo with a smile.

Since they had already completed their supper, the Marquis invited Lucia to take a stroll in the gardens. Mateo and Genaro were left sipping their cognac and smoking their cigars in the solar. It was a warm evening but comfortable. "Marquis these gardens are splendid; I particularly am enjoying your extensive assortment of roses. How many varieties do you have here?" "We have over fifty different kinds of roses. I have a gardener whose only job is to tend these flowers. He has been with me for forty years but alas, he grows old and is now training a young man to take his place when he can no longer fulfill his duties. Auriella loved roses they were her passion in addition to art. She was an extraordinary woman who loved to surround herself with beautiful things. You would have loved her Lucia. You remind me very much of her when she was your age."

They walked for a while, Lucia stopping to smell the different perfume given off by the enchanting flowers. "Please sit. Let us chat for a moment in comfort." The old man waited until Lucia had seated herself and then joined her on a bench. "Dear Marquis, may I ask you a very personal question but, if you wish not to answer I will understand?" The handsome older man took her hand and gently stroked it "I will answer as best I can." "You loved your wife that is obvious to see. I feel her presence and spirit everywhere, but sadly, that was so long ago. You are a healthy man filled with love and vitality why did you never remarry?"

Once the words left her mouth Lucia instantly regretted asking so personal a question "I am so sorry, forgive me my ignorance. Sometimes I cannot hold my tongue." He turned to face her directly "There is no harm. I know you are a curious woman. I thought of remarrying many times over these years but my heart held me back. I will tell you something that because we are now old, and all scandal has been wiped clean, that I had asked Marchesa Sucretti to marry me many years ago when we had been lovers." Lucia was not hurt or shocked by this revelation; she could see how this man would have swept her aunt off her feet. "Why did she not accept your proposal?" He looked away toward the vast beauty of the manicured gardens their perfume scenting the very air they were breathing, "She would not relinquish Monteforte, and for the love and memory of Auriella I could not leave this place, and so the two of us spent the greater part of our lives in loneliness for fear of losing our past. Fortunately for your Aunt she found Giovanni Romano and they seem happy and for that I am grateful."

"Marquis de Fauntil I am sorry for having intruded into your privacy. Please forgive me." "Dear Lucia there is nothing you could say or do that would displease me. You must call me Henri and that I must insist." Lucia smiled with a peach blush coloring her cheeks. "Henri it shall be. By the way, how is our little venture going with the shipbuilding?" "Ah, I am pleased you asked. We are progressing very well. Piro has done marvelously well and has earned a name for himself among those in the shipping business. The day after tomorrow we shall go to Le Havre and you can see for yourself how it is coming together. Piro has hired a well-known international shipping magnate and engineer to oversee all the structural aspects of our first project. His name is Lord Danford Stevens of Wallingston and is highly regarded for his knowledge of shipbuilding. He is quite wealthy with a large estate and many tenants on his property. I find him most pleasing to speak with and I am sure you will as well." "There are two things I treasure in our relationship, one is your guidance and friendship and the other is your knowledge, if you are pleased than I shall be also."

Lucia leaned over and gave him a kiss on the cheek. The older man smiled warmly and stroked her hand. "I need to caution you about Piro" he said his expression becoming sullen. "When I returned from your gala I told him you might be coming for a visit. His initial response was 'Why?' and I told him that you wanted to check on all your holdings. At first he seemed happy then as time wore on, he became agitated. I asked him what was troubling him, but he refused to confide in me. Many things have changed for this young man, as it has for you. Time has a way of altering people. He no longer sees himself as an ignorant, indentured, groom, but as a man who has made something of himself. The worst of it is he thinks he did it on his own merit. Soon, I shall have to tell him it was you who made all this possible. I am afraid that will not be an easy conversation." Lucia looked sad at the prospect of having Piro know that he alone did not make his success but it was made possible only by her feelings for him. "Let us not tell him just yet. I still feel responsible for what happened to him." Henri de Fauntil was a man who knew pain and loss, success but few failures. He turned to look at her directly "You have done everything possible to erase what has happened in the past. You cannot carry that burden forever. No one was given more opportunity than Piro. To his credit, he has done remarkably well, with what was given him. The one thing he should never forget is that you could have had him killed not just beaten." Lucia saw that the Marquis was very concerned. His handsome features became contorted at the thought that Piro was becoming out of control.

"Does he know I am here?" "No I have not seen him in several weeks since he has gone on a buying trip with Lord Stevens. The two of them have become good friends." Lucia had such mixed emotions regarding these new revelations. "I will need to approach this with much diplomacy. I do not want to hurt him again." Hearing voices, they turned to see that Mateo and Genaro were approaching. "So here you two are, we were searching for you. I just received word that Giancarlo Marzoni will be in concert tomorrow evening. He has invited all of us to attend."

"That sounds like a wonderful idea. Shall we all get ready to go to the city? I maintain apartments near the boulevard of Sant Germaine. I am sure we will be comfortable there. We will use those rooms as our base for visiting the shipyard." Lucia was all excited "Henri will I be able to go shopping?" The three men looked from one to the other "I think we can arrange such an outing" he said tongue in cheek. Genaro said, "Do you not own every piece of garment God ever created?" Mateo rebuked him "Genaro leave her alone she is a gorgeous young woman who must be properly outfitted. Don't worry little sister I shall bring you around." Genaro was pouting, "Will you bring me too?" Mateo had a devilish look in his eyes "Perhaps if you behave!" They all laughed.

CHAPTER TWO

THE CITY OF LIGHTS

PARIS

The Rue de Sant Germaine was a lovely tree lined boulevard with classic French architecture and a view of the Eiffel Tower as a backdrop to the River Seine. As soon as the carriages approached, the building owned by the Marquis de Fauntil that the majordomo came bustling to greet them. "My Lord I just received word of your arrival today. I will assure you that even though it is short notice we shall have everything you require for your guests." The older man who was dressed in a black waistcoat and powdered wig bowed very formally to the Marquis. "Do not concern yourself Pierre we shall be here for a while. This evening we will be dining out and then going to the Opera. If you would however, please send word to Lord Giancarlo Marzoni that Marchesa Banfi and guests will be attending the concert this evening and if Lord Marzoni would like to join us for dinner before the show?" Pierre bowed with no further explanation necessary then bowed to the rest of the party. "Marchesa Banfi I am honored to make your stay in Paris comfortable and enjoyable. If there is anything you require please do not hesitate to ask me or any one of my staff." "Well Pierre if you would not mind please escort my maid Sophia to my quarters and assist her in preparing my room. I wish to prepare myself for this evening." "Of course Marchesa, as you wish." Sophia who was as excited as Lucia to be in Paris was barely able to keep her mouth from gapping open in wonderment. "Mademoiselle Sophia follow me," said the majordomo with the authority of his position.

"Dear Henri again I am overcome by the beauty of these apartments. The view is magical. I cannot wait to see it in the evening." "I am happy that you are so taken with the view." "I do not believe there is anything you could do to improve my spirits." Lucia heard Genaro's voice "Would shopping improve your spirits even more baby sister?" "Genaro do not mock me, but, perhaps, only a little more." They all laughed heartily. "Lucia, why don't you and your brothers go shopping while I complete our arrangements for this evening as well as the next several days? We will need to travel to Le Havre tomorrow, and I want to make sure of our transport. Go, have some fun, but, sadly there is nothing you can purchase that will improve on your own natural beauty." Henri kissed her hand and sent them to explore the city.

Lucia was enchanted. As they rode in their carriage through the cobbled streets of Paris, she was struck by the elegance of the city. As their carriage made its way down the Champs Elysees, they passed the Jardines des Tuileries she was thrilled by the sight. "Ah dear brothers if only we could see the inside of this magnificent structure." "This is not the residence of the royal family," said Genaro. Lucia was surprised "Are you sure? It is so massive and beautiful." "No this was built by the predecessor to King Louis XIV. The royal palace which is the residence of His Highness is located at the Chateau de Versailles about twenty odd kilometers from here." Mateo answered, "I have been inside, and it is such as you would imagine. The King is a great collector of all things of beauty. With any luck between the Marquis and myself, we might be able to press for an invitation to one of their grand banquets. I hear that they are extraordinary and all the ladies are costumed in the height of fashion."

"Then I could not possibly attend!" frowned Lucia. "Why?" both of her brothers asked. "I have nothing suitable to wear." "Oh poor little Lucia has nothing to wear! Well then we shall just have to remedy that problem." Mateo shouted instructions to their driver to take them to the Place de la Concorde where the dressmaker to the Queen herself maintained a shop. When they arrived, Mateo got out first and told the driver to wait. He entered the shop and was there for quite some time but finally emerged all smiles. "Come the proprietor is someone with whom I am acquainted and she has agreed to fit you for the latest fashion." "Really Mateo she will have time to make me a gown so quickly?" "Yes, she has many ladies who sew all day for her special clients."

Lucia had never been to a haute couture shop in her life. All her gowns were custom made by her own seamstress who came directly to the castle. Her eyes were trying to take in all the sights and sounds of the place. The elegantly appointed shop was small but busy. Several women were in various stages of being fitted for their gowns. When she entered there was a woman overseeing each of the fittings giving instructions to each seamstress. She was a petite woman, yet her appearance spoke volumes as to her place in high society. Upon seeing Lucia, the woman left her clients standing on their pedestals and came over to Lucia.

Mateo was beaming "Madame Francine Richaud I am pleased to present the Marchesa Lucia Banfi of Monteforte." The petite proprietor curtsied deeply and then said to Mateo in French "The reports of her beauty were not exaggerated. She is a stunning creature." Lucia felt the heat rise to her face and responded in her perfect French "Why thank you Madame Richaud, I do not know who is spreading such rumors, but as you can see me now in the flesh I am but a modest woman." The proprietor was shocked "I did not mean to speak of you in such a common way, please forgive me, you obviously speak my language and so well. Let me apologize and start over once again. I created many of the gowns that were worn to your Gala. When my clients returned the talk was of a young woman so beautiful she looked like a Goddess. They described a young woman with hair the color of sun kissed strawberries, skin like polished marble and eyes the color of azure. I thought they were lying but now I can see they did not do you half the justice of what my eyes see. I am jealous that you could wear a flour sack and be breathtaking. If all my clients looked like you I would be out of business."

Genaro came forward "Dear Madame, you will be filling my baby sister's head with all thoughts of grandeur, we shall not be able to fit back into our carriage when we leave, for her head will take up all the space." Lucia slapped him playfully on his arm and the tension of the initial introduction was broken.

"Please Marchesa come with me I will dress you myself as I do Her Majesty Queen Marie Antoinette." Lucia could hardly contain her excitement. By the time she was done, she had purchased three gowns. The first of which would be ready for a fitting in three days. "Marchesa did you receive an invitation to the King's ball?" "No I did not." "Well when I go to fit Her Majesty this evening I will let her know that you are in Paris. I am sure she will contact you."

With their business completed the trio left in their carriage. "Oh Mateo thank you so much for bringing me here but how did you know of this woman?" Mateo had a coy smile on his face "My beloved Lucia, there are many people one needs to know in my business. A well-placed suggestion, a mention in the right ear for a much sought after invitation, can all mean the difference between success and poverty.

My clients are men and women of extraordinary refinement and fat purses."

***

The evening came quickly. Lucia told Sophia about what happened at the shop of the dressmaker while she was dressing. She would wear her purple silk gown and the diamond broach that her Aunt Maria had given her. Sophia was plaiting her hair and intertwining it with pearls. "Sophia, I would like for you to come to the opera tonight. Would you like that?" Lucia, knowing that Nicko and her two bodyguards would be going with her to the opera, asked her maid if she wanted to come along. Sophia was so excited to accompany her mistress to the opera. "Oh yes Mistress. I shall wear the gown you gave me. Isabella fitted it for me." She had been given one of Lucia's old gowns, which she had altered to fit her more petite frame.

The Marquis, Genaro, and Mateo greeted the two women. "Oh how lovely you ladies look. You will be the talk of all Paris this evening," said the Marquis, extending his arm for Lucia. As they were leaving Lucia could not help but be amused by Nicko's reaction upon seeing her maid. When Nicko saw Sophia, he was hard pressed to contain his pleasure. Lucia knew that they loved each other and when they returned to Monteforte, she was going to invite them to wed.

Hotel de Crillon, which was located on the square of the Place de la Concord, was where the elite went to be seen. Often frequented by Her Majesty Queen Marie Antoinette it was an elegant building and was the home of one of Paris' best restaurants. As their carriage pulled up there was a gathering of all of Paris' high society. Men in fine waistcoats and powdered wigs and women dressed in the latest fashions all chatting and observing. The men emerged first from the carriage without much of a stir but as soon as Lucia stepped foot onto the cobbled walk all eyes, male and female, focused on her. The men with their licentious grins were sizing her up and the women with their heads together were trying to figure out who was this gorgeous young thing on the arm of one of France's most eligible bachelors.

Many of those gathered greeted the Marquis, their expressions were ones of askance, but he did not give up any information and just proceeded into the hotel. "Marquis de Fauntil always a pleasure to see you my Lord. Your usual table is prepared and Lord Marzoni has just arrived and is seated." "Thank you Camille, please send over two bottle of the Chateau le Fete." "Qui my Lord."

Lucia was flushed from her head to her toes. The Marquis escorted her and following just behind were Genaro and Mateo. Upon seeing them Giancarlo rose to his feet and came to them "Marchesa you are breathtaking as always." He kissed her hand with a deep bow. "Marquis de Fauntil how generous of you to invite me this evening. I have reserved the best seats for all of you at my concert." To Genaro he embraced him with a manly hug "Old friend, I almost did not recognize you. I must say that you look wonderful. And who do we have here?" "Giancarlo this is my brother Lord Mateo Sanfranco Rizzo." The two men eyed each other and gave a bow. They were both handsome but in very different ways "How do you do?" replied Mateo with a cordial bow. "It is so nice to meet you and I can see the resemblance is so strong. I am very fond of both your brother and sister. I hope you all will be coming this evening." Genaro was excited to see his old friend but somehow he did not hold the same sexual arousal as he once did for the handsome composer "Yes and we are most anxious to hear your new concerto." They finally settled to their dinner. Lucia was seated between Henri and Giancarlo, as all of Parisian society observed her every move.

Once their dinner was complete, the party left in their carriage for the opera. The *Palaise Garnier Opera* house was one of the most elegant buildings in all of France. When their carriage turned on the Saelle des Capuccines Lucia gasped at the sight of the grand façade. The scale and symmetry of the architecture was amazing. Seven porticoes sat upon seven arches. Sitting atop the grand structure at the east and west end were sculptures cast in gold. On the west end was L'Harmonie and on the east end was La Poeier each one standing twenty feet tall. Multicolored marble graced the façade. When their carriage finally came to a halt, footmen surrounded to open the doors.

Lucia's eyes grew wide at the expanse of the building with all its detail and the size alone was impressive. Once again, the Marquis escorted her with his head held high and Lucia could see that the older man was proud to have her draped on his arm. As in the restaurant, all eyes fell upon Lucia, from admiring smirks from the men to the whispered inquiries behind the women's fans. Who was this beautiful woman? Lucia did not pay any mind to the frivolous scene, she was consumed with the style and stunning appointments of the architecture. They were ascending a massive marble grand staircase with its sweeping design and golden ornate handrail. There were sculptures and paintings of such exquisite design that she was completely absorbed in the decorations. Musicians were roaming the halls on every level playing such fine melodies their tunes being overridden by the sounds of continuous chatter. For a moment Lucia stood fixed on the stairs and wanted to remember this moment forever. The sights, sounds, and smells were enveloping her in their magic. She thought to herself 'it is so wonderful to see the world with all its beauty.'

They were escorted to a private balcony box with its rich, soft, velvet wall coverings, gilded railing, and fine upholstered high back armchairs. Perched at this height and location Lucia could see the entire stage as well as all the room. It was so huge and sitting in the middle of the frescoed ceiling was the enormous crystal and gold chandelier she had ever seen. It was perhaps fifteen feet in length from its place at the ceiling and twenty feet across. There must have been a hundred candles shimmering against the crystals casting a prism of color throughout the cavernous space. Lucia looked down over the rail to see that Giancarlo was setting up for the concert, which was scheduled to begin shortly. Looking up to the box he spotted Lucia and gave her a hearty wave and bowed formally to her. All those looking toward the stage followed his movements, and caught sight of her waving back.

"Oh dear Lucia this is such great amusement for me. All tongues are waging like tales on happy puppies. "Everyone wants to know 'Who is that magnificent creature with the Marquis de Fauntil'. I am afraid that your character might have been compromised for they are thinking that you are my young mistress." Lucia was enjoying the reaction of not only the notoriety, but that Henri was so pleased, they laughed together companionably. Mateo and Genaro had joined them having ordered bottles of champagne to be served once the performance began. "Genaro is this not the most wonderful place you have ever seen?" Lucia could not contain her excitement and sounded like a young child. "Yes it is of such splendid design and ornamentation I was admiring all the grand paintings and sculptures. Perhaps, someday, I will have works displayed in a place like this." Mateo now joined in to their conversation "Your work has a much higher calling. Such talent as you possess must be given to the Lord to grace all his churches, and in that way all, even the poorest among us, can see the beauty that you create." Genaro lowered his head in recognition of Mateo's admiration for his work "Thank you Mateo I often forget that my abilities are gifts from the Lord. You are right that I should not seek such vanity." The Marquis chimed in with "Yes but it is great fun to dream. You are young and to dream is the privilege of youth."

The concert was the dessert of the evening. Giancarlo's performance was flawless and the audience was overwhelmed by his mastery. They stood and applauded, cheering and begging for more. The Marquis had arranged for them to have refreshments at his apartment in Sant Germaine and Giancarlo agreed to come. "How did you enjoy your first evening in Paris?" asked Henri. Lucia was still reeling from the grandeur of everything. "Dear Henri, thank you so much for this evening, for being my friend, for teaching me. I am beyond words." The old man was thrilled; she could see it in his eyes "I am very pleased that you enjoyed it. There will be more to come."

An hour later Giancarlo finally arrived "I do apologize for coming so late but there were so many people who wanted to speak with me. I must admit that I am slightly offended that they were more interested in the identity of the bella cappezzi rosa than in my music but for that I cannot fault them." Genaro asked "And what did you tell them?" "I told them that she was a Goddess from Monteforte the land of Vesuvius." They all laughed but Lucia was anxious to know what he really said, "Truly what did you tell them?" Giancarlo hesitated and was going to quip another tale but relented and said, "I told them that you were the Marchesa Lucia Banfi of Monteforte one of the most powerful women in the world. The men wanted to know if you were married, some wanted to know if you were having an affair with the Marquis and the women all wanted to know the name of your dressmaker." This information elicited much laughter from all gathered.

"Marquis, I hope you do not mind, but I have taken the liberty to invite two of my fellow composers to meet me here. Our now famous Marchesa has smitten them with her beauty. Surely you know Johann Bach and George Handel?" The marquis was very amused "I know, and have heard their music, but have not had the pleasure to meet them in person. This is going to be a great treat for all of us."

Giancarlo was playing the harpsichord when the two composers arrived. Lucia who was intently listening to him was delighted at their appearance. She had never heard their works but they, like Giancarlo, were the talk of Europe. The moment Giancarlo caught sight of his friends he quit playing and greeted them with much enthusiasm.

The three men in turned embraced each other with pounding slaps on the back and warm banter. Lucia was waiting patiently. Giancarlo led his friends to where Henri and Lucia were seated "Marquis de

Fauntil, Marchesa Lucia Banfi, I am pleased to introduce my friends Lord Johann Bach and Lord George Handel." The two newcomers gave formal bows and each in turn reached to kiss Lucia's hand.

Lucia was astonished at the sight of them. They were only a few years her senior but she thought they looked much older. Bach was the taller of the two and thinner. He wore no wig and his hair was chestnut brown with a widow's peak and thick curls that fell to his shoulders. He had a long aristocratic nose and full lips. He was not a handsome man but not unattractive to look at. Handel was full figured, and wore a big powdered wig that covered his shoulders, which from the expanse of his huge forehead Lucia imagined that he had already gone bald. His puffy eyes gave his fat cheeks a look of sadness, which seemed in stark contrast to his arrogant nose. Although Lucia thought that, it was a blessing that these men made beautiful music for their appearance was not so attractive. "So pleased to meet you, Giancarlo has spoken often of you. Usually one prone to exaggeration, he could not have painted a better portrait of you if he were the greatest artist. I trust you enjoyed his mediocre performance." That was Bach mocking Giancarlo's concert. Giancarlo feigning indignations stood to his six feet and puffed out his chest "How dare you? I challenge you to a duel for such solicitous slander." With that remark, Lord Bach reached into his waistcoat pocket, pulled out his gloves, and promptly slapped Giancarlo across the face. "High noon tomorrow, and don't forget to bring your bow this time." "Ah, yes, the last time I did forget the bow. The violin bow that is." The whole group broke into great laughter. Lord Handel gave an apologetic bow, "I do regret that you have suffered through their childish antics." Lucia could see that the portly young man was no match for his two counterparts, but there was something very endearing about his homely face that she liked. He was very soft-spoken and almost shy in his manner. "Lord Handel do not concern yourself, I have been raised with four older brothers. I am quite familiar with this type of banter but I thank you." His chubby face lit up with her attention to him.

Before long, the three composers were entertaining the guests. As the wine flowed freely so did the music. It was a very entertaining night.

It was already late by the time the evening ended. Before leaving Giancarlo found a quiet moment alone with Lucia, "Dear Mistress Lucia I am so pleased to see that you are finally fulfilling your dream of traveling across the continent. To say you look beautiful is never really quite enough. My heart throbs to hold you in my arms." Lucia whose own heart was fluttering wildly retorted, "I believe Lord Marzoni that it is an organ that is a touch lower on your anatomy that is throbbing." Giancarlo tried to look crushed but he suddenly burst out into a bellowing laugh. "Ah, you are too wise My Lady. Nevertheless, truly I am happy that you are enjoying your stay here in Paris. The Marquis de Fauntil is a fine man, and I am sure you will be comfortable here. I must bid you good night for I have been told by your brothers that tomorrow you will be leaving for several days to Le Havre." He came to her and kissed each cheek so intimately that Lucia felt her womb tingle with desire. She inhaled his scent a mixture of sandalwood and lavender. "Thank you Lord Marzoni, until we meet again I wish you much success with your concert."

Lord Bach and Lord Handel came to join them, "Upon your return to Paris you must come to our concert. The three of us will be performing together. We would be so delighted if you would come." Lucia was thrilled at the invitation "Oh how kind of you. Yes, I would love to come." They were leaving when Lord Handel turned and took Lucia's hand and kissed it very tenderly and whispered "Thank you for your kindness Marchesa. You are an extraordinary woman whose beauty is only surpassed by your generosity. I shall look forward to seeing you again. Good evening."

Before retiring, the Marquis gathered Lucia and her brothers and informed them of the events for the next day. "I was able to secure passage on a riverboat which leaves tomorrow morning at seven o'clock. We must be at the dock and prepared to embark before then. I must assure you that these captains are very punctual with departure times. We shall be in Le Havre for three days and I have arranged for us to stay at the home of Lord Danford Stevens; he is the man running our new shipbuilding facility. So, if you would please excuse me I shall retire and I recommend you all do likewise."

Lucia kissed Mateo and Genaro good night and walked to her rooms with Henri on her arm. "I am so grateful Henri to have had such a wonderful evening, and it is all thanks to you. Thank you so kindly." The old man took her face in both of his hands and cradled it "I have not had this much fun in many years. To think of all those rumors going around and around, and for crediting me with having an affair with someone like you was worth every moment. It is I who must thank you my darling Lucia for giving an old man great pleasure. I see our composer Lord Handel has a soft eye for you." Lucia blushed but did not respond. He bent and kissed her tenderly on her forehead. "Get some rest we will leave early in the morning."

CHAPTER THREE

Le HAVRE

France

"Mistress it is time to get up" urged the soft but insistent voice of Sophia who was shaking Lucia out of a most passionate dream involving Lord Marzoni. "Leave me alone I am kissing my lover." "What, I see no one" answered Sophia who had already turned back the luxurious blanket filled with goose feathers, and was nudging her mistress into a sitting position. "All right if I must but it was so real." Lucia felt as if she had just laid her head upon the pillow and now she was up once again. "Come, you need to make your toilette and dress. I understand that we shall have breakfast served aboard the boat. I packed what I thought you might need for three days." "Dear Sophia I don't know what I would do without you." "I don't know either."

Finally dressed, Lucia found her brothers and Henri already to leave standing by the carriage waiting to load the trunks. "Good morning sister, ready for a sail on the Seine?" "Good morning gentlemen, I am ready for all my adventures. Shall we go, what are you waiting for?" The three men looked at each other and shrugged knowing there was no hope for it.

It was a short carriage ride to the dock. Already waiting was Nicko and her two bodyguards. "Good morning Mistress Lucia, this is a fine day for a boat ride. Shall we get you settled onboard?" Lucia was quick to see that Nicko had given Sophia a board smile "Yes thank you Nicko, if you would help Sophia with our bags that will be fine. Nicko, I would like just you to accompany us on this trip. Have the others wait back at the Marquis' apartments until our return." He was just about to protest then saw the set of his mistress' jaw and knew he could no longer press the issue. "As you wish Mistress, I shall instruct them to stay here." She could see that Nicko was not happy with this arrangement but she did not want to converge on Le Havre with an army.

Once settled on board Lucia became excited for the trip. She had known of Le Havre from her readings as well as stories she had heard over the years. It was a bustling city of international trade set to the northern most region of France. If she truly wanted to be honest with herself, she would admit that the thought of seeing Piro was very appealing to her, yet she bore in mind what Henri had said regarding his reaction when told of her impeding trip.

The boat was now fully loaded with passengers and cargo. It would be an all day trip down the Seine but the weather was most pleasant and she was enjoying the sights of the small towns and fishing villages along its picturesque banks. As they approached, she could see the locals waving toward them. She waved back and more than once a fisherman gathering in his nets shouted "Beauté rouge tête va vous arrêter pendant un certain temps." Lucia just giggled and found Henri by her side "You see Lucia you draw the attention of everyone just by your presence." "Oh, Henri, they would speak to the fish if that would make their day pass easier."

It was an easy trip and as they neared the harbor, Lucia was caught up in the sights and sounds of the busy port. There were many large vessels waiting to be loaded to sail across the Channel to Great Britain and other ports of call. The smell of raw sewage, tar and turpentine, as well as the mass of bodies, filled her head with past memories of Naples and the day Vesuvius destroyed her village. She was roused from her thoughts by Sophia "Mistress, this is so exciting, I am anxious to see all the shops in the city, Madeline, she is the kitchen maid, told me that some of the finest items can be found here, and very inexpensive." Lucia was also excited and said "Sophia, I know that you and Nicko are in love, when we get back to Monteforte do you wish to marry?" The maid's mouth dropped and she looked stunned "Mistress, I am so sorry, did we do something to offend you? Have we done anything wrong?" Lucia grabbed her by the shoulders and said "Dear Sophia I love you like a sister, of course you did nothing wrong, I want you to be happy. You can marry Nicko and still be with me. Tonight, while I am otherwise engaged with my social obligations I want you and Nicko to take some time off to be alone that is why I told him to leave the other two back." Sophia was giddy at the thought of spending private time with Nicko, but quickly her expression changed "Oh Mistress, Nicko would never let you be alone and unattended." "Do not concern yourself, I will not be alone, Genaro, Mateo and the Marquis will be with me. Surely, I will be safe. I will insist that he obey my request." Sophia nodded but there was definitely a dubious look on her pretty face.

It took a little while before they were unloaded and sitting in their carriage. Henri had made the necessary arrangements for them to spend the next few days at Lord Stevens' manor, which was not too far from the port. Lucia was quietly enjoying the ride to their final destination when Henri interrupted her thoughts "Lucia tomorrow we shall go to the harbor to see the progress of the new shipyard I hope all that I have done pleases you." She leaned toward him and grabbed his gloved hand "Henri I am sure it will be wonderful." The handsome face lit with joy.

Lord Stevens' manor house was not grand but nicely appointed, the lack of feminine touches was markedly noticeable, yet, it was a warm place that spoke of its owner's tastes. The house had an underlying scent of tobacco and polished wood. The main salon was a massive room with tall ceilings and trussed beams supporting its expansive length.

There was a model of a sailing ship, which occupied a large corner of the room. It was a marvelously detailed miniature and Lucia was drawn to it. She was bent over intrigued by the model and busy investigating the perfectly scaled design elements, when she was interrupted by a polite cough. She spun around to find herself staring at a handsome young man. He was very tall and broad shouldered. His dress was not formal but the cut of his waistcoat was of a fine weave. There was something captivating about his face. He had a ruddy complexion from being outdoors no doubt, which complimented his auburn hair, which was not powdered. His features were clean and chiseled with a strong chin and full lips. It was his eyes that drew her attention; they were of the deepest shade of green.

"Oh, excuse me I was just admiring the view of this beautiful model." The handsome stranger, which Lucia already surmised, was the master of the house smiled ruefully and said, "So was I." Lucia felt the immediate rush of heat to her face and silently cursed herself for it. The man walked over to where she was standing and bowed formally "Please let me introduce myself, I am Lord Danford Stevens of Wallingston, Great Britain, and it is an honor to welcome you to my modest home." Lucia was trying to find her tongue "Thank Lord Stevens, I am the Marchesa Lucia Banfi of Monteforte" she responded in accented English.

At that very moment in came the rest of her party, it was Henri who said, "Ah, there you are and I see you have already introduced yourselves." The Marquis came over to Lord Stevens and they greeted each other in a familiar embrace. "Henri it is always so good to see you. I trust your trip was uneventful?" By the older man's face, it was obvious that he liked Lord Stevens and enjoyed his company. "Ah, it is so good to see you as well Danford. It was very pleasurable except we had to beat the fishermen back from wanting to take Mistress Lucia as their prize." Lucia was mortified "Henri stop that," she protested in French. The big man laughed heartily "Well I cannot say that I would blame them" he replied in flawless French. Again, Lucia could feel a bead of sweat forming on her upper lip and wanted to beat herself.

"Please let me introduce Lord Genaro Banfi and Lord Mateo Rizzo, brothers of the Marchesa." The two men stepped forward to make his acquaintance. "Welcome to my home. Please make yourselves comfortable and if there is anything, you need be sure to let my servants know. I am sure you are weary from your trip and famished. Once you are settled we will dine around seven o'clock," he bellowed in a strong but pleasant voice. All the while he was speaking the handsome lord did not release Lucia from his stare, it was most disconcerting. "With your permission I will take my leave to give instruction to my staff." He bowed formally and retreated from the room. As soon as he disappeared, a small army of servants appeared in his place and escorted them to their rooms. Sophia was already being settled into the space they had been assigned. It was a lovely room, spacious and airy, with a view of a small, but manicured English garden. There was a magnificently carved bed, and what looked to be layer, upon layer, of goose down blankets, which were piled high; it looked so inviting. The furnishings other than the bed were simple in design but of a good quality. In the corner of the room was a desk that had been furnished with fine vellum paper and several fresh quills and ink. Lucia was very pleased with the accommodations.

"Mistress I saw Lord Stevens he is very handsome, don't you agree?" Lucia tried to be coy and replied, "Oh, I hadn't noticed" but could not stop herself from giggling. "Yes he is very handsome and very sure of himself. I think I shall like him very much." "I think you should wear the blue gown to dinner this evening. It brings out your eyes so nicely," said Sophia as she was unpacking the very garment from the trunk they had brought. "Well, if you think so."

When she made her way to the dining room Lucia was surprised by the formality of the setting. It was a large room with a long, grand, table, which had been set with fine linens and equally elegant china. Fresh flowers had been set in vases and there was a warm glow from the many candles. An interesting scent of cinnamon filled the air. The men had been enjoying a glass of wine and otherwise engaged in lively conversation. When they saw her standing at the threshold, of the room, all eyes fell upon her and she flushed from the attention. It was Lord Stevens who left the group as he was in the middle of his sentence to come to her "Good evening Marchesa Lucia you look radiant in that gown it matches the color of those beautiful blue eyes" he said in perfect Italian. Lucia curtsied and slipped her arm over his "I see you are a man who possesses command of many languages." Pleased that she noticed he replied, "As do you My Lady."

It was Henri who softly said to Genaro and Mateo "They make a handsome pair, do you not agree?" Mateo who was watching Lord Stevens was careful not to show his wolfish grin "Indeed." Genaro who caught sight of his reaction gave Mateo a sharp elbow in the ribs and he feigned injury.

They found their places at the dining table. Lucia surprised by where she had been seated, which was not to the right of Lord Stevens, which would have been customary, but opposite him at the end of the table. Four other guests had been invited, an English couple who were visiting, Lord Morgan and Lady Winifred North. They were a middle-aged couple of considerable wealth as was evident by their manner and dress. Two gentlemen, Sir William Bradford, Esq. a barrister, and Lord Montague Parker, both of whom were on assignment from his Majesty King George of England. In all, it was a lively evening with much conversation regarding the recent political events in America. Lucia was much intrigued with news from that part of the world.

It was a hearty and well-presented feast but certainly not sumptuous, Marcello would have had many criticisms of this meal. While it was lacking in gourmet preparation and presentation it was savory and well cooked. Again, the lack of a feminine touch was quite evident. Yet, Lucia felt warmly welcome and enjoyed not only the food but also the company. She caught Lord Stevens staring at her several times and each time he made that, it was purely accidental. She smiled at the obvious attempt on his behalf to act casual.

After dinner, cognac and cigars were served in the library, and the men continued their discussion of the problem of pirates on the high seas. They were focusing on the shipping trade that the Dutch now more or less controlled and the demand for goods from America. Lucia would have loved to continue with the conversation but politely joined Lady Winifred North in the solar for sherry and gossip.

"So my dear, what brings you to France?" Lucia was intently watching the Lady North and thinking to herself that she would become just like that in twenty years from now and shuddered at the thought. "I am embarking on a tour of several countries to see firsthand the progress of the companies and holdings that I have inherited." Lady North could hardly contain her surprise "You are the heir to a family fortune?" Lucia was not surprised by her question and answered, "Why do you seem so shocked? Is it because I am not a man?" Lucia realized that the tone of her voice had suddenly taken one a sharp bite. "My aunt, from whom I have inherited my fortune, was one of the most powerful women in all of Europe perhaps you have heard of the Marchesa Maria Sucretti?" Lady North's beady little eyes grew wide with this revelation "Of course all of Europe knows of her vast empire. She has left it all to you? Why, are there no male heirs in your family? Did I not just meet two of your brothers?" Lucia could feel the flames of anger heating her cheeks and was about to give Lady North her opinion when Lord Stevens stepped into the solar.

"Lady North I hate to interrupt what seems like an engrossing conversation but would you mind if I stole Marchesa Banfi for a while?" The old biddy had hardly voiced her reply and Lucia was on the arm of the handsome lord of the manor. As they were already leaving the room, they heard a faint "Of course not." Lucia was angry and felt the heat upon her face, but was trying desperately to control herself by biting the inside of her cheek. Her rescuer's arm was strong and muscular and his grip was steadfast on her arm. She felt him pulling her into a salon which was off toward the opposite end of the manor. Finally, they arrived and she looked around the room. Models of ships in various stages of construction filled the space. There were tables laid out with strips of wood and the room reeked of green wood and turpentine. Sketches, charts, and paintings of sailing vessels adorned the walls. There were collections of compasses and clocks in glass cases. There was an array of carving instruments, were neatly arranged according to size, their use attested to by the littered wood shavings that decorated the floor. Overall, it was the workshop of a man who enjoyed designing sailing vessels and she found it most appealing.

Lucia heard the heavy door close behind her and she spun to see what was going on. "I must apologize for Lady North she is a crotchety old busybody but her husband is a good friend of my father. Lord North is much more tolerable than she is but unfortunately, she accompanies him wherever he goes. I hope she did not offend you in any way?" By now, he was standing very close to her and because of their height difference; she had to look up to see his face.

"Thank you Lord Stevens for coming to my rescue for in another moment I would have told her some uncharitable things. You have saved my honor and her pride." He laughed with such warmth and gusto that she found that she too was laughing, the anger she was holding was starting to dissolve. "Lady North does have that effect on most people, very much akin to a bug that you cannot catch but keeps buzzing in your ear."

"This is a wonderful room. Have you made all these models?" Lord Stevens seemed to have stood just slightly taller and he was obviously pleased that she appreciated his talents. "I find that making scale models helps me with the life size ships that I build. If I find a flaw in the models design I can correct it on the real one." Lucia was now truly impressed. Not only was this man gorgeous to look at, but he had a true sense of who he was and was confident in what he did. She could truly find herself liking this man.

"That My Lord Stevens is very impressive. May I look at some of your sketches?" He gave an appreciative smile "I would not think that a woman as beautiful and educated as you would care to bother herself with such details. I find it rather refreshing." Lucia, her blue eyes, now shielded under a hood of lush thick strawberry lashes replied, "I have many interests My Lord." She saw that he seemed just taken a little off balance but quickly recovered "I hear you enjoy riding horses would you care to join me tomorrow morning before breakfast?" Lucia was very excited at the prospect of going for a ride, she missed Apollo, and her daily runs with him "Yes that would be delightful. Dawn?" His handsome face wore all his emotions and Lucia could see that he was amazed by her response "Yes, I shall be waiting at the stables."

Lucia did not want to leave the room. She wanted to look through all his drawings and ask him many questions, but she knew that their absence would already we provoking speculation as to what they were doing. "I believe Lady North has probably attached herself to another unwitting victim, so perhaps we should join the others, before they think you have kidnapped me." He came closer to her and she could smell his scent, which was a pleasant mixture of leather and cinnamon. She thought to herself what an odd smell, but very pleasing. "You are most interesting My Lady is there no end to your appeal?" Lucia felt the flush rise from her toes to her face and as always cursed herself for it "I love life and I enjoy learning something every day of that life. Perhaps you will teach me things that I have yet to learn." The handsome lord was speechless. He searched her beautiful face and seemed to dissolve into those eyes the color of the sea "It would be my honor and my pleasure to show you all that you want to see and teach you all that you would like to know."

"Perfect, it is then settled, before I leave France I shall have you teach me to sail a ship? Will you?" Lord Stevens was taken aback by the forthrightness of this lovely young woman. He hesitated for a moment then said, "Well, if that is your desire then you shall become a sailor." They laughed in the comfort of their own sudden awareness of their feelings.

"Lord Stevens I would like to thank you for your hospitality." The young lord was nearly touching her he was so close. "It is I who am thankful for such a beautiful woman to grace my humble home. May I kiss your cheek?" Lucia was stunned for a second then recovered "Yes." Again, she felt the heat paint her cheeks the most appealing shade of crimson. He bent his head and his lips brushed first one cheek then the other. When he pulled back, his breathing was a little quicker and then he moved suddenly toward the door. "We should join the others." Lucia was cemented to the floor but recovered and met him at the door. His large hand upon the small of her back gave her a shudder "Thank you" came his hot breath on her neck. Lucia's knees were weak and she had to catch her breath.

"Mistress Banfi I see my Master of Horse has secured a worthy steed for you." Lord Stevens came over to the handsome animal and scratched his nose. "He seems most agreeable. We have introduced ourselves." Lord Stevens smiled and helped Lucia sit the horse. His own horse, which was a magnificent animal, was anxiously waiting to be mounted. "We shall follow the path along the forest," he shouted over his shoulder as he took off at full cantor. Lucia whispered into her horse's ear "You are not going to let them beat us now are you?" and she slid a sugar cube into his mouth. Fixing her reins Lucia gave him a swift kick and off they went. It was a crisp morning and she could see the breath forming billows of steam from his flaring nostrils he was hoofing steadily down the well-worn path. In a matter of moments, Lucia was already two lengths ahead of Lord Stevens.

They ploughed on until she could sense that her horse was straining. She had made her point; that she could out ride the lord of the manor. As he was catching up, she brought her horse to a stop, jumped off, and tethered him to a branch. It was a beautiful forest thick with pine trees and their fresh clean fragrance. He came to where she had tied her horse and jumped off to join her. "You truly know how to ride a horse." Lucia chuckled "He is a good horse but tiny in comparison to my beloved Apollo. I love to ride. I love the feeling of being free." Lord Stevens had taken a blanket and a basket from his own horse and was laying them on a bed of pine needles. "Please, come join me, let us have a bit of food." Lucia sat down and waited while he unloaded the basket. The aroma of fresh baked bread and a pie filled with cheese and ham made her mouth water. He doled out a portion of each and she ate with gusto. "This pie is wonderful, what do you call it?" The lord, his mouth filled, waited until he had finished then answered "Quiche. It is a pie made from eggs, ham, and cheese. I like the taste and have it often. It travels very well."

He took a silk scarf from his waistcoat and reached over to wipe her mouth. She did not pull away. "I have made a pig of myself. I apologize but it was too good. I shall impose upon your cook to give me the recipe to bring home." The lord laughed and Lucia's expression made him answer an unasked question "Of all the delicacies in France your favorite is a simple pie that all the peasants eat. You are so remarkably unmarred by the vast fortune you possess. It is a gift that you have Mistress Banfi. It is the gift of honesty and truthfulness." Lucia felt the flush wash over her face "Dear Lord Stevens I would lie, if only I could command my face not to tell the truth." He laughed so hard he spat out a mouthful of food.

Lucia's expression changed and she was now quite serious, the young lord sensed that something was troubling her "Mistress Banfi what is pressing on your mind that you look so serious?" Lucia's intense blue eyes met his and she said, "I wish to ask you a deeply personal question but I am ashamed for my forwardness." He seemed concerned "Please if there is something that is troubling you ask me, I will tell you all you want to know." Lucia took in a deep breath and said, "Do you have a wife or are you contracted for marriage to anyone?" He just stared at her in amazement "No I am not married, nor contracted to anyone." Lucia smiled "That pleases me." He leaned over and gently kissed her cheek. "Mistress Banfi I have never met a woman like you. You have in two short days already cast your spell on me." " Lord Stevens please address me as Lucia when we are alone and may I call you Danford?" "That would please me very much Lucia."

He stood, unfolding his strong muscular frame, and extended a hand to help her to her feet. "Sadly, we must be heading back or we shall miss all the light of the morning and you do want to see how your ship is progressing. Yes?" He held her in an embrace for what seemed a long time and then bent and kissed her on the mouth. It was soft and full of promise. They rode back to the manor house.

CHAPTER FOUR

A CHANGED MAN

Le Havre, France

It did not take too long for them to reach the shipyard. Nicko and Sophia had arrived in another carriage. As soon as she got out Sophia ran to her mistress the glow on her face told Lucia what she needed to know. "Is it settled Sophia?" The pretty maid nodded shyly "Thanks to you we will be able to marry and still hold our places. I cannot even begin to express my happiness." Lucia hugged her maid and kissed each of her flushed cheeks. "I am so happy for you dear Sophia." Lucia then caught Nicko's eye and he bowed deeply to his mistress. "As soon as we get back to Monteforte we shall have a wonderful celebration."

There was a commotion in the shipyard where a crowd had gathered. A man was shouting and cursing. Lord Stevens was ushering Lucia forward to see what was going on. The man had a young boy, perhaps ten, or eleven, by the collar of his shirt and was pummeling him. The boy's face was already swollen and bloody. His assailant was wild with anger and cursing at him. The boy's face was stricken with fear, as were the onlookers. No one approached the man to save the boy.

Suddenly, in a loud voice Lord Stevens shouted, "Piro, let that boy go" as his long strides closed the distance in seconds. Lucia was shocked first by the sight of how much Piro had changed and by his ruthless behavior toward this boy. Piro either did not hear him or chose to continue to strike the child. Lord Stevens ran from her side, caught his arm in midair, and pushed him violently away. "Have you gone mad, he is but a child?" Piro was enraged not only at whatever misdeed the boy committed but now Lucia could see the vehemence in his face as he looked at Lord Stevens. "What do you know of the daily workings of this place? You come here the Lord of the Manor and think everything runs to perfection. It runs that way because I must keep everyone in line. I am the person who takes the responsibility to see that the work is done." The young lord who was taller and heavier than Piro had his fists clenched and would surely have hit him but held his temper. "If it were not for my design and abilities you would not even be here. I warn you to bear that in mind."

Lord Stevens bent to whisper to the boy who was crying and shaking. Lucia could see that he had been badly beaten. "Nicko get that boy and have him attended to immediately. Make sure that he receives a full purse for himself and his family." "But Mistress we do not know what crime the boy committed." Lucia's face grew stern "What could a child of his years have done. No child should endure such punishment. Do it now and not another word." Nicko bowed and went to do as he was instructed.

Nicko quickly went to Lord Stevens, drew him aside, and told him what Lucia had said. The lord nodded and let the boy into Nicko's charge. Piro was furious "How dare you come here and disrespect my authority?" By now, Lucia was only a few steps from where he was standing with his back facing her.

"It was not Lord Stevens who removed the boy from you but me." He swung around to face Lucia. "Mistress I was not aware that you were coming here today." Lucia was visibly upset as was evidenced by her expression "Would you not have beaten that child had you known I was coming? Piro, I will not tolerate such abuse." He was so angry she was sure he would have struck her as well. "You cannot come here and disrupt the order of things," he protested. Lucia closed her eyes for a moment to gather her thoughts "I see you have forgotten that I am your Mistress and you serve at my pleasure. I will tell you, from this day forward, I shall appoint someone to oversee the workings of this shipyard. If you step out of line, I will discharge you from your duties. Do you understand Piro?"

Henri had made his way to the center of this mayhem "Piro what is going on here? You would have seriously injured that boy. Do you forget that Marchesa Banfi is in charge not you?" The marquis was angry that Piro had disrespected Lucia with his arrogance. "I have worked day and night to make this successful and now I am but a mere servant. Did you all not even bother to ask what that ignorant wretch did?" Lucia looked him in the eye "A boy of that age could never have done such a crime to warrant being beaten half to death. Che cosa è accaduto a voi Piro?"

Piro bowed deeply to Lucia "Mistress I am sorry if I have offended your delicate sensibilities. I am striving to make everything perfect. I lost my temper with the boy and I now regret my actions. I shall see to it that he is properly cared for." Lucia still upset but calm answered "There is no need I have sent Nicko to make sure he receives treatment and money." Again, the anger was so obvious but Piro kept it under control and replied, "As you wish Mistress" came his tart reply. Lucia would have slapped his face but restrained herself. Lucia spoke softly and in their native tongue "Go home and gather your thoughts and find out what troubles your mind. I shall see you when you have recovered." Piro looked like a whipped dog, his jaw clenched so tightly he could have cracked his teeth, bowed, kept his head down, turned, and walked away.

Lord Stevens wisely stood silently to the side and observed the workings of this capable young woman. Henri spoke "Mistress Lucia I am so sorry that you were witness to this terrible scene. I do not know what has come over Piro." Lucia now composed once again "Henri this is not your fault, but, I require that someone is here at all times to manage the situation. I am afraid that Piro would have killed that poor boy. Do you know if this has happened in the past?" Henri shrugged "There was talk, but, then there is always talk. One cannot trust all that is said." "But perhaps the talk had truth behind it. If that ever happens again I shall dismiss Piro and strip him of all that he has acquired."

"Well, shall we try to salvage this day by reviewing the progress of the construction?" said the strong baritone voice of Lord Stevens with an attempt at sounding lighthearted. Lucia drew in a deep breath and wrapped her arm over his "Yes let me see what my new ship will look like." The small group toured the shipyard and Lord Stevens gave explanation as to the design and construction of the merchant vessel. It was a massive undertaking with many men and boys performing various tasks. Lucia was caught up by the sights and sounds of this busy, noisy place. Huge planks of green timber were being dried and cured so that they could be formed to bend and shape the hull of the ship. Huge raw trees were being boiled in massive cauldrons, which spewed clouds of smoke that hung in the dampness of the enclosed cavernous space. Carpenters were cutting and sanding the newly bent planks. The floor was covered in a blanket of sawdust and bark which was at least an inch deep. Another cauldron of tar and turpentine was brewing to seal each piece that was nailed to the giant skeleton of the vessel. Lucia imagined this would surely be what a beehive looked like on the inside. There was a symphony of banging, clanging, sawing, and singing. The men were keeping a steady pace by singing a tune. It was pure chaos and she was delighted.

Lord Stevens excused himself to speak with a man who was overseeing the placement of each plank. The lord was giving him instructions and the older man was nodding in agreement. Lucia watched him as he masterfully showed the other what he required. He was a powerful man, intelligent and kind and she could see that the workers respected him. Henri came to stand by her side "Lucia I see how you are watching Lord Stevens are you attracted to him?" Lucia flushed "Yes I am he is a wonderful man and very kind." "My dear Lucia, he is a good man but do not forget he is a man and you are a beautiful woman. You have confided that you wish to experience life and I am happy for you but just be careful. Promise me you shall be careful." Lucia, her cheeks aflame with embarrassment replied, "Dear Henri I shall be cautious at all times do not fear" then she kissed his cheek.

"Well Marchesa what say you?" shouted Lord Stevens above the cacophony, as he puffed up his chest with pride. "It is simply wonderful. I am so impressed with the size of this massive vessel. When the ships are in the water one does not realize how large they are since half their height hidden below the water line. I am so happy I could see the birth of our first ship. Thank you Lord Stevens for all your hard work, someday we shall sail on her together." The young lord his handsome features enhanced by the deep emerald of his eyes smiled broadly "It would be my honor My Lady."

By now, Mateo and Genaro had joined them in the bowels of the shipyard. "Brothers come see what a fine vessel we are building. Someday we shall all sail to America on this ship. Will you both come?" Lucia was as excited as a little girl. Both men were walking around looking, pointing, and watching. "Dear Lucia it is a marvelous vessel, Genaro and I would be grateful to accompany you to America. Lord Stevens, is this ship your own design?" "Yes but I must confess I studied the basic design concept from a master engineer and then modified its structure to suit my own construction. I am pleased that you both find it worthy for your sister."

"Lord Stevens, will you join us for supper this evening at my apartments?" ask Henri. "I regret that is not possible. I have a prior commitment with Lord North and Lord Parker, Sir Bradford has been commissioned by my father to relinquish all his holdings to me, and we must finalize the details of the transfer. However, tomorrow evening I am hosting a small party for my friends Francois Boucher and Giovanni Tiepolo who are both here in Paris for a few days. I would be so happy if all of you could come." He then turned to Genaro "I am sure you are familiar with their work?" Genaro eagerly replied, "Of course, who does not know of these two masters of the arts, even if the others don't come, you, My Lord, would be hard pressed to keep me away." They laughed, "Well then until tomorrow evening, I bid you all a good evening." He turned to Lucia "Marchesa thank you for an interesting day and

I look forward to seeing you tomorrow evening." He then bowed deeply and kissed her hand. Lucia was glowing.

Lucia was left standing next to Genaro "This was a difficult day for you dear sister, I heard what happened with Piro. What will you do with him?" Her expression had turned sad at the thought of the ugly incident with Piro. "I don't know brother. I had sent Piro to Henri with the hopes that an education would give him the tools to become a better man. If what I am hearing has any basis of truth, Piro has become a vile man. He nearly beat that poor child to death. I cannot, I will not, tolerate such cruel treatment from those who work for me. I will need to speak with him and try to understand what has caused him to become this violent and bitter young man. He was given every opportunity and Henri tells me he was doing so well, yet, something has changed within him." "I see that this transformation has hurt you deeply. Did you have feelings for Piro?"

Lucia took a deep breath and clutched her brother's arm as if she needed to support herself. "Before Piro was sent here to apprentice under Henri there was an incident that involved the two of us. He got the wrong impression to a simple act of kindness and reacted poorly. For his trouble, Gandolfo found it his duty to administer a severe whipping. I was not Marchesa then and so did not have the authority to prevent it. That very night, I was attacked by a man and nearly killed. It was Piro, who, sick with fever from the whipping, found me, and carried me to safety. I cannot forget his act of love for me. Now, after seeing what he has become, I find that I have lost any affection I would have held for him. I will not have him administer cruelty to those who work for me. I feel that I have repaid his sacrifice and laid before him the opportunity to become a wealthy man. He seems determined to destroy what I have given him. What shall I do brother?"

Mateo had come just as Lucia was telling her story and he joined in "Lucia no matter what you do you must step carefully. Piro is a proud young man, who was humiliated by your actions this morning, and was dishonored in front of those he thinks are his servants. His pride has been shattered and he will seek revenge. I tell you to be wary, for once a man's honor is destroyed he can never be the person he used to be. Piro now feels like he did when he was a stable boy at Monteforte."

Lucia was upset "Did I do wrong this morning Mateo?" He came to her, kissed her forehead, and brushed a curl from her face "No dear sister you did nothing wrong because you saved that young boy from serious harm or death. We do not know how many others have suffered in silence and fear at Piro's hand. No one would have given him the chance to change his life as you did. Do not hold yourself in contempt for his actions. Obviously, this is a man who cannot handle the challenge of being in charge." He turned to face her and said "Lucia I want you never to be alone in this man's company. He is dangerous and violent. I am afraid for your wellbeing." "But Mateo we grew up at Monteforte together, he loves me, and would not hurt me." Mateo gave a sad little chuckle "You are wise in so many things but so naïve in the ways of men and life. It is because he loves you that he has become so dangerous. You have publicly whipped him again. Piro is a man now Lucia and you have shamed him in front of Lord Stevens whom he tries to compete with but cannot. Do you understand?"

A small parade of tears marched down her beautiful face and she blinked furiously to hold them back "I am so sorry, I never meant to hurt him, this is my entire fault. Had Piro stayed at Monteforte something bad would have happened to him, so I sent him away with hopes for a better future. I don't know what to do, I don't want to bring him any more pain, but I know in my heart that I cannot let him continue on here and possibly hurt someone."

"It is truly a difficult situation you are facing little sister. Piro needs to go. Perhaps, Mateo and I could talk with him and send him off with enough money to start over again elsewhere. Would you want us to talk with him?" Lucia squared her shoulders and straightened her chin "I will not ask either of you to clean up my soiled linens. I made the mess I shall have to deal with it. I will make him an offer to leave and if what you are saying about his pride is true then perhaps he will agree, quietly leave, and start fresh somewhere other than here. We shall see soon enough."

When they arrived back at Henri's apartments Sophia greeted Lucia "Mistress I have two letters that have arrived for you." Lucia was happy to receive word from home and looking at the letter saw that it was from her sister Antoinetta. The other letter, which was beautifully engraved, carried the official seal of His Majesty Louis XVI; the sight of it filled Lucia with excitement. "Sophia please prepare a bath." Lucia needed to rest and tried to sort out how she was going to dismiss Piro, the mere thought of it made her head ache. "Nicko told me of the incident with Piro, I know how much that hurt you. I remember how he always looked at you with those big sad eyes. Does he not realize that he can never be with you?" Lucia sat down with what seemed the weight of the world on her head. Sophia came over and undid the plaited braids she had done early that morning and then rubbed Lucia's temples. "Mistress you have done more than he deserved, I know your heart is broken, but he has become someone else." Lucia loved Sophia and reached to grab the hand that was massaging her head. "Thank you, I know what I must do, but it pains me to do it. I tried to repay him but he is not the Piro I knew."

She opened the letter from Antoinetta, which was written on good velum in her fine hand. Lucia closed her eyes to bring the image of her sister to herself.

Dearest Sister,

While I have been so busy with learning how to be Lady Catalano and all that it requires of me, I still find time to miss you. Tomaso has already proven to be a kind and gentle man, and his parents have welcomed me with open arms. I could not be happier except that I miss you and Monteforte.

You will be happy to know that Tomaso rides Nero every day. I would swear that he loves that horse more than me. When I see him, upon that great beast, I think of you astride Apollo and I want to cry for our separation.

I have seen Zia and Zio who have come to our estate to visit. They are counting the days until you come home. They seem so rested and in love and Zia does not regret that she has placed you in charge. They are so proud of you Lucia as we all are.

Oh, and there is another small matter that I would share with you. I have missed my courses this month and so you may be an aunt sooner than we had planned. I have not yet told Tomaso for I want to be sure. If I am with child, please pray with me that it is a healthy child. I know that Lord and Lady Catalano would be most pleased if I were to produce an heir to the Catalano family. I am afraid that it might be too soon for Tomaso and I have just begun to know each other. It is in God's hands and I trust He will show us the way.

Write to me soon. I love and miss you very much,

Your Loving Sister, Lady Antoinetta Catalano

Lucia was thrilled to hear from her sister and sat quietly reading the letter. She too missed her sister. These two women, who were so truly different, but so much alike, shared their love for each other and for Monteforte. Lucia felt a pang of jealousy that Antoinetta was so happy but then quickly dismissed it from her mind. She would never find happiness being the property of some man.

Antoinetta, her sister, having a baby, the idea of it was so foreign. Of course, she knew that if you lay with a man there is always that possibility but it was so soon after the marriage. She tried to envision her petite sister with a big belly and the visual image was absurd. Lucia smiled to herself and again fought back the demons of jealousy. A baby! Her sister was having a baby! She would be an aunt. Lucia suddenly found her spirits lifted at the thought of a baby.

She was thinking of Zia Maria and Zio Giovanni and was pleased to hear that not only were they in good health but that they had gone to see her sister. The burden of the Rizzo fortune was now lifted from Maria Sucretti's aging shoulders. Wait until Mama and Papa hear the news, as well as Zia, and Zio. How wonderful and such a blessing.

"Mistress" came the soft voice of Sophia. "Yes Sophia what is it?" "Your bath is ready shall I help you?" "No, that will not necessary, but I would like you to bring a glass of cognac and set up my writing tablet. I will send some letters once I have completed my bath." Lucia tried to relax and wash away the thoughts of the day's trouble with Piro. She tried to focus on her sister's letter but she found herself too distracted and grew angry and hurt. Piro had stolen her happiness for her sister.

When she had finished her bath, she saw that Sophia had done as she had instructed and found the glass of cognac sitting by her writing materials. She made herself comfortable and took a sip of the amber liquid, which slid, down her throat with sweet heat. She closed her eyes and thought back to a day long ago when she had seen Piro for the first time as a young man and not just as a stable boy. He was growing tall and his once narrow shoulders were filling out. He had a kind face with large expressive eyes and handsome features. She could almost feel the touch of his lips on her own as he had stolen a kiss. She felt the wrenches of bitterness taint the sweet taste of the alcohol. Damn him. Why was life so complex? All she wanted was to give him a better life. She tried to push the thought of him out of her mind once again.

In the hopes of putting her ailing mind at rest, she reached for the beautiful note with the seal of His Majesty. Her hand trembled ever so slightly with anticipation as she carefully broke the wax seal. The parchment was so fine and perfumed with the scent of roses.

Marchesa Lucia Banfi,

It has come to my attention that you are currently visiting our beautiful city while a guest of the Marquis De Fauntil. I would be very pleased to meet you as I have heard splendid things of you.

I am hosting a gala in three weeks and would be delighted if you would care to attend. As I am told, you are in the company of your brothers I extend this invitation to them as well and the Marquis De Fauntil.

I look forward to your arrival,

Her Majesty the Queen of France,

Maria Antoinette

As excited, as she was at the invitation, Lucia felt a dark cloud hang over her. No matter what she did to distract her mind, she was trapped by her own doing. Feeling that she would not be a desirable dinner guest Lucia sent word to Henri and her brothers that she would take her supper in her rooms for she was tired and upset. Mateo gently knocked on her door "Come" she answered. "Lucia, are you ill?" He came to where she was sitting on the settee by the terrace doors and joined her. "Physically I am fine but my mind and heart are heavy." Mateo took her hand and lifted it to his lips "Baby sister I know you are preoccupied with the thoughts of that young man and how to discharge him, but I also know that you harbor feelings of guilt and responsibility for actions that were taken against him a long time ago. Actions you could not control and were not your fault. Non tenere se stessi responsabili per le azioni degli altri per se fate si nutre. I have carried the guilt of my birth my whole life and it nearly destroyed me."

"Thank you Mateo for coming to me I have grown so fond of our relationship. My brother Genaro has never been more content, please never hurt him for he loves you and it would break his heart." "Once again, I implore you not to worry, especially about my feelings for Genaro, for I too love him. I love you very much Lucia and I do not want to see you hurt. Come down and join us for supper Henri and Genaro are looking for you." Lucia relented and followed Mateo to join the others for supper and they were pleased to see her. "Ah, there you are, and as lovely as ever."

"I have received an invitation from Her Majesty Queen Marie Antoinette to attend a gala in three weeks. She has graciously extended that invitation to the three of you. Of course, that is if I wish to have you escort me, after all it is me who received the invitation." Lucia was trying desperately to act regal and so above her dinner companions. "Ah that would be a sad turn of fate for you not to include us in your invitation, but, alas we shall survive," said Genaro with a look such as the fox that just emerged from the hen house. Lucia was trying to surmise what he was up to when the three men all reached into their waistcoats and produced identical invitations as the one she had received. Lucia's eyes grew wide and her cheeks instantly glowed with heated surprise. "You have all been invited?" she asked with suspended indignity. The trio all nodded as if to feign their arrogance. After a moment of incredulous resignation, Lucia started to laugh and they all joined in the merriment. "To Versailles" bellowed Genaro his face fixed into a broad smile.

They ate and drank and Lucia felt comforted in the warmth of their companionship.

CHAPTER FIVE

A FIRE STARTS

Paris

The next morning Lucia, accompanied by Sophia and her brothers, made their way to the shop of Madame Francine Richaud dressmaker to the rich and famous. "Good morning Marchesa Banfi, are you here to be fitted for your gown to wear to the Queen's gala?" Lucia was going to ask how she knew that but then realized that this woman knew all the intimate secrets of Parisian society. "Yes, is it ready?" she asked breathless in anticipation. "But of course, please follow me, and we shall make whatever adjustments are necessary."

Mateo and Genaro were shown to a comfortable salon and offered cognac and pastries, which they gladly accepted.

Lucia and Sophia followed Madame Richaud to a sumptuously appointed dressing salon. Standing by were a small army of women ready to make whatever alterations as were needed. With her maid to assist, Lucia was outfitted in her first gown that was purchased from a shop.

It was a deep rich shade of royal blue in dupioni silk imported from the Orient. There were interlaced threads of both silver and gold and a most subtle design of embroided bumblebees on the long flowing body of the skirt. The bodice, which was lined with whalebones, lifted her full rounded breasts and a filigree of gold lace traced and caressed their voluptuous mounds. Her curvaceous waist was enhanced by the tight fit of the bodice. The sleeves were of the sheerest silk organza dyed to match the rich hue of the body of the dress, which gave a sensuous reveal of her bare arms. A bustle of matching silk was attached at the waistline and trailed a yard beyond her hemline. The overall effect was nothing short of spectacular. Madame Richaud presented her with a pair of matching silk shoes, which sported silver heels. Bumblebees of silver and gold, studded with diamonds, were set into her thick strawberry tresses.

"Marchesa I am stunned that this garment fits you so perfectly. You are truly a perfect model" the petite dress designer extended her hand to help Lucia from the raised platform. "Please walk so I may check the hemline for proper length." Lucia walked several feet and was confident that she would not trip over her skirt. "I think it will be fine Madame Richaud. I love the feel of this garment and the fit is very flattering." Lucia was admiring herself in the long full-length mirror. Sophia could not contain her excitement at the sight of Lucia "Mistress you are breathtaking. Every eye will be fixed on you." The diminutive shop owner was looking up at Lucia who stood at almost six feet and admired not only her own creation but was delighted at how her model displayed her work. "Magnifique! By the morning after the gala there will be a hundred women at my door begging for this very gown."

"Come let us seek the opinion of your brothers" and they made their way to the outer salon. When Mateo and Genaro saw Lucia, they stood with their mouths open. "Oh dear sister you are beyond words. You are a Goddess and very tall" chuckled Genaro. "My Lady you will leave everyone speechless. Madame Richaud you have outdone yourself" said Mateo. "You are fortunate that I am your brother for I would have to sweep you off your feet." The shop owner curtsied "I only sew the garments it is this beautiful woman that gives it life."

When they had made their purchases and were about to leave Lucia went over to Madame Richaud "Thank you for this beautiful gown I shall wear it with pride." The shop owner once again curtsied "Be sure to tell the ladies where you got it, but I vow that I shall never make another just like it because no one could do it as much justice as you."

They got back to Henri's just in time to change for dinner at Lord Stevens. Lucia loved the fast pace of being in Paris there was always something to do or see. Sophia was helping her dress when Lucia said "Sophia I shall not need you or Nicko this evening. Stay here and enjoy yourselves. Has Nicko asked for your hand in marriage?" Sophia's eyes lowered as if in sadness "He has not and I will not ask him. Perhaps he does not want me for his wife. I don't know Mistress I thought he loved me but now he seems distant." Lucia blew out her cheeks and shook her head "Men, I tell you Sophia I cannot understand what matter of reason flows through their heads." Sophia, her chin on her chest nodded her agreement. "Do not despair he shall come around."

As soon as their carriage pulled up to the manor house, Lord Stevens himself greeted them. "Welcome to all. We have a special treat this evening. Monsieurs Boucher and Tiepolo are going to select someone to sketch. It shall be a contest. Genaro please would you like to join in the fun. When it is finished the lucky person will be able to buy the sketch and the money will be donated to the coffers of Notre Dame for the poor." Genaro hesitated and Mateo spoke up "Of course he shall, it is for charity after all." Genaro looked frightened "I don't know Mateo, do you know who these men are? They are renown throughout the world." Mateo got angry "You are also renown throughout the world; do not sell yourself short Genaro how many times must I tell you that." Lord Stevens interrupted "It is settled then that you will join in this little exercise for charity." Genaro did not speak but just nodded.

The large main salon was filled with men and women and Lucia picked up the guttural tones of German, she heard French and some Italian, and so there was a mixture to many languages. She had worn one of the three new creations from Madame Richaud. The one she had chosen for this evening was a rich purple in a style that the dress designer said was the latest in high fashion. "You must always wear deep, vibrant, colors against your alabaster skin," said Madame Richaud. When she removed her cloak, Lord Stevens drew in his breath and his eyes devoured her with their penetrating stare so much, so that she suddenly felt very self-conscious. "My God Marchesa Lucia you are stunning. That color against your pale skin is astounding." By now, Lucia's face was aflame with embarrassment. The handsome lord realized he was embarrassing her and quickly apologized "I am sorry Marchesa I didn't mean to discomfit you with my remark. Please forgive my forwardness but you are so beautiful I cannot control my mind from speaking its peace." Lucia had to smile at that statement. "Thank you Lord Stevens."

Lucia was like a nymph, wherever she went people just watched her. Tonight was no exception. Lord Stevens with his chest puffed escorted the red haired beauty into the main salon and as expected, all eyes were upon her. Even at her ample height, the young lord was still almost a head taller than she was. They were a handsome sight, which did not go unnoticed by those watching. It seemed as if all the women's fans went to their mouths in one movement.

The two artists Boucher and Tiepolo, whom Lucia could see were about her own age, approached

"Who is this divine being?" asked Boucher. "This Monsieurs is the Marchesa Lucia Banfi of Monteforte." They both gave a deep footed bow "It is a pleasure to make your acquaintance" chimed in Tiepolo in Italian and he kissed her hand but lingered a little too long for her taste. "I am charmed Marchesa" replied Boucher his eyes surveying her up and down. Genaro and Mateo had joined the little group and Lord Stevens introduced the two men "Ah, are you the famous artist Genaro Banfi?" Genaro nodded "I have seen your work Monsieur and I am most impressed. I understand that you are in much demand by His Holy Father to embellish all the churches of Europe." "I have done a fair number." Lucia could see that her brother had gained a quiet confidence now that he knew that someone with Tiepolo's notoriety knew of his work.

"And this is my brother Lord Mateo Rizzo" said Genaro. "Ah, Monsieur, and I heard that you are an antiquities trader." Mateo, so handsome and sure of himself, nodded slightly with a coy smile on his swarthy face. "I have been known to dabble in the arts for preferred clients." Genaro stood just to Mateo's side and watched his every move; his every gesture like a faithful dog watches his master. "Tell me Lord Rizzo what has been the most exciting artifact you have ever found?" By now, Mateo knew he had captured their attention "I was once engaged by the Sultan of Tunisia to locate a sacred stone that had been stolen from his harem by a disgruntled mistress." It was Boucher whose curiosity was peeked "Did you find it?" Mateo had withdrawn a cigar from his exquisitely tailored waistcoat and was leaning over a candle waiting for it to light. The soft glow from the candle cast his face in amber light. The years had been kind to the man who still looked so youthful in spite of his true age. He took his time savoring the taste of the cigar and blowing puffs of its aromatic clouds into the air. Finally, with the rest of them waiting, he replied "Oh I found it after a while, as well as the girl. I am sorry to say it was unfortunate for the young wench who had stolen it. I was instructed to return both the stone and its thief back to the Sultan. I shall not tell you of the girl's fate but the Sultan is not a very sympathetic man." Lucia looked horrified "Brother that is a very sad story. Why did you bring back the girl?" "For two reasons my sweet sister. First, she knew the consequences of stealing from the most powerful man in her country, and, second, if I did not I would not have been paid. The Sultan is a very wise man, and, whilst he was fond of this girl he had to set an example to those who would disrespect him." They all nodded soberly. Mateo grinned with satisfaction.

The evening progressed with much enjoyment. Lucia had the regrettable misfortune of encountering Lady Winfred North once again. "Ah, Marchesa Banfi, I am delightful to see you once again." Lucia bit the inside of her cheek and curtsied slightly in acknowledgement "Yes, very nice to see you as well Lady North. I thought you were preparing to return to Great Britain?" The portly woman was fanning herself with such ardor that her hair was moving with each swipe of her fan "Quite so my dear, but, our young host Lord Stevens received legal documents from his father that needed to be reviewed by my husband. Once we assist Lord Stevens with settling some of his father's affairs we shall be heading back to Yorktown." "Well, I hope you enjoy the evening."

The talented musicians Handel and Bach seemed to be inseparable and Lucia speculated internally whether they were lovers. Perhaps it was her imagination but the way they moved gave off the impression that they enjoyed each other's companionship just a little too intimately. Lord Stevens had convinced them to entertain his guests who were all delighted at the prospect. Everyone's attention had drifted to the rapturous sounds of their music.

Lucia felt nearly faint with the heat, smoke from puffing cigars, and perhaps a little too much cognac. She made her way to the terrace to gather her thoughts and drink in some cool air. She was standing peacefully looking up at the evening sky admiring the stars, the music drifting out to the world beyond.

She closed her eyes for a moment trying to find her composure. Her head was swimming in fog. Unexpectedly, she felt a strong hand seize her across the mouth and with the other drag her off her feet. She was stunned, disoriented, and tried to fight this phantom from pulling her into the darkness. Lucia started to kick and was thrashing about but whoever her assailant was, he had a death grip on her.

A cold voice whispered in her ear so close she felt the brush of his mustache "Do not fight or scream for if you do I shall cut your throat from ear to ear. Come with me and I will not harm you. Do you understand?" Lucia knew she had little choice but to abide by what he was saying his strength was overwhelming her efforts at escape. She nodded in the affirmative but he kept a tight hold over her. He dragged her for a long distance. It was so dark she tripped several times but he did not loosen his grip. They came upon what Lucia thought to be the stables and once he withdrew his hand over her mouth and nose, she could smell the familiar scent of horses.

Quietly he opened the door just enough to push her through and then bolted it from the inside. He threw her down to the ground and she fell in a pile of hay. In the struggle, her hair had come undone and she could feel the bruising from where he had been squeezing her arm. She did not move for it was pitch black. Her first instinct was to make a run for it but in the dark, she knew he would quickly find her; apparently, he was familiar with this place. Out of nowhere, she felt his presence by her side. "I saw you in there laughing and dancing with Stevens. You are a whore and a witch. You cast your wicked spell on me and now on him." Lucia knew the voice but it was so distorted with loathing she was sure it could not be him. He reached out in the darkness, took hold of her hair, and turned her face toward his. She could smell the whiskey on his breath and his male odor. She was repulsed as he drew her to himself. She tried to turn away but he held her head so tight she was afraid he would tear her hair from its shaft. She cursed herself for not having had Madame Richaud sew in the secret pocket into her gown to hold her dagger. She was too embarrassed to tell her what it was for; and now she might die for her stupidity. Lucia could hear the voice of her uncle Giovanni in her head "Always keep this with you."

He kissed her hard and wet and she tasted his putrid saliva mix with her own. She gagged and tried to bite his lip. He reached back and let his open hand find her flushed cheek. Her eyes began to tear from the searing pain. "What is the matter you have no taste for me?" Lucia was choked with fear and anger "Who are you? What do you want of me?" Without warning, he landed another blow to her face with such ferocity it jerked her neck. "Whore, you've forgotten who I am. So short is your memory. Well I guess I must shake your memory loose."

Abruptly he stood and yanked her to her feet. "Come with me." She stood her ground but could not fight him off; she was no match for this lunatic. He took hold of her arm and pulled so hard she fell. He was furious. He bent down and hoisted her over his shoulder slapping her bottom with great force. Lucia was punching him in the back and trying to kick him but he kept up a relentless pounding on her bottom. "This is just the beginning. I shall teach you to respect me. I have lost everything for you." This voice was haunting and familiar and it frightened her. She was trembling as he carried her to the farthest recesses of the stable. She thought to scream but being so far from the manor house with all the music and conversation no one would hear her. She must keep her wits about her and make her move when the opportunity presented itself. Again, she cursed herself for not taking her dagger, the words of her uncle echoing in her head "Never be without your dagger. It will save your life one day."

They came to what she would suspect was the Master of the Horse's quarters. He dropped her on a low pallet that was covered with a blanket and pillow. Winded from the exertion of carrying her, his breaths were rapid and shallow. He was searching for something. Finally, he found a small taper, matchbox, and lit the candle. Lucia gasped. "Dear God, Piro, what are you doing? Have you gone mad?" Once again, he came over and slapped her face this time catching her lip and she began to taste blood. She started to cry. "Why are you doing this?"

He came to where he had dumped her on the pallet. He stripped off his shirt and turned his back toward her. She was shocked at the sight of his naked back. There were rows of crisscross silver scars that caught the light even in the dimness of the small room. She turned her head not to look upon his back. He turned on her like a viper on a mouse "Look at me, go on, feast your eyes on my back. You did this. You have disfigured me. Every lash, every scar, was because of you." Lucia was weeping, "I didn't know. I am so sorry Piro. It was not my doing." He fell upon her and pushed her down flat on the pallet "It was you even though you did not hold the whip in your hand; it was you who drove Gandolfo's hand." She was sobbing so hard she could hardly find her breath. "I am sorry."

Piro, his eyes wild with hatred, straddled her and torn at her bodice. "Sorry, that is why you humiliated me in front of my men at the shipyard. Sorry, that you have dismissed me and taken all my property. How sorry are you Mistress?" Piro savagely tore the front of her gown to the point that her breasts were fully exposed. "I loved you so much that I endured one hundred lashes for it. I dreamt of you day and night. I prayed to all the saints that someday, if I worked until my flesh fell off my bones that you might have me. I built that shipyard, made all the contacts with suppliers and would-be merchants, and it is that English cock who you desire."

Lucia knew there would be no reasoning with him he was beyond all sensibility. She was truly fearful for her life. "Piro, I will give you money, even land, just let me go." He slapped her again this time her nose began to trickle blood down her face. She was sobbing more from fear than pain. "There is no amount of money you can give me. You have stolen, like a thief in the night, my heart, and my manhood. I am and always will be your servant. Yet, tonight, tonight, I shall have my satisfaction. Tonight I shall show you who a real man is, not that English whoreson."

He took a dagger from his sash and slit open her gown. Now she was fully exposed. He stared at her but not with love or desire but as a predator. Lucia's mind went back to that dreadful day near Montecassino and she withdrew inside herself. This cannot be happening again. She started to flail, her arms catching him about the head and face but he just swatted them away like a nat. She was desperate and half out of her mind with fear.

Lucia was thrashing about punching and kicking. He was trying to hold her down. He tried to kiss her and she bit his lip with such force she spat out a piece of it. He cursed and gave her another slap.

For some reason, he suddenly let go of her arms. He sat upon her just looking at her and then started to cry. "I am no better than the man who tried to kill you all those years ago. That night I rescued you from him I vowed to protect you, yet here I am. What have I become?" Piro began to weep. "I am a dead man. You have killed me and taken my soul." He slowly got to his feet leaving her lying there. "I cannot violate you. I have loved you all my life. I prayed that you would give of yourself willingly. I see that is not to be. You are the muse of the devil. Your curse is in my soul. I am a dead man." He turned and started running toward the door from which they had entered.

Lucia curled up into a ball and lay there crying not for herself but for this poor wretched soul. Soon she heard a commotion outside people calling her name. They threw open the stable doors and saw the candle light. Genaro, seeing the light, ran toward the back room. When he saw her he fell to his knees "Lucia, oh caro Dio, che cosa ti è successo?" Lucia was in such a state of shock she could not speak. He wrapped her in the blanket and scooped her up. Lord Stevens was right behind him "What has happened here? Is Marchesa Banfi ill? Is she hurt?" Genaro was moving rapidly toward the door, he needed to preserve her honor "She is fine just feeling overcome by the heat. I will take her directly to Marquis de Fauntil's apartments." There was no stopping him or questioning him. Mateo was at his heels.

Neither Genaro nor Mateo asked anything of her, and gently but firmly laid her in the carriage. They drove as fast as they could back to Sant Germaine. When they arrived, they had the servants call for Sophia. She came instantly and upon seeing Lucia became frantic. "I am fine, but a little bruised. Help me to my rooms." Once again, Genaro carried her like a child in his arms to her rooms. Still swaddled in the blanket he softly asked, "Who did this to you?" She was going to lie and say she did not know her assailant but she knew that if he was not stopped next time he would surely kill her. "Piro" and she began to cry with such deep sorrow he held her tightly and stroked her head. "Did he abuse you?" Lucia knew what Genaro was asking and she answered "No; he did not, even though he could have. I am afraid that he is sick in his mind."

Genaro was enraged "I shall hunt him down and kill him with my bare hands." Lucia was too tired and hurt to argue. Genaro said "Sophia, help get her cleaned up." Sophia was crying and just nodded she could not even speak.

Sophia undid the threadbare blanket and began to wash her Mistress with the gentleness of a mother toward her infant. She wept and prayed as she went about her task. Lucia laid there and welcomed the comforting ministrations of her maid and friend. "What happened?" Lucia closed her eyes and told her the events of the attack. "I am so sorry. My sweet baby girl" Sophia was stroking her hair and kissing her face. "Did he damage you?" Lucia shook her head "No." Sophia brought her some cognac "Here sip this it will help you sleep." Lucia held her hand "Sophia, stay with me tonight." Sophia hugged her with the love of a mother "Of course." Lucia wept softly, her body hiccupping with emotion. "He betrayed me, Piro, he betrayed me," she repeated until she fell into a restless sleep.

Dawn had not yet broken when there came an urgent pounding at the door. The voices that wafted up to her bedroom were anxious and loud. She was hurting all over her body more from the tension of what she had endured the night before than the actual physical abuse. Now frightened and curious as to what was the cause of the commotion she and Sophia came to the top of the stairs, which from there they could clearly see the foyer and front entrance. There was a young boy accompanied by a slightly older young man, both, were panting from having run from wherever it was they had come from. "My Lord there has been a terrible accident at the shipyard" said the older breathlessly. He hesitated for a moment he was bent with his hands resting on his thighs. "What is it boy. Tell me quickly," demanded Henri who was in his nightshirt. "What has happened?" The younger boy jumped in to the conversation "My Lord the shipyard is on fire. We have called the alarm. They are coming with help."

Henri digested the news. He grabbed the older boy by the shoulders, "All is lost?" The boy now recovered stood upright "No My Lord it appears that the alarm was sounded just in time but there is much damage." Henri stood still contemplating his next move "I shall be there as soon as I dress. Does Lord Stevens know?" The boy nodded "Yes they told us to go to his manor house first so that he might salvage the ship." "Yes, that was good. Who are you boys?" They both stood taller for the moment "We work at the yard with our Papa. He first saw the flames. He sounded the alarm and sent us with this news." Henri said "Well done, you shall be rewarded for your deeds. Now go and tell them I am on my way. Go. Hurry." With that, they were gone and Henri nearly ran to his rooms to dress.

"Hurry Sophia, I must dress." Sophia's eyes grew wide with concern "Mistress you cannot go you are still hurt." Lucia spun to face her "I am fine. I will not sit idle while my ship burns. Now please help me before Henri leaves without me." Lucia dressed quickly in her riding gown and made her way down to the carriage house where Henri was just getting into the carriage. "Where are you going? You cannot come it might be dangerous." Lucia held the door and extended her hand for him to help boost her up into the cabin "I am coming." Just by the tone of her voice and the look in those eyes, Henri knew it was a lost cause to try to dissuade her from this mission.

It was a ten-minute ride to the shipyard. Even a mile away they could smell the scent of burning pitch. As they got closer, the flames were licking the side of the great building. Twenty, maybe more, men were hauling bucket, upon bucket, of water to put down the flames. The cauldron of turpentine was fueling the fire. She could see that Danford, whose height made him a clear target, was there at the head of the line of water bearers. He was talking with an older man. There were countless other people running here and there trying to salvage lumber and other materials. A number of wagons were waiting to haul off large wooden casks filled with some unknown substance. The hard part was trying to keep the horses calm for they were stamping and nervous from the smell of the smoke and the level of activity around them. It was plain that Danford was giving the man some instruction but he seemed to be arguing the matter. Of course, she could not hear the conversation but it was obvious that they were in disagreement.

As soon as the carriage pulled up Lucia jumped down not waiting for the driver to assist her. She ran, holding up her riding skirt, her hair loose and blowing in the air, to Danford. "Lord Stevens" she shouted for he had his back to her. He turned to see her coming up the line. "What are you doing here woman are you mad?" he was angry. "Do you forget this is my ship? I have a right and a duty to see that all is well." She too was angry. By now the older man, he had just been speaking with appeared with a leather apron and a leather hood. "Yes, that is exactly what I need. Thank you. Now get the rest of what I want ready. We can spare no more time. Quickly! Go." The pace was frantic. The wood from the vessel was dry as was all the hundreds of pieces of lumber that were stacked almost to the rafters of the mammoth building. It was the perfect kindling for this out-of-control blaze. Danford, with no time to exchange in any trivial talk, donned the leather apron. He was making his way toward the smoke engulfed entrance to the building. Lucia scurried along with him, curious as to what his plan was, but said nothing. The older man reappeared, and this time he was hauling a wheel barrel filled with sand, and behind him were two more men doing the same. Danford paid no mind to Lucia's presence but was intent upon what his next move would be. He spoke to the older man who called to one of the water bearers with a filled bucket to come over. He told him to douse the bucket over Danford. The water bearer looked fearful and with precious little time to spare Danford yanked the bucket from his hands spilling some of its contents on the ground. He then dumped the whole bucket over his head and it covered the lord's body. He then placed the leather hood over his head. He called for a scarf to cover his nose and mouth but no one had any. Lucia heard this, picked up her skirt, and began tearing at the hem of her petticoat. She ran toward him and handed him the torn scarf. "What are you going to do?" He was starting to tie the material around his face when she walked behind him and started laying a knot to secure it around his nose and mouth. "I am going to try to extinguish the fire that is in the cauldron. If we do not stop it we will be left with a mountain of ashes." He turned suddenly, and took her hand "If I should not come out of there I want you to know that I have fallen deeply and madly in love with you." Not waiting for her to answer he seized the handles of the first wheel barrel and proceeded into the burning building. As he entered through the huge opening, the smoke so thick and malodorous with the smell of pitch, all she could think of is what he had just said to her. A single tear rolled down her swollen cheek. The older man instructed the others to bring their barrels as close to the opening as possible and not to inhale any of the smoke.

Only minutes had passed but it seemed like forever. By now Henri had made his way to her side "I am so sorry Lucia. I was informed that this was the work of Piro. I blame myself for not seeing this coming." Lucia knew in her heart that this was in fact the work of Piro and her heart was broken for both of them. "Do not blame yourself for Piro's actions my only concern now is for Lord Stevens." As they were standing there, they saw the figure of Danford emerging from the smoke. He retrieved another barrel of sand and ducked back into the burning building. The smoke seemed to have gotten thicker. Black smoke was spewing from the blown out windows and doors. Henri was excited "Look Lucia, the flames are dying. See the black smoke. I believe Danford has smothered the cauldron."

Lucia started a silent prayer to the Blessed Mother "Dear Mother, Queen of Heaven, watch over Danford. Save him from the burning flames. Ave Maria." She closed her eyes and invoked all the saints and angels in Heaven to bring him to safety. It was early morning but the sky was dark, the wind was picking up over the water, and within moments, it started to rain. "Henri, it has been too long that Lord Stevens has stayed in there. What shall we do?" Henri looked very tired and forlorn "There is nothing to be done my sweet girl. We must wait. My fear is that he has been over taken by smoke." Lucia could not sit idle, she instructed the older worker to have clean water ready. She silently prayed, "Dear Blessed Mother, I beseech you to watch over this man and bring him safely back to me." A lone tear trickled down her pale cheek.

Eternity passed before they saw some movement at the opening to the giant building. Danford was on all fours crawling slowly out, he was wheezing and coughing and covered in soot. He had pulled off the leather hood and was gasping for air. He was barely clear of the belching doorway when he keeled over onto his side and lay there retching up black bile. Lucia ran to him "Danford are you all right?" She motioned for the bucket of water and once again tore at her petticoat hem for a clean cloth. She soaked it in the water and began mopping his face, which was red and angry looking. "Fetch me a cup or ladle, something with which to give him water to drink," she shouted. Within moments, a cup appeared which she dunked into the bucket and half filled. Scooping his head off the ground and laying it upon her lap, she coaxed some water into his mouth. He drank but then just as quickly gagged and coughed until it drooled out the side of his mouth. Henri, who was at her side, began instructing several of the men to retrieve a pallet or board upon which to lay the big man. Once found, it took six of them to carry Lord Stevens' inert body to a waiting wagon. "Quickly, take him to my apartments and send for the doctor. There is no time to spare."

Lucia turned to see her brothers emerging through the crowd "Lucia, what has happened. When we got up and inquired as to where you and Henri were Sophia told us that you were here. What has caused this terrible fire?" Lucia was so upset she could hardly speak "Piro set it on fire as revenge against me. Please we must help Danford I fear for his life." Mateo gathered her in his powerful arms and spoke into her ear "Fear not Lucia, he is a strong and healthy young man, he will recover." He kissed her lovingly, he and Genaro escorted her to the carriage. Henri rode with the wagon to insure Danford's safety.

When they reached the house on Sant Germaine, Danford's lifeless body had been brought in and placed in one of the first floor bedchambers. Sophia met Lucia. "Mistress you look so pale. I will get you some broth and a cup of wine." Lucia did not hear a word she said but asked, "Where is he?" Henri, Nicko, and Henri's maître d' were working quickly to strip him of his soot-encrusted clothes. One of the kitchen maids had a bucket filled with warm water and a bowl with soap and clean linen cloths. Not wanting to waste time Nicko cut the garments off his body. Lucia ran down the hall and burst into the room only to find Danford's stark naked body stretched across the bed and the three men washing him down. Her eyes grew wide at the sight of his beautiful body and a heated flush colored her face. She stood there paralyzed for the moment until Genaro and Mateo ushered her to the solar.

"Sit down before you fall down. You look dreadful. Here have some cognac it will calm you" came the distant sounds of her brother's voice. Genaro was holding a crystal glass filled with the amber liquid to her lips. Her eyes were glazed over, she began to sweat, and her whole body was trembling. Mateo caught her seconds before she would have fallen to the floor. "Let's get her to bed. Sophia, I believe she is suffering from exhaustion and anxiety." He lifted her off the settee, carried her to her bedchamber, and laid her on the bed. "Will you need help to undress her, if so I shall get one of the kitchen maids to assist you?" "No My Lord I can manage by myself." The two brothers thanked Sophia and instructed her to come and fetch them when she woke up. "I will have the doctor stop in to see Lucia when he is finished attending to Lord Stevens." "That will be wise My Lord."

Sophia drew up a chair and kept watch over her mistress. She prayed for Lord Stevens and Lucia for she knew they had serious affection for each other. It was some time before she heard a soft tap at the door and went to see who it was. "Oh My Lord my Mistress still sleeps. Has the doctor come for Lord Stevens?" It was Genaro at the door "Yes, he is here now. The doctor says that he will be fine in a couple of days. He instructed the cook to make a special broth and prepare a salve for his face and hands, for the burns. How is my sister? Shall we have the doctor look in on her as well?" Sophia turned to look toward the bed "I believe she will be herself by tomorrow. She is not hurt physically, but her heart has been broken by the betrayal of Piro." Genaro looked sad "Yes I know she really cared for him and now this is her repayment. I shall kill him with my own hands one of these days, coward that he is. When she awakes come and get me. Thank you."

Lucia was so exhausted she slept most of the day and finally awoke just after supper. Sophia had been relieved of her post by Genaro and so when she opened her eyes she saw her brother's handsome face. "Genaro, what are you doing here?" Genaro smiled at her "I told Sophia to take some supper so that I could be here when you woke up. How are you feeling?" She propped herself onto her elbows and said, "I'm not sure. I am only slightly bruised from the beating Piro gave me, but now I feel a pain in my heart. It is hard to speak of such feelings." Genaro reached for her hand "No, you must speak of them if you are to heal. I know the feeling of betrayal by one you have loved. For so long you held an idea of what Piro had become, and when you saw the real man you were broken. He has tried to hurt you, and will do so again, if he is not caught and punished." Lucia lay back down on her bed and was quiet. "I will have them bring you a light supper. I know Mateo and Henri are anxious to speak with you, and before you ask, I shall inform you that your Lord Stevens will be up and working in a week or two." Genaro was smirking, a mischievous grin, "You, my baby sister, are very fond of this man. Yes?" Now she too smiled "This is not fair, you know it is impossible for me to withhold the truth. Yes, you evil man; I am very fond of him." He came to her and gave her a gentle but loving hug. "I knew it and I believe that big hunk of man feels the same for you. He is a magnificent beast, lucky for you I have my heart pledged to Mateo or I would have to fight you for his affection." They laughed and hugged each other. "I love you dear brother and I am hungry."

CHAPTER SIX

VERSAILLES

France

Danford slept restlessly for almost two days. On the morning of the third day Lucia ever present at his bedside was administering the special salve that the doctor had prescribed for his face. She was leaning over him gently brushing the mixture on his handsome face and humming as she worked. Without as much as a change in his breathing, he grabbed her hand and brought her to himself in one swift movement. Lucia, startled at the sudden advance, yelped, but did not pull away. He opened those beautiful green eyes and looked through to her soul.

"What a magnificent sight to wake up to. That face is like looking at a rendering by the greatest artist in the world." He did not wait for her to respond but brought his hand to her head and kissed her full on the lips. His lips were dry and his skin was red and blistered but there was no denying how handsome he was. Lucia kissed him back getting the sticky salve all over her face. He smiled when he saw that she was covered with the salve. "I'm sorry, I did not mean for you to get that all over your face."

Lucia was flushed with excitement "It is fine. I am happy to see that you have returned to us. I was very worried, you have slept for so long, this will be the third day. How do you feel?"

"I'm not sure" he answered honestly. "Can you get someone to help me up I should like my toilet. I must smell like a goat." Lucia was enjoying this banter "Well now that you mention it I did smell something akin to the barnyard. I shall get Henri's man to give you some help and then I shall have the kitchen bring you some food, do you desire anything special?" He looked at her with such longing "I desire you. Lucia what have you done to me? When I was in such a deep sleep I dreamt of you." Lucia was giggling like a little girl at his words. "Do not mock me, I am entranced by you, and you laugh at my heart." She stood and proceeded to leave the room when he called after her "Lucia I love you." She spun around and with her wide-eyed innocence; she replied, "You do?" He tried to get up then realized that he was naked and quickly caught at the sheet that was covering him "Yes, with all my heart." Her head tilted, cheeks flushed, and a smile on her face she curtsied and responded, "I am happy for it for I too have dreamt of you. Rest for now. I will send someone to assist you and when the food comes I shall return." With that she left him and as she made her way down the hall toward the kitchen she could not stop humming and smiling.

She returned an hour later to find Lord Stevens sitting up in the bed. He had washed, and his hair was combed and pulled back into a neat cue. Coming directly behind her was a male servant carrying a tray overflowing with food. "That smells wonderful I am as hungry as a bear. Will you join me?" Lucia had the servant set a small table near the bed and place the tray upon it. "Yes I will share your supper." He was smiling but she could see that he grimaced with every movement. "Will you require my assistance My Lady?" inquired the servant. "No thank I shall manage. When we are finished, I shall ring for you. Please close the door behind you." The servant bowed deeply "As you wish My Lady."

Lucia began by pouring a glass of wine for each of them. "Now you need to go slowly or you will disturb your stomach." He nodded obediently. She brought the glass to his mouth and he took a deep swallow "That is so good. I feel as if my throat has been tanned like leather." "The doctor said that he will come tomorrow to check you. He said it will take some time for the blisters to heal but the salve will help." He watched as she prepared his plate. Lucia cut his meat and vegetables for him since his hands had been badly burnt; they were wrapped in a tincture of roasted garlic, goat milk, and honey.

"Thank you for feeding me, I am starving," he said with love in his eyes. Lucia felt herself flush "It is the least I can do since you risked your life to save my shipyard." "Is that the only reason you are playing nurse maid to me?" She grinned but did not want to fall into his trap. "Here, eat, you need your strength."

When they were done eating, Lucia wiped his face clean dabbing gently at his face. "I am so sorry that Piro did this terrible act. I fear that he has gone mad and will not stop until he kills either himself or me." The young lord looked her in the eyes and said, "As long as I am alive he shall not harm you, I pledge this on my honor." She kissed him on his lips with such affection but then quickly sat back in her seat.

The days passed and Lucia and Danford spent most of their time together talking and reading. Danford was now almost fully recovered from his burns. After the first week, they ventured down to the shipyard. Danford had placed the father of the two boys who had come to tell them about the fire, Maurice, in charge of rebuilding the damage caused by the fire. Every day either Maurice would come after work to report what was going on or he would send his boys. According to the reports, all was going well. Even Henri would go down every couple of days to check on the progress.

It was early morning and the crews were just getting settled to their work when the carriage carrying Danford, Henri, and Lucia pulled up to the yard. All eyes went to see who was coming. When Danford emerged from the carriage, everyone came running to greet him and a universal cheer went up. He was touched by this apparent show of affection. He took his time but made a careful and thorough inspection of the place. He called Maurice over "You have done a fine job restoring all that was lost. I will not forget your hard work. I wish you to elevate your sons to a greater position for they too have been invaluable to me." The new overseer was pleased that his efforts did not go unnoticed "You are too kind My Lord Stevens, my elder son is ready to move ahead and I shall be pleased to make him my assistant but the younger boy must wait and learn to move through the ranks." Danford was impressed with this man and replied, "You are their father, and overseer, do with them as you see fit. Now, I should like to go over some of these new design ideas with you. Do you have a moment to spare for me?" The man bowed "Always My Lord. Come and sit inside, I had them replace your worktable. It is as you left it before the fire." All was going well and when he was finished, he escorted Lucia back into the mammoth building and showed her the changes he told Maurice to implement. "You love what you do and it is clear that you have taken great pains to make this right." They spent about two hours with Danford making adjustments and taking the time to thank each man and boy individually for all their hard work.

Lucia and Danford shared their time with her brothers and Henri. It was most pleasant and they all enjoyed each other's companionship. One evening at the dinner table, Mateo announced, "While this has been some of the most enjoyable weeks of my life, sadly, I must return to Milan to attend my business and Genaro must meet with the Holy Father for his next appointment. We will be leaving in three days."

Lucia was crushed "Why must you leave? You can conduct business from here, can you not?" She was acting like a small child that was told her guardian was leaving. Genaro spoke up "Lucia, you knew that our company was only temporary when we embarked on this grand journey with you. We must be about our own business. Now, the more important question is; what shall you do? Will you come home with us or continue on?" She looked confused and was clearly upset "I do not know. I must take a little time to seek the answer to that question." It was now Henri who joined the conversation "Lucia, my dear, you are always welcome to stay, for as long as you wish. The presence of all of you has been a great joy for me. I almost dread to go back to Paris." She looked to Danford, waiting for him to say something, which he did "I have been called back to Wallingston because my father is gravely ill. I was going to ask you in private but since we are all making our plans known I should like you to accompany me to my family home. I know you spoke of your intentions to visit with Lord Brunswick in London and my father's house is not far from there."

Mateo spoke "Lucia, we would all rest knowing that you were under the protection of Lord Stevens as you continue your journey to England. With Nicko, and his men, to insure your safety, together with Lord Stevens, we would be much more at ease. Do we all agree with that assessment?" He looked from one to the other for approval. Genaro agreed, "I for one would be much comforted at the thought that you were accompanied by Lord Stevens as well as Nicko. You must remember there is a madman on the loose who would not hesitate to do you harm." "Listen to your brothers and go with Lord Stevens, or, go back home with your brothers. You must keep yourself ever vigilant as regards Piro. I do not trust him any longer," said Henri was a sad expression.

Therefore, in a matter of moments Lucia was persuaded to join Lord Stevens on his return to England. Secretly she was thrilled, but with the approval of all those concerned, it did seem like the right choice. "It is settled, I shall write this evening to Zia Maria and Antoinetta to let them know of my new plans. Of course you will stay until the Grand Ball at Versailles?" Genaro spoke "I would not miss that for ten Popes. God forgive me."

After dinner Lucia retired to her rooms and dismissed Sophia "Go join Nicko, it is still early, I will be up writing. We will be going to England shortly so you will need to prepare all our things." Sophia was excited at the prospect of going to England "Will we see the King?" Lucia chuckled "Only if he is a friend of Lord Stevens." Once Sophia left, she sat at the finely carved writing table and wrote first to her sister.

My Dearest Sister,

I think of you every day and wonder how you must look now with your belly growing round. I hope this letter finds you feeling strong and happy. What did Tomaso, Zia, Zio, and the Catalano's say when you told them? Have you written to Mama and Papa? Can I tell Genaro and Mateo? I am so happy.

I will be leaving France in a week or more and then going on to England. After I conduct my business there, I shall find my way home. I will write to let you know of my arrival. I must see you as soon as I get home.

You are in my prayers always,

Lucia

For a moment, she thought of telling her about Piro and the fire but considered it unwise for she knew her sister would worry too much. She sat back for a few minutes, thought of Monteforte, and realized how much she missed the tranquil splendor of the place. Lucia also reflected on the Abbey at Montecassino and Abbot Vittorio. When last she saw him, it was a painful experience for both of them. She would write to him as well and let him know that she would be returning in several months.

Dear Zia Maria,

I am having a wonderful time here in Paris. Sadly, Mateo will be leaving to return to Milan, and Genaro must go to Rome. I will be going to England with Lord Danford Stevens who is the engineer for the new shipyard. Zia, he is a good man and I am sure you and Zio will like him. I will invite him to come to Monteforte upon our return. We have been invited to Versailles tomorrow evening, to attend a Grand Ball, it is all very exciting. I shall write to tell you how it was. For now, Henri has been the most gracious host and he sends his fondest wishes to you.

As soon as I am settled in England, I will write. I love you and Zio very much.

And, yes, I will be careful. Do not worry.

Lucia

She knew the next letter would not be so easy to write but she felt compelled to do so. Lucia sat back and closed her eyes, remembering with sweet bitterness the last time she saw Abbot Vittorio. She breathe in deeply, made the sign of the cross, and set her mind to her task.

Dear Abbot Vittorio,

It has been some time since last I wrote to you. I am presently in Paris overseeing my new shipyard. I must confess that I had put Piro in charge of this new venture, but he changed. He tried to kill me, and then set the shipyard on fire. Both the shipyard, and I, escaped with minor damage, but Piro is now a wanted criminal and will stop at nothing to exact his revenge. Please pray for him for I know he is now consumed with hatred for me, and will not stop until he succeeds in killing me.

I will be leaving shortly to journey over to England to check on my holdings there. Upon my return to Monteforte, I shall let you know of my arrival and shall stop at the Abbey. I trust you might have some news for me by then.

I am sorry for our last encounter and blame myself for what happened. Please pray for me for it is not my fault but the curse under which I was born. Che Dio perdoni i due di noi.

God Bless You Always,

Lucia

It was late by the time Lucia had finished all her letters. She had sealed the three letters and would have them sent tomorrow. She felt better having confessed herself to Abbot Vittorio. Her heart was still broken to think that she almost caused him to break his vow of chastity. She laid her head down on her folded arms and silently wept that God would cleanse her of this wretched curse. She did not remember falling asleep until Sophia came and gently woke her "Come Mistress let me put you to bed." Lucia followed obediently, climbed into the bed, and fell fast asleep.

Today was the day they would go to the King's Grand Ball. Lucia was so excited she was humming and dancing around the solar. Henri found her there as she almost knocked him over during a twirl. "Oh dear Henri I am so sorry, I did not hear you approach, are you all right?" The old man was delighted to see her so happy "Yes, yes, I am fine. Lucia it warms my heart to see you so joyful. I shall miss you when you leave." Lucia stopped and came to him "You have been so kind to me with your loving heart and gracious hospitality but you know I must go." He nodded and the sun coming in from the beautiful arched windows caught the silver glint in his wavy hair and framed his face in a soft glow "I know, but I will still miss the spirit that you have infused into this musty old place. Will you stop back here on your way home?" Lucia grabbed his hands "I am not sure, it all depends on what news I hear from home. I shall share a very private secret with you. I received word from my sister Antoinetta that she is already with child and I am most anxious to be there with her during the end months." Henri's old eyes lit up "That is wonderful news. I shall keep her in my prayers." "I shall be an aunt. I hope I shall be as good as Zia Maria." Henri kissed her forehead "Of course you will. You have so much love to share." Lucia spun around and then turned back toward Henri "Would you like to come to England with us?" "Oh dear Lucia if only I could. I should love to, but we are progressing to the final stages of the new ship, and Danford has asked me to oversee all the last details until his return. After all he has been through I feel it is my obligation to assist him." Lucia pouted her lip in a feigned attempt to look downtrodden "Yes I understand, but I should have liked your company nevertheless." She went and hugged the old man and he in turn embraced her with great affection. They were held in that position when Mateo walked into the solar "Good morning. I see that the two of you are celebrating something. Is it private or can we all share in the good news?"

"Ah, dear brother, I had invited Henri to come to England, but sadly, he cannot leave just now for the ship is in its final stages of completion and Danford, I mean Lord Stevens, has asked him to oversee the progress until his return." Mateo smiled and nodded "I wish to thank you Henri for all your hospitality and care over these weeks. I hope we were not too burdensome. I am sure Lucia was a great deal of trouble, and for her I apologize." Lucia gasped at the insult and rushed over to give a gentle pat to his cheek "How dare you defame my name and my temperament?" With that they all laughed.

Henri spoke "I hate to leave this little merriment but I must go to the yard. The masthead is being delivered today, and I must see to its condition and placement. I shall return in time to get ready for this evening."

They were left alone in the solar. Lucia winded from all her dancing sat in the settee just opposite the window. The sun was caressing her beautiful face. Mateo joined her and could not help but touch her face. She looked at him and smiled "What troubles you brother?" He did not answer immediately but reached into his waistcoat and extracted a soft leather pouch. He held it in his hand and hefted it as if it were filled with gold or silver. Lucia sat and waited for she instinctively knew he wanted to tell her something. He reached for her hand and placed the small pouch in it while covering her hand with his own. He looked at her directly and cocked his head to one side "I am not sure how to say this but I shall come to the point. I see how you are with Danford and I can sense that there is a strong connection between the two of you. You are a grown woman now dear sister, and he is a very handsome man, with physical needs. I am not condoning or disparaging any relationship that might develop between the two of you for that is not my business. However, in this pouch is a very potent cure to ward off becoming with child."

Lucia's eyes grew wide and her mouth was open as if to speak but she shut it tight as a clam. He continued, "I have the formula written inside the pouch. You must use it exactly, for if you deviate from my instructions, you will poison yourself. This is highly effective when used properly." She took a deep breath and spoke in a whisper "I have never laid with a man. I am afraid, for all the kitchen maids have said it hurts, and that I will bleed from down there. Is this true, or did they lie to me to frighten me?" Mateo tried to control himself from laughing at her childishness but coughed to conceal his mirth. "Yes it can hurt just for a short time, but once you and your partner find your rhythm it will be quite pleasurable." Lucia seemed confused "How do you know this given your appetite for men?" At this, he did chuckle "I did not always understand my body's desires, and so in my early years I thought I preferred the sexual relationship with women. I assure you that I am well versed on both sides of this coin." Lucia relaxed and felt the tension of the initial conversation pass over her. "Mateo will you tell me what to expect when the first time comes?" Now, for the first time he felt a pang of discomfort. "It will be different for you Lucia because I know that when you do choose to be intimate with a man he will be very special. You will love him. For me it was just sexual desire, and something that was expected of a young man. Do you understand what I am saying?" "I think so. But how shall I behave?" Now he put his arm around her shoulder and drew her in close, "Sweet baby sister, you will know how to act by the man you are with. If he loves you, he will be kind and gentle and teach you not only how to please him, but to please yourself. You must relax and enjoy the act. It is natural and enjoyable when shared between two people who love each other."

Lucia pulled away and had an expression of urgency on her face "Will my lover think I am a whore if I lay with him and we are not married?" Mateo contemplated that question for a moment "That depends on the man. It also depends on you Lucia. Do you wish to marry in the future? If so, then the man you pledge yourself to will want a virgin. If you have no intentions of marrying then discreet relationships with men are possible. You are one of the wealthiest women in the world, it should not matter to you what anyone thinks. Do you understand?" She bent her head and nodded her assent. He picked her head off her chest and said "Lucia do what is in your heart. I know you do not want to marry, but if the right man should ask, you may want to consider his proposal. Do not let forbidden intimacy sway your judgment, and, for the love of God, forget about that senseless curse." "Yes but how will I know when it is the right man?" He was a patient man and sat back in the deep cushions of the settee "When you can think of nothing but him, and your mind and heart are distracted beyond all reasoning. At the sight of him, your womanhood begins to flutter. That is when he will be the right man."

They were interrupted by the appearance of Genaro, "Ah here you two are, and what is going on, you both look so grave." "Lucia had some questions as to knowing when the right man will come into her life." Genaro sat on the other side of her and now she was flanked by both of them "Oh that is a weighty conversation, I am happy that I was not part of it." He looked at Lucia and said "Did you learn anything from Mateo?" She looked down at the small pouch and fingered it; the feel of the leather was soft and supple, "Yes. I learned a great deal." "Well that is marvelous since it is almost time to get ready for tonight's gala. Are you excited sister?"

Lucia was engrossed in her thoughts and almost missed her brother's question "Yes. It is going to be wonderful. Don't you agree?"

Sophia was busy laying out her garments, humming to herself, and failed to see Lucia enter the room. She turned with a start, "Mistress, I did not hear you enter." Lucia smiled and replied, "Someone seems very joyous? What did I miss?" Sophia smiled sheepishly "Nicko has asked me to marry him as soon as we return to Monteforte." Lucia rushed to her side and grabbed Sophia and started dancing around the room "That is wonderful. I am so pleased. We shall have a grand feast and you shall have a beautiful gown." Sophia stopped suddenly, the tears rolling down her face "Mistress you are too kind to me, to all of us, I love you so much." Lucia was so touched she too started to cry. "Oh, see what you have started. We must be about our business.

Stop that and help we get ready." They then hugged each other and started to half-cry; half-giggle.

The gown that Madame Richaud had made for her fit her like a second skin, with the feel of the imported silk caressing her. It was light in weight but so intricately detailed. The color, which Madame had dyed just for her, was a deep rich shade of royal blue. Lucia loved the simple design of bumblebees that had been hand sewn on the long flowing body of the skirt. The bodice, with its corset design lifted her breasts, she was happy that Madame had trimmed the neckline with delicate gold lace. Her favorite thing about this gown, beside the color and the bumblebees, were the sleeves. Lucia liked the sleeves because the silk was so sheer she could see her bare arms. She hated the bustle, which she thought was much too long, but Madame Richaud assured her that it was the perfect length.

Lucia felt pretty. She slipped on the matching shoes, which, again, Madame told her were the same design she had made for Her Majesty. They pinched her little toe but the tiny gold and onyx bee that sat upon each one delighted her. Sophia had fashioned her hair in a style that was very Parisian. The women from the kitchen had told her exactly how to do it. The result was nothing short of lovely. Lucia was just about ready when there came a soft knock at her door. "Enter." It was Henri. The older man gasped at the sight of her. He came over to where she was standing "My dear Lucia, you look magnificent. May I ask you a very personal favor?" Lucia could not imagine what Henri would need but "Yes, what is it that you require?" He reached into his waistcoat and pulled out a box. It was so intricately carved that it immediately peaked her interest. He opened the box with great care and presented it to her. "These were my wife's jewels. It would be such an honor if you would consider wearing them this evening." Lucia was stunned. She looked into the box "If that would please you. I shall be honored to wear such a precious memento of your wife." He laid the box on the table next to where she was standing, and then extracted a necklace made of sapphires and diamonds. It was the perfect match to her gown. He came around and gently secured the piece around her neck. Coming back around to face her, the old man had tears in his eyes, "You are so beautiful, just like she was. Thank you for this gift you have given an old man." He embraced her with great affection and kissed her on each cheek. Lucia took his hands, "It is I who have received a beautiful gift. I only hope I am worthy to wear the jewels of such a special lady?" "Auriella would have loved you, as I love you."

Henri, bowed deeply, proffered his arm, and they left to go down to their waiting carriage. Both Mateo and Genaro were waiting anxiously for Lucia and Henri to appear. Genaro upon seeing her smiled broadly as did Mateo. "Henri, do you have any pistols at the ready?" Henri grimaced, then asked, "Why, is there trouble about?" With a serious face, Genaro replied, "There might be once the single men lay eyes on my sister. Is she not the most beautiful woman you have ever seen?" They all laughed, but, Genaro continued "I am serious, Lucia, you cannot be my sister, you are far too beautiful. Mateo and I shall be beating back the men with sticks."

Lucia was blushing "Stop that nonsense. There will be countless beautiful women. I must confess I do feel very elegant this evening." Mateo, came to her, bowed formally, "Marchesa Banfi, I am honored and delighted to be in your company this evening. All eyes, male and female, will be upon you my beautiful sister. Be proud, stand tall, and, most importantly have some fun. Now, let us embark on this wonderful event. Shall we?"

Lucia's stomach was fluttering as their carriage stood in line on the Rue de Palaise waiting their turn. The gates that enclosed the long drive were at least twenty feet high and forged of ornamented steel. Guards in the royal house colors stood at attention, while young grooms outfitted with similar uniforms scurried behind each carriage scooping up horse droppings. There were two grand sweeping drives. Each drive lined with orange trees, their perfume scenting the air with a clean citrus smell. When finally they reached the main entrance, they were surprised to see two brick and stone obelisks surrounded by stone balls. The palace was set far back from a sweeping lawn with a reflecting pool in the center. Shrubs, which had been planted in symmetrical beds, flanked the walkways that led to the Grand Chateau. There were ponds, and hundreds of flowering plants, all sitting in stone beds that were raised off the ground. Statues, cast in marble and in shrubbery, were placed strategically along the way. Every few feet hanging lanterns lit the way. The overall effect was magical. Musicians strolled the paths, lending their soothing sounds to the bucolic scene. The general feeling was one of walking through a serene painting. Lucia was fascinated by the brightly painted and gilded structures that were scattered throughout, which were in sharp contrast to the sand colored stone of the main chateau. There were buildings dispersed throughout the grounds that encircled the palace. One would have to climb to the highest turret to take in all that was there.

Taking center stage, along the main axis of the promenade to the chateau, was a fountain of such magnitude and design it is difficult to put into words. Rising out of the depth of the fountain was Apollo, God of the Sun, in his chariot, drawn from the bowels of the sea by his four horses. Apollo is rising to bring the illumination of the sun to Heaven. King Louis, who was celebrated as the Sun God, naturally, would have chosen this particular statute of Apollo as his symbol. The figures were so perfectly executed they looked to be living and breathing. It was truly an amazing sight. Lucia, so mesmerized by it, she almost fell right in, if not for the quick wittedness of Genaro. "Careful dear sister, we should not want to spoil that lovely gown before the gala."

Everywhere the eye landed there was a new delight to encounter. Off to one side was a stunning building that was completely gilded. When asked what that was, she was told it was the Grotte de Thetis. It was a shrine to the Gods of the Sea. The array of things to see was overwhelming. Strolling amongst the ponds and gardens were exotic birds and animals, the likes of which Lucia had only seen in books. It was a mythical experience. "Mateo, Genaro, do you see that horse with the stripes. I have read that this animal comes from Africa, the Dark Continent." Lucia was like a child and filled with excitement and wonder.

By the time they reached, the entrance to the Grand Chateau Lucia was dizzy with wonderment. They were greeted by two guards that were clad in the royal colors, who escorted them to the main foyer, there they were asked, by yet another set of uniformed servants, their names, once found on the list, were then free to roam the palace.

The palace was by far the most extravagant structure on the property. The halls, were covered from floor to ceiling, with tapestries of such fine quality and detail, they looked like oil paintings. Gold leaf had been applied to every exposed surface. Ferns, the size of full-grown trees, sat in gigantic pots that lined the expanse of the entrance hallway. A Swiss Guard, was posted every twenty feet, to assist guests, answer questions, or generally keep an eye on things.

Their party was directed toward the grand banquet hall. They had to pass through the now famous Hall of Mirrors, which extended over seventy meters, to get to their destination. Along the way, they passed more than three hundred gilded mirrors. This was truly a magnificent room. Even the floor was of the purest bisque colored marble, and had been polished to a mirror finish. The windows, which reached nearly to the top of the groin-vaulted ceiling, captured the sunlight and brought its shimmering rays into the room. The sun, which had not yet set, had cast such an illumination that the room was ablaze with light. It was Genaro, so excited at the sight of the ceiling, he started telling them, and "This ceiling was painted and inlaid with over thirty frescos by the artist Charles LeBrun, who is known as the First Painter to the King. Each fresco depicts a battle wherein France was victorious." Lucia was so thrilled she was walking with her head gazing at the ceiling and walked into one of the other guests. "Ah, pardon me Monsieur; I am overwhelmed by the splendor of this room. I am afraid these magnificent paintings have cast a spell on me." The man, a distinguished looking middle-aged man bowed deeply, "I am most pleased for it. I am myself in awe of your beauty. May I introduce myself, I am Charles LeBrun."

Lucia was taken aback for a moment. "Charles LeBrun, the painter, who did this magnificent ceiling?" The man once again bowed and reached for her hand, kissed it, but did not let go. "Yes I am he. Now, more importantly, who are you my lovely bird?" Lucia, momentarily speechless, recovered soon enough, "I am Marchesa Lucia Banfi, Mistress of Monteforte." "Yes, I have heard about you. Everyone is talking about a beautiful redheaded Enchantress. Now, I understand what all the fuss was about now that I see you. May I escort you to the banquet?" Lucia, flushed from head to toe, looked for her brothers and Henri. "I am not alone. I am accompanied by my brothers and the Marquis Henri DeFauntil." "Well then, shall we find them so they can join us?" The painter, who had not yet released her hand, with his eyes filled with laughter, walked with her to find her party.

They walked a few yards when Mateo saw them and came over. "Dear Sister I see you have found a new friend. May I introduce myself, I am Lord Mateo Rizzo of Milan" he turned to face Genaro, "This is our brother Lord Genaro Banfi and this is the Marquis DeFauntil." Henri was already acquainted with the famous artist "Monsieur LeBrun always a pleasure to see you." "Marquis DeFauntil, Monsieurs" and he made a deep bow. "I had to save this beautiful dove from falling, and now have asked her to join me at the banquet, but, sadly, I come to find out that she is not unescorted." Mateo ventured "Please Monsieur LeBrun, it would be our pleasure if you were to join us." "Perfect, it is settled. Now, Marchesa, come, I shall tell you all about this wonderful room. Yes?" Lucia was all smiles "Yes."

"What great fortune to be seated with the great LeBrun" said Genaro. Mateo, looked him in the eye and said, "You are also great. When you finish your next commission for His Holiness all will be calling you the Painter of the Church of Rome." Mateo always made Genaro feel important and successful. "But", he added swiftly, "Unfortunately, we shall only be famous as the brothers of the Enchantress Lucia." They both laughed heartily and followed closely behind their sister and LeBrun. Henri had stopped to chat with some friends.

"Do you see these arches and the flourishes that are on top?" Lucia nodded. "The Fleur de Lys is the symbol of His Majesty and signifies the royal sun, which sits between two French cockerels. This is known as the "French Order". What do you think?" Lucia looked at the arches, there was seventeen in all, and each one was massive in height and circumference. "I particularly like the design. It is a great deception for hiding the support of the ceiling. The gilding, the mirrors, even the colossal dimensions of this room all lends the effect of being bigger than life." The painter stopped suddenly and looked directly at Lucia "Marchesa, not only are you extraordinary in your beauty, but, you have a keen mind. How did you come to have knowledge of architecture?" "Ah, Monsieur LeBrun, you, like most men, believe that a woman cannot possess both beauty and intelligence. I have knowledge of many things."

As they were talking two of the Royal Swiss Guard came to them. "His Majesty would like the presence of your company Mademoiselle, if you would please follow us." A slight panic came over

Lucia, she looked around for her brothers, but she did not see them for the crush of guests had all now just arrived. "Monsieur LeBrun, would you be so kind as to inform my brothers where I have gone." The painter looked disappointed, "Of course Marchesa, we shall meet up with you at the banquet." Then, just before she was about to leave he whispered in her ear "Do not upset His Majesty." Lucia looked puzzled and was about to questions him when the guard said more insistently "Mademoiselle, His Majesty awaits." Off they went.

Lucia, with butterflies in her stomach, followed discretely behind the two guards. Their colorful uniforms and polished silver helmets caught the light cascading from the parade of crystal candelabras that were placed every few feet, keeping the grand hall illuminated day and night. She was more than anxious to meet the King. As they were making their way through the crowds that had now gathered, everyone looked at her. Some of the women nodded with a strange expression, while the men, smiled lecherously.

Finally, they arrived at the farthest point of the grand hall. There were three glazed doors, which separated the east, and west wings of the palace. Behind was an alcove that was separated by a gilded wood balustrade that divided the rest of the chamber. "Wait here Mademoiselle; we shall inform His Majesty of your presence." Lucia felt the sweat bead up on her upper lip and she cursed herself for her nerves. Looking around the room, she was surprised at the subtle sparseness of the decoration, as compared to what she had already seen. If this was the King's Chamber, it certainly did not fit with the rest of the palace and grounds.

She was deep in thought and did not hear the King's approach. A soft cough made her spin around to face a chubby figure who was dressed in an exquisite waistcoat and enormous powdered white wig. He had a kindly face and poufy whimsical eyes. "Your Majesty" she stammered and curtsied deeply, her knee actually touching the floor. "It is true. You are flawless! I heard rumors of this lovely creature with flaming red hair and skin like polished marble, and, here you are." His voice was excited and high pitched, which she thought was odd for a King. Her cheeks were on fire and she could feel the moisture between her full round breasts. "Come here to the light so that I might have a better look." Lucia took his proffered hand and came toward the window. The room was facing the gardens and the sun was just reclining into the horizon, its russet rays casting a peach hue on her silhouette. "What is your age?" Lucia was surprised at the question "I will be eighteen years next month." He was so close she could smell his breath, which reeked of onions. With his finger, which was as soft, and delicate, as a woman's, he traced the contour of her face, her chin, curving down the hollow of her throat and down to the top of her breast. He was stroking her décolletage. Lucia was confused and aroused. "Have you yet lain with a man?" At this question her eyes grew wide, and she became angry "No, but that, Your Majesty, is not of your concern." She instantly realized that her tone was harsher than it should have been. He drew his whole hand around her neck and tightened his grip, lifting her chin upward. He kissed her with his mouth open and stuck his tongue inside. Lucia did not know how to respond.

"Tell me, is your cunt wet?" She was embarrassed but answered honestly, "Yes." "Good. I have not lost my touch." The king laughed at her indignity, "I am sorry if I have offended you. I only asked because I wanted to lay with you. But, alas, you are still a virgin and I shall not spoil such a perfect creature. Most women give themselves willingly; it is I, who reject them. I must say that you have surprised me" he laughed again and finally, Lucia, joined in his merriment, at her own expense. "Lucky the man with whom you share your womb." "I should ask one more question of you. Are you redheaded between those long legs?" Again, she just shook her head "Yes." He once again moved his finger to her breast and now slipped it into her neckline and brushed her nipple, which was hard. Lucia gasped which made the king wiggle his finger. "Ah, the joys of a virgin, I never have one anymore. Quite a pity I should have liked to have seen a redheaded cunt." He removed his finger from her bosom, bent over and kissed each soft mound, then, casually walked over to a screen, and she could hear him relieving himself. "I have not been this aroused in a long time. It feels good."

When he was done, he emerged from behind the screen with a lustful grin on his face. "I hate to have to satisfy myself, but, under the circumstances you left me no choice. Let us join the rest of my guests their tongues are already wagging. Are you hungry my dear?" Lucia felt at ease for the first time since arriving at Versailles, "Yes Your Majesty, I am famished." He put out his arm, Lucia took hold, and together they strolled to the Grand Banquet Hall. "Your Majesty, I am in awe of this fantastic palace, the grounds, the decoration, everything. Thank you for inviting me here and I am sorry if I have disappointed you." He stopped, turned to her and smiled, "My dear young woman, it would have been my great pleasure to bed such a beauty as yourself, but, I am a man of God and respect the virtue of a young woman. It shall be my great loss, however, the next time you come your situation may have changed, and then you shall not disappoint me." He laughed and leaned over to kiss her on each cheek.

The second the Swiss Guard opened the doors that led to the Hall of Mirrors shouts of "Long live the King" arouse to an almost deafening pitch. The King was a man of great humor. He stepped away from Lucia and raised his hand. There was an immediate silence. "May I present Marchesa Lucia Banfi, Mistress of Monteforte." Another resounding cheer rose up from the crowd. "Let us eat."

His Majesty whispered in her ear, "Of course they all now think that I have bedded you. There will be much talk. I apologize for your honor, but, what great fun for me. Go, find your party, I must be a good husband and sit with the Queen and my children. It has been a pleasure to meet you Marchesa; I hope you enjoy the evening. Remember, the next time we meet you must let me see that beautiful body." Lucia curtsied deeply and upon rising whispered "I might have let you see it a few minutes ago, if only you had asked." The King laughed with such robust joy he had tears in his eyes. "You, my redheaded beauty are an Enchantress."

Waiting for her to leave the King's side were her brothers, Henri, and Charles LeBrun. Each one eyeing her for any signs of damage, but there was none. "Are you all right?" asked Henri, who was well aware of what normally occurs in the King's Chamber with young women. "I am fine. Nothing happened. We just talked." They let out a collective sigh of relief. From across the hall she heard her name being called and looked to see who it was. To her amazement, it was Lord Stevens. He pushed his way through the crowd that was by now working their way en masse into the banquet hall. "Hello, I did not know you had received an invitation to come. May I join you?" "Yes. I am so happy to see you." Lucia was flushed just at the sight of him. He looked particularly handsome. With all the scars from the fire already healed his skin look fresh. He was a big man and stood a head over most men. His broad shoulders looked even wider by his small waist and high ass.

Their eyes met and Lucia's womb tingled with excitement. She would like to rip his clothes off his back and devour him right there on the polished marble floor. He must have felt the connection because she saw that he had moved to bring his waistcoat tails closer toward his crotch. She gave him a wicked smile at his apparent interest in her. "You look more resplendent than the Queen. I cannot take my eyes from you." He took her hands and kissed each one lingering for a moment longer than necessary.

They were making their way toward the grand banquet hall when he announced, "I shall go ahead and find a table." As soon as he left, Mateo came to her and grabbed her arm drawing her close, "Did that fat pig do anything to you?" Lucia was not surprised by the question, apparently, it was the King's custom to take a woman before each banquet. "If you are asking if he bedded me, the answer is no. He did ask me if I was redheaded all over and if I was a virgin. To which I answer yes and yes." Mateo was not amused by this, but did say, "Well, with the looks of you and our young shipbuilder, you may not be coveting your virginity for too much longer. Be wary of what I have told you, and, for God's mercy, definitely do not forget the potion I gave you." He kissed her neck and she giggled.

She found her way through the throng of guests, feeling their eyes upon her, but she decided there was no way to stop their minds from thinking she was the King's latest conquest, so she held her head as high as she dared. Looking around she noticed for the first time the opulence of the room. It was gilded, just like all the other rooms, with statues as tall as a full-grown man, holding torches, their bodies were made of black marble and their costumes were gilded, and inlaid with jewels. They were everywhere around the room, casting their glowing flames. The tables were arranged in such a fashion that they formed a horseshoe pattern, with the Royals in the middle, with long tables on either side. At the Royals table, which was divided equally between the King and his courtiers to the right, and the Queen and her lady's to the left. Seated on either side in descending order were nobles, merchants, and guests. There were twelve enormous crystal candelabras hanging from the ceiling. Massive windowed doors were placed around the room this was to circulate the air when opened during the warm weather. Tapestries, hung from suspended armatures, would be lowered during the colder months, to stave off the chill. The floor was an intricate wooden inlaid, with designs of the royal fleur des lys, in repeating intervals, polished to a high finish. Toward the back, shielded by massive plants were the toilet screens. Perched high above the room to one corner was a balcony where the musicians were playing, the sound resonating so beautifully in such a vaulted room. It was like being in a dream.

As far as the banquet, it could not even hold a candle to the feasts that Marcello prepares at

Monteforte, but, alas, she was not there for the food. Everyone was looking at her and whispering. Men were coming up to her and congratulating her on her beauty, while the women asked who her designer was. There was much merriment and toward the mid-point of the evening, a courtier came over and informed Lucia that Her Majesty the Queen would like to speak with her.

Again, Lucia followed the young man to where the Queen was sitting surrounded by her ladies in waiting. All eyes focused on her and she felt the heat rise to her face. Marie Antoinette was a handsome woman. She exuded a sense of serene elegance. The women parted so that Lucia could come closer, she curtsied, and waited for Her Majesty to address her. "I have heard many things of you Marchesa Banfi, most of which have come from my own dressmaker, Madame Richaud. Generally, I dismiss stories that circulate around the Royal Court, but for once, they have not exaggerated your beauty. Please, come sit with me for a while I am most curious to learn more about you." The lovely young woman who was occupying the seat next to the Queen immediately vacated it so that Lucia could take her place. "Your Majesty, I am so honored to be here, I cannot even put into words how in awe I am of this fantastic palace, for that matter, I have been enjoying all of your picturesque country."

"Tell me Marchesa of where you are from. I am somewhat familiar with the Kingdom of Naples but have never been to Monteforte, yet, that is not to say that I have not heard of it, or, of your family." Lucia was smiling, "Monteforte is an ancient castle, built as a fortress, high upon the cliffs overlooking the sea. It is a sprawling structure with land as far as the eye can see. We grow everything that is needed to sustain the estate." She had a kind face and soft brown eyes, Lucia was sure that she truly did not want a description of Monteforte. The Queen, who feigned interest in this statement, leaned closer and lowered her voice so that Lucia would be the only one to hear, "His Majesty shared with me what happened in his chamber. I must apologize for his behavior. I hope he did not offend you too deeply?" Lucia instantly turned a deep shade of red. "I was just taken aback by his actions, but, he was very kind and we parted laughing. I cannot believe he told you what happened, your customs are far different than my own." The Queen, a patient woman, shook her head and replied, "He is a good man, but, this behavior has always been the custom of all the Kings. I tolerate it because I know it means nothing. I hope you enjoy your stay in my country and if there is anything I can do to assist you please do not hesitate to ask." Lucia sensed, more than was told, that the audience with Her Majesty had ended. She stood, kissed the gloved hand of the Queen, curtsied, and took her leave back to her table.

Lucia was impressed by the poise and grace of Her Majesty. She thought that she and King Louis were ill matched. The Queen was tall, almost willowy, with delicate skin and fine features. The

King was portly, self-possessed and the fact that he openly had sex with whomever he chose was abominable. She would never tolerate such behavior if she were Queen.

Genaro was anxiously waiting for her return "Well, what happened?" Lucia did not know if Mateo had told him what had transpired earlier, she simply replied, "She wanted to know about Monteforte and said that if, during my stay, I needed anything to ask her for assistance." It was getting late and some of the guests had already left. Monsieur LeBrun came over and asked Lucia to dance.

He was a good dancer and she was enjoying herself. As he held her close during the revel, he whispered in her ear "Did His Majesty hurt you?" Lucia did not know whether she wanted to protect her honor, or, that of the King. "No he did not. He was very gentle." The painter's eyes narrowed and his jaw set but he said nothing further. When the music stopped, he escorted her back to the table. "It is late, I shall take my leave. Monsieurs it was a pleasure." He came over to Genaro, and spoke with him "Whenever you are back in France please come visit me, I am always in need of a fine artist. You are young, yet already, you are known as an accomplished artist, I have great hopes for your future." Genaro was so pleased, it was written all over his face, "Monsieur, coming from someone of your artistic genius I am much flattered. Thank you for the offer, and, when I return I shall look forward to the opportunity to work with a Master such as yourself."

"As to you my beautiful bird, come sit for me, I should relish the prospect of painting that magnificent face. I will make you immortal. You have cast a spell on every man in this palace, and, no doubt, where ever you go. Until we meet again, I bid you much happiness." He bowed deeply, kissed her on each cheek, and left in a rush. "What a charming man, and, a very good dancer. I should like him to paint my portrait one day." Lord Stevens interjected with a bit of a sour tone "I trust it is not just your face that lecherous rogue wants to paint." "Do I detect a note of jealousy?" teased Mateo. "I know this man, and, have heard wild stories of his particular appetites. There is no doubt he is a genius, but, along with it somewhat of a madman." By now, Henri jumped into the conversation, "I fear that Lord Stevens might be correct on some account, but, then again, he might be slightly tainted by his feelings for our young Mistress as well. What say you Genaro?" Genaro, still smitten by what the grand master had said about him, but did add, "I don't care if he beds monkeys, and if he can further my position I will like him fine."

They were all standing rather close and the music started up again, in the resounding noise Mateo spoke softly into his ear "You shall be punished this evening for that remark. I shall whip your bare bottom until it is on fire, and then I shall rape you like the whore you are. Now what say you?" At the mere thought of what was to come Genaro was panting and felt the blood rush to his groin, "Yes Master!" "Good. I want you to think about what will come, but, do not stroke yourself, for, if you do, I shall have to give you more lashes." Genaro's face had flushed to a bright red, even his ears, were on fire. "I am growing hard just at your words. You are cruel to me, but, I love it." They laughed haughtily and Mateo told him to sit down at the table, then reached under the table linens and was stroking Genaro's cock, which by now, was rock hard. "Do not spill your seed here, for everyone will see what you are about" he whispered in his flaming ear. There was a delightfully pained expression on Genaro's face.

Henri announced, "I shall be home late, some of my friends have invited me to a card game. You may take the carriage; I shall get a ride home later. If you will excuse me, I shall see you tomorrow. Good evening." It was the four of them standing by the table. "Lucia would you like me to take you back? Mateo and Genaro can take Henri's carriage?" She looked to her brothers and they nodded their approval.

Lucia was ready to leave and asked Danford to take her home. "Shall we leave I am quite tired of this place." Danford agreed and they walked back through the gardens to where they might retrieve their carriage. They were about halfway through when Danford stopped, took Lucia by the arm, with a little more force than he had meant, "I cannot stop thinking of you with that pig of a King. Everyone knows what he does before each banquet. I must know if he violated you?" He was angry, and his voice, while low, was filled with vehemence. "Nothing happened." He now took her by the shoulders and looked down into her face "Don't lie to me Lucia. Did he lay with you?" Now, Lucia was angry. "I told you honestly that he did not. How do you dare to be my keeper? I shall lay or, not lay, with whomever I choose. I am not your wife, or your mistress. I am not a liar." He was shaken. She was fuming with anger. She started to walk ahead of him. In a moment, he caught her, grabbed her, spun her around, and kissed her hard on the mouth. Instinctively she slapped him across the face with such force her hand stung. "I am not your property. If you should like to kiss me you will be a gentleman and ask if that is what I too desire." Now, for the second time, she chastised him. It took him a second to recover "Lucia, I am sorry. I was consumed with the thought of the King making love to you. I love you. I want you to marry me. Will you marry me?"

Lucia was befuddled. Marry him, but she hardly knew him, or his family. "I don't know. I shall need time to think on such an important question. Danford I have strong feelings for you, but, I will not be the property of any man, ever." They continued walking until they came to the main entrance. They waited in silence until their carriage was brought up.

Danford helped Lucia into the carriage and they sat there in an awkward silence for what seemed a long time. Finally, not being able to withstand the agony any longer, he asked, "Will you promise to give this your most careful consideration?" He hung his head and looked sad. She stroked his face "Do not be sad. I am not sure what I want. At least not, right now. I care deeply for you, but I hardly know you. If you are seeking an obedient wife, who shall bear children, I am not the woman for you. I want to be my own person; to seek adventure, and not be burdened by children. Let us talk when we have settled our minds." He nodded but was sullen. "Shall I book you a passage to England?" Lucia looked at him and replied "Of course. I should love to meet your family. No matter what my decision, I shall always have feelings for you. It is you, who needs to weigh the answers to the questions I have posed to you. Being a wife and bearing children are not what I want. I want freedom and perhaps a lover. Can you handle that?" He took a deep breath and closed his eyes and answered as honestly as he could "No. I could not live knowing that you were in the arms of another man, and I have always dreamt of being a father. Therefore, the truth is, I am not sure. The only thing I am truly sure of is that I love you and think of no one but you. Damn you woman, you have possessed my soul!"

CHAPTER SEVEN

THE BROTHERS DEPART

Milan

"Ah, there you are, I have been searching for you. It's time for us to leave." Lucia was pouting at the thought of her brothers leaving. "I detest that you are going and will not be with me in England. I shall be all alone." Mateo took her hand, "My little dove, you shall be with Lord Stevens, Sophia, Nicko and those two brutes that follow him around like dogs on a rope." At the mental image of the two bodyguards Lucia started to chuckle in spite of her sadness. "There is one thing I shall beg you to promise me, do not go anywhere without Nicko and his pets. With Piro on the loose, it is far too dangerous. You must promise, or I shall bind you hand and foot, and carry you all the way home." With her chin on her chest and her pouty mouth, she answered, "Yes, I promise."

"Shall we bring any word home to Zia or Antoinetta?" "Yes, I have had Sophia load a small trunk with some special items, which I have marked for each person. Please see that they are distributed." Genaro, ever the jester, gave his best formal bow saying, "Yes, Your Majesty, we, your lowly servants, shall insure that your instructions are carried out to the letter." Lucia came to him and tweaked his ear "You my dear brother are too smart for your own good. It is only luck that I still love you deeply." Mateo was chuckling at this little banter and then turned serious "Lucia when shall we tell Zia of your return?" I am hoping within two months but I shall send word." They each kissed and hugged her and wished her a safe journey. Before she realized it, they were gone. Suddenly, she felt a tremendous sense of loss and started to cry. She thought to herself, 'how foolish am I for I shall see them in a short while', and thus tried to comfort herself, but wept in spite of her brave words.

Mateo and Genaro found the return trip not as enjoyable without the exuberant Lucia. They pushed themselves to complete the journey in far less time, not having to make as many stops to accommodate their sister. It was Genaro, who asked, "What was it that you gave Lucia that day in the solar?" Mateo smiled coyly "It was a potion to prevent her from getting with child. Someone had to help her, for you know that the wolf is at the hen house door." Genaro chuckled at the analogy. "Do you think she will lay with Danford?" "Well I would be very surprised if she did not. Did you not see how she looks at him? He is a good man, but even good men have needs. It is only a matter of time, and, of that I am sure."

Finally, they arrived back in Milan, and Alba, the ever-faithful servant, was anticipating their arrival from the letter Mateo had sent ahead of them. "Ah, Master, it is so good to see you and you

Master Genaro." They were sure that Alba knew what was going on with their relationship, but like all servants feigned any knowledge. For their part, they exercised a high level of discretion. They were happy to be home and enjoyed the fine meal Alba had prepared for them. That night, knowing that they would be separated for a long while, they made love with great passion. "I shall miss you so much, perhaps you could find time to come and stay with me in Rome?" Mateo, who was stroking Genaro's wavy hair, began to nibble his ear "I think I might be able to arrange something. I am not sure how long I can be left on my own without someone to comfort me." "Since this is our last night together for a while, I should like to give you whatever you desire." With that said, he walked over to the wardrobe where they kept a special trunk filled with an assortment of items. "Close your eyes, I should like to treat you."

Mateo closed his eyes and waited, he enjoyed the creative side of Genaro, ever the artist in all things. "Open." Standing there in nothing but a leopard loincloth and a mask that was supposed to resemble the same animal, Genaro growled and purred. He brought with him a silk rope and a horsehair whip. "Now, what shall I do with those?" lecherously asked Mateo, who just at the sight of him had grown rock hard. Genaro, getting down on all fours, turned so that his hind end was facing Mateo, purred, "I think you can think of something. Yes?" Mateo licked his lips which had suddenly gotten dry "Yes, I can."

The realities of life returned the next day, as Mateo went to his shop, and Genaro packed a bag for his trip to Rome, and his audience with the Pope. It would take Genaro the whole day to reach the Eternal City. The Curia would have rooms for him, and then he would see the Holy Father for his assignment.

Genaro found his rooms to be comfortable, but certainly sparse in decoration, and, definitely not like the luxurious furnishings of Mateo's villa in Milan. The mere thought of him made Genaro sad. To comfort himself he rubbed his very sore ass, which held the signs of a great night shared with his lover. He was thinking of Mateo and his hand moved to his erection. He could still taste his cum and smell his sex, and in a very short time, he had spilled his own seed all over himself. Genaro felt guilty for having done such a thing especially sitting under the statue of the Virgin but, knelt down and prayed for forgiveness and for Mateo.

***

Mateo, upon arriving at his shop, found that his assistant had carried on his business with great diligence. All was in order, several large purchases had been made, and the security notes had been posted at the Bank of Milan in his account. Soon he would have to go to the Magistrate to officially change his name. All his accounts were in the name of Antonio Sanfranco, which now sounded so foreign to him now, but it was not so long ago that he owned that name. He would no longer be the bastard child of a whore. Mateo thought of his mother and tears came to his eyes. She was a good woman who loved him beyond all imagining and sacrificed her own happiness for his sake. He now owned a name that meant something to both his mother and himself. He would carry the name of the man who was his father, Mateo Rizzo, but, for now, until it was legal and recorded, he would have to settle to keep his old name. He shook off his melancholy for his mother and suddenly thought of Genaro and realized how much he missed him.

Mateo, who was older and more versed in the ways of the world, felt a pang of pride at his ability to share and teach his younger lover. Genaro was a brilliant and talented artist but, more importantly, he was a kind and giving man. He trusted Mateo in all things and tried desperately to please him. The transformation of Genaro was the first visible sign of his desire to please Mateo. He went from a scrawny, ill-kept vagabond, to a handsome, muscular man of style and grace. One of the many things that Mateo loved about him was his sense of humor. Genaro could always make him laugh. He sat there dreaming of his lover and felt a longing that he had never experienced. He also thought of Lucia and a smile came to his handsome face. He ran his fingers through his thick wavy black hair and thought to himself "She is a handful. Pity the man who tries to tame that wild creature. I pray for her safety and happiness." He was holding a very expensive Venetian crystal ball and gazing into the prism of colors being radiated by the light it was catching from the open window. Without warning, a burning anger grew within him at the thought of Piro, who was now a wanted criminal on the loose. The sheer thought of him hurting, or worse, killing Lucia, made the bile reach his throat and he clenched his jaw. Mateo, now furious, knew he would have to intervene to protect his baby sister. He vowed that he would find a way to destroy Piro before he harmed Lucia.

***

Genaro, who was dreading his audience with His Holiness Pope Clement XII, sat nervously outside the gilded door to the papal office waiting to be called. His hands were wet with anticipation. While he had received commissions before, it was always in writing, he had never met him in person. He withdrew the silk scarf, which Mateo insisted that he always keep in his waistcoat pocket, was thankful now for his instruction, and mopped the sweat from his brow. He had just put it back in his coat when the door opened silently and a small priest dressed in the papal colors emerged. He bowed slightly and said, "His Holiness will see you now Signore` Banfi. Please follow me."

His mouth was dry and he prayed that he would not start coughing. The office was not what he expected. Although there was a massive and exquisitely carved desk in the middle of the floor, there was not much else. Genaro was struck by the overwhelming scent of sandalwood, which was fresh smelling and fragrant. Two large chairs were set at the front of the desk, and a small settee was situated in front of one of the floor to ceiling windows. At the back of the room, hidden in the shadows was a prie dieu. The only decorations were the century's old painted frescos, which adorned the walls and ceiling. Large windows, inserted with beautifully designed stained glass depictions of various saints and Jesus, brought brilliant light into the cavernous space. Standing in a corner was a life size statute of Jesus and at his feet were baby lambs.

His Holiness, an old man, was slumped over the prie dieu. Genaro stood there swallowed by the silence and was afraid that the noise from his pounding heart would disturb the ancient priest. After, what seemed an interminable time, the old man, moaning from the effort, stood up. He was a slightly built man who seemed to be hiding under the protection of his embellished robes. A shriveled head on a skinny neck protruded through the neckline. The jeweled crucifix, which hung from around his scrawny collar, appeared as an anchor on a tiny raft. He almost made Genaro laugh at the sight of him, which closely resembled a turtle in its shell.

"Come" he instructed, his voice was strong, which surprised Genaro, as he made his way to the settee. Genaro, just by instinct, kneeled before the pope, and the old man extended his hand so that he could kiss the papal ring. "Your Holiness, it is an honor to be here." The old man smiled warmly and patted his head. "Get up and sit with me, I have many things to discuss with you." "Are you familiar with Alessandro Galilei?" Of course, Genaro knew of the famous architect "Yes Your Holiness. I understand he has almost completed the new Arcibasiclica Papale de San Giovanni in Laterano. I am most anxious to see the finished structure." A broad smile appeared on the old man's face "That, my son will be your next accomplishment. You shall decorate the Church of the Bishop of Rome. What say you?" The pope, a gaunt man with hair thin as silk, sat hunched, his keen, sharp eyes, assessed the man before him as if he could read into his soul. Genaro was dumbfounded, he never, even in his wildest dreams, would have thought that he would have been asked to execute such a task. "Well?" Genaro, overwhelmed by the honor, slipped off the settee and came to his knees before the withering old man "Your Holiness, this is an honor too great for a simple painter such as myself, I am without words."

The pope, his knurled fingers reached for Genaro's face. "You, my son, are a great artist. All over Italy, they are singing praises to your work. You will be known as the Artist to the Church of Rome. I have every confidence that you shall carry out this mission for the greater honor and glory of Our Lord

Jesus Christ." When he finished speaking, he made the sign of the cross on Genaro's head. "Now go, my secretary, Cardinale Corsi, will explain everything to you. May the inspiration of Jesus be your guide." Genaro knew the audience was over and once again kissed the papal ring and whispered "Thank you. I shall do everything in my power not to disappoint you" and then rose, bowed, and followed the petite priest out the door. There were tears trailing down his handsome face.

Cardinale Corsi turned out to be a pleasant and highly competent man. His size could not be viewed as a suggestion to his power or ability to command respect. As they walked through the halls of the Papal Palace all those they met stopped and bowed at the sight of him. They walked and talked companionably, and Genaro felt at ease with the man. When they reached the site of the nearly finished cathedral Alessandro Galilei met them. Genaro, who only knew this man by his reputation, was stunned to see that he was of his own age. He greeted the cardinal with warmth and affection "Your Eminence, it is always a pleasure to see you." The Cardinal in return embraced the young architect with sincere affection "Alessandro I should like to introduce Genaro Banfi. As you know, the two of you will be working on the final completion of the cathedral." Alessandro was nearly as tall as Genaro but gaunt, with soft brown eyes that nervously darted from here to there, and a prominent nose. "So I finally meet the famous artist that His Holiness has been bragging about for so long." He must have seen the expression on Genaro's face at that statement then quickly added "It is an honor to meet you. Your work is well regarded, and I am thrilled that we shall work together to bring glory to this holy place."

Genaro's greatest flaw was his lack of self-worth. He felt intimidated by the magnitude and grandeur of the structure that stood before him. It was a brilliant manifestation of Galilei's talent. Genaro felt dwarfed by the scope of the work, but then he heard Mateo's voice in his head "You are a gifted artist, and one day they shall sing praises to your name." The thought of Mateo, who was strong of mind and body, calmed him and infused him with confidence.

"Let us escape this burning sun, I would like to show you the drawings, and then we shall get your opinion." As they walked up the granite steps to the massive entrance doors Genaro's eye caught the inscription above the door, it read "*Christo Salvatori*". It was very hot outside and the coolness of the interior of the cathedral sent a shiver up his spine. There was no doubt that this church was truly worthy of being the Cathedral of the Bishop of Rome, where the Popes will celebrate Mass. He had been in many churches throughout Europe but this one was different. It felt fresh, not because it was newly built, but the design was unusual, it felt like a palace. It was as if Alessandro could read his mind "Yes, the design is not what you are used to seeing. I had many a conflict with His Holiness regarding this new concept, but in the end, He liked it. What do you think?" Genaro, did in fact like the new look, which in some ways he thought would work better for the parishioners, "I like it and believe it will help with the circulation of both people and air." Alessandro suddenly became very animated, and his voice echoed in the hollow emptiness "Ah, Cardinale, you see, I told you, and this man has vision." The tiny priest nodded his head and smiled, as if appeasing him after many similar discussions over the design. The architect came over to Genaro and put his arm around his shoulder "We shall work well together. I like the way you think. Now, let me show you the drawings and tomorrow we shall lay a plan. Yes?" Genaro felt comfortable with this man and replied with a resounding "Yes." In the background, they could hear bells tolling, calling all clerics to vespers. Cardinale Corsi bowed to the two men before him, "I must go, it is time for vespers. I shall see the two of you tomorrow. Please, before I go, I should like to bless you." The two young men knelt before the diminutive figure. He placed a hand on each head and prayed "Jesus, bless these two young men, whom you have bestowed with boundless talents. Let them embellish this holy place with lasting beauty. May the God of all mercy inspire you to do great things, Amen" and then he made the sign of the cross over each of them. "Domani" he called over his shoulder as he scurried out of the church.

In a moment, he was gone. The two men stood there in the cold barrenness of the space, yet Genaro felt the warmth that emanated from Alessandro. They would work well together of that, he was sure. The architect brought him over to the battered workbench that was strewn with page, after page, of drawings, each one illustrating a different elevation. Genaro was captivated by the exactness of every detail with endless calculations written on the side of each diagram. He thought that his newfound friend was a genius and remembered with longing his own brother Andrea, the mathematician. His mind wandered for a moment, and he thought back to their childhood days when Andrea would spend hours scribbling numbers on whatever surface he could find. An unexpected pang of grief for a brother he had not seen in far too long weighed heavy on his heart. "What troubles you Genaro you look miserable, are you ill?" Genaro shook it off, "I am fine." The other man was not convinced, and thought perhaps it was the amount of work that needed to be done, "Don't worry; we shall hire many apprentices to assist you in this task" at that statement Genaro found himself relaxing as he contemplated this daunting task.

The two men poured over the volumes of seized design sketches, Genaro trying to absorb the space, saying little but intently listening to the architect explain the various functions of each space. Genaro, at one point walked away from the table. The sun had not yet set, and the light captured through the newly installed stained glass windows. The light held him in a trance, envisioning what he would create for each space, and how it would play against the various forms of light, from day to night. Alessandro, an artist in his own right, silently stood back, waiting, and watching Genaro's every move. When he was finally satisfied with his mental plan, Genaro now filled with great energy, announced, "It shall be magnificent. I will start immediately. Tonight I will compile a list of materials I shall require and how many laborers will be necessary" his voice was strong and high pitched from his excitement. Alessandro, himself caught up in this enthusiasm, replied "Excellent!"

"It is late, will you join me for supper?" asked the architect. Genaro, with only a small, bare, apartment in the Vatican to call home, thankfully agreed. They made their way to a nearby cafe, which was already overflowing with patrons. The proprietor, upon spotting Alessandro, rushed over "Signore` Galilei, I shall set a table for you on the terrace. Will this man be joining you?" The architect, who was obviously a steady patron, thanked the man and they were escorted to a quiet terrace in the rear of the building. It was cool and there were only a few other people pleasantly enjoying their meals. "Are you hungry?" asked the architect. "As a wild boar" answered Genaro with a broad smile on his handsome face. "Well then, we shall ask Lorenzo to prepare us a feast." The serving girl, who knew the young architect, came over, curtsied "Signore`

Galilei, what can we make for you this evening?" "Please tell Lorenzo to surprise us with the specialty of the house, and bring a jug of your finest wine. Oh, and be sure to put the charges on the account for Cardinale Albani." The young girl smiled, showing crooked teeth, curtsied once again, and went off to fulfill the order. "Cardinale Albani, my patron, affords me an allowance beyond what the Vatican pays. I shall talk to him about giving you a stipend as well. You will probably meet him in the next few days. Do you know of His Eminence?" "I have never met him but have heard that he is a great champion for the arts and has a vast collection of priceless antiques." Alessandro continued, "He is a powerful man who has a long reach to some very hefty coffers. You would be wise to pay heed to him, beside; he does have exquisite taste, and an educated eye for art, and those with talent.

"So, where are you from, and what of your family?" Genaro told him his whole life story, including Lucia. The architect then shared his own story. "I was born in Umbria, my parents died when I was quite small. I was sent to live with my father's brother and his family, perhaps you have heard of him, Galileo Galilei. I was placed with his son. He was kind and when I was of age, they sent me to be schooled in Pisa. I have been living on my own since the age of twelve. I have no regrets and have made a name for myself." The architect stopped speaking for a moment and seemed to be deeply engrossed in his thoughts. "Tell me, do you have a brother, who is a mathematician?" Genaro seemed shocked "Why yes, his name is Andrea. Why do you ask?" "I was at universita` with a man by that name. You bear a remarkable resemblance to him. How is he, it has been a number of years since I saw him last?" Genaro was sorry to say, "I too have not seen my brother in many years. We have been unable to find him. He was always different from the rest of my brothers and sisters. His mind was consumed with numbers." "Yes, I understand that affliction." They changed the subject and enjoyed a relaxing supper. The food was good, but the wine and company were better. Genaro finally decided that he needed to get back to his room "I shall bid you good evening. It has been most pleasant. I will compile my list of items I will need to embark on his very extensive mission." Alessandro made no move to leave "Are you not leaving?" Genaro asked. The architect lowered his voice "Sadly, I stay out late for I have no one who greets me at home. I live alone and so the nights are long and lonely, that is why I stay late. And what of you my friend, who comforts you when you are home?" Now, for the first time Genaro was conflicted. He knew he could not answer honestly, his relationship with Mateo was forbidden. "I too find myself to be alone. Our choice of work does not leave much time or energy for others. I shall once again say good night. I will see you in the morning." He left with a heavy heart, knowing how his new friend felt, but, grateful to know that he had someone who loved him waiting at home.

CHAPTER EIGHT

THE CROSSING

Calais ~ Dover

Lucia was delighted to see Henri and Danford, who had just returned from the shipyard, she ran to greet them. She had been trying to distract herself in the solar by reading, but had failed miserably. They both looked exhausted, but upon seeing her, they came to her asking, "What troubles you?" She felt somewhat foolish and sheepishly replied, "I know it is childish, but I do miss my brothers, and, I am anxious about going to England." Danford brought her to the nearest chair and sat her down "There is no need to fret. I shall be with you for the entire journey, and, you shall be comfortable at my family home. I will make time to squire you around London or wherever you shall need to go. I promise you will be safe." He was kneeling at her side and had been holding both her hands in a tight grip and then kissed them, lingering over each one. Henri smiled but said nothing, until Danford rose, then added, "You shall not need to worry for too much longer, your passage has been booked for the day after tomorrow." Lucia took in a deep breath "Then it is done. I shall begin collecting my things."

They sat for a simple but hearty supper and discussed the day's events. "How is the ship coming?" Danford smiled with great satisfaction, and replied, "With Henri's help and careful supervision it is progressing very well. We have a fine, hardworking crew, and most of the damage from the fire has been repaired. While we lost some time and material, considering the extent of the fire, it could have been much worse."

Lucia looked at him and added, "The worse loss would have been you. To think that a few short weeks ago you were covered in blisters, and barely conscious. It is nothing less than a miracle that you survived. I am so grateful for your courage, but you must promise me that you will never do that again. If something should have happened to you, I would never have forgiven myself."

Henri, took his time, and announced, "I have taken the liberty, since tomorrow is our last day together for a while, to invite some friends over for a farewell dinner. I trust that will not displease either one of you?" He turned to Danford, "Given the hour would you like to stay the night?" Danford declined "I have much to do to secure the manor house for my departure. I shall come as soon as time permits for the dinner." Since they had finished, and the hour was late, he rose, kissed Lucia on both cheeks, embraced Henri with a manly hug, and said good night.

Lucia was alone with Henri who rose, and invited her to join him in the solar for a glass of cognac. They were quiet, but Henri wanted to talk to her. He gathered the glasses and they sat on the settee. Lucia took in the perfume of the finely aged liquid, turning the glass to admire its purity of color. Lucia could sense that Henri was nervous, so she reached over and took his hand, "Do you wish to speak with me?" His handsome face broke into a smile, "Yes, I do. When I was with Danford, who seemed disturbed by something, which at first I thought was due to the extreme illness of his father. Yet, in speaking with him, he may have revealed a situation that has placed me in an awkward position. If what I am about to say offends you please forgive me." Lucia put down the glass and now had both his hands in hers "I could never be angry with you. I know you love me." He smiled but it was a sad smile "I wish that my beloved Auriella and I would have had children. I see you and think how much I have missed. Danford has asked you to marry him, yes?" Lucia was not surprised, or upset, by the fact that he had confided in Henri. "Yes he has. I have not committed to any betrothal. Not because I don't love him, I do." Trying to hold back her tears, but with no success, Henri reached into his coat and produced a silk scarf. Rather than hand it to her, he gently patted her cheeks to dry her face. "I am so sorry if I have upset you. Please forgive me." "Dear Henri I am upset with myself." He looked confused "Yourself. How is that possible?"

Lucia sucked in a deep breath to steady herself. "I do not want to be the property of some man; to be told where I can, or, cannot go. What I can buy or, what I must sell. I will not bear children, and I have already told Danford so. What is wrong with me?" Henri folded her into his arms and held her with such tenderness. "There is nothing wrong with you. You, my darling child, are a free spirit. Unfortunately, the world does not account for women who think as you do. Where you are going, England, there have been powerful women, Queens, who have ruled by their own sword. None of them married, but took lovers as they wished. You are a powerful, wealthy woman, and you can do as you please. Just be careful Lucia, there are those, both men, and women, who would seek to destroy that spirit. Do what is in your heart. You are still young, and beautiful, there is so much time ahead of you. As for Danford, I regret, he may not understand or appreciate a woman you thinks as you do."

For now, she had calmed herself. "It is late, we cannot resolve anything here. Let us go to our beds, tomorrow is another day to ponder these questions. Alas for now, content yourself with the knowledge that Danford loves you. He is a good and patient man, I am sure you will make the right choice. Come, I will walk you to your room." When they arrived, he cradled her face in his hands and kissed her lips so gently it was almost imperceptible. "Sleep well my beautiful flower."

Lucia was grateful that Danford was gone for the entire day. She and Sophia had much to do before their next journey. All her newly acquired gowns would have to be packed in traveling trunks. As she was sorting through her gowns, she came upon the gown Madame Richaud had designed for her the night Piro savagely attacked her. She was not aware that Sophia had brought it to Madame Richaud to be repaired. "Sophia, I did not know that this gown had been repaired." Sophia, her chin lowered, spoke softly, "It was so pretty Mistress I did not have the heart to discard it. I hope I have not overstepped your wishes. If it brings you discomfort to use it I shall get rid of it." Lucia thought for a moment, "Sophia, it would please me very much if you were to wear it. I am sure the fit will be perfect." The Sophia's eyes lit up, "Really Mistress. I may keep it for myself?" She picked it up and stood in front of the long mirror, but then her smile turned to a frown. "What is it?" asked Lucia. "Will it trouble you every time I put this gown on?" Lucia looked at her holding up the gown and realized that it truly would look beautiful on her. "No. It is not the fault of this beautiful garment. It is the damaged heart and mind of Piro for whom I once cared for very much. Please, I would be very happy to see you wear it." Sophia ran over, hugged, and kissed Lucia. "Thank you Mistress, I will treasure it."

The day passed quickly with all the preparations that were needed for the next part of their journey. Lucia was not sure if she would be returning to Paris and so all her belongings needed to be packed and ready to move. She heard a knock at the door and one of the serving maids announced that the Marquis was going to take his midday meal on the terrace and would like her to join him. She had not realized that she was in fact hungry and so welcomed the break. It was a lovely day with just a light breeze. Henri, who was seated at a table covered with mouthwatering delights, but when he saw her, he immediately rose and invited her to join him. "A little rest from all your packing and fussing will clear your head." "I am so happy you sent for me. I am ravenous." They ate with hearty appetites, talking and enjoying each other's company.

Henri told her that the ship would leave from the Pas de Calais and would take almost the entire day to arrive in Dover. They would spend the night there, embarking the next day to begin the two-day trek to Northumberland to Wallingston, the estate of the Duke of Northumberland, Lord Stevens, family estate. "Lucia, I would like to give you one of Auriella's fur capes to take with you. The northern regions of England will be turning quite cold this time of the year. I will also supply a woolen one for your maid, as I know you were not expecting to travel through cooler climes. Will that be acceptable?" "Henri, you think of everything. I should not have known about the change in weather, so thank you for your thoughtfulness." After they ate Lucia went back to finish the packing but Sophia had already completed it "Oh thank you Sophia." She shared with her what Henri had said and then went to lie down resting for the party that evening. "Sophia, is Nicko all ready to leave?" Sophia still perky from the morning replied "Yes Mistress. He has told me that he will meet us at the dock so that he can secure all the trunks and make sure that all is in order." "I am pleased. That is very good."

The farewell party was delightful. Henri had thought of everything. Every favorite dish Lucia said she liked was on the table. The guests were all people she had met during her stay in France. It was a wonderful evening. Before he left for the night, Lucia spoke with Danford to finalize their plans for the next morning. "I shall arrive here at dawn to pick you and Sophia up. We will then travel for two hours until we reach the docks at Calais. We will board our vessel and sail to Dover. I have made provision for food and drink and when we make land, I have reserved us rooms at a quaint inn. It is not fancy, but, it is clean and the food is palatable." Lucia listened and nodded, then added "Thank you Danford. I am very excited to meet your family." He was pleasant, but she knew he was trying to keep her at arm's length. Lucia wanted to express her affection for him, but knew that in her heart she would never marry this man, or, perhaps, any man.

The guests had all left and Henri was sitting quietly in the solar, "Henri, it is late are you going to retire for the evening?" The old man who was sitting on the settee, beckoned her to join him. "Please, come sit with me for a few moments." Lucia joined him and said, "What troubles you?" He looked forlorn and for the first time since she met him, his age was visible. He drew in a deep sigh, as if it were difficult for him to breathe, "I will miss you terribly my dear child. You have made me happier than I have been in so long. You have filled not only this house, but also, my heart with joy. I am worried for your safety. I know Piro, and he can be a vengeful man. You must promise me, on your honor, that you will exercise great caution." Lucia slid off the settee and came to her knees, her face lit by the warm glow of the candlelight, "I pledge on my honor to be diligent for my safety, you need not worry. Henri, I too am heavy of heart at the thought of leaving you and this beautiful country. I have learned many things in the short time that I have been here with you. I shall hold your love in my heart always." She reached up and kissed him on the lips, her heart fluttering at the act. "I love you Lucia. Promise you will come back to see me." Lucia, not sure what the future would hold said, "We shall be reunited again." Henri, nodded, "It is late we will need to be ready by first light. Go to bed. I will come up shortly." She stood, kissed him on the cheek and said "Good night dear Henri." He watched as she disappeared from his sight, a single tear kissing his cheek. Henri prayed that he would see his beloved Lucia again.

Morning came swiftly, and Lucia was tired from a restless night. "Mistress let me help you get ready, Lord Stevens will be here shortly" said Sophia, who was already dressed and ready to go. Lucia rose, washed, and dressed in anticipation of Danford's arrival. She had butterflies in her belly at the prospect of leaving the security of Henri's home and love. She busied herself until she went down, only to find Henri waiting for her. He looked tired and sad. They were talking companionably with each other when Danford arrived. He seemed anxious, Lucia was not sure if it was because she was going home with him, or, because of his father's illness. It was time to leave, "Lucia, my dear sweet flower, I shall pray for your safety and always hold you dear to my heart." Lucia with tears flowing freely down her face, embraced him with such love, "Henri, I shall be back to see the launching of our first ship. We shall celebrate this great event with a fabulous gala. I was thinking would you mind if we named the vessel after Auriella?" Henri's eyes grew wide and a smiled immediately came to his face "That would be such an honor for both of us, but, that honor should be yours." Lucia, hugging him replied, "There will be many more ships, but, this one, like Auriella, will always be special. Please give me this special gift." The old man, kissed her, and she felt his tears on her face. "Thank you Lucia, this is the perfect gift. I will send word of our progress and then we shall set a date for the maiden voyage, God's speed."

Henri turned to Danford. "I will move forward with all that we have discussed. In the off chance there is a problem I will send word. I beg you to watch over Lucia and guard her with your life." Danford, caught up in the emotion of the moment, fought back his own tears, but, cleared his throat as he responded, "I am confident that all will be well under your supervision. Do not worry, I have pledged on my honor to protect Lucia. We will send word when we shall return. Keep well old friend and thank you for all your support. Now, we must make our way to Calais or we will miss the boat."

As the carriage pulled from the drive Lucia, her head out the window, waved, and called to Henri, as if she were a child leaving her parent. She continued to wave until the trees that lined the broad boulevard swallowed the house. She was sad, and Danford tried to comfort her, "Do not concern yourself; we will see him in a few short weeks." Lucia blotted her eyes with her linen scarf, "I have a terrible foreboding that I shall never see my dear Henri again." They sat in silence, Danford respecting her sorrow, until they were approaching the port city of Calais.

It was a relatively warm morning and Lucia had left her carriage window open. She could smell the briny fragrance of the sea and her spirits lifted. The carriage had to snake its way through the maze of people and carts making their way to the docks. It was just past eight o'clock in the morning and already the place was alive with activity. Merchants, standing about, animatedly talking with one another, while waiting for their shipment on the arriving ships, still others were ready to load their wares on departing vessels. Young men clad in seamen's attire scurrying between ships either looking for work, or, reporting to their ships. The general atmosphere was one of organized chaos. Lucia remembered fondly thoughts of her father and brother loading their boat making ready for the day's fishing. A large man who was barking orders at their driver rudely interrupted her thoughts. "Move that carriage to the side. Do you not see you are blocking a whole line of carts that need to be unloaded? Bring her around to the port side of the dock and let out your passengers." Obediently, the driver followed the big man's orders and brought them to the port side of the vessel. Waiting for them was Nicko and the two guards, he bowed at them and cheerfully announced, "Good morning Mistress, Lord Stevens, all your trunks have been loaded and I have secured a comfortable spot for the two of you. Once we are underway Sophia will serve you breakfast." Lord Stevens offered; "My valet, William, who is due to arrive shortly, can assist her as needed" Nicko nodded. Lucia noticed that Nicko coyly smiled approvingly at Sophia who blushed at the sight of him. "I am told that the trip will only take a few hours. We shall arrive in Dover for the midday meal." "Yes, and I have sent word at a tavern I often use to expect our party." All was set and they made their way onto the vessel, which was not huge, but packed to the rails with merchandise and passengers. Danford volunteered, "At this time of the day, as it is the first ship to leave for Dover, is the busiest. In the evening the returning vessels are equally as full." The sun was just burning off the sea mist and a warm breeze was whispering on the wind. Lucia was starting to relax. The sea always made her calm.

After their light morning meal Danford relaxed by playing a card game with Nicko and his men. Lucia and Sophia sat reading and enjoying the general movement of those sailing aboard the ship. Lucia started to doze, lulled by the swaying vessel and Sophia leaned into her to keep her from falling off the bench they shared. Lucia awoke about an hour later with a chill and the bouncing of the ship on the strong current. The weather had turned much cooler and the waves were sloshing heavily against the bow.

She got up to look over the side and caught a glimpse of the distant shoreline. It seemed closer than it was. The sky was a dark grey and the wind had picked up bringing with it a cold sea spray. She steadied her stomach and closed her eyes. She was thinking of the day Vesuvius destroyed her village when she was a little girl. That was the turning point of her life. Lucia always held mixed feeling as to the events of that day and how her fate had been determined in the ashes of the 'unextinguished'. She reflected on the first time she laid eyes upon Giovanni Romano. He was a wretched sight and to think of what he has become, not only in appearance, but also to her heart. Lucia had been told terrible stories of Maria Sucretti, with whom she then came to live; the woman the whole family hated. The same woman who became a mother to her, who has given her everything she has, and taught her everything she will become. The dramatic way her life, and the lives of all those she holds dear, have changed in a decade. As she looked into the roiling waters, the blackness of its color, made her wonder what fate has in store for her now. These waters, so different from the blue seas she loved, seemed ominous to her and she shook with a chill that fell upon her.

From high above her head the mate who was shouting, "Land ho. Land ho" broke her reverie. She looked up and there straight ahead was the coastline of England. Lucia was thrilled and frightened in the same breath. She felt the powerful arm of Danford engulf her in his grip "There is the land of my birth. I am finally coming home." She felt, more than heard, the pride in his words. He bent over and gently kissed her cheek "I am so happy you are with me. I should greatly like for you to meet my father, before he..." He did not finish his sentence but left the thought of his father's death hanging in the sea mist. Lucia did not answer, but squeezed his hand. She felt dwarfed by the form of this man, a man for whom she held great affection.

The water was tumultuous and the vessel swayed and dipped with each crashing wave. The sky had turned dark, and a light drizzle kissed all it encountered. The cool damp air, filled with the stench of a busy, dirty, harbor perfumed the air. Much like Calais, the harbor and dock were alive with activity. It could have been the same scene, if not for the language. Lucia knew English and could speak it, but the sound of it hurt her ears. Bedraggled boys were running up and down the dock, each in their turn shouting their services. One was holding up a bulletin board with the menu of a nearby tavern; a younger boy was passing out leaflets with articles printed on it. Carts, horses, casks of any number of items, were all being transported on and off the docked vessels. A tattooed man, with a long braided beard, and gold earring, was yelling for seamen who wanted a good day's wage. Lucia was fascinated by the comings and goings of the place and was caught up in the mayhem when Nicko came to secure her arm and lead her to a waiting coach. "Mistress, Lord Danford has gone ahead to the tavern to arrange the accommodations, I will escort you and Sophia to the place." Sophia brushed against his arm and he pinched her waist, at which she drew in a silent yelp, and flushed. Lucia enjoyed watching this banter between the two, she knew they were in love, and it made her happy.

Lucia's initial impression of Dover was not very pleasant. It was a tired looking place, with grey buildings to match the darkened sky. It was musty and damp, and the foul odor of unwashed bodies and mold seemed to permeate the air. They made their way to the tavern and Danford greeted them at the door "I've secured us our own room which I had them wash down and tidy up for your arrival. It is not luxurious, but, the food is good and it is now very clean." "Thank you for your efforts, but, I do not wish to cause undue measures on my account."

Walking through the busy establishment was an adventure in itself. Loud, drunk, men were shouting and calling after her. She could see that the mere act of it was infuriating Danford, who was practically growling back at them. "Don't get upset, this always happens. Pay them no mind." His eyes were narrowed, and his jaw was set, "I will not have men treat you as a common whore. You are a Marchesa and should be treated as such." Lucia would have liked to slap his face, but of course, she did not. She knew that the only reason he was upset was that he considered her his woman, and, did not want other men to lust after her. Just to antagonize him, when they reached the doorway to the room, Lucia, turned and curtsied to her adoring fans. This sent up a roar of cheers and laughter.

Danford, now visibly upset yanked her by the arm into the room and slammed the door shut, to the sounds of yowling and uproarious laughter. Danford brought her to a small room in the back of the tavern, which had indeed been swept up and clean linens on the tables. "How dare you do something like that? Do you like when men call after you like a street slut?" He was holding her arm so tight she grimaced. Danford's size blocked the sight of Nicko who was standing in the rear of the room, who had come forward, and pried Danford's hand from his Mistress' arm. "My Lord, I am sure you wish to wash up before supper is brought." Instantly the young lord, his pride wounded, regained his composure, "Yes, is there a place?" Nicko replied, "Follow me."

Danford followed Nicko to the rear of the tavern where there was a privy, and a basin with water. Nicko came to speak directly in his ear while he was bent over the basin, "My Lord, never address my Mistress in that manner again. I understand how you feel, as a man, but do not dishonor Marchesa Banfi like that ever again. Thank you My Lord." Danford rose to his full height, which was a head over Nicko, squared his shoulders, and set his jaw. Nicko was preparing himself for a fight with the young lord. "Yes, you are right Nicko; I overstepped myself, with your Mistress. That woman is driving me mad with desire." Nicko bowed deeply, as if to accept the young lord's apology, but cordially responded, "I will defend her to my death." Danford, his shoulders now relaxing, replied, "I do understand. I too have pledged to protect and defend her, but, damn that woman, she is so defiant, I should like to take her across my knee." "Yes, I agree, she has a mind all her own." The two men understood each other, and, Danford knew that if he ever crossed the line Nicko would not hesitate to kill him or, anyone else, to defend his Mistress.

When they returned to the room Lucia's face was flushed with anger. Danford knew he had to apologize, but he felt awkward while Nicko and Sophia, and his own valet William were in the room. "Will the three of you excuse us for a few moments?" The trio, left immediately. "Lucia, I am afraid that my feelings for you have caused me to act like a tyrant. I only want the best for you. I want always to protect your honor." She did not look directly at him, "You see, now, if I were your wife, your property, you would have hurt me." Danford felt the heat rise to his own face, "Why did you taunt those drunks, acting like a whore?" He knew the second those words left his mouth that he would regret it. This time, she turned to face him, her eyes were smoldering, and she stood. "I will do and act, as I say, not as you say. I was teasing you, not them. You were not so worried for my honor, but, for your own. You are a man, who must defend his property. You think I am your property, to do as you wish. I assure you Lord Danford that I am no man's property." Danford was furious, "I would like to take you over my knee and thrash you pretty pink arse until you beg for mercy." Lucia, aroused at the thought, yet would not relent. "I am sure you would My Lord, but, unless I had such an inclination for you to do that to me, it will never happen." Danford was crazed with anger and desire; he lunged toward her and kissed her hard on the mouth. Lucia did not anticipate the move, but did not reject him. His large hands were all over her neck, back, and finally, her breasts. Lucia was gasping from yearning. He moved his hands to her waist, pinching the smallness of her, and then he grabbed her ass and moaned. His erection was so pronounced she was sure it would tear through his breeches. He kissed her again, his tongue filling her mouth. She felt herself become wet between her legs. She wanted him.

There came a soft knock at the door, to which they both moved to opposite ends of the room, and Danford announced "Come." It was his valet William, "My Lord, your supper is ready to be served. Shall I have them come in to start the service?" Lucia, was not very familiar with William, but, liked his easy way and knew that he had been with Danford all his life. Lucia looked to Danford and nodded her approval, "Yes William, have them serve the food, and, bring us some of their finest wine. Thank you." He had pulled his waistcoat as tight as he could to conceal his ever-growing desire.

The food was brought and Sophia, Nicko, and William joined the party; the two guards ate by themselves in the bar. Lucia, while she thought the meal was palatable, was not impressed with the taste or presentation. She thought to herself, everything in this country is grey and flavorless. The first course was a watery porridge of some kind, which smelled foul; the second course was a hunk of steamed meat dressed with a pudding, the likes of which she had never seen. Finally, the third course consisted of a battered fish dish. She ate enough to fill the empty void in her gut, but did not take a morsel more than necessary. For his part, she had never seen Danford devour so much food. "Do you enjoy this cuisine?" He smiled broadly, "Yes, but, I see you do not." The wine however, was quite good, and so Lucia drowned her appetite with its consumption.

They were going to stay the night in Dover, making the three-day journey to Northumberland on the morrow. After they had filled themselves, Lucia, a little unsteady on her feet, was escorted to the room Danford had secured for her. There were not enough rooms in the tiny inn, so William, Nicko and the two guards all made their way to the barn where they were given a threadbare blanket and small pillow. Sophia was fortunate enough to get her own room, the size of which was no bigger than a cupboard, but at least she did not have to share her space with the animals.

Morning seemed to have come quickly. Sophia, already up, had gotten a cast iron pot filled with clean hot water so that Lucia could bathe. Fresh linens were laid out for her, as was her own scented soap. Sophia helped her wash, combed her hair, and then dressed Lucia in her riding gown. "Good morning. Porridge is hot and on the table. Come now ladies it is getting late." Lucia recognized the high-pitched voice of the innkeeper's wife. Lucia was starved and made her way down to the room where they had dined the night before. A large iron pot of steaming gruel was sitting in the middle of the table, a ladle hanging from the side. The men, having gotten up earlier, were already spooning it up into wooden bowls. It smelled horrible and looked even worse.

Upon seeing her Danford and the other men rose and bowed. "Good morning Marchesa? Did you sleep well?" asked Nicko in a lighthearted way. "Yes, thank you Nicko." Danford came around the table and kissed her hand, and holding it brought her to the table and sat her down next to his own place. "Porridge?" She looked distressed, "What is this "Porridge?" Danford gave out a hearty laugh "This, my beautiful lady, is the national food of England and Scotland. It is a soupy mixture of barley, sometimes oats, that has been ground into a finer texture, and then it is cooked slowly in milk and butter, over hot coals. We use it for many things, but, we love it for the first meal of the day, because it is hearty and sticks with you." Given the explanation for its preparation and use did not comfort Lucia, but she could see there was little in the way of an alternative. She remembered Gandolfo making the same concoction for Apollo and the other animals at Monteforte.

Sophia spoke, "Mistress, I shall prepare a bowl for you, and top it with berries and honey. It will be delicious." Lucia just nodded, but there was no joy. When the bowl of gruel was placed before her Lucia's stomach growled, but, being a good sport, she dug right in and tasted it. Her initial reaction was one of surprise. Everyone was watching her, "It is not terrible. Actually, with the berries and honey it is quite enjoyable." Again, Danford roared with laughter, "Ah, I shall make an Englishwoman of you in no time at all." Lucia thought to herself, 'I sincerely doubt that I shall ever want to be an Englishwoman'.

Once they had completed their meal, Danford settled the bill with the innkeeper, and the other men brought around the horses that the young Lord had bought for the journey. Lucia was mounted upon a pleasant looking steed that was about fifteen hands, not as big as Apollo, but a sturdy animal. Once they were mounted, Sophia joined William in the wagon they had also bought that was loaded with trunks and casks of every description. The small caravan started out on the three-day trek to the farthest region of England. Lucia was excited, as well as anxious to be here. What would she find once she arrived? Would Danford's family accept her? More importantly, her relationship with Danford, to this moment in time had been strained. He loved her, and there was no doubt in her mind, yet was she willing, even able, to be the wife and mother he so desperately wanted her to be.

Dear Lord Jesus, please deliver me from the curse of my birth.

CHAPTER NINE

THE DISCOVERY

Montecassino Abbey

After weeks of painstaking study Brother Angelo, emerged from the library of his beloved monastery at Montecassino, exhausted but triumphant in his discovery. He was anxious to share his astonishing news with his superior Abbot Vittorio. He had finally unraveled the ancient text of the dozens of manuscripts found in the cave at Monteforte. He was elated at his own knowledge, but then chastised himself for the sin of pride. The young monk, who had been working exclusively on this portion of the manuscripts, had become enthralled by the story.

He found himself staggering toward the private chamber of his superior, boosted only by the knowledge he claimed as his own. He was almost delirious with joy at this very moment. Softly, he padded down the dark hallway to the suite of the Abbot of the Abbey de Montecassino. It was very late but he could not contain his excitement and needed to share his findings. The monk tapped gently on the abbot's door, he knew he was still awake by the glimmer of candlelight seeping from under the door.

There was a quiet shuffle and the bolt was thrown back to open the heavy carved door.

"Brother, what brings you to my chamber so late?" inquired the abbot. Breathless with anticipation Brother Angelo answered softly "I have just now finished the final translation of the last manuscript and I was too anxious not to share the news." "Come, then we shall share your discovery." Abbot Vittorio was a kind and generous leader of the men who inhabited the great monastery. He was a highly intelligent man in his late thirties with sharp, but kindly eyes, who oversaw this magnificent ancient center of worship and learning. It was a great honor both ecclesiastically and intellectually for a man of his age to be ordained Abbot. He was not a boastful man, yet he knew that he held great power, not only over those in his abbey, but because he was the curator of the Abbey de Montecassino, with all its antiquities and repository of priceless books and manuscripts.

"Let us have some port to compliment this sweet success." The younger monk bowed to his superior and welcomed the sweet wine for his efforts. He poured two glasses and then they set to their work. "Tell me Brother, what have you discovered?" Brother Angelo took a deep breath as if to savor the moment then said, "There is a book, an ancient book, written in approximately 700 B.C. which describes, in detail, the Creation of the world and the Gods who brought forth life. This book, which was presumed lost or destroyed over many centuries, was discovered by a Greek fisherman in a cave of glowing waters. That was approximately around 650 A.D. He brought it to his local priest thinking it was something possessed by the Devil. When the priest asked him where he found such a book the fisherman, according to the story, fell to his knees, covered his face and wept. He told the story of finding a cave in the middle of the sea from which a brilliant light was glowing. Surely, he thought, this must be the work of the Devil, for he had been living off the sea his whole life, and had never seen such a sight. It was in this cave that he found the book.

The priest, was a wise man, and knew he could not decipher the book, but knew it was important. He left his parish and travelled due south to a monastery inhabited by Byzantine monks of considerable repute. They examined the book and knew, without a doubt that it was of such great importance that they would have to bring it to the Holy Father. Feigning ignorance of its content, the monks sent the priest back to his home thinking it was just an old book of no value. After toiling over its translation, the monks journeyed to Rome to seek an audience with the Holy Father.

It was said that this is the only true tome of creation and all others are impostors in its wake and that the Bible, with its story of Genesis was created by the Roman Church in support of the birth of the Prophet Jesus. There was such love, fear and devotion to the Greek Gods that Holy Mother Church knew that in order to destroy this blind faith to the

Gods of Mythology they would have to destroy the very book from which it came." The younger monk stopped to organize his thoughts then continued, "The story, according to the ancient manuscripts that I have read and translated states:

That on the Mount of Helicon, the sacred and holy dwelling of the Gods, with its vast and glimmering waters, a brilliant light glows from deep within its depths. That springs of holy water gurgle and roil from the bottomless wells. The water that spills forth is the light of life from which all things live. Helicon is the home of the God Zeus who is Father of all living things.

One day, the horse of ancient fable Pegasus, and bearer of Zeus, travelled to Earth. Wherever his hooves landed, it is written that springs of glimmering light sprung forth. It is out of these springs of light that life was created, and took the physical form of Muses. Out of these springs came the nine Muses, or daughters of Zeus, they are the mothers of the Earth. They brought forth creation. They are the mothers of Fertility, Art, Music, Literature, Science, Philosophy, Mathematics, Astronomy, and Love. It is from these nine daughters of Zeus that our Earth, and all its inhabitants, were created. That the life's blood of the Muses lies in the mystical waters of the springs, the glowing lights of the waters holds the key to creation. Whomever drinks of the waters of the glowing lights shall live forever!

The young monk was so taken by his rendition of what he had uncovered that he was on the verge of collapse. He stopped to take a deep swill from the glass, and drained its contents, without regard for his superior; he then poured himself another draft.

Abbot Vittorio was sitting in rapt attention to this story and was watching his friend and colleague with a keen sense of awe. The abbot knew of the fine mind of his subordinate, and was impressed with his ability to have translated so much in such a short time. They both were aware of the importance of their find and that Mistress Lucia's very life might be held in the outcome.

The Abbot now broke the silence. "Dear Brother Angelo, it is hard not to make the correlation between the glowing underwater cave and secret chamber that Mistress Lucia brought us to and what you have just read. The ancient mosaics and frescoes are all in testament to what is contained in the manuscripts. It was no wonder why such places were kept secret. Yet, this book, where has it gone? Does it say what has become of it?"

Now it was Angelo's turn once again to hold the attention of his master. "Yes Abbot, the manuscripts are clear as to the place that the ancient Monks hid the book so as not to be found by any person who would bring the true story of Creation to the common man. Let us not forget, that the Byzantine monks were praised throughout the then known world for their ability to read and write, and thus their word was held to be sacred. If they were to divulge the contents of this book of knowledge to the common man, it would be considered truth. This explanation of the creation of the Earth lies in direct conflict with the teachings of Holy Mother Church."

The story goes on to tell of a group of faithful and devout monks, who toiled their lives in the service of our Holy Mother Church, who discovered the knowledge of this book, and after centuries of being hidden in the southern most regions of Italy, was found by an unwitting fisherman. They brought their findings to the Holy Father. We must not forget that the Church was still in its fledgling years, and was mistrusted by many. Persecution for their faith was still on going in many parts of the world. Any teachings from the past that could upset the beliefs of the new Christians had to be destroyed. In his fear that the common man would come to believe in the power of the Muses, and not the Church, his Holy Father commanded that this powerful book be destroyed.

The monks were commanded to take back the book and destroy it. They were administered an oath of silence and obedience to its execution, yet, being learned men they could not abide by destroying such an important and potent piece of history so they hid it in a secret place, a place where no man would venture for fear of evil spirits descending upon him. The little band of monks, each swearing a pledge of loyalty and silence, knew they would have to rid themselves of this book. If their conspiracy against the Holy Father were discovered, they would be tried as heretics and burned at the stake.

It is at this point that the mastery of these monks becomes apparent. They conspired to build a secret chamber from which to study these manuscripts. Apparently, there were many more manuscripts than the ones we found, and so they embarked on the construction of what we discovered in the cave, which at that time was no simple task. The structure was set upon the very spring of eternal light of which the book spoke. With the fear that they would be found out, together with the terror of the power of the eternal light, that these men were kept in constant dread for their lives.

One day the mountain, Vesuvius, erupted and those that were working within the secret chamber were sealed within forever. Thinking this a sign of God's wrath, whether they thought it was their Christian God or Zeus, it is not clear, but the few who were still alive did not venture back and all died in the silence of its existence."

"Brother this is a formidable tale. In the manuscripts does it speak of where this Book of Muses is hidden?" The younger monk, his hair tousled, with dark circles under his reddened eyes from lack of sleep, seemed to awaken with the question, and smiled with the slyest of grins, "Yes Abbot it does. It is hidden in the darkest, farthest recesses of a catacomb." "But Angelo, there are perhaps hundreds of catacombs scattered throughout the world. How shall we know which one it is? " It was now that the young monk, rejuvenated by the telling of the story, sat taller than he ever had, squared his shoulders and announced "It is not hard dear Abbot, the secret chamber that we discovered holds the passage way into the catacombs, at least according to the manuscripts."

The Abbot was stunned, "here, right here under our own nose. Can this be true?" Brother Angelo looking somewhat smug said, "Why would they lie? These manuscripts are ancient and they would have had no way of knowing that centuries later they would be found. Let us not forget, that had it been discovered that they had deceived His Holy Father, surely they would have been burned at the stake as heretics. What these men did was in direct disaccord with their orders. They would have to swear themselves to secrecy and find the best hiding place. No one, even the thought of it makes my spine crawl with fear, would dare to desecrate the final resting place of the dead, for to do so is a mortal sin."

The Abbot was deep in thought. "So Angelo, what do you think happened? It must have been a thriving monastery and from the looks of the remnants, a most wealthy one at that."

"I believe, from later manuscripts, that the monks lived in fear at the rumbling of Vesuvius. They came from where we are standing, and with no more than a dozen or so of them, built the cave and secret chamber we found. They knew it was the right place because of the glowing waters. I can only assume, and from what few documents are remaining, that there was an eruption and those fortunate enough to escape did not reveal their secret. When they died, so did the knowledge of the Book of Muses, and its hiding place."

The older monk seemed to find this explanation very plausible yet he seemed confused. "But we, you, me and Lucia, searched that whole chamber but could not find any means by which to escape into another antechamber. So where are these catacombs? Are they here at Montecassino?"

Brother Angelo sat back in his chair for the first time and seemed as though he would fall fast asleep, he closed his eyes, and was breathing deeply. After a few moments, he turned to his superior and said, "It is hidden under Monteforte." "Are you sure?" asked his superior in an incredulous voice. "Yes, I am positive. I have in my possession a detailed map of where they hid the Book of Muses." The young monk was suddenly so overcome by exhaustion that he nearly fell off his chair. The Abbot seeing his fellow at the point of collapse said, "Brother, go to your bed. We shall talk further when you have rested." He got up to help the young monk to his feet. "I am very proud of you Brother Angelo. If what was detailed in these manuscripts is true, we must find it, and safeguard it for all of history." The younger man just gave a sleepy nod like a child who is too exhausted to fuss, and then staggered to his chamber.

Even though the hour was late, the Abbot knew that he needed to write to Lucia and inform her of this latest development. The mere thought of the redheaded beauty made his heart flutter. He cursed the frailty of his flesh and dropped to his knees to pray for strength against his desire for Lucia. "Lord Jesus, I beg thee to give me strength. Punish me for my weakness and my lustful thoughts. I have served You, My Lord, my whole life without blemish. Deliver me from my sins of the flesh." Abbot Vittorio wept for his weakness. He knew he needed to put thoughts of her out of his mind and serve up penance for his sins. Walking resolutely to his wardrobe he withdrew a whip, then slowly removed his robe and knelt on the cold, stone, floor and taking hold of the horsehair whip began to whip his bare skin. The sting of the whip made him flinch, but, until he could control his desire, which was evident by the erection he now had, he would chastise himself with no mercy. He continued until he felt the warmth of his blood trickle down his back. The pain had eased his desire and he made his confession in silence, weeping as he prayed.

When he was done, with hands shaking from pain and fatigue, he dressed, and went to lie in his bed. He slept restlessly, and, realizing that sleep could not keep him from his desires, got up, changed his blood stained robe, washed and prepared for morning prayers.

After morning prayers Abbot Vittorio, skipped breakfast, he would fast today in penance. He returned to his chamber and tried mentally to prepare himself to compose a letter to send to Lucia. He took in a deep breath and picked up the quill, his hand started to tremble; he then reached for the vellum that he kept for special letters and began to write. He stopped for a silent prayer and pleaded, "Jesus, make me strong of mind and will. I have sinned in my thoughts and in my deeds. I love Lucia and I know that it is wrong. Help me I implore Thee."

Dear Marchesa Banfi,

I send this missive with knowledge that Brother Angelo has found the information we had been seeking. Upon your return, we will plan a course of action to bring this matter to a close.

I hope you are enjoying your stay abroad. I have been speaking with your beloved sister Antoinetta and the impending birth of their child. She is well but tired from carrying such a big belly. Marchesa Sucretti and Lord Romano are happy and healthy.

God bless and keep you in His heart,

Abbot Vittorio Fermelli

When he had completed the note, he set the wax with his official seal, and would have it delivered to the Marquis De Fauntil. He vowed never to be alone with Lucia for his flesh was weak. He would spend the day in prayer and fast for his sinful thoughts. While his back ached from the chaffing of his rough robe against his battered flesh, his heart ached even more, for he loved Lucia, as he had never loved anyone.

CHAPTER TEN

NORTHUMBERLAND

Wallingston Castle

For the next two days, they rode hard stopping only for food and lodging until they reached the outer borders of the Duke of Northumberland's estate. As they made their way through miles of barren, rocky sheep farms, the villages became fewer and fewer. The landscape was harsh and the weather, which was usually overcast, had a dampness that set into the fibers of your clothing and penetrated into the bones.

Lucia cursed the weather as her hair, became one giant mass of ringlets, in spite of Sophia's efforts to tame it with scented oils. On the second night, the inn they found was small and dirty, Lucia whispered to Sophia, "I hate this abominable country. It is always damp and grey. I long for the warm sun and the smell of the sea and lemons." Sophia was trying to shush her up for the walls were thin. "Mistress, how long shall we stay here?" Lucia understood the underlying need for her maid to know the length of their stay, for it was that much longer before she could wed Nicko. "I do not think it shall be too much longer. I long for Monteforte, Zia and my sister. It will not be too much longer for you either Sophia." The last statement was said with tongue in cheek, and the maid blushed. They finally fell asleep only to be abruptly awoken by the shrill sounds of horns blowing and baying dogs.

"What is that God awful sound?" Sophia got up and peered through the grime-encrusted windowpane. A thick fog blanketed the ground, the unmistakable sound of riders and dogs could not be unnoticed. Since they had slept in their riding gowns, for fear of being infested with lice, they quickly washed their faces, combed their hair, and made their way down to the commotion.

"Ah, there you are. I apologize for the rude awakening. Today is the first day of the Hunt. Everyone is here to gather for the traditional opening of fox season." Lucia could not help but see the excitement in Danford's face as he inspected the hunters on their fine mounts, their dogs yelping and excited for the chase. There was a tension in the air. The young grooms at the ready, holding their horses reins, the dogs pulling at their ropes, the scent of their prey already in the snout.

Lucia felt the exhilaration of the impending start of the hunt. Looking over those gathered she saw the crème de la crème of the local nobility. Each man dressed in his finest hunting plaid. Black velvet hats, adorned with dyed feathers and fastened with a pin with their family crest. Their red waistcoats, so meticulously tailored, even the buttons, which carried the family crest, glimmered in the dull morning light. Boots to the knee, polished to a soft patina, covered riding jodhpurs. There was no detail left undone. Each wore supple leather riding gloves, a crop, and one even carried a mask fashioned after the fox prey. To a man, they were a remarkable sight, in all their splendor and power.

A robust greeting came from one of the men "Lord Stevens, when did you arrive? Are you joining the hunt?" Danford stood taller than usual and replied "Lord Bentley it's so good to see you. I have only just arrived. I am on my way to Wallingston. My father has summoned me. I regret I cannot join you today." The other man dismounted and came to Danford's side, he embraced him warmly, "I was so sorry to hear that the Duke has taken ill. My best regards, and if there is anything I might do to assist, please do not hesitate to send word to me. My mother will be relieved to know of your return." Danford had lost his smile and inclined his head, "Thank you Samuel that is very kind of you. I shall see for myself the extent of the Duke's illness."

Lucia, not wanting to intrude on their conversation, had stayed back in the shadows of the inn. Now, she saw that they were no longer engaged in personal conversation, stepped into the light. "What have we here? Who is this delightful dove?" Danford stepped forward and extended his hand to Lucia, which she took and came closer. Bentley was scrutinizing her from head to toe. "This is the

Marchesa Lucia Banfi of Monteforte, Italy. She is a dear friend, and will be a guest at Wallingston for as long as she wishes to grace us with her presence." Bentley, licked his lips, removed his hat and swept it in a gallant gesture, coming up he took her hand and kissed it, "The pleasure of your acquaintance is purely mine Marchesa Banfi." Lucia felt herself flush and she gave a slight curtsey. "Welcome to my country, if there is anything I can provide during your stay, please, I beg you, send word for me." Danford, doffed him on the ear, "I believe you best be getting to the hunt before there are no foxes left. I shall send around William, my valet, and we will arrange another private hunt on my estate." Samuel Bentley, took the implied dismissal bravely, bowed formally to Lucia, and mounted his handsome horse. "Farewell, Mistress Banfi, I hope to see you soon" his voice trailing behind him as he rode off to join the others. Lucia followed him with her eyes, and thought, that he was indeed a fine-looking man, about the same age as Danford. "Have you been friends for a long time?" asked Lucia, still holding her attention to the young lord who was well into the distance.

Danford kept his annoyance in check, "Yes, since childhood, Lord Bentley is the son of my mother's sister, we are cousins. Why do you ask?" Lucia brought her attention back to him, "No reason in particular, he seems rather interesting, and now that you mention it, I do see the resemblance." Danford surrendered to this line of interrogation, but, interjected that they should have breakfast and be on their way. "Wallingston is but another half day's ride from here." He looked up to the sky, which always looked the same shade of grey to Lucia, and said, "We best be getting underway, I see rain clouds in the sky." Lucia could not control herself and blurted out, "How can you tell; the sky has been grey since we landed?" Danford smirked, "You get used to the weather. Women say it is good for the complexion."

Lucia managed to get down a decent amount of the gruel they called porridge, mounted her horse, and was ready to travel in very little time. She hated living from dirty inn to dirtier inn, and was longing for a hot bath, a good bed, and well-prepared food.

They rode for a long stretch in companionable silence. Lucia was drinking in the sights of the vast, and mostly barren, landscape. "Do you enjoy the hunt?" she asked just to break the silence that had fallen between them. "Yes. All my friends come. It is a time to rekindle acquaintances that were dormant over the winter. It is also a time to demonstrate one's hunting skills, as well, as your dogs. A good hunting dog can fetch as much as a good horse in these parts." Lucia just nodded, truly, she was not interested in a poor defenseless fox being chased and killed by a pack of yelping dogs. They continued with idle talk for the better part of the morning. It was noon when they stopped to relieve themselves and take a small food break.

"It will not be much longer. Wallingston proper will be coming up over that ridge within the hour. We are now on the estate's outer perimeter." Danford had spread his riding cloak on the ground so that she might sit upon it. "Are you anxious to get home?" Danford was stripping the bark off a small limb he had found, she could see that he was trying to distract himself, "Yes, I am. I have been away for quite some time." "What will happen if your father dies?" At this he picked up his head and looked directly at her, "Then, as is the legal custom, Wallingston, and all that my father possess, will become my property. I will assume the title, and, the responsibility, of being the Fifth Duke of Northumberland." Lucia could see that there was no joy in this statement, she felt sorry for him, and, reached over to grab his hand. "Danford, this does not please you? To be a Duke of such a rich and vast estate would be most men's dream. Why does it not please you?"

Danford, closed his eyes, sucked in a deep breath, and replied in a soft voice, "I never wanted this position which will require that I become tied to this place. I will be responsible not only for my mother and my siblings but, a vast array of servants, tenants, and will have to pledge fealty to the King." Lucia understood the burden of inheritance. "I too have been placed in such a position. I had never thought that I would be the Marchesa of Monteforte, with so many lives to worry about and business to run. It can be overwhelming. At least, I am sure;

you were born and reared for this station, I, on the other hand, was not." They held each other's hands as if they were mourners grieving a common loss. "Let us get to the task," she said and rose not waiting for Danford to help her up; he caught her in his arms and gave her a tender kiss on the mouth. "The servants will talk," said Lucia. "Talk to whom? I don't care, I love you Lucia, and I need you." She did not respond but walked to her horse. Nicko, was holding her reins, and gave a knowing nod. As he helped her mount he whispered, "If you need my protection I am always here for you my Mistress. Men have needs that sometimes cloud their judgment." As he handed her the reins she patted his hand, "Thank you Nicko, I am fine."

Just as Danford had said, as they ascended the ridge they could see across to the next ridge upon which sprawled an ancient stone castle. Even from this distance, Lucia could see its turrets, which supported flapping flags, each one designating allegiance to, family, God and King. It was still a long way off, but the landscape took on a dramatic change in appearance. At this elevation, they held an unobstructed view of acres of manicured lawn, with copses of ornamental trees and shrubs. Several small structures were scattered around a dene surrounded by a low stonewall. There were stables, and pastures for grazing animals, as well as acres of tended vegetable gardens. All, in all, it was a most bucolic scene. Lucia could see that Danford leaned forward in his saddle, surveying all that would be his, and in spite of himself, could not hide his sense of pride and duty. "It is quite magnificent Danford; fate has chosen our lot in life. Duty, honor and love for our heritage, makes us do what we must. You will be a fine Duke, and, much beloved by your wards." He held his head high, his noble blood lurking just below the surface of his skin, "I pray to God it will be as you say." He then spurred his horse and galloped hastily down the ridge with Lucia and the others in pursuit. The castle was rising before them was a medieval structure constructed of thick grey granite it was a formidable edifice. The sight of it gave Lucia a chill that racked her body.

They rode hard across the glen and back up the opposing ridge. Coming around the crest of the ridge, they followed the well-worn path and passed over a moat, the gate open, welcoming them from their long journey. Someone must have spotted them along the way, for when they rode into the walled courtyard there were servants and grooms at the ready. Upon seeing him, they all bowed deeply, the little ones running up to him and clutching to his legs, all crying "Lord Danford is home. Lord Danford is home." It was a touching sight to be sure. He could barely dismount for the flood of children and servants gathered around him.

He was patting heads; he picked up some of the tiniest ones and kissed them. Suddenly, there came a blast from a horn, all activity stopped, standing in the arch of the doorway was an elegant woman, frail but with delicate features. She was dressed in a deep burgundy gown, her white hair, was white, and was plaited into a bun. She carried the pallor of one who has not been well. Dark shadows fell upon her gaunt cheeks. Danford instantly put the little girl he was holding down, ran to his mother, and went down on bended knee. Her eyes filled with tears, as she stroked his wavy hair. He stood and this giant of a man engulfed his mother with such love and affection. They remained, coddled in each other's arms for what seemed a long time. Everyone stood in silence, even the youngest of the children.

It was an awkward moment and Lucia felt like an intruder. Nicko assisted Lucia in her dismount and Sophia came to her side. They stood there waiting to be presented to the Duchess of Northumberland. After a few moments, the duchess told her son to present his guest. Danford came to Lucia, took her arm, and walked slowly over to where his mother was standing, "Mother, may I present Marchesa Lucia Banfi, the Mistress of Monteforte. Marchesa, this is the Duchess of Northumberland." Lucia, eyes shrouded under her thick lashes, kept her head bent and curtsied formally to the older woman. Despite the dampness in the air, she could feel the flush on her cheeks. "Duchess, it is an honor to meet you. Your son has spoken so highly of you and his father. I hope my presence, under the circumstances, will not be the cause of any inconvenience?"

Lady Evelyn Stevens, Duchess of Northumberland, had been born and bred for her position, and whether or not she thought that Lucia's presence was vexing, she did not exhibit any change in demeanor. "Welcome to Wallingston. Danford has written to me about you as well. Please stay as long as you wish, perhaps, a new face will lighten the Duke's mood. Come, you must be exhausted from your long trip, they will show you to your rooms." Lucia curtsied once again, "Thank you Duchess for your hospitality."

As they entered the ancient castle, which had withstood many battles during its long history, Lucia was surprised at the light and grandeur of the place. Candelabras were lit and filled the space with soft light. They were walking through the main hall, which was decorated with eight huge murals, each one chronicling the history of Northumberland. Danford, knowing her love of art, noticed her interest in the murals, "These were painted by Sir William Bell Scott. They are a pictorial account of our history." Lucia was fascinated, not by the subject matter of the murals, but by the composition and colors used. "What a brilliant use of color and form. I had read about Sir Scott, never to believe that I would actually see his work in its original form. It is rather grand." Danford was pleased that she appreciated the art, "Tomorrow I shall take you around the castle and grounds and show you everything. For now, I know you want to refresh yourself, dinner will be served at eight o'clock, and I will come for you then. If you need anything just ask. I too am anxious to wash the road from my body."

Lucia, accompanied by Sophia, were escorted to her rooms. It was a spacious suite of rooms, simple, but, tastefully decorated in English fashion. There was a giant bedstead in the middle of the room, which she yearned to crawl up into, but knew if she did, she would fall fast asleep. Sophia was thrilled by the place, and told the maid who had taken them there, that her mistress required hot water, in which to bathe. As Sophia unpacked, she took out a particular gown from the trunk that was filled to the brim. "Mistress, will you wear this gown tonight?" It was one of the dresses Madame Richaud had made for her everyday use, but it was well cut and of the finest silk. "Do you think this would be appropriate?" Sophia knew that Lucia would follow her suggestion "Oh yes Mistress, it is demure, but accents your lovely curves." "Well then, how could I refuse to wear such a garment?" They laughed, but, then Lucia became serious, "Sophia, I am so conflicted. Lord Stevens has asked for my hand in marriage, yet, even though I have strong feelings for him, I could never live in this God forsaken land, and, besides which, he cannot give up his inheritance as Duke of Northumberland." Sophia was holding her hands, "You cannot rule Monteforte from here. He is a handsome, kind, man, but, he is a man who, by the nature of his birth, must stay here to rule his people."

There came a knock at the door and three young men labored under the weight of steaming buckets of water. Lucia was delighted. They filled the porcelain tub with the hot water and Sophia helped her to her bath, which she had been dreaming of since they left France. Scented oil was dripped into the steaming water and Lucia felt her tired, sore, muscles relax for the first time in almost a week. It was glorious!

Sophia got her dressed and plaited her hair, which, she still could not control, no matter how hard she tried. Curly tendrils framed the alabaster flesh of that beautiful face. Lucia hated when her hair was all curls, "Mistress, you would look beautiful even without hair." "Someday, we may just see if that statement is true. However, for what you had to work with, it does look rather nice. Thank you Sophia, I will not need you tonight, so if you want to spend the evening with Nicko, which I am sure he would prefer, over those two bulldogs that follow him around, please feel free to do so." Lucia knew that her maid and her bodyguard were sleeping together, and, she was happy for them. They had not been together since they left France, she was sure that Nicko was in need of Sophia. "Well, if you think it will be fine, I shall see if he is around. Thank you Mistress."

"Sophia, I know that you and Nicko sleep together, how do you keep from getting with child?" The maid was mortified, but answered her mistress with honesty, "Prendere una pozione che uso tutti i servi. Spero che il nostro stare insieme non sia causato voi qualsiasi disagio o imbarazzo?" Lucia came to her and embracing her said, "Of course you have not embarrassed me. You and Nicko love each other and have every right to your own happiness. I will be happy for you when you can live as husband and wife. For now, your secret is safe with me." Lucia kissed her maid and felt the heat on her face, "There is only one thing?" Sophia seemed confused, "Yes Mistress, what is that?" Lucia smiled at her, "Can you give some of that potion to me?" Sophia narrowed her eyes, "Are you considering sleeping with Lord Stevens?" after the words left her mouth, she realized that she had overstepped her position. "I am so sorry Mistress; I had no right to ask such a personal question." Lucia giggled, "Sophia, you are not just my servant, you are my friend, and, to answer your question; yes, maybe, I am not sure, but, I want to be prepared." Sophia understood and replied, "I shall get some for you and leave it by the bed. If something, you know, should happen, then you must drink the potion. Do not take it if nothing comes." Giggling, like two friend, they embraced each other.

A tapping at the door broke the shared intimacy of two women sharing a common desire. Sophia went to the door and opened it; Lord Stevens, tall and handsome was dressed in a well-tailored waistcoat, which was draped by a paid shawl, which was secured at the shoulder with his crested broach. He looked resplendent as Lord of the Manse. "Shall we go to dinner?" Lucia, was leaving and squeezed Sophia's hand, then turned back to smile conspiratorially at her. "Yes, I am famished.

Danford, please tell me there will be no porridge for supper?" Danford bellowed out a resounding laugh, "No my darling there will be no porridge for supper, but, I am sorry to say, it will reappear at breakfast."

They walked to the dining hall, the castle was huge, but they kept it well lit. As they entered the room, Lucia immediately noticed that there were several people already seated. She recognized Lady Evelyn, to her right was a rather plump young woman, whose face was pretty but the features were slightly askew; to her left was another young woman who resembled the other woman but was slim and pretty. On either side of the table were seated two young men, both of whom looked exactly like Danford, and finally at the opposite end of the table sat the Duke. All eyes fixed on Lucia and she felt herself flush. Danford sat to the duke's right and Lucia to his left. Still standing Danford announced, "May I present Marchesa Lucia Banfi, Mistress of Monteforte." He then systematically went around the table introducing all those seated. The two young women were his twin sisters, apparently one of them had been born abnormal; the two young men were his brothers, who she surmised were also very close in age; and the Duke. "Father, it is so good to see you. How are you feeling?" The man, who was in his late forties, looked old and withered, but his eyes were still sharp. "Son, I am so pleased you are home, it will not be long now. I am coming to the end. With that, he burst into a violent fit of coughing, so much so, that Lucia could see traces of blood on his linen ascot. His nurse, who was standing behind him, quickly wiped his mouth and beard. The poor man could not eat but a few spoons of soup. He instructed his valet to take him back to his room. Therefore, he, the valet, and the nurse all exited, leaving Lucia and Danford at opposite side of the table with little conversation.

It was a dismal atmosphere, and, while his sisters were only slightly younger than she was, they seemed old and dull, so unlike Danford. Dinner was served, which was a welcomed relief from the lack of conversation. It was roast boar; a blood pudding; gravy and some kind of root vegetable. It was tasty and satisfying, but Lucia thought it would have been more elegant, especially since it marked the return of their son, and heir apparent, as well as a guest. Perhaps, this was the English way of entertaining guests. The English, she was finding, had no flair for frivolous decoration in dress or food.

After dinner, they retired to the music room, where the pretty twin, whose name of Rachel, played the harpsichord and one of the boys played the violin. They were very talented and Lucia was enjoying the music. From behind her came the other twin, Elizabeth, who came to sit between her and Danford. She was a dimwitted young woman. She was staring at Lucia so intently it made her uncomfortable. Suddenly, she reached up, took a handful of Lucia's hair, and gave it a strong pull. "Ouch, what are you doing?" cried Lucia. The girl's eyes grew wide with fear and she began to cower.

Lady Evelyn came over to her and smacked her hard across the face, she did not utter a sound, but the blow left the imprint of her mother's hand on her pudgy cheek. "I am sorry my dear, this one is a dim witted cow, she doesn't think about what she does. Please forgive her." Lucia saw the fear in the girl's eyes and said, "It is fine. Would you like to touch my hair, but, just don't pull at it?" Elizabeth nodded, and her fat fingers came up to touch Lucia's hair. "It is so pretty. I want hair just like it." The girl then stroked Lucia's face, "Smooth." Lucia then stroked her face and felt the welt left by the duchess; Elizabeth cringed when Lucia's fingers touched the bruise, "I am sorry you got punished." Elizabeth smiled, lowered her eyes, and said, "I like you. Will you be my friend?" "Yes, of course I will."

Of course, by this time, the musicians had stopped playing and all was quiet again. Lady Evelyn announced, "Well, I shall retire, to look in on the Duke. Good night all." Her children did not kiss or embrace her, but, formally, one by one, came to bow or curtsey before her. It was the oddest scene Lucia had ever witnessed. Lucia got up and went to her, curtsied, "Lady Evelyn, thank you for your gracious hospitality. I bid you a good night's rest and I shall remember the Duke in my prayers." The duchess simply nodded without reply, and seemed to have floated out of the room.

As soon as she had left, the conversation became animated. Both Lucia and Danford were bombarded with questions. Apparently, none of them had ever left Northumberland, and, so, they were all anxious to hear of our recent exploits. "Mistress Banfi, where is Monteforte?" Lucia explained who she was and gave a brief detail of her life at Monteforte, where she had been, and, where she was going. Danford told them of his shipbuilding adventures and of the places he had been in the past several years. Stories and news of the goings on in Northumberland were traded back and forth. It was late by the time they had exhausted all their questions. Lucia was very tired from their days spent traveling, and asked Danford if he would walk her to her room. "Good night. Thank you for a most enjoyable evening. I hope we can continue this conversation tomorrow." Danford had already gotten up and offered Lucia his hand, which she took. "Sleep well dear ones. I know it has been hard for all of you since I was gone, but, I promise, things will change." He singled out Elizabeth, "I am sorry Lady Evelyn treats you so poorly. I shall have a chat with her. Are you well?" he spoke very softly and directly at her, she was just a little younger than Lucia, but was perhaps the mental age of a much younger girl. "I can't tell you how happy I am to see you dear brother. Life, without you here, is unbearable." Even as the words left her mouth, the others, looking toward the door, echoed her sentiments. "Well, have no fear, I am here now. Tomorrow, the weather permitting, we shall all take Mistress Banfi, on a tour of Wallingston. Is everyone in agreement?" All four gave a resounding "Yes." "Splendid, we shall leave promptly after breakfast. Now, please excuse us, we have been traveling for three days, and are weary to the bone. Good night." Each one, even the young men, came over pounding him on the back, in a display of manliness, while the women hugged and kissed Danford. They came, at first formally toward Lucia, the young brothers, each in turn, kissing her hand, and bowing, but the girls, Elizabeth in particular held her in a strong embrace and kissed her cheek, several times.

When they came to her room, Lucia invited Danford in to join her in a glass of cognac. "It was difficult to see Lady Evelyn act so coldly to your brothers and sisters. What is wrong?" Danford invited her to sit with him on the settee. "Lady Evelyn is not their blood mother, nor mine, for that matter. She was my mother's youngest sister, and when my mother died in childbirth, with the twins, my father, in need of someone to care for his children, asked her to marry him. Since he had six children already he refused to let her have any of her own. She has resented us since the day my father forbade her from getting with child." It all made sense to Lucia. "Danford, where is the sixth child?" Danford, lowered his head, an expression of sadness pressed upon his face. "My brother, Harold, died when he was eleven years old." Lucia, touched his arm, "That is awful, how did he die?" Danford cleared his throat, she could see the pain in his eyes, "My mother was very near to her time of birthing with the twins, Harold, was told by my father to help her with gathering some vegetables from the garden. Instead of going with my mother to help, he went off riding his horse. As she was picking she encountered a large snake. She dreaded snakes, and in her panic to escape, tripped over a log and fell. The fall caused her to go into labor, but it was too soon, the babes were not ready. As you can see Rachel was the first to arrive, but mother struggled with Elizabeth. The cord was wrapped around her neck and she could not breathe. That is why she is dimwitted. Mother, from the loss of blood, and the exertion of bearing two babies died that night. Harold, who was a sensitive boy, blamed himself for our mother's death, not old enough to know that it had nothing to do with him, was found the next morning hanging from the stable rafters."

"The death of my mother, coupled with the fact that she would never give birth to a child of her own flesh, has made her bitter and mean." "Yes, but, she received you this afternoon with what appeared to be great affection." Danford, a smirk on his handsome face, replied, "My Aunt is no fool; she knows that the second my father draws his last breath that I shall be the Fifth Duke of Northumberland. Little does she know that on that very day she shall be sent from Wallingston." Lucia asked, "Does she not have any heirship to your father's estate?" "In England, as in most of Europe, all estates pass through the eldest son, if he should die, it then passes to the next son, and so forth; when all blood sons are deceased the estate then passes to the brother of the deceased. I have arranged, in anticipation of my father's grave health, a small estate, outside of London, for the new Dowager, Lady Evelyn Stevens. She will be given an annual stipend, staff, and she will be able to keep her social status, until she either dies, or, remarries. I suspect she will remarry as soon as is socially proper, which is after one year of mourning."

"But Danford, how will you conduct business in Le Havre if you are here? As the new lord of this duchy will you not be required to spend all your time overseeing your property and tenants?" Danford smiled, "I've thought of that aspect as well, and have decided to place my brother, Michael, as Regent, at those times when I am not here. I was also contemplating the relocation of the shipyard to England. Would that present any problems for you?"

Lucia, who was following Danford's logic, liked that he had given all of this great thought. "I do not have any problem with relocating the shipyard. The only thing is that Henri will be lost without something to do, but I suppose he could continue being my liaison with the various merchants. How do you propose to get the merchants to come to England?" Danford stood, walked over to a side table, and poured two glasses of cognac from the crystal decanter. Handing her a glass he responded, "Well, we are building ships after all, so therefore, we shall sail our ships from here to Le Havre, or Paris, or Naples, or America. We shall sail our ships anywhere we wish to go." Lucia stood up, "Salute, you are a genius." They clanked their glasses; it was a toast to the launching of a new adventure.

Danford, set aside the glasses, and drew Lucia into his massive arms. "I cannot begin to express how happy I am that you are here with me. The next few days will be quite difficult; your presence will lift my spirits. You were very kind to Elizabeth this evening, and for that I thank you so much." Holding her face in his hands he peered into those beautiful blue eyes; he gently kissed her on the mouth. She stood stone still, but knew she wanted more. He moved so that his arms engulfed her and kissed her again, with passion, his tongue separating her lips. Lucia was not sure what she needed to do, she cursed her inexperience. She tasted the sweet cognac on his tongue, and, she instinctively moved her own into his waiting mouth. His strong hands were caressing her back. His kisses were growing longer and with more urgency. He was kissing her face, her neck, the hollow of her throat.

In one sudden movement, he scooped her up in his arms and brought her to the settee. Still holding her like a small child he continued to kiss her, his mouth nibbling her ear, gentle bits on her neck and shoulder. Lucia was aflame with desire. She felt a tingling in her clit. Her breasts had swollen and were pressing against the bodice of her gown, the bone stays restricting her breathing. His hands were roaming her torso; he pinched her tiny waist, and, his hand was working his way up to her bosom. "I want you so bad; my love for you is painful." His mouth came to the soft mound of her swollen breasts; he kissed them, nuzzling his face between her décolletage. Lucia was panting, beads of sweat trickling down her gown. This new sensation of passion; this aching need for release, was making her heady. The big hand finally reached its intended target and Danford cupped her supple breast, feeling the weight of it, he began to fondle it pulling tenderly at her erected nipple. He was panting with desire. He pinched it and Lucia responded with an excited gasp; he did it again; and again. It was an agonized ecstasy. She was moaning with pleasure. He slipped his hand down her bodice and closed his eyes at the feel of her. He wiggled her nipple and Lucia's body trembled. With his other hand, he crawled ever so slowly up the skirt of her gown. His hand reached her thigh, he knew she wore no pantaloons, she was Italian, and they did not wear such garments. He silently thanked God that she adhered to her traditions. He made small circles on her upper thigh, while continuing to knead her breast. He was still kissing her, his tongue pushing the limits of its own reach. Painfully, slowly, he trekked up her hip, she giggled, until he came to her flat belly. He squeezed her nipple; Lucia thought she would faint from the heat he was generating in her body.

His fingers were walking down her belly and soon reached her curly nest. This time Danford gasped as his middle finger slipped into her hot, wet clit. He was so hard he was hurting her hipbone. She spread her leg ever so slightly. He acknowledged the movement by stroking her burning cunt. Lucia was so aroused she could not even continue to kiss him. He worked her nipple, putting his mouth on her chest, licking it. He slipped another finger in her slit and together they were performing a rhythmic tattoo. Lucia was wild with lust; he knew she would climax in a few seconds. He knew she was a virgin. His hand was moving rapidly, flicking her pulsing sex, she was wet; she arched her back as he plunged his finger deep inside her waiting cunt. Lucia let out a guttural growl of satisfaction. He did not withdraw but waited a few seconds and flicked her clit and once again, he plunged deep inside her until she purred with pleasure. He removed his hand from under her gown, and smoothed down her skirt. He took his hand out of her bodice and sat her upon the cushion next to him.

Lucia was confused, excited, and somewhat afraid of what would come next. She stared at him with wide-eyed innocence. He put his arm around her and drew her to himself, "My darling, I want you more than I have ever wanted any woman, but, I will not take you to my bed until we are wed. You cannot even begin to imagine, nor can you understand, what restraint I am forcing upon myself not to tear the clothes from you and ravage that magnificent body? I will not make a whore of you; I love you too much. Be my wife, come live here with me forever." He pressed a finger to her lips to keep her from speaking, "Do not answer me now. I am a patient man. Let me show you who Danford Stevens is." He kissed her forehead, stood up and walked to the door. Turning to face her, he asked, "Did you enjoy that?" Lucia nodded in the affirmative. "That my sweet virgin, is only a tiny morsel of what pleasure I can bestow upon you when we are husband and wife. Sleep well my beauty." He bowed formally and left closing the door behind him. e HHe

Lucia sat there for quite some time, thinking about what had just happened. She held deep feelings for Danford, perhaps, even love, but she would never live at Wallingston castle, or any other part of England. If she did marry him, which would probably never happen, what would become of her heirship in Monteforte? There were so many questions, and, sadly, few answers, or, at least answers she would not like. She undressed, the thought and feel of his touch upon her body, still lingering. Lucia knew she would enjoy sexual intimacy, and, if that was a prelude to what was to come, she wanted more, much, more.

CHAPTER ELEVEN

THE WANNEY

Northumberland

Lucia slept well, and was awakened by Sophia, who seemed anxious. "What is wrong Sophia?" The maid busied herself but did not pick up her head to look at Lucia. "Sophia?" something was troubling her maid and she wanted to know what it was. "Mistress, I see that the potion I left is unused. Please tell me you did not forget what I told you?" Lucia, now understood the concern her maid held, "No, unfortunately, Lord Stevens and I, did not consummate anything." Sophia's face was a little unreadable, "I see." Lucia was smiling, "No you don't see. He says he will not bed me until I marry him." "Oh, truly I now see," said Sophia with a little tongue and cheek expression. "What shall I do?" Sophia came to sit by her mistress, "Mistress, there are things happening here, the depths of which we cannot understand. Everything here will change upon the passing of the Duke, of that I am certain. Lord Stevens must then assume the title and duties of Duke of Northumberland, which, from what the servants tell me, is quite formidable. A Duke, in this country, is a very coveted title, and it holds much responsibility."

"Do you love this man?" Sophia was very serious about the question. Lucia knew she did not have to answer, but she was desperate to seek some advice. "I truly am not sure. I want to be with him, yet, when I am with Danford, he tries to control my every thought, action, and behavior. I do not want that life. He wants children, and I do not. He must be lord over all of Northumberland, and I hate this place. However, in my heart, I yearn for from him. I am so confused. What am I to do?"

Sophia took her hand, "Mistress, do not make any hasty decisions. You have driven some difficult arguments against this relationship, but I sense that you have deep feelings for this man. Give yourself some time; do not let him pressure you into making a decision. I want you to be happy. When a man wants you to bear his child, and, you refuse, that is a serious matter both in the eyes of the law, and, in God's eyes. You must make certain that you make that desire clear and have him write up a legal document that he understands the terms of any marriage contract."

Lucia, for the first time in her long relationship with her maid, was so impressed with her commonsense and wisdom. Apparently, she had underestimated her servant's intelligence for far too long. "Sophia, I cannot help but admire the advice you have given me. How do you come to be so wise?" "People possess much knowledge, if only they stop to learn and listen. As a servant to your aunt, I watched and listened to how she would conduct her business, she is very keen of mind. Mistress Sucretti, when I was young, made sure that I was educated, so that I could assist her with her work.' Lucia said nothing but just nodded her acknowledgement of all that was said.

Coming down to breakfast Lucia found that everyone was dressed and ready for their day's outing. "Good morning Mistress Banfi. Did you sleep well?" asked Elizabeth in her childlike manner. "Oh yes, thank you Elizabeth." Her twin just nodded but said nothing; however, her eyes followed every move Lucia made. The brothers, Michael, the older of the two, soon to be named Regent, stood up and greeted her cordially, "Good morning Mistress Banfi, please let me help you with your chair." When he came around to hold her chair, he brushed against her unnecessarily, and as she sat he pushed her toward the table, his mouth coming close to her ear, "How is that?" he whispered, she could feel his breath on her neck. Lucia was unnerved by his manner, and, moved slightly to adjust herself, "Fine. Thank you." The other brother, Jonathan, was watching this little scene and smirked when he caught Michael's eye. He remained silent, but like his sister Rachel, was observing everything. Lucia was angry and uncomfortable, but she would not give them the satisfaction to think they had upset her. She smiled cordially to all of them. "Where is Lord Danford?" she asked.

Elizabeth came to her and sat next to her "Oh, our Father, has taken a bad turn during the night. Danford is with him, and Baron Humboldt and the physician are all together. Will you eat now?" Lucia, so unaccustomed to all this intrigue, replied, "Yes, I suppose. Did all of you have breakfast?" Each one nodded their heads in affirmation. One of the kitchen maids was standing in a corner waiting to serve whomever wanted something, "Bring Mistress Banfi some porridge and toast", ordered Michael. The maid who was not much young than him, nearly flew out the room. There was something about him that made her skin crawl.

Just as the breakfast arrived, Danford came into the dining room, "I am sorry, my Father is not doing well. I will have to postpone our outing for today." Almost before the words left his mouth Michael jumped into the conversation, "Brother, I can take Mistress Banfi around; that is unless you need me?" Lucia felt the toast stick in her throat, "Oh, that is too much of a bother, but, thank you Lord Stevens, I shall stay and read." Danford, not wanting to disappoint Lucia, said, "Mistress, I would be so pleased if you would let Michael take you around the property. I would not feel any guilt for keeping you inside, it is going to be a beautiful day. I regret that I cannot take you personally, but Baron Humboldt and I have many matters to discuss. It would please me very much." Lucia felt cornered, "Well, I suppose, if it would make you happy." "Yes; very much so." Thinking quickly Lucia asked, "Well then everyone should come with us, as was originally planned." Michael's eyes narrowed at his siblings as if he was defying them to say they would join us. He spoke for the others, "That would have been grand, but, sadly, Lady Evelyn has requested that Rachel and Elizabeth join her today to prepare for guests who will be arriving for the funeral, and, Jonathan had made arrangements to join the hunt, which is already in progress. Therefore, I regret it is only I who is left. I am afraid you will have to make due solely with my company." His wolfish smile made her feel unsettled. Danford smiled at her and taking her hand kissed it, "It is agreed, Michael shall stand in for me. I shall see you both at dinner this evening. I hope you have a good day. If you will excuse me I need to return to business."

Michael came to her side and extended his hand. "Well, shall we embark on our adventure?" As he held her hand he gave her a little squeeze, she quickly pulled it back. "Will you ride, or, shall we take a carriage?" Lucia, for the first time this morning, heard something that did please her, "We shall ride."

They made their way to the stables and Lucia found the horse she had ridden to the estate. He was a good animal, sturdy and sure-footed. She sensed that Michael might try to out ride her and she wanted to be prepared. The stable groom brought the horse, whose name she did not know, around. He was saddled and seemed excited to see her. She let him sniff her, and she in turn scratched his ears, and snout. She whispered in his ear, "I hope you do not mind, but I shall name you Apollo, after my beloved horse at Monteforte." Oddly, the horse whinnied, as if to acknowledge his approval. Lucia stealthily reached into her pocket and brought out two cubes of sugar, which she had taken from the breakfast table, and gave them to her new Apollo. The horse was delighted, and stamped his hoof. She had made a new friend.

The young groom bent to give her a leg up to Apollo, and she sat the horse with confidence. "Well, shall we embark on our adventure?" asked Michael with a snide smirk on his face. "Yes, I am ready, lead on."

For as far as the eye could see there were rolling lush lawns. Large and small ornamental ponds were scattered about in what appeared to be an oval pattern. He took her past what was called the Edwardian conservatory, which was the first structure past the stables. It was framed on all sides by ceiling to floor windows, and although they did not dismount, she could see that it was filled with plants and flowers. "This is where Lady Evelyn keeps all her exotic plants and flowers. The temperature and moisture in the building are very conducive to such specimens. If you like, on our way back, if it is not too late, we can stop in." Lucia was enthused at the prospect of seeing unusual and exotic plants, "Yes, that would be nice. I enjoy gardening, but, right now do not have the time for such pursuits." He did not comment.

"The grounds are divided by an East Wood and a West Wood, with the River Wansbeck rising above the Sweethope Lough and the edge of the Forelaros Forest. My father inherited all of this from his father, and so on for many generations. Upon his death, my brother Danford, as you know, will become the next Duke of Northumberland." Lucia detected a sour note to his tone of voice. "Does the fact that your brother will reign over this vast estate, as well as over you and your siblings, give you concern?" He reined up his horse, "Why do you ask such a personal question?" Lucia braced herself and answered honestly, "Because I have noted your actions, and heard the catch in your voice, when you said that Danford would be the next Duke. I understand that you may feel cheated, since, for all these years, while he was away, you and your siblings, have endured the trials of staying here. Danford has shared with me the circumstances of how Lady Evelyn came to be the Duke's wife, and, your step-mother."

Michael, head facing the vast sweep of sprawling vistas, replied, "I will not deny my resentment, but, not towards my brother, for it is his right and his duty, but toward my father. He saw, and was aware, of the abuse my siblings and I have had to endure at her hands. He did nothing to protect us. Even Danford does not know the worst of all that has befallen us, especially, Elizabeth. He has made me aware of his plan to remove Lady Evelyn immediately upon my father's death, and, for that alone, I am grateful. It is more than that wretched bitch deserves." He was angry, but, then he turned to face Lucia and she could see the pain in his eyes. "I am so sorry, for all of you. With the grace of God, Danford will make it right." He bent his head, as if in supplication, "May God forgive me, for my thoughts. I pray that His strength and wisdom be showered upon my brother."

They rode for a while in silence as they left the confines of the estate compound. The landscape was mostly scrubby, low shrubs, with a smattering of large oak trees here and there about the vast grounds. "Would you like to stretch your horse's legs?" "Yes, I thought you would never ask." With that they both spurred they horses into a full gallop and Lucia felt renewed and exhilarated. She closed her eyes and envisioned riding Apollo along the sandy beach of Monteforte with the sun caressing her face and the sea breezes cooling her heated skin. She opened her eyes and saw a grey sky and barren, craggy, hillsides. The spell was broken and she longed for Monteforte, Zia Maria, Zio Giovanni, and her sister.

It was as if Michael read her mind, "You are homesick?" Lucia brought back from her reverie answered, "I am. I long for the sun upon my face and the soft perfume of the lemon trees. I miss my family, and, I am anxious, for my sister is with child. I want to be there for the birth." Michael, his face, for the first time, was softer and he seemed to care.

"Come let us stop here, I had them prepare a basket with refreshments."

They found a spot under the tree and Michael came around and helped her dismount. He then laid down a blanket and untied a bulging pouch from his saddle. They sat and he spread the items from the pouch on the blanket. There were small round baguettes, cheese, fruit, and a skin of wine. He offered her one of the small baguettes. It was hard, but tasty. "What is this bread you offer me?" Michael smiled, "It is called a scone, it is an oatmeal cake, cooked on a griddle, or heated flat iron. We stole it from the Scots, and made it our own. It travels very well, and is used by the military. Do you like it?" Lucia, did like it, but, she liked that he had taken the time to tell her the history behind the tiny treat. "Yes, but, when they get old, one must be wary of cracking a tooth." He laughed heartily, "You are so right. I have seen it so." They settled in a comfortable companion and talked of inconsequential things. Lucia felt more at ease.

They were relaxing watching the different species of birds and small creatures that were residents of the adjoining forest, when Michael casually asked, "Mistress Banfi, will you marry my brother?" Lucia was shocked, she was not aware that Danford has shared that bit of news with anyone. "I do not know." Michael seemed surprised by the response. "It is not that I do not hold deep feelings for him, he is a good and kind man, but, I am not willing to relinquish my freedom. Upon pledging myself in marriage, I would become the property of your brother, perhaps, I would even lose claim to my own vast estate." Michael's expression was one of concern, "I am sorry to hear that you harbor such feelings. My brother has confided to me his deep love for you. He will be rich and powerful, surely all women desire a good man, who possesses such wealth, do they not?" Lucia was concerned, "Yes, I am sure you are correct, but, I am not ready to wed, to bear children, and, certainly not to give up Monteforte. I will need to pray very hard to Jesus and all the saints regarding this most ponderous matter."

"It is getting late in the day, if we are going to see the river, and, make it back home before dark, we must be on our way." They packed what was left and mounted. They rode for a long time, each keeping their own thoughts, until they reached the crest of the hill and stopped at its peak. From this vantage point, they could see the fast running river. Michael, his voice elevated over the rushing sound of the water, said, "They call this the Wanney, it is from the wilds of the River Wanney that the icy waters marry with the North Sea." The rushing water fascinated Lucia. "Is it always cold?" she asked. "Yes. In the dead of winter, if one were to fall in, they will die of frost in minutes; but, it is just after All Hallows Eve, that we secure all our best fish, which we save for the long winter months. The fish is then salted and stored in the root cellar." Lucia could feel the cold wind coming off the water, coupled with the grey, sunless sky; she caught a chill, and began to shiver. Michael saw that she was cold, "Let us head back. The weather is coming off the water and we shall we drenched before long."

Upon their arrival back at the stables, barely escaping a heavy downpour, they were aproached by the stable master, "Lord Michael, your brother Lord Danford, is seeking you." Michael's carefree expression of just seconds earlier, changed to dire concern. Without any additional conversation, he took her hand and they ran toward the castle. In just the few moments it took to reach the kitchen entrance, they were soaked. "You best go and change before you catch your death. I shall seek out my brother to see what he needs." Lucia did not reply, but turned on her heels to go back to her room, she suddenly felt herself spun around, and now was practically nose to nose to him, "Thank you. If you do not wed my brother it will be a great blow to this family." He bent down, kissed her on each cheek, and then ran off.

Lucia found her way back to her room, there to find Sophia preparing her black mourning gown. Upon seeing her, the maid jumped to her feet, "Mistress have you heard?" Lucia assumed that the Duke had died, "Is the Duke dead?" Sophia nodded anxiously, which seemed out of place given the fact that his death was expected. "What is it?" Sophia excited related the events of the day, "After you and Lord Michael left, William, Lord Danford's valet, was summoned. I was in the kitchen when he was called to the Duke's chamber. We all knew what had happened. When he returned an hour later, he was white as marble, and announced that Lady Evelyn was dead as well." Sophia waited for her mistress' reaction, "What are you saying. That Lady Evelyn is dead? But how did that happen?" Sophia paused for effect, "Well, upon the pronouncement that the Duke was dead, Lord Danford then informed Lady Evelyn of her fate. I am sure you were aware of what was to become of her. According to William, who was there, at his master's side, she said nothing, did not shed one tear, and excused herself to her rooms." Lucia was impatient with Sophia's theatrical rendition of the events, "Sophia, I shall kill you, if you do not commence with the conclusion of this story." "She called for her maid, who set out her most exquisite dressing gown, took her bath, and then sent her away. When the maid returned later, to see if she would take her midday meal in her chamber or in the dining hall, she found her dead in her bed. She left the room and ran to Lord Danford for help. He found her as the maid had described, lying, fully dressed, hands folded in a death pose. Immediately, he dismissed the maid and told her not to give any more information other than to say Lady Evelyn was dead." Lucia asked, "Where is Lord Danford now?" Sophia shrugged but ventured a guess, "I last saw him in the library with Baron Humboldt." Lucia, her mind racing in many directions, sat with a thud on the settee. "This is a strange turn of events. These English have such a flair for spectacle. I shall go and find Danford and ask if I can be of any assistance to him. This is all very dreadful."

As if he had read her thoughts, there came a knock at the door, and Sophia rushed to open it. Standing there was the young lord of the manor, disheveled. Lucia got up with a start and came to him, embracing each other she said, "I have just returned and have heard all this terrible news. I am so sorry not only for your father, but, for Lady Evelyn. What happened?" Danford turned to Sophia, "Sophia, please leave us. Your Mistress will ring when she needs you." Sophia curtsied deeply and removed herself instantly.

Danford, his eyes reddened from sorrow, took Lucia back to the settee. The same settee, which just the night before he had shown her what pleasures lie ahead, but now it was overcast with the shadow of death. "Can I help in any way with this heavy burden you now bear?" She was holding his hands and stroking him with great tenderness. "I must do something that it not only morally wrong, but, legally wrong, for a person I hated." Lucia, wide eyed, searched his face for an explanation to this profound statement. He saw that she did not possess any inkling as to what he was talking about.

"Lady Evelyn has taken her own life. I saw the cup from which she had drunk the poison. If anyone finds out that she killed herself, she will be declared a heretic and denied burial in the sacred burial grounds of the church. By law, as my father's wife, she is entitled to be laid to rest in our family crypt. Yet, if she is found to be a heretic, who died in mortal sin, she cannot be entombed in the crypt. She must be burned in a pyre and her ashes scattered to the winds. There would be forever a stain on our family name, to, think that the Duchess of Northumberland died a heretic."

"Who knows of the circumstances of her death?" asked Lucia, her voice as steady and calm as possible. "Only me, and now you." Lucia felt heaviness in her throat; she was both pleased and frightened that Danford had confided such a tremendous secret to her. "What does her maid think happened, and how long has she served the Duchess?" "Why?" "Well, if she was her personal servant, for many years, than she would know every detail about her mistress, the room, and everything that was usual or unusual. If she served with her for a short time, then, she would not be as familiar with her particular habits. Do you agree?" Danford seemed to relax ever so slightly, "This is a new maid; the maid that had served her for the past twenty years died only days ago. Yes, I do agree, and, I thank you for your brilliance. I knew you would give me sound advice. I love you Lucia."

Danford became sullen once again, "Is it wrong to create this deception?" Lucia, did not answer quickly, but, sat back, sinking into the goose down pillows. Finally, she said, "Lady Evelyn lived her whole life as a deception. She pretended to be a dutiful wife and mother, but was neither. It is only fitting that this charade should follow her to her grave. When she comes for judgment before Our Lord Jesus Christ that she will be called to atone for her sins. You and your siblings have suffered enough at her wicked hands. Let it be done." He did not speak but gathered her in his arms, the tears shamelessly falling from his eyes, and kissed her with such love and passion. She too found herself filled with emotions she did not know existed. Did she love this man? She wiped the thoughts from her mind; this was not the time to contemplate such questions.

"Will you have any problems with the doctor?" she asked. "No, he is my father's nephew. He, as well as I, does not want our good name besmirched by association with a heretic. She did this last final insult to my father, and to us, as an act of revenge, knowing what would happen. She was such a wicked woman that she would rather take her own life, rather than let us live in peace. I hope she rots in the fires of hell!" "It is settled. What will you tell Michael and the others?" Danford who by now had regained his customary demeanor of lordship, replied, "I shall tell them nothing; the more who know the more chance of exposure. I trust you with my life and my honor. I pledge my love and respect to you forever." He kissed her again, this time with more urgency; he knew he would need to be about his business.

"We shall have the wake, which will take place in two days, here at Wallingston. On the third day, we shall consecrate their bodies with a Requiem Mass, and then they will be entombed in the family crypt. May God have mercy on my soul." Lucia added "On our souls." He nodded gravely and squeezed her hand. "I must leave to make preparations, may I impose upon you to help organize the staff, and to get things ready with the food and drink?" Lucia felt a twinge of uneasiness, "Will your siblings not feel slighted if I take control of the situation?" Danford smiled for the first time, "They better get used to it if you are going to be my wife?" Lucia wanted to scream at him but they were interrupted by a knock at the door, "Enter" he commanded, not giving her the opportunity for rebuttal.

It was William his valet, "Your Grace, there are many decisions that are awaiting your attention; the least of which is a dispatch to His Majesty to inform him of your father's death and your written pledge of fealty to his throne. Shall I send word for your cousin, Lord Monroe, to draft the letter?" Danford was on his feet, but still held tight to Lucia's hand, who, was now standing at his side. "Yes, send word immediately to Charles. William, I want you to inform the entire household that Marchesa Banfi will be head of the house, and, that whatever she commands is to be followed without question. Do you understand?" William, who was older than the two of them, bowed formally, and, facing Lucia directly, replied "Marchesa Banfi, I am your devoted servant, please command me as you will." To his master he turned "Your Grace, I shall do all that has been said, if I may beg my leave, I shall need to act swiftly; there is much to be done." Danford, his massive hand on William's shoulder said "Thank you William you are a good and faithful friend." With that, the valet bowed again and left the room. Lucia's ear did not miss the new title now assumed on Danford of "Your Grace" which was to designate his recent elevation to Duke. Lucia was proud of him, and, in spite of all her fears and reservations, was growing much too fond of him. Danford took her in his arms and kissed her once again. "I must be off. Thank you for everything." "Oh there is one last thing; Lady Evelyn left two notes, please read them, then, carefully make sure they are destroyed." Before he left, he enfolded her in his strong arms, and began kissing her, his tongue searching her mouth. His hands roaming over her torso, he cupped her breasts and gently fondled them, she gasped, and he did it again, then he felt her erect nipples against her bodice. He reached down, cradled her firm, full, ass in both his hands, and squeezed her cheeks, pressing his erection into her. Lucia was wet. He was bulging nearly out of his breeches. "You have driven me to become a mad man. I am overcome with lust. I merely need to look upon you and my cock becomes so hard it pains me. I want you. I love you." He was gone in a breath, and Lucia was left panting with desire. Would it always be like this she wondered?

She was so aroused that she almost forgot the two notes he had slipped into her hand. Each note had been sealed, and, on the face was neatly written the names of both Danford and Elizabeth. She felt the fine vellum paper and caught the faint scent of lavender. With reservation, she unfolded the note addressed to Danford. There was no salutation.

You have always hated me, and I you, for I knew that this day would one day come. You believe that you will exile me, dismiss me like a common servant, but you are wrong. I have endured a loveless marriage to your father, and have been hated by his children. What I am about to do will forever stain the name of Stevens, Duke of Northumberland. Enjoy your misery. I will see you all in Hell.

Duchess Evelyn Stevens

Lucia was now convinced that they had taken the right path in covering up her death. This woman, even in death, tried to destroy this family. She dreaded to open the letter addressed to Elizabeth. Why had she singled her out from the others? Her hand trembled slightly as she drew in a deep breath and opened the note.

Elizabeth,

By now, I will have succumbed to the deadly poison, and, already your family has been pitched from its throne. I know you tried to love me, out of all of you; you were the one that showed me affection. I was vicious to you and abused you to exact revenge upon the others. Only to you will I say that I am sorry, for not only this last act of hatred, but also, for all the years that you needed a mother, while I used you as a dupe, for my own miserable satisfaction.

Please forgive me

Lucia started to cry for the pervasive suffering all those involved had to endure for such a long time. This woman, so consumed by her own plight, was incapable of love. Her heart was broken for dear, sweet, Elizabeth, but she wondered what has been the toll on the others, who by the nature of their strength, have suffered as well. She instinctively knelt down and prayed for all of them. She begged God to forgive her for her complicity in covering up the nature of her death. "Dear Lord, please forgive us, but, this family, these children, have endured, all their lives, unrelenting abuse, at the hands of a loveless mother. In Your mercy Oh Lord, forgive Evelyn, and bestow love and comfort upon this family. Jesus, help me to know what choices I am to make for their good and for mine as well. Thank you."

She got up and walked to the hearth that was in her room, and placed the letters in the smoldering embers. They caught the flame almost instantly and Lucia felt a chill crawl down her spine. She jumped at the sound of a solid knock at the door. "Come." It was William, "Marchesa, His Grace, will be addressing the staff shortly and asked me to come and invite you to join him. Shall I wait?" Lucia was still reeling from having read the notes, but knew it was important for Danford to show her support. "Please give me a moment to collect myself. If you would wait outside, I shall not be but a moment." William did not reply, but, bowed deeply and did as she instructed. She went to the basin with water and splashed her face, she desperately wanted to weep, but, could not understand why. So much sorrow had been festering in this old castle. Perhaps, with the grace of God, and, the death of these two selfish people, it would purge itself of its malignant spirits. She straightened her gown, and standing as tall as she could, she marched to the door.

CHAPTER TWELVE

A SHROUD OF DECEIT

Wallingston Castle

The entire castle was bereft with the loss of both Master and Mistress of Wallingston Castle. Danford had concocted a viable story for the passing of Lady Evelyn. He assembled the entire staff into the grand ballroom. Standing beside him were his brothers and sisters, Lucia was standing in the shadows of the far end of the room. When Danford saw her he walked over to where she was and extended his arm for her to join them at the head of the room. "Dear Servants, as you are all aware, the Duke, and Duchess of Northumberland are dead. Early this morning my father left this earthly home for Heaven. Lady Evelyn, his devoted wife, our mother, was so overcome with grief at the loss of my father that she died of an apparent broken heart, according to our family physician, Dr. Robert Heathrow. As you know, we will follow the customary funeral program, with two days of waking and the third day reserved for immediate family and select friends for church services and burial. Now, as the Fifth Duke of Northumberland, I Danford Stevens, Lord of Wallingston Castle, pledge to uphold the honor and dignity of my father and my ancestors before him. I would expect your complete obedience in all matters. I hereby appoint William as my personal aide. There is one last matter that I will bring to your attention, my guest, Marchesa Lucia Banfi, will be acting Head of House. You are all to obey her every command as if it came from me. Anyone who disrespects the Marchesa, or fails to fulfill her orders, will be dealt with harshly. I hope I have made my wishes expressly clear. Thank you for all your years of dedicated service to our family, and I pray that the Lord Jesus blesses my reign as Duke of Northumberland. That is all." From somewhere in the far back a loud gruff voice declared, "God bless Duke Danford!" It instantly became a chant to cheers and whoops and whistles. Danford was pleased but embarrassed. He bowed, and held up his hands, "Thank you all. Now let us be about our duties in preparation of all our guests who will be descending upon this castle. Let us make my father and mother proud." With that last statement, they disbursed to get on with their jobs.

Lucia, addressing his four siblings, said, "I have not asked for this position, but, was asked by your brother to assist in the preparations. I hope you do not resent my place here, and, if you do, please inform me. I am here to help." It was Michael, the senior member of the group, who said, "We are honored that you have assumed this mantel. Please delegate to us what we must do. We have talked amongst ourselves and are so happy you are here with us." Lucia was relieved. "Me too" said Elizabeth in a childlike voice.

"How many people will come? Will those who have travelled a great distance need to sleep here? Where is the wine cellar?" Danford, having anticipated her anxiety over heading up such a sudden undertaking called over to an elderly woman, "Marian, this is Marchesa Banfi please answer all her questions and make sure that all of your staff follows her instruction to the letter. Marchesa will find you in the kitchen. That is all." Danford turned to his siblings, "Each of you knows what you must do, as we discussed earlier. I will be making the necessary notifications. Let us get to work." "We will all gather again at dinner."

He would have liked to kiss Lucia, but dare not do so in public. He just bowed deeply and kissed her cheek. "I have many things to attend to; I shall meet up with you at dinner. Thank you for helping me." He leaned very close to her and whispered in her ear, "Were you wet when I touched you earlier?" She tried to control her smile, but could not, "Yes. You are a demon beast." He again came close "Did you stroke yourself after I left?" She was horrified at the question, but, being Lucia, she could not lie, "Yes." He gave up a roar of a laugh and said, "Well we may have to attend that matter this evening. What do you think?" "I think you are evil, but, we should." This time they both laughed heartily. Just at the thought of him touching her, she became wet.

As it turned out Marian was indeed a great resource for Lucia. With her help, they organized the kitchen staff in preparation of the days ahead. Lucia met with the purveyors for meats, cheeses, and fish. Most of the food would come directly from the estate, but, due to the number of people who would be attending, she thought it wise to supplement their supplies. She also spoke for quite some time with the head chef, but, of course, he being English did not possess any ability for delicacies, it was strictly meat and puddings. She would at the least try to get him to add a few spices. The food was like the weather; always grey.

The chambermaids were next on her list. There were twenty guest bedchambers, all of which needed to be cleaned, the linens needed to be washed, and all the little details had to be attended. Lucia was going from room to room to inspect what was being done. She made sure that each guest was provided a small bundle of vellum, sharpened quills, and an inkpot. That each had a basin and pitcher, chamber pot and a sufficient amount of linen towels. For the most part everyone was following orders and doing their assigned tasks.

By the end of the day, she was exhausted and hungry. She had asked Burton, the chef, to try out, for the family, a dish she helped him prepare. He was reluctant but, after he tasted it himself, was pleased with the outcome. All were gathered around the table, Lucia was the last to arrive. The men stood as she found the place Danford had saved for her. Lucia was anxious that they would not enjoy the meal she helped prepare. It was one of her favorites from Monteforte, which consisted of fresh rabbit, in a tomato, vegetable stew. She even showed Burton had to make bread in the Italian style.

They all chatted about the day's events, each sibling giving a report to Danford, who listened and asked appropriate questions. Lucia said nothing but just listened. Burton, whom she had never seen in the dining hall, had come himself to oversee the food service. "What smells so good?" asked Elizabeth. The chef, a wiry little man, with the face of a rodent, said nothing, but instructed the maids with the service. Once they were plated, Danford said, "Burton, this smells marvelous. What is it?" The chef, who had been born and raised on the estate, bowed, "It is rabbit stew Your Grace." Danford dug right in to the steaming bowl, "Burton, I must say you have outdone yourself. I am enjoying this stew." Everyone was enjoying its taste. "Is this a new concoction?" Michael asked Chef Burton, who for a moment, had let down his guard and smiled, "Yes My Lord, but, I must confess it is not of my own choosing." Danford seemed confused "What do you mean?" The chef walked over to where Lucia was seated, "The Marchesa prepared tonight's meal, the stew and bread, are of her own making."

All eyes turned to Lucia and she felt the heat reach her cheeks. She lowered her head in embarrassment. "Lucia, this is marvelous, the taste is equal to any delicacy that I have eaten in France. Bravo. You see, not only is she beautiful, but, keen of mind and spirit; and she can cook." Michael, put down his spoon and clapped his hands together in recognition of her accomplishment. "This is so good, can we have it every night?" asked Elizabeth. "Thank you Burton, I could not have managed without your expert assistance." Seeing that the meal was a success Burton bowed and left. "Lucia, where did you learn to cook like this?" She was pleased that they were all enjoying this simple meal. "When I was a little girl I would help my mother in the kitchen. Then when I got older, I would go to the kitchens at Monteforte and Marcello, our chef, taught me many things. He would say, "A woman must know how to prepare a meal, even if she is a Marchesa, for if she is ignorant, she will not know how to instruct her staff." Danford, a broad smile on his face, said, "I must thank that man; he is truly wise." They all raised their glasses in toast to Lucia's ability as a chef.

It had been a long day and everyone was tired, after dessert, they all excused themselves from the dining hall, except Danford and Lucia. "Imagine it could be like this every day. You and I; together we could manage Wallingston. He came over to where she was seated and put out his hand and she took it in her own. He raised her to her feet and embraced her with great affection. "Thank you for today, and, every day since I first met you. Come, let me give you a proper good night kiss."

They walked slowly and silently to her rooms, Lucia began to feel her heart beating more rapidly, her mind wandering to thoughts of delight. When they reached their destination, Danford, reached for the door and opened it. He entered first then, still holding her hand, led her in. By now, she was flushed. He was very sure of himself, and she hated him for it. Once again, he led her to the settee, sitting himself and then scooping her upon his lap. "Had you been thinking of this very moment all day?" Lucia was nearly breathless, while he was calm and talking softly, his hand stroking her back. "Yes." He drew her closer and his mouth latched upon her own, his tongue darting in and out, in and out. His big hand was tracing her back from the neck to the top of her buttocks.

He found the laces of her bodice and deftly with one hand began to untie them. Lucia closed her eyes and yielded to his every move. She could feel his growing desire. His kisses became more urgent. When he had reached the last loop, he took both hands and slipped the bodice seductively from her shoulders, her breasts, full and hard, were nearly exposed. He held her firmly in his grip and stood up. She was now facing him, her bodice caught at the top of her mounds. He stepped back just a little and slowly, carefully lured the fabric to slip away from her. As if this handsome man was seducing even the material of her gown, it gave way without the slightest struggle. Lucia did not feel ashamed or uneasy; she loved when he touched her.

The massive hands cupped the suppleness of her young, taut, breasts, the skin so pure and white, the palest shade of pink kissing the hard nipples. She was beautiful beyond all imagining. He made tiny circles around the outside of each one, coming closer to the center with each turn. Finally, he found the prize, and ever so lightly brushed each erect knob in the center of each breast. She was so wet she thought she would drip her lust on to the floor. Her heart was pounding in her ears and she wanted to cry out from desire. Danford gently squeezed each one; she gasped with pleasure. He then bent down, took the left one into his mouth, and nuzzled it with his tongue; then finally he began to suck. They grew harder and longer. He abandoned the left and started on the right. Lucia was wild with wanton craving; she had never wanted anything more than to have Danford inside of herself.

He took her hand and brought it to his groin. She was shocked at the size and hardness of him. Her hand probed the length, then the width of him. He loosened his ties and guided her hand into his breeches. Lucia was thrilled at the feel of him. With so many brothers, she had seen the male organ, but never had she touched it. Her fingers toyed with the clutch of nested hair, tracing the length to the tip then encircling with a soft touch the slit at the end. It was wet and sticky she wondered what that was.

Now Danford was breathless. "Touch it all around; squeeze it hard and move your hand up and down its shaft." She did as he asked. He closed his eyes and once again suckled her. She felt him growing; and thought to herself that he would surely burst apart. His hands were hiking up her skirts until he reached her bare bottom. He took each cheek in his hands and was kneading them, groaning and moving. Her fingers skimmed over the tip only to find that it was dripping a sticky substance from the tiny slit. He was panting heavily; she could feel the heat radiating from his body. "Move your hand faster, up and down; I am almost ready." Lucia was not sure what he was ready for, but he seemed very much in need of what she was doing. She liked the feel of him.

He moved one of his hands to her clit and began stroking her. She was hot and wet. He slipped his big finger into her waiting sex and wiggled it around. She spread her legs apart and was panting so much her mouth was dry. He found her hard little clit and worked it until she nearly collapsed with pleasure, and, he found himself covered in his own seed. They feel into each other's arms in a heap upon the floor. They were spent. "Thank you." He said breathlessly. Lucia, now exhausted, draped her arms around his neck and buried her face in his neck. He managed to hold her while he rose from the floor and carried her to the bed.

Danford laid her on the bed and gazed upon her magnificent breasts with such longing. "You are so beautiful. Look at these breasts; so perfect, with skin as white as freshly fallen snow." He kissed each one, as if they were infants, so pure and new. Lucia saw for the first time his exposed sex "I never saw a man with such a big sex. Will it hurt when it comes inside me?" Danford brought her hand to him and she tenderly fondled his cock. "Do not worry, the pain is only temporary. It is the pleasure that last forever. I will not hurt you. I love you. Marry me Lucia. Make me a happy man. I shall leave you with one last indulgent delight."

He removed her hand from his sex and lifted her skirts to her waist. When he saw her clutch of red carnality, he was weak from longing. He came to her, his head nudging her legs apart. He sniffed the muskiness of her; he was kissing her outer thighs, then moving ever closer toward the middle. His mouth fell upon her, his breath hot on her skin. With his hands, he spread her lips apart. She did not resist. One hand moved adroitly in tiny concentric circles while his tongue licked and sucked; licked and sucked. He drank in the taste of her sex, the perfume of her cunt imprinting its scent on his brain. In only a few strokes, she was succumbed to her own release, her juices of erotic sensuality dribbling into his mouth. He sucked her hard and fast and swallowed her essence into his soul. He too had found his own release. He came up from his font of delight and brought his mouth to hers and she tasted her own sex. It was truly bliss. For a long while, they just laid there basking in the contentment of their intimacy. "Will we always be like this?" she asked him in a raspy voice. "Yes. I hope so."

CHAPTER THIRTEEN

AN INTRUDER

Paris, France

He was hungry and his clothes reeked of sweat and grime. It had been weeks since he had enjoyed the comforts of a good meal and clean clothes. He cursed himself for what he had done. His life was ruined, and, everywhere he turned, he faced the dangers of capture. Piro had never enjoyed the sport of hunting, always believing that the prey had an unjust disadvantage, now, he was the prey and confirmed his beliefs.

Out of desperation, he concluded that he must face Lucia and beg for her forgiveness. He knew in his heart that she would grant him his life, but he would be banished from any association with her forever. The thought of never being with Lucia was agony for him; he knew that was his only chance for salvation. He would go to Henri's apartments in Paris and plead for forgiveness.

It was under cover of darkness that Piro arrived at Henri's apartments. He decided to spend the rest of the night in the stable; at least he could find a clean shirt and wash up to make some sort of presentable audience with his Mistress. He crept in, trying not to alert the animals of his presence; but he was fully aware that the stench of him would arouse them. True to his knowledge, the horses started to whinny and stamp; he tried to calm them; to talk softly to them, but they instinctively sensed an intruder. Piro knew horses, but his fear was so sharp that it came to the animals' sensitive noses. He cursed them, and, himself. Their agitation was growing and soon the lantern came on in the Master of Stables rooms. Again, it would be just a matter of moments before he was discovered. Would there ever again be rest for him? He was wild with lack of sleep and his stomach, which had been empty for days, growled fiercely.

He made a break for the house, knowing that the kitchen door would be unlocked. He tried to be as quiet as possible. Climbing the servants' stairs, he made his way to where Lucia had been staying. All was quiet, only a muffled snoring filtered through Henri's door. He was pleased that so far his presence had gone undetected. With a steadied confidence, he proceeded as noiselessly as he could. When he reached Lucia's room, his heart was pounding so hard he was sure it would crack through his chest. His mouth was dry as sand. He was sweating profusely and his hands were shaking. He closed his eyes, swallowed a deep gulp of air, and placed his hand on the knob. His hand was so sweaty he could not grasp hold of the metal handle. He wiped his hand on his filthy shirt and he was then able to turn the knob. The lock disengaged from its hole with what seemed a loud click.

Piro was shaking with fear, confusion, and arousal. The mere thought of Lucia could give him an erection. He tried to clear his befuddled mind. He admonished himself and tried to calm his head. It was very dark inside. He could make out the outline of the massive bedstead that was in the middle of the room. He quietly made his way to it; there were no other noises, except the pounding in his chest. He reached the bed and felt for her body; it was empty. His mind swirled in confusion. Had he gone to the wrong room? He was sure that this was where she had been. He made a cursory survey of the room; it was devoid of any sign of her presence. Where was she?

Unable to control his frustration, Piro bounded toward Henri's room. He did not hesitate but pushed open the heavy door, which slammed hard into the wall behind it with a loud thud. Henri moved, but, did not fully awake. Piro ran to the bed and shook the old man as hard as he could. Henri, who was still in the fog of sleep, was startled and dazed. "Where is she? Where has she gone?" Piro was now screaming at the old man. Henri realized who it was. "Are you completely mad? Lucia is not here. Get out of my house and never return. Leave or I shall have you sent to the Bastille." Piro was so crazed with anger he did not even comprehend what the old man was saying.

Piro grabbed Henri by his nightshirt and slapped him hard across the face. "Tell me where she is or I swear I shall beat you to death." Henri was already breathless, but he was calling for help. "Where is she?" screamed Piro. "She is in England you fool. Leave her alone; you are nothing, she will have a good life with Danford. Go away. Leave all of us." Piro was momentarily halted by the thought that Lucia was in England with Danford. The thought of the two of them, together, only fueled his fury. Henri continued to call for help. Piro could not tolerate the sound of the old man's voice, picked up a brass candlestick from the bedside table, and began bashing in Henri's head. The old man tried to stave off the onslaught of pain. He was crying out and moaning from the blows. Suddenly, the moaning stopped; but he could now hear that there was coming a rush of shouting and heavy footsteps. He took one last look at the man who had been his mentor; who was now covered in blood; and ran for the balcony door. They ran in through the open door and shouted after him to stop. Piro knew there was no other means of escape. He threw the door open and leapt over the rail, falling to the dew covered grass below. Blindly he ran, with no direction, until his chest heaved with pain from the lack of air. Wherever he was, he collapsed and felt himself drifting away.

CHAPTER FOURTEEN

A MESSENGER ARRIVES

Wallingston Castle, England

It was just after breakfast when the young man arrived. Having been dispatched from London he had ridden hard to Northumberland. William received the small stack of letters and then led the rider to the back of the castle; he gave the kitchen maid instruction to give the messenger some food and drink and a clean pallet to rest. The young man was grateful for the hospitality and followed the maid.

William gave the letters a cursory glance and headed to see his master. Danford was with his cousin, the barrister, composing his letter of fealty to His Majesty the King. The door was open so William walked in, "Your Grace" he bowed, and waited for Danford's acknowledgement of his presence. "Yes William." The servant approached and handed the stack of letters to the duke. "Thank you William." He gave them a quick glance; there were two letters addressed to Lucia and several for him. He stopped at the one marked from the "Estate of Henri de Fauntil" he thought that an odd way for Henri to sign his letter.

"William please take these two letters to Marchesa Banfi. Do not send the messenger away until I have read these notes, they may require an answer." "As you wish Your Grace." William bowed once again; then walked out to wait for further instruction.

"Charles would you mind terribly if we took a short break; I would like to read these missives; perhaps they are notes from persons who will be attending the services. I shouldn't take too long." Charles, a good friend, and childhood playmate of his, bore the family resemblance. He was just around Danford's age, tall and handsome, but his coloring was dark and he had raven black hair. He was very distinguished and styled his beard in the new Spaniard way. He was a very striking man who was equally as intelligent. "Yes, of course, I was getting tired from writing so many drafts. I shall go to the kitchen for a pint of ale, shall I bring one back for you?" "Now, that is a most generous thought. Yes indeed, perhaps, two pints, this is tedious work." They laughed in familiar camaraderie.

Danford waited for Charles to leave; for some unknown reason he felt hesitant to read the contents, but then opened the note from Henri.

Dear Lord Stevens,

It is with a heavy heart that I must inform you of the death of your dear friend, The Marquis Henri DeFauntil. He was killed at the hands of his former apprentice, Piro, who has escaped. I write to advise you that he may be coming to England in search of the Marchesa Banfi. There is now a price on the head of Piro and bulletins are up everywhere. I hope he is caught before he makes his way to you.

The property of Marquis DeFauntil has been bequeathed to his niece, the Marquise Noelle Givenchy, the daughter of his sister. There are no other heirs. The Marquise will be in residence within the next week.

Your faithful servant,

Renee Blanchard

Danford could not put the letter down, but stared at it in his hand, as if it were an object he had never seen. He remembered with great fondness his old friend Henri. He was a kind and fatherly man, who, had pleaded with him to take Piro under his tutelage. How he had convinced him that the young man had great potential. At first Danford would have to agree; Piro was eager to learn and took well to instruction. He learned quickly and worked hard, but then one day he seemed to change; he became distracted and just thought about making money. Everyone saw the transition and all wondered what had happened. Yet, Henri would not give up hope of molding this young man into something special.

Danford, with tears streaming down his face, was hurt and angry. He wanted to kill Piro with his bare hands. First, the attack on that hapless boy at the shipyard; then the night he tried to kill Lucia; the fire he set at the shipyard; and now the one man, a good man, who believed in him, whom he killed. He must to be stopped. He would inform the sheriffs in the surrounding counties to be on the alert for such a man fitting his description. He would ask Charles to have notices printed and posted with a reward of 10,000 pounds sterling to the person who captures and brings him to Wallingston.

Now, he dreaded the thought of having to share this terrible news with Lucia. After all, she had sent Piro to Henri to be apprenticed. She will be devastated to hear of Henri's death; and to think the very hands of the person she tried to help killed him. Danford was trying to evolve a plan of how to bring this news to Lucia when she suddenly appeared at his door. He saw that she looked happy and was smiling; he on the other hand could not contain his pain.

Seeing him in such a state of sadness, she rushed to his side, "Danford, what troubles you?" He held the letter in his hand, she caught sight of it, and "Did you receive bad news?" Danford braced himself and told her to sit down, "What is so terrible that I must be seated to hear?" "Please my darling, sit down, I want to share something important with you." His voice was so strained with sorrow, and his manner so urgent, Lucia obeyed. She waited until he was ready to tell her. He came to her, knelt before her, holding her hands; he looked into her eyes and said, "I have just received word that our dear friend Henri was killed." At the sound of his words Lucia's eyes darted back and forth, as if the words had caused her to not comprehend their meaning." He waited. "How did it happen? Who? When, did you find out?" Danford, his shoulders slumped, his head bent, "Just after we left. According to his houseman, Renee, Piro had come to Sant Germaine looking for you. When he did not find you there, he asked Henri where you had gone. At first, Henri tried to fight him off, not wanting to tell him of your whereabouts. Piro would not relent, until he learned that you came here; then he beat Henri to death. It is all here in the letter Renee sent. Do you want to see it?" Lucia was numb with shock. She did not cry at first; but took the letter.

She finished the letter and threw it to the floor. She put her face in her hands and began to weep. Danford embraced her with great tenderness. "This, this terrible thing, it is all my fault. I asked Henri to take Piro. To spare him from death; to give him a new start; to have him become a man of means. It was I who told Henri to start the shipbuilding company and let Piro think he was the one in charge." By now, Lucia weeping with such depth of sorrow, her words were almost inaudible. "It is my entire fault that he is dead; as surely as if I killed him. I loved Henri; he was kind and generous; now he is dead. Dead; he is dead, because of me." Lucia was racked with pain at the loss of her friend. "How will I tell Zia Maria, that I killed her dearest friend?" Lucia was on the brink of hysteria. She was gasping for air. Danford was scared for her. He tried to comfort her, but she was too distraught. He stood up and grabbed her by the arms, and began to shake her with such violent force. "This is not your fault; you did not kill Henri; that motherless bastard killed him. I will not rest until I see his sorrowful body swinging from the gallows." Danford was angry and did not realize that he was shouting; his hold on her arms was intense. She stopped crying and looked at him with fear in her eyes. He came to his senses and let her go; she nearly collapsed on to the chair. It was suddenly quite; the only sound was the intermittent whimper from Lucia.

Charles Monroe had reached the threshold of Danford's office just as this drama was unfolding. He said nothing; but watched as the intensity of their grief purveyed over the scene. He was not sure if he should leave them to their privacy or try to lend some comfort. Before he could decide, Lucia, who was facing the door, discovered his presence. She saw him for the first time and recognized him as the man from the foxhunt that she met at the inn. Danford followed her gaze and found Charles awkwardly standing in the doorway; in his hands, he was holding two tankards of ale. The expression on his handsome face was so telling. He was embarrassed and confused at what he had just witnessed. He said nothing but came into the room and set down the two glasses. He was about to leave when Lucia said, in a voice riddled with pain, "You do not have to leave; we are mourning the loss of a good man, whom we both loved." Charles, again in his confusion, thought they were talking about Lord Stevens. "Ah, the Duke, my uncle was a wonderful man." For a second Danford and Lucia looked at each other in complete puzzlement, Danford replied, "Not my father. The Marquis Henri de Fauntil was murdered by a man whom he had befriended and given great opportunity." It seemed as if Charles was now totally lost. "I am sorry; I thought you were bereft by the loss of the Duke. Shall I leave the two of you?" Lucia answered, "No, there is no need; the deed has been done and we must face our grief." She turned to Danford, "I am sorry I intruded on your work. I shall find work to keep me busy."

Danford, took stock of the situation, and recalled that when Lucia had bounded into to his office, before he broke the news of Henri's death, she was joyful. He came to her and standing so close she could feel his breath upon her face, inquired, "Why were you coming to see me? You looked so happy, and, then I shared this letter with you." Lucia for a second nearly forgot her reason for coming to see him, "I too received a letter; it was from my sister, she came early for the birth of a son." "That is sterling news, a boy, her husband must be so proud. Are both mother and child well?" "Oh yes. Even though he came too soon he is a big, healthy boy. She is fine. They will baptize the baby, but, will wait until I return to have the celebration party." "I am so happy for you Lucia, but, I know how much you wanted to be there with her. I am sorry; it is because of me that you came to England. Can you forgive me?" Lucia felt bad that she missed the birth but knew it was not Danford's fault, "She came early, and there was nothing either of us could do."

Charles was pretending to be interested in his writing, but was watching their every movement. Lucia caught him staring at her and she felt herself flush. He had the most penetrating eyes, undoubtedly a good asset for a barrister. She was sure he frightened his opponents, and yet there was something erotic about him that intrigued her. Lucia flushed, she felt as if he could read her thoughts, for he was smiling lustfully at her. Very ill at ease, Lucia said, "I am sorry for Henri, he will be missed. Piro must be stopped, he has become completely mad. What can we do?"

Danford was squeezing her hands, "Do not trouble yourself; I will send word to all the sheriffs to be on the hunt for him. I will post a reward for anyone who brings him to me, then, I shall deal with him." Lucia felt a cold shiver, Danford could be sweet, and gentle, but she knew he could also be ruthless when needed. "As you wish; I shall be cautious until he is caught." Lucia now met Charles' stare and her mouth was so dry she had to lick her lips. He was a wicked man, but she was attracted to him.

"Charles" barked Danford. Charles distracted by this nonverbal banter with Lucia had not heard him. "Ah, yes, what it is My Grace?" Lucia thought it odd that the cousin addressed him so formally. "Forgo the letter to His Majesty for a bit. We need to send word to all our neighbors, of a dangerous man on the run. I shall give you a detailed description to be sent around to all the sheriffs." Charles was listening to the young duke but his thoughts were fixed on the redheaded beauty before him.

"I shall leave the two of you; it appears that your work is endless. Your Grace shall we dine together this evening?" Danford, so distracted by his thoughts, he merely said, "No. I have business at Lord Branson's manor this evening." "Pity, then I shall have to dine alone." "Where are the twins and my brothers?" "Everyone has gone to purchase additional supplies because there has been an overwhelming response from those who will be attending the services. Well, I should be off, there is still much to attend to before tomorrow." Danford, his head down, deeply engrossed in writing something, "Charles, would you be a gracious fellow, and stay to dine with Marchesa Banfi?" Lucia was both surprised and dismayed at the thought, "Oh that will not be necessary, you are both so busy."

Charles came around from behind the desk he was sitting at, bowed formally, and responded, "I would be delighted to keep you company. It is settled. Now, if you will excuse me, I suddenly have a much longer list of letters to compose. I shall look forward to our dinner together." Bowing deeply, he retreated to his desk and took up his quill.

Lucia left in a state of rare depression. She loved Henri and at one point held great feelings for his killer. She remembered with great sorrow how each of these men had played a significant role in her life. Tears for the both of them falling from her swollen eyes. She found herself in the chapel. It was another grey day, and the chapel, which was nestled between two great wings of the castle, was dank and dark. She wanted time, in peace, to think, to pray, to beg Jesus for his direction. In her grief, she nearly fell over the caskets of His Grace the Duke of Northumberland and the Duchess. Their bodies lay in state for all to mourn, the picture of a perfect couple, even in death they would not separate. Lucia wanted to scream, "It is all a lie!" but she dare not. Boughs of pine were swaged around each casket, tied with ribbons, which was to mask the odor of death. There was no mistaking the scent of decay.

She found a pew in the darkest shadows of the sanctuary, a lone candle casting its flickering glow from the altar. There was no corpus on the ornately carved oak cross. The altar, a massive slab of granite, was simple and austere. The windows did not portray intricately detailed pictures of saints and angels. It was a sad and desolate place. Lucia, in her misery, longed for the beauty of her home, of, Monteforte. The chapel there was petite but so magnificently decorated as to make one feel the presence of the Lord, to lift one's spirit. Lucia, in spite of her surroundings tried to concentrate on her prayers. "Lord Jesus, please show me the way. I want to love Danford, I do love him, but, in my heart, I know that I cannot be his wife. He is a good man, yet, I will never give him what he wants." She remained there for a long time, and, eventually began to nod off to sleep. She was awoken as if by the will of someone's presence.

Lucia felt his presence before she saw him; the strong smell of sandalwood was near her. A strong hand came around her mouth and nose and held them so that she could barely find her breath. She was thrashing about trying to free herself, when he came around to face her. She was shocked! He removed his hand and replaced it with his mouth, his tongue licking her lips, the inside of her mouth. His hands were large, and he had a vise like hold on her throat. He moved his mouth to her ear and his hot breath was on her, "Do not scream; do not speak; for I shall snap your neck like a chicken. Do you understand? I will not hesitate to kill you." She nodded. He began licking her face, his hands roughly seizing her breasts. "Come with me. Say nothing." He held his powerful grip on her throat, she believed he would certainly kill her, and there was no doubt in her mind. He dragged her behind the sanctuary to a hidden door. It was dark, yet, he knew his way. He pushed her along, half dragging, half carrying her. They were descending stairs, it was getting cold, and the passage was getting narrower. Her hands brushed the stone walls for support, they were wet with dampness; he never eased his grip; she was struggling for air and felt herself becoming lightheaded. He felt her body becoming inert and eased up a little; she was grateful; it was enough so that she could gasp for some breath. He pushed her along, her foot missing a step here and there. Further, and, further they descended into the bowels of the castle. The stench of mold and decay was so strong. He did not speak. She was astounded that he could move so swiftly in this oppressive blackness. By now, Lucia's eyes were adjusting to the darkness and she was imprinting a mental map. She realized that the deeper they went the wetter the stones became. Then finally he stopped, they had reached an open space. It was a dungeon. Still holding her tight enough to prevent her from escaping he came to a steel door. He opened the door, and it squealed on its hinges. He threw her inside, her leg encountered a steel object, and she fell upon it with such force she went down with a thud. The pain was so searing she nearly fainted. "Sporco figlio di puttana, spero che brucerai all'inferno." She cursed him in Italian. "Pensi che sono ignorante e non capiscono la lingua di polli? I can speak seven languages you bitch. Therefore, you think I am the son of a whore, and, that I should burn in hell. Well Madame, I assure you, my dear mother was not a whore, but a saint. My father, that miserable excuse of a man, did indeed marry a whore, and thankfully I am not of her flesh." He was so calm and calculating that it made Lucia more frightened than if, he had been a ranting lunatic. There was something so odd about him that she shook with fear. "What do you want of me?" He laughed, "I don't want you. It is my brother, Danford, whom I despise. You, unfortunately, are my means of punishing him." Lucia was confused, "Why do you hate him so? He is a good man; he will care for you and your siblings."

By now, he had found and lit a small candle. It was nothing but a tiny cell, but to her shock, there were children's play objects. Why, she thought to herself, were these objects in this awful place. She continued to survey her surroundings and found chains fixed to the walls, a rack, which held various sticks, all, arranged in order of size and thickness. The object she fell over was a bed, which had been chained to the wall, with leather strapping attached at several intervals along its sides. He just stood there watching her reaction to what she was seeing. She looked at him with questioning eyes. "This is the place that sick bitch took us when she decided we needed to be, as she called it, enlightened." Lucia could not contain her curiosity, "Enlightened?" He walked over to the rack, which held all the sticks, "Yes. A word she invented to tell my father why we were gone for hours, even a day. She would drag us down here and teach us things." He was fingering the stick he had withdrawn from its place. "What would anyone need to learn in this God forsaken place?"

Suddenly, without warning he wielded the stick with such power and struck the bed so hard it shattered. The clang of the metal reverberated within the confined space. Lucia squealed with fright. "She taught us hate. She taught us depravity. She taught us pain." His eyes were on fire. Lucia was afraid. "What does this have to do with Danford?" she was trying to control her fear, but, her voice was stammering. He turned on her, "It has everything to do with him. Everything I tell you. He left us. He went to live with my father's brother. We were just tiny babes, and she beat us and made us please her in the most sinful of ways. She nearly killed Elizabeth she beat her about the head so badly. That is why she is dim witted." He was so deranged with hatred the spittle was foaming from his mouth. "That evil cow would make us get naked and touch each other's privates. Then she would get naked and make us touch her. If we refused, she would strap us to that metal bed and whip our naked little bodies. If she deemed we were truly misbehaved she would lock us down here, in the dark, without food or water, for a night sometimes two."

Lucia could see that he was not right in his thinking. "But Jonathan, your brother was a young boy; he would have had no choice where your father sent him. Surely, you must understand that. Lady Evelyn is dead, and, for that matter so is your father. Neither one of them can ever hurt you again." He was silent and stood stone still. Then, without warning, he screamed, "NO! He must pay. He knew what was going on here, but did not save us. He knew. He knew." Jonathan kept repeating that Danford was aware of their plight and did nothing to stop it. "What could he have done, he was ten when he was sent away?" She knew it was futile to argue with him. He had been so abused that his mind would never be right. She needed to find an escape before he hurt her. "My father did not believe us when we told him that his wife was doing these terrible things. He too then beat us, calling us liars, and troublemakers. There was no escape for us; no love, no comfort for us. He would have believed Danford, the would-be heir, the next Duke of Northumberland. Danford was always favored, even now, his life is perfect."

"Why did you take me here? It is your brother that you wish to punish for abandoning you." Lucia was trying to draw him out, to find out what his true intentions were going to be. "That Madame is really quite simple; I am surprised that a woman with your apparent intellect did not find that to be plain. You are the object of my brother's love and desire. When he speaks of you, it is with pure love; when he looks at you there is lust in his eyes. You are the one person that I can use to exact my revenge on Danford. I am sorry; you have become the bait in my trap." Not for the first time, but, certainly now, Lucia was genuinely terrified. Jonathan spoke in a soft, almost reverent tone. He had apparently thought this plan through and was now fully prepared to execute it. "What do you plan to do with me?"

He came very close to her, stroked her cheek, and took hold of her hair. "I can see why my dear brother adores you, I could fancy you myself, for you are a beautiful creature, but, I must forego any desire, at least for now, and concentrate my efforts on claiming justice for my brother and sisters." "Do they know what you are planning to do?" He smiled in such a way that it sent a chill down her spine, "No. Why would I tell them? They are the weak ones. They always obeyed that wicked bitch to escape punishment. She hated me the most. I was the object of her most perverted inventions. I withstood her worse punishments in defiance, while they cowered under her gaze. Fortunately, for them, I shall be the one, as in the past, to stand against evil." "How will you do that?"

Jonathan, a handsome man, tall and muscular, with a clean, youthful face, turned and was leaving, "Where are you going?" He reached the door in two steps, turned to fully face her; his eyes filled with hatred, and said, "Don't trouble yourself Madame in a day or two this will all be over for all of us." Lucia rushed to the door but he was too quick. He pushed her hard and she fell backward, falling onto the metal bed, she yelped in pain. He slammed the steel door with such a bang a few clumps of mortar fell to the floor. She jumped up and ran to the door, pounding on it, screaming "Jonathan, please do not do this. I will talk to Danford, we can work this out. Please Jonathan, don't leave me here." He opened the tiny viewing hole in the heavy iron door,

"Madame, I told you not to worry. Oh, by the way, there is no use in calling out for help, no one can hear you down here, trust me I know. For years, I called out in pain, in fear, in loneliness, and no one came. Goodbye Lucia, I am sorry."

Lucia knew from her own castle, that these dungeons were buried deep in the bowels of the foundation. No one would think to look for her. No one knew where she had been taken. How long would she last in this prison? It was she thought, nearly dinnertime, perhaps, Lord Monroe, Charles, would ask the servants where she was since they were supposed to dine together. Everyone was gone her only hope was Sophia. Where was she?

What a sad story Jonathan had told her, and, from the looks of her confinement, he was telling the truth. She went around the tiny cell, picking up small objects, lifting the heavy chains that protruded from the walls. She touched the wooden rods that stood like sentinels in their rack. Picking one up she felt the heft of it, she slapped it across her palm and smarted at the sting. She thought to herself "Dear God what happened in this room at the hands of that vile woman? What suffering did this family endure? It is no wonder the poor soul has gone mad." Lucia was overwhelmed by the depravity of the tiny cell. Her imagination was wandering in all directions as to what Jonathan and his siblings had endured.

Lucia did the only thing that made sense, she knelt down and prayed. "Lord Jesus, help all of us. I am sending my prayers as a warning to Danford, let him heed my message. Guide someone to find me and release me from this prison before I too perish." As she completed her incantations it instantly became pitch dark, the candle had gone out. She had not thought to look for flint and stick before, now she would have to try to find it in the blackness.

A feeling so terrifying as to make her struggle to find her breath descended upon her. It felt as if the very walls were closing in on her. She tried to calm herself, talking to herself, trying to reason her mind back to reality. "These walls are made of stone, they cannot move, get a grip on yourself", she chastised. Lucia realizing her situation was virtually hopeless, removed her petticoat, fashioned it into a pillow, and curled up on the metal bed. The iron rods digging into her ribs, with her leg throbbing with pain, she began to weep. At first, her tears were for the utter bleakness of where she was, and the fear of what was to come, but then her tears fell for the children that had been tormented and abused in this very cell. The fear they must have faced as little children lying here strapped to that very bed, in the dark, with no love or comfort. She wept with great sorrow. Eventually, she fell off to sleep.

CHAPTER FIFTEEN

SOPHIA'S SEARCH

The dungeons, Wallingston Castle

Danford left to meet with one of his father's oldest allies. Lord Lionel Branson, a distant blood relative to his father, who had pledged his loyalty to the Duke, in exchange for a fifty-acre plot on the north ridge of the Wallingston estate. It was important to continue these types of relationships. Northumberland was on Scotland's border, and many of the inhabitants of that region were intermarried with Scots, thus, their loyalties ebbed and flowed with the tide. Since there was much political unrest in all of Europe, Danford thought it prudent to personally make the notification of his father's death to Lord Branson. Even though his new title and authority did outrank that of his neighbor, Danford was a cunning politician, a trait he learned from his father. "Keep them in your pocket," his father would always tell Danford, his favored firstborn, and heir to his duchy.

It took him an hour to reach Lord Branson's manor. It was dinnertime and he was invited to join the Lord's family. His valet William and his brother Michael accompanied Danford. Danford wanted to show Branson that even in his absence his Regent

Lord Michael Stevens would be in charge. After dinner, they and Lord Branson retired to the library to discuss future arrangements. "It was so thoughtful of you to come yourself to notify me of the passing of your parents. I am sorry for this double tragedy to your family. Your father and I served in the military together and remained close friends for all these years. I hope to continue that relationship under your family flag." Danford, always heard from his father that Branson, who was related distantly, but related nevertheless, replied, "I believe, if I am to recall the stories my father so willingly shared, that you are kin to us. Is this true?" The older man beamed that his pedigree had been acknowledged, "Yes, it is true. Your grandfather and my grandfather were first cousins." Danford was tired, still upset from the letter regarding Henri just wanted to get home, "Then it is settled, I shall be able to call upon you and your tenants, in times of trouble. And for your continued loyalty and service to my family, I shall deed you twenty more acres of prime pasture land." Danford rose from his chair, it signaled that the audience was finished and the deal sealed. Branson, a middle-aged man, portly and balding, came over to him, knelt down on one knee, Danford extended his hand to the man, who said, "I pledge my lands, my coffers, and my people to you Your Grace." It was complete. "Thank you Lionel, I pray we never need to face an enemy, but, if we do, I feel secure knowing of your loyalty. I trust I will see you at my parent's funeral services." "Of course Your Grace, I shall be there. Again, I wish to impart my deepest sympathy upon you and your family." Danford thanked him for the dinner and bid him farewell.

William was anxiously waiting for him to emerge from the library. He drew up close to him and whispered discreetly that he had just received word from one of the stable lads that Marchesa Banfi was missing. "Your Grace, Marchesa Banfi is nowhere to be found at the estate. They have searched all over for her and fear for her life." Danford was enraged, "Will this day never end its misery upon me?" "What troubles you brother?" asked Michael seeing the reaction of whatever it was William had whispered to him. "Wait until we leave." Lord Branson was just ahead instructing his grooms to bring round the duke's horses. Danford was infuriated, but tried to conceal his anger to his new supporter. His farewell was brisk, "Thank you again Lord Branson I will see you soon."

They just cleared the drive of the Branson manor, when Danford turned to Michael, "William has gotten word that Lucia is missing. No one knows of her whereabouts. No one has seen her since she was last with us this morning. I fear Piro, that lunatic may have taken her. Upon our arrival we shall begin a full scale hunt for them." Michael, concerned, but practical, said calmly, "It is already dark, we shall find nothing. It would be more prudent if we commence at first daybreak, but first we must begin a full search of the castle and grounds. When we get back I shall assemble every servant and assign them sections of the castle and grounds to begin searching." Danford was pleased with his brother's logical thinking. He was too emotional to formulate a workable plan.

The ride back went swiftly; they were riding hard at full gallop. When they reached the castle, Danford and Michael jumped off their horses and stormed into the castle. There waiting for them in a frantic display of total confusion were Sophia, Elizabeth and Rachel. The three of them began speaking simultaneously. "Stop! One at a time" he barked. "Sophia, where is your Mistress?" She so nervous and was stammering, "I do not know Your Grace. I saw her after she received the letters, we talked a while, and then she went off to look for you. I did not see her again. Lord Monroe came to get her for dinner, but, she was not there." By now Charles appeared on the scene, he too seemed agitated, "Your Grace, it is most vexing Marchesa Banfi seems to have vanished." By now Danford was half out of his mind with worry, "It is that whoreson; he has taken her, but, where?" He was pacing back and forth. Michael, said to William, who now was back from tending the horses, "William, assemble all the servants, go now." William just bowed and ran to do as he was told. Danford was looking for his brother "Jonathan; where is he, has he returned yet today?" Elizabeth was stuttering, "I, I, saw him after breakfast, he was hiding in the chapel." Danford came to her, "What do you mean? Was he praying in the chapel?" Elizabeth's eyes grew wide with fear,

"He told me not to tell anyone." Danford took her by the shoulders and held her very tightly, her face contorted with pain, "I shall ask you once more, where is Jonathan? What was he doing in the chapel?" She started to cry, he immediately regretted yelling at her, he fell to his knees, "Sweet sister, I am sorry, I am so worried for Lucia's safety, can you bring me to where Jonathan was hiding." The girl instantly recovered, wiped her runny nose on her sleeve, and took hold of his hand.

"I will go with Elizabeth, the rest of you, plus the servants, divide into smaller groups, search everywhere, leave nothing unturned." He was shouting orders as he was walking. Elizabeth, headed toward the chapel, "Why were you in the chapel this morning Elizabeth?" Danford was trying to remember that he was talking to a child, not the full-grown woman, he saw before his eyes. She put down her head, and spoke so softly he could hardly hear her, "I wanted to see Lady Evelyn. I wanted her to get up. I wanted Father to get up. I thought that if I prayed to God very, very, hard, He might wake them up." They were inside the chapel; he stopped, and embraced his little sister, the child was sad at the loss of her father and the only mother, albeit a wicked one, she had ever known. "It will be fine sweet sister, I will care for you now. " Tell me, where was Jonathan hiding when you saw him?" Elizabeth liked this game, she led him to the exact spot she had seen her other brother earlier in the day. "Did Jonathan see you there?" "Oh, yes, he told me that I must keep it a secret, and, especially not to tell you." Danford was befuddled as to why his younger brother would tell her such a thing, "Perhaps, you are confused Elizabeth." The girl became annoyed, "NO, I know what he said, "He said do not tell anyone where I am. Do not tell Danford where I went." Danford had no choice but to believe her. "Was anyone else in here at the time?" "No." "So Jonathan was hiding and he told you not to tell anyone, especially me, where he was. Why?" Elizabeth shrugged her shoulders, "Maybe he was playing a game with Mistress Lucia?" Danford came right into her face, "Now, Elizabeth, this is very, very, important; was Lucia in here this morning?" She nodded her head to acknowledge that she had seen Lucia earlier in the chapel. "What was she doing? Did she know Jonathan was there?" For the first time the girl smiled broadly, "She was praying, I heard her talking." "Did she talk to Jonathan?" "No. Jonathan was hiding. I wanted to play with them but Jonathan gets angry with me all the time." Danford did not want to upset his sister, "Then what happened?"

At that question Elizabeth broke away from him, she went to the pew where Lucia was praying and was mimicking Lucia's movements. She was kneeling, talking to the unadorned cross; then feigned sleep. Danford was not amused, "What did Jonathan do next?" Again, the girl rose from her seat, came around to the pew behind, and crouched down behind the spot where she had been pretending to be the sleeping Lucia. "What did Jonathan do next?" She instructed Danford to sit where Lucia had been he complied. She came from behind and put her hand over his mouth and nose, then pretended to be able to drag him out of the pew. He was playing along in order to gather what had happened.

Elizabeth led him behind the altar; he suddenly realized where Jonathan had taken Lucia. There was only one place those stairs led, that was to the dungeon. "Stay here, go find Michael and tell him where I am. Go." She wanted to stay with Danford, but, obeyed, and went off to find her brother. Danford was incensed, wondering why Jonathan would have taken Lucia down to the dungeon. He knew the way; they had shown him the place where Evelyn had tormented them. He cursed her soul to the deepest regions of Hell. He had never been her victim. He left soon after his mother died; he would be groomed to become the next Duke of Northumberland. He would visit every few years, but for the most part, he was not truly part of what had happened. Michael and Rachael had told him stories of her wickedness. Jonathan was always defiant, and, so, he bore the brunt of her wrath. He could not even think of the suffering they had endured at her hands.

It was dark but he knew the way. He found a torch and lit it. In his hast he faltered once but recovered his stride. Even with the torch, it was so densely dark it made him feel disoriented. Finally, he reached the last step, the dungeon was on his right; he felt for the key to the steel door. Finding it, he turned the heavy iron ring and the bolt threw back. He opened the door and it squealed at the intrusion. "Lucia, darling, are you hurt?" "Danford, is it you?" Her eyes so unaccustomed to the light did not focus for a moment or two. Her heart was pounding. She stood; he went to her, "Are you harmed?" Lucia was crying from relief, "No, he did not hurt me." "Who did this? Was it Jonathan?" Lucia was so sorry to have to say that it was "Yes, it was Jonathan. Danford, he is ill, he needs help." Danford was still too angry to think of how he would deal with his brother, "I shall deal with him later. For now you are safe, I love you my darling." For the first time Lucia truly felt that she could love this man, she was not sure how she would grow to become his wife, but she was now certain that she would marry him. Something within her had changed. "I love you Danford. I will marry you." He kissed her with deep affection.

He was holding her in a loving embrace, then, she heard a sharp crack, and Danford went limp. "I don't think he will be marrying anyone," said Jonathan. He pushed Lucia away, "I do not intend to hurt you, I have the one I want dead. Stay out of my way, for your own safety." Danford was moaning but coming around, "Get up you pitiful excuse for a man. You will die at my hands so swear me God. I have dreamt of this day for the better part of my whole life." Danford was groggy from the blow to his head,

"Jonathan, what are you talking about? I have never harmed you." Jonathan's voice grew louder and held an unusual tone, it was guttural, almost a growl, "You, the fair one, the chosen one, you were not here to endure the torments, the suffering, the anguish of that bitch. To live with a father, who knew what she was doing, but closed his cowardly eyes to our pain. You, and, only you, could have stopped her, but, even after we told you, you did nothing. I have hated you, more than her, at least she did not pretend to love us; she hated us, and told us so every day of our lives. It was only when Your Grace came home, that she put on her motherly face. You make me sick. You, like our father, are a coward! You will go on to rule much in the same manner as he, with your new beautiful wife, living a charmed life, while I cannot close my eyes to sleep for the dreams of what I endured haunt me." Without warning, he lashed out at Danford with a dagger. He cut him across the chest. The young duke was stunned but before he could recover, another vicious gash came across his lower abdomen. "I will not kill you quickly. You must suffer for a while." Jonathan was wielding that knife with the mind and strength of ten madmen. Danford was struggling with him, trying to wrestle the knife from his hand. He was by now covered in blood from the gapping wounds Jonathan had inflicted.

Lucia was waiting for a chance to help Danford. She took out the dagger she always kept secreted in her sash. She held it, feeling its weight in her hand. She took the hilt and held it tightly with both hands, just as Giovanni Romano had taught her. Jonathan had Danford pinned on the steel bed; his full weight was on him and the blood was gushing from his belly. Danford was trying to reason with his younger brother, "Jonathan, I will get you help. I am sorry for all that has happened here. I was but a child myself." Jonathan who was beating him about the head and face could not be reasoned with. Lucia could see that Danford was getting weaker; he would not be able to hold Jonathan back too much longer. The blood was pooling, coming through the slats of the iron bed. Jonathan did not relent for a second. His insane fury was uncontrollable.

Lucia, with her hands wrapped tightly around the dagger, lunged toward Jonathan catching him in the back of the neck with such force he instantly collapsed upon Danford. She backed away.

There was shouting coming from the stairs. Michael was the first to enter the cell holding a burning torch in his hand. "Dear Mother of God, what is going on here?" Lucia had retreated to the farthest corner of the cell. Jonathan, with her dagger protruding from the back of his neck, was sprawled out on Danford their blood flowing and mixing. It was a scene of such carnage that she could not contain the bile in her stomach and vomited all over herself.

Michael, momentarily stunned by what he saw, stood frozen in his own footstep. The scene was a picture of complete mayhem. With William and Nicko at his side, he gathered his wits about him. "Help me get Jonathan off Danford," he commanded. The three men lifted Jonathan off Danford. He was dead. Danford was unconscious and still bleeding profusely. William reacting to his master's situation, he addressed Michael. "My Lord, let us leave His Grace directly on this metal bed and carry him out of here. I shall strap him down to keep him from moving." They did as William suggested. It was only after they tried to move him that they realized that Lucia was crouched in the corner. She was covered in blood, dirt, and vomit. Nicko ran to his mistress, "Mistress, where are you hurt?" Lucia was in shock. William who had served time in the military and had assisted the field surgeon knew the symptoms. "She is suffering from shock. Let me see if she is injured." William made a cursory examination and determined she was not hurt, at least physically. He told Nicko to carry her up, while he and Michael would manage Danford. The passage was narrow and they had a difficult time for Danford was a big man.

They made it out of the dungeon, Michael shouted, "Send someone to get the physician. Waste no time, he has lost so much blood" he instructed one of the servants. Those gathered were alarmed by what they were seeing. William and Michael assisted by several house boys carried the young duke to his room. William cut the blood soaked clothes from his body, and barked orders for boiled water, clean rags, leaches, poultices, linen wrappings, honey, and a needle. Servants scattered in every direction to fulfill the list.

When Nicko emerged from the passageway, Sophia, Elizabeth, and Rachel greeted him. The three of them cried out when they saw her; they had not even recovered from seeing Danford and now Lucia. "Where is Jonathan?" asked Rachel. Nicko, too concerned with his mistress, curtly answered "Dead", and walked toward her bedroom. Sophia was running ahead of him, with her was Elizabeth and two kitchen maids. Sophia told them to bring hot water and linen towels. She was weeping loudly. "What happened?" she asked Nicko in Italian. "I don't know, we went down there and found Lord Jonathan dead, His Grace bleeding to death, and the Mistress just as you see her." Sophia was crying so hysterically that Nicko could not console her, "Sophia, my love, you must clear your head, Lucia needs you." She continued. Nicko grabbed her by the arms and shook her hard then gave her a smart slap on the face. Her eyes bulged as she realized that he had stuck her, he then embraced her with great affection, she was still crying but now it was a soft expression of her love for her Mistress. Nicko was stroking her head that was nestled to his chest, "Cara, don't cry, she is not harmed, she is in shock at what has happened. She needs you and all the love you can give her. I need you to be strong. I count the days until our return to Monteforte, to the day when we can be wed. I love you Sophia."

Sophia was now under control. Nicko's strong, steady voice had calmed her and she knew her Mistress, her friend, needed her care. She took a deep, hesitant breath and pulled away slightly from Nicko. "I love you very much, I will be fine now. I am ashamed for my behavior." "Do not beat yourself, you saw someone you love in pain and it brought you sorrow. It is only important what you do now to help her. Come Cara, I will help you get her to bed, then, I will go get some food and wine for her." "Thank you Nicko. I too dream of our wedding day, and, our wedding night." He smiled and grabbed her ass with both hands and she moaned, but that must wait.

There was much chaos in the castle. Servants running here and there to fulfill assigned orders, family members all caught up in this mire of misery. William, with the aid of one of the male servants, was proficiently cleansing and dressing his master's wounds. He was grateful that they seemed to be more superficial than he had originally assessed. Whenever there is a belly wound, there is a lot of bleeding, and the exertion of trying to fight off his assailant only aggravated the blood loss. He was confident that in a few weeks he would be totally healed and fit. He washed the wounds with distilled vinegar and water, and laid a poultice of smashed roasted garlic and a layer of raw onion. Smearing honey all around the cuts, he then laid strips of linen cloth over the wounds. He sent his assistant to fetch some wine and a bowl of broth.

William, who had been Danford's valet since he was a young boy, loved his master like a son. When he had completed his ministrations, he looked at his handsome face and seeing that all color had drained from it, he began to weep. He swept the hair from his face and drawing a cloth from a bowl of water, gently washed his bloody face. Already the bruising was shades of purple and red, but after a while that would also fade. Danford was naked and William washed his whole body, careful not to wet his bandages. His large, muscular body was now showing signs of bruising but they would heal. What worried William, who knew his master better than any other person could have known him, was the fear that armed with the knowledge that the one woman he so truly loved had killed his brother, would forever hang like an ominous cloud over their relationship. He put the thought out of his head.

Michael was present when the hailstorm occurred within the confines of the dungeon. He also knew that Jonathan had been showing signs of being ill for quite some time, but, he never realized to what extent his younger brother would go to exact his revenge on Danford. One thing was certain; he needed to protect not only his family's reputation, but to insulate Lucia. After all, Jonathan was still the son of the Duke of Northumberland, and, now brother to his successor, the Marchesa Lucia Banfi of Monteforte, Italy, was a foreigner, who had just killed a native son. Michael was thinking quickly, it was only William, the trusted valet, himself and Nicko, Lucia's bodyguard present when this all happened. He would confide in them what their story should be.

Wasting no time, Michael set a plausible story in motion and began by telling it to the gathered household. "There is lurking amongst us a cold blooded killer. He has already killed several people that we have knowledge. This very night, he captured Marchesa Banfi and the Duke, and would most certainly have killed them if not for the valiant efforts of our dear Lord Jonathan. Make no mistake, this man is mad, and will stop at nothing to escape. He goes by the name of Piro. He is from Italy, but he is proficient in both French and English. I have contacted all the surrounding counties and their sheriffs. Go about the grounds and the castle with caution, and for the love of God, bolt the doors and windows. If you encounter this man, do not attempt to capture him, notify William, the Marchesa's bodyguard Nicko or myself. Now, go about your business, in two days we shall be overrun with mourners."

Michael was pleased with his story, and, from what he knew of this Piro, he did not lament over having marked him with the death of his brother. William and Nicko had heard the story and both nodded their approval. He went to his brother's room and sat by the side of his bed. He reached for Danford's hand and he opened his eyes, "Dear

Brother, how do you feel? I see that William has done a remarkable job in patching you together." Danford was weak from the loss of blood but his eyes were alert, "How is Lucia? What happened to Jonathan?" At these questions Michael held his brother's hand tighter, "Lucia is badly bruised, but, will heal without damage. As for our brother" he hesitated "he is dead." Danford closed his eyes but spoke in a mere whisper, "Michael what happened to him? He cursed me and called me a coward for not rescuing the rest of you. Did he not understand that I was but a child in my own right? Is what he said true?"

Now, at this line of questioning, Michael rose, and walked to the other side of the room, he landed at the fireplace and pretending to stoke the fire, waited a few moments before he responded. "He was a troubled boy, who grew to be a troubled man. Sadly, it was not his own doing that drove him mad. Yes, Evelyn was a wicked woman, who tormented all of us, but she centered her deepest hatred on Jonathan. He, we, all hated her and ultimately father, because he knew what was going on but shut his eyes to her abuse." Michael stayed fixed to the mantle, leaning on it for support.

Tears were trickling down Danford's bruised and battered face, "I am so sorry, forgive me, I had no idea what was going on here, of course, at that age what would I have done. What shall we say happened?" At this question, Michael, regaining his usual quick-witted composure, came to his side, "I have concocted a story that this man Piro, a wanted killer, is responsible for Jonathan's death and the attempted murder of both you and Lucia. Since it was only William, Nicko and me as witnesses this story will be taken as truth." Danford who reached out for his brother's hand, "Tell me Michael, who killed Jonathan?" Michael did not hesitate, "It was Lucia. Had she not killed him he would surely have killed the two of you. She saved your life." He closed his eyes tightly but could not stop the tears from marching down his face. He let go of his brother's hand and covered his face, not in shame for his weeping, but to block out the image of Jonathan's face as he tried to kill him. Michael left silently, closing the door behind him.

CHAPTER SIXTEEN

THE WAKE

Wallington Castle

"William, get my finest waistcoat, my father's jewels and help me dress." The valet looked aghast, "Your Grace, you are in no condition to walk about, that dressing will open, and you will begin to bleed like a stuck pig." Danford was weary and lightheaded from the pain and loss of blood, "I must put on a good show for the Lords who will come to pledge themselves to me. I cannot receive these men in my nightshirt like a crying newborn." William knew that his master had a very valid point "Well, in that case, shall we set up court in the library, and you can sit in your father's very well worn comfortable chair and the writing table will serve as a barrier between you and your lords." Danford had to admit it was a very plausible plan, "Once again my dear and faithful friend, you have demonstrated your wisdom. I think it shall work marvelously. William I am anxious to see Marchesa Banfi, would you ask her to join me for a light supper here in my rooms." "Of course Your Grace, I saw her this morning walking the gardens." William was about to leave, then suddenly stopped and turned to his master, "Your Grace, I would not mention her present appearance, woman can be mightily sensitive of their looks." Danford smiled, "A point well taken, I shall bear it in mind. Is she that damaged?" "She has lots of colorful patches about the face neck and arms. All of which will heal in a few weeks." Danford, closed his eyes and shook his head, William left quietly, closing the door after himself.

Mourners came from all across Great Britain to pay homage to the late Duke of Northumberland whose reputation, as a brave military man and just lord of this vast territory were famous. To their shock, not only was the Duke and Duchess laid for waking, but their youngest son Lord Jonathan Baynan Stevens was reposing as well. All three caskets lined up in the grand ballroom. The servants had bales of pine boughs formed into swags and wreaths to mask the odor of decaying flesh. When asked as to the nature of what happed, people were simply told that upon receiving the news that her beloved husband had died the Duchess' heart was so broken she also died. As to the death of Lord Jonathan, the story of the mad intruder had already been posted and circulated, which gave a foundation to why the new Duke was unable to attend services due to the injuries he sustained in combating the killer. There was no issue as to the validity of the circumstances. Bulletins with a good likeness and details of his crime had been posted throughout the territory.

Each Lord that came under the rule of the Duke of Northumberland sought an audience with their new liege to pledge their fealty to his reign. Danford, still weak, but aware of his duty, received each Lord in his library. It was paramount that he demonstrated his strength and ability to lead. One by one, they waited their turn to speak with the new Duke, each bringing an offering of their best crop, sheep, cows, and one even offered the pick of one of his six daughters. A robust older man, with a long, plaited beard, dressed in the tartan of his clan, more Scot than English, but an old friend of his father, Lord Slatterly leaned in close, "A fine looking man such as yourself should be fixing for a wife for making babies. I got just the pick of the litter for you, My Grace, strong, healthy women folk, with big tits for nursing and round arses for keeping a man satisfied. You say the word and I'll bring all six around for your picking." Danford was amused at the offer and a stark image of Lord Slatterly in a dressing gown flashed before his eyes, the bile came to his throat, "You are much too kind Lord Slatterly, I shall give your generous offer serious thought. For now, however, I must concentrate my thoughts on learning the office to which I have been born. Sadly, for now I must put aside my own desires." The old man came around and gave Danford a crushing bear hug that sent arrows of pain throughout his body. He shuddered from the pain. "Don't deprive yourself too long. A man must get laid every day to keep his mind and body strong. Look at me, I am fifty and two and still strong as a bull. I keep a wife and two servant girls very happy." He laughed so heartily that despite his pain even Danford laughed.

A steady parade of lords from the vast territory that Danford would now command came to pay their respects to the new duke. Finally, William, himself exhausted from all the extra duties, came to assist his master to his bed. "Is it done? Can I now rest, at least for today?" William took his very large master and half walked, half carried the now pale duke to his bed. "Thank the Lord Jesus; they had finally retreated to the dining hall. My Grace, there are bodies everywhere. I will get you settled then bring you a tray for supper. I am sorry to say, but, you are looking rather dreadful." Danford, pale and in pain, did not argue the point with his valet, "William, where is Marchesa Banfi? Can she spare some time to see me?" William who was diligently assisting his master in getting ready for bed replied, "Marchesa Banfi has been working all day, overseeing the staff, and doing a fine job of it, if I might add." "Do you think she will come see me?" William looked him straight in the eye and said, "I think our beautiful young Mistress would be very pleased to come see you. She had been concerned that you were overtaxing yourself." Danford smiled, pleased at the thought that Lucia was concerned for his wellbeing. He was exhausted, and in pain, both physically and mentally. He could not stop thinking of the confrontation with his brother Jonathan. Every time he closed his eyes, the wild, savage eyes of his brother reached into his soul. Danford now feverish from all the exertion of the day, felt as if he would pass out. His skin was damp and his pallor was grey. His body started to shake from the chill.

William saw that his master was feeling the pressure of having to perform all day; keeping up the pretense that all was well and so he suggested "Perhaps My Grace would take this evening to rest. I could ask the Marchesa to stop by after she has her supper. I am concerned that you are with fever." Danford had to admit that he was not up to entertaining anyone, "That may be a reasonable solution. Please ask Mistress Lucia to come to me when she has had her supper. William I will have just a light meal." The valet took his leave and went to prepare his master's food. He came back in a short while and assisted Danford with his meal. "Shall I go and get the Marchesa now My Grace?" Danford was weak but wanted to see Lucia and to thank her for all she had done. "Yes William, but please tell her I am feeling ill and need to rest." William bowed and left.

Danford was starting to doze when he heard a soft knocking at his bedchamber door. "Come" he managed to say with a strained voice. Lucia entered the room, which was dimly lit, "Danford, I was told that you are with fever. Here let me see." Lucia bent down and placed her lips upon his forehead; he was burning. "Oh you poor thing you are burning up, I shall get some healing tea and cold rag for her head.

If your fever does not break by the morning I shall send for the doctor." There was no point in arguing with her; beside he was much too weak to fight.

Lucia went running down the hall calling for William, the tears streaming down her face. She finally caught up with the valet, "William His Grace is burning with fever. I want the cook to steep a pot of boiling water with Yarrow. I also want a bowl of distilled cider vinegar, and clean, dry rags, all as quickly as possible. When you have everything ready bring them to His Grace's bedchamber." The valet, who was by now very tired, just nodded, and scurried about to fulfill her orders.

Lucia had been on her feet working all day. She was tired and in pain from the beating she had sustained while trying to fight off Jonathan, yet, she knew that such a high fever could be deadly and so she pushed herself harder. William, accompanied by a kitchen lad, laid the iron pot to the hearth that was burning while the boy brought over the small bundle of rags and jug of cider vinegar to his master's bed. The boy, a scrawny little lad, with huge brown eyes and the beginnings of a handsome face, stood wide-eyed at the appearance of his master. Lucia caught the subtle gasp the boy let out upon seeing the present state of the big man. He was plainly scared at the sight of him. There was much concern circulating around the castle. First, there was the death of the Duke, which even though expected was shocking; then the mysterious and unexplained passing of the Duchess; and to complete the macabre events of the past week, the brutal mayhem in the dungeon resulting in the death of Jonathan. Sophia, who was superstitious by her nature, had told Lucia that all the servants now believed that there was a curse on the castle and all those who were within. Lucia's reverie was rudely broken by the sharp voice of William. "Ian, that will be all, I'll call if I should need your services." The boy, his eyes still fixed on Danford, bowed and walked trancelike out of the room.

Lucia placed the rags in a bowl and poured the vinegar over them. Wringing them out, she tied one around each wrist. William was watching but said nothing. "William, pull back the bedclothes." William looked horrified and spoke in a whisper, "Marchesa, the master is not fully dressed shall I ask you to turn around? Everyone will be talking that you are in His Grace's bedchamber." Lucia was too tired to worry about her reputation, "No. We do not have much time; he will become deathly ill if we do not get his fever down soon. Do as I say. Just help me; I shall worry about my honor tomorrow when his fever is broken." The valet gave a tired but satisfied smile and replied, "Tell me what to do Mistress."

They rolled back the bedclothes and Lucia tied a soaked rag around each of his ankles. "Pour the steeped mixture into a cup and we must make him drink it. Even if he protests he must take it down." William poured the liquid into a cup. Lucia by now was changing out the rags on his wrists. "Help me plump up his pillows so he can drink." Danford was in either a deep sleep, or, unconscious. Lucia was not sure. "William you take one side, I shall take the other, and together we will lift him into a sitting position." They struggled to get the big man to where Lucia wanted him, but finally managed to have him propped up. Danford was stirring and moaning.

While the herb mixture was cooling, Lucia was wiping his head and face with the cold cider vinegar. William never left her side. "William let us try to get him to drink." Lucia came to him and was patting his cheek, "Danford I need you to get up; you must drink this elixir you are burning with the fever. Please my Darling, you must try." Lucia was now crying and pleading with the young duke to wake up. William now stepped up "Master Danford, get up, you must drink." The valet took his master by his massive shoulders and shook him hard. Danford groaned but opened one eye. When he saw that Lucia was there he tried to rouse himself, but the fever had sucked all his strength.

"Danford, my love, please you must drink." He gave a weak nod, and she placed the cup to his lips." William offered his help, "Let me do it. I would get him to take his castor oil when he was a small boy, I am sure I can get him to drink this." Sure enough, William got the cup into his master. In the meantime, Lucia was busy changing out the soaked rags that were bound to his ankles and wrists. After he drank, they set him back down so he could sleep.

"William, go get some rest, I shall stay with His Grace. Come for me in the morning, but first go tell my maid Sophia where I am." The valet began to protest, "Marchesa, this is my duty to stay with my master, you need to get some rest. I am most concerned for your well-being." Lucia was barely able to speak she was so exhausted, "I wish to be with him and take care of him. Please do as I have instructed. Thank you William for your concern, for His Grace, and for me, but I must stay and care for him. If I need you, I will call. You must get some rest; tomorrow will be another long day." The valet knew she was right and was grateful that she would tend to his master. "I shall take a blanket and sleep right outside the door." "That will be fine but first you must find Sophia before she alerts the entire castle that I am missing." They wearily smiled, each sharing in the other's misery.

Danford slept restlessly throughout the night and Lucia kept her vigil, changing the vinegar soaked rags, and mopping his face. She was at the point of collapse and dozing lightly between ministrations. "Lucia." Her name drifted through the air on a whisper. She thought she was dreaming. It came once again and she opened her eyes Danford was looking at her. Lucia got to her feet and bent over him to press her lips to his forehead, he felt cool to the touch. "Cara madre di Dio, la febbre ha rotto. I Santi essere lodato." She was speaking in Italian so rapidly that Danford had trouble keeping up with her. He smiled "Yes I shall thank God and the Saints, but, it is because of you that I am feeling better." Lucia, pushed beyond her limits, was so overcome with emotion she started to weep. "Lucia, my Darling, why are you weeping?" She could barely control herself, her chest heaving with relief. "Come to me" he said in a hoarse voice. She knelt down by his bedside and he stroked her silken mane of wild curls. "I love you. You have saved my life now for the third time. How can I ever repay you?" They suddenly realized that life had changed for the both of them, and they wept together.

BOOK THREE

CHAPTER ONE

THE MANHUNT BEGINS

England

Piro knew it would be just a matter of time before he was captured for the murder of the Marquis Henri de Fauntil. Henri had been a member of the ruling aristocracy and a distant cousin to the King. At every turn, he saw bulletins calling for his capture and execution. A handsome reward was also mentioned. Piro was now a wanted man with a price on his head. It would not be much longer. He was half crazed out of his mind with nowhere to go and no one to turn to for help. By now, his beard was long and uncut and his clothes were tattered; he needed to find a place to hide, some food and money, but where could he go. Fear of someone recognizing him and calling the authorities was more than he could manage.

It was three days since he had been to Henri's house. He kept revisiting the scene in his head, and every time he wept. Piro had loved the old man who had been kind and fatherly. He had not meant to kill him; he only wanted answers. He only wanted to know where Lucia had gone. She had destroyed his life, yet, he could not erase her memory from his heart. He would find her and explain before it was too late. Piro was resigned to the fact that he would die for his crimes against the Marchesa Lucia Banfi and for his murder of the Marquis de Fauntil, two people who had tried to help him but failed.

Sitting in the dark shadows, consumed with fear and guilt, Piro dreamt of the earlier years back at Monteforte. After the death of his parents, Gandolfo took the responsibility of raising him. He was stern and held no tolerance for disobedience, but he was fair and taught him everything he knew of training and caring for horses. He saw the old man weep the day he flogged him nearly to death. The same day that Gandolfo knew that it would have to be Piro to go in search of his missing Mistress Lucia. That day changed his life forever; he became a man.

Oh the pain and sorrow upon finding his beautiful mistress, that perfect body so abused; that flawless face so damaged. Piro wept more for himself than for her; he almost thought that if she had been truly damaged, and the animal who attacked her had taken her womanhood, he, the one who loved her unconditionally, would have a chance. When he found out days later that, her wounds were superficial and her virginity was unblemished; his heart was broken and his dream shattered.

When Mistress Sucretti called him to the castle he knew that something would happen, what that was he was unsure. The Mistress spoke kindly, her eyes were soft and wise, and he was actually shocked at her beauty, for he had never been so close to her in all his life spent at Monteforte. "Piro, I have heard many good things about you. Master of the Horse Gandolfo has spoken highly of your abilities and your intelligence. I know that you have been hurt, and I know why. I shall share with you a story that happened just about when I was your age. I fell in love with a man who was not of my station. My parents had signed the marriage contract the day I was born pledging me to Master Sucretti. Neither he, nor I, had any say in the matter. Yet, my heart belonged to another. Not to disgrace my family, I obeyed my father and married my chosen husband. I lived everyday with the pain of a broken heart for the man I truly loved, but there was no hope for it. Soon, I realized that to want what I could not have would soon destroy not only me, but also the man I loved. Do you understand what I am trying to tell you?"

Piro remembered the look on her face, he could see the pain in her eyes, he said, "I do understand my Mistress and I am sorry for the both of us." With that, she reached for his hands and held them strong in her own. "I shall not torment you and leave you to languish here with dreams and desires that cannot be fulfilled. I have arranged to have you sent to a dear friend of mine in France. He is a wonderful and very powerful man. I have instructed him that you are to be groomed in the ways of a gentleman. He will send you to be educated at one of the finest institutions in Europe. I ask only one thing from you." The Mistress Sucretti, with fire in her eyes said "On your honor you must pledge to me that you will never dishonor my niece Mistress Lucia; and that you will put your mind to your studies and become an honorable man." The young groom put his head down and fell to his knees at the feet of his Mistress "I will pledge on my life never to dishonor you or Mistress Lucia. I am moved beyond all words for this generous opportunity. Someday I will repay your kindness."

Mistress Sucretti drew the boy off his knees and stood herself. She was still tall and their eyes met, "You will leave in the morning. All has been arranged for your journey. Go now and say your farewells. Make sure you say farewell to Mistress Lucia I am sure she is waiting for you. Here is a purse and a letter of introduction. You will be under the apprenticeship of the Marquis Henri de Fauntil. Gandolfo has all your instructions. God bless and protect you Piro. Become a good and trustworthy man."

When she had finished speaking, she pressed a heavy purse into his hand along with a letter written in a beautiful hand on the finest paper. She did not say another word and he knew he was dismissed. She turned suddenly, took his face in her hands, and kissed both cheeks "I am sorry for I understand your agony. Be strong of heart and spirit and keep your mind to your work. Time and distance will help you heal." She turned and walked out of the room. Piro stood there with tears marching down his handsome face; he knew he would never see Monteforte ever again.

Just as he was about to leave the castle he spied Lucia sitting in the garden reading a book. He did not make a move to go to her; he remained hidden by the bushes, and gazed upon her beautiful form. She sat tall and straight, her wild strawberry curls cascading over her shoulders. It was the hour when the sun was crimson and it cast long shadows. The golden rays of the last beams of sunlight caught the peach in her cheeks. She sat there so serene and lovely; so natural and unaware of her own beauty. His knees grew weak; his mind drifted to the night he had seen her naked and the blood rushed to his groin. He would miss her so much; yet he knew he could not stay, the temptation to have her as his own was so overwhelming he could not think of anything but her. His hand found his swollen cock and he undid his laces; he could not stand the pain any longer and after a few strokes found his release. Piro felt guilty for lusting after his Mistress but there was no hope for it. He waited until his mind once again controlled his body and straightened himself to present himself to her.

It was nearly dusk, a warm breeze was coming off the sea, and it playfully caught the errant curls that had escaped her combs. Piro, not wanting to startle her, walked around to the front of where she sat. She heard his approach and immediately closed her book and laid it aside. "Good evening Mistress Lucia, I am sorry if I have disturbed your reading. I wanted to say goodbye, I am leaving by first light." Lucia was well aware of his departure and saddened by the thought of it. "Yes Piro I know. I shall miss you. Please know that your dismissal from Monteforte is not a punishment, but a reward. If you had not come in search of me, I would surely be dead. You put aside your own suffering to help me. We can no longer be here together; you know that better than I do. I am sorry for all that has happened to the both of us." She stopped talking and waited. Piro fell to his knees at her feet and spoke in a desperately hushed voice "Mistress I would lay down my life for you, but you are right we can no longer exist here together it would be certain death for me; I cannot continue to pretend that I am not in love with you. My desires are so strong I fear them myself. Thank you for this chance to better myself. Someday I shall return to Monteforte a rich man, and then perhaps you will consider me worthy of your love." Lucia could hardly contain herself, "Piro I do love you and that is why you must leave. It is not that you are not worthy, it is not our time. We must both make this sacrifice. I wish you all good things." He got off his knees and stood before her, his hand reaching for hers. Lucia took his proffered hand and stood. Piro held her close and kissed her mouth so gently it was as if a feather had brushed her lips. He kept her in a tight embrace and kissed her again with more passion. She kissed him back. He disengaged himself from her, turned, and left, the tears imprinting both their beautiful young faces with the stain of unrequited love forever marking their hearts.

Piro made his way back to his pallet in the open room he shared with all the unmarried stable servants. They were all waiting for his return, "Ah Piro there you are. We were able to get Maria to get a skin of good wine, some roasted pork and some cheese. Let us have a farewell celebration for you." He was touched by their efforts to make his last night memorable. They drank, ate, and shared memories, hopes, and laughter. There was not one among them that did not envy the gift Piro had been given.

Morning would not come soon enough as he lay on his pallet with thoughts of the soft tender lips of the woman of his desires. Finally, sleep came with dreams of Lucia.

Gandolfo had woken him early on the day of his departure from Monteforte. Gandolfo had taught him all that he knew; the man who had been like a father to him since the death of his parents, he waited for him to get ready. When Piro was finished they stood there, the familiar scent of the stables like perfume to his nose, the old man gathered him in his still powerful arms, "Piro, my boy, you will come to realize this is the greatest opportunity you will ever receive. It is a gift beyond all imagining; use it well.

The Marquis de Fauntil is a good man and he will help you become a great man. Listen to him and make me proud. God bless you." He kissed the young man who was no longer a boy, their tears mingled together and then Piro left.

He remembered with longing the day he arrived at the magnificent estate of the famous Marquis de Fauntil. It was massive but in a different style from Monteforte. The color was a soft rose color and beautiful potted trees and plants surrounded it. At first it took Piro a moment to figure out what was different, and then it struck him, the castle presented itself on flat ground. Making it appear longer than taller. When his carriage pulled up to the front entrance there was no one to greet him and a cloud of anxiety fell upon him. He thought to himself, "what if the Marquis changed him mind?" as a wave of panic engulfed him; the door suddenly opened and standing there was the Marquis de Fauntil. "Come, come here, welcome to your new home." The handsome older man, so elegant in his finely tailored waistcoat, embraced the shocked servant with warmth. "Now that you are here we must make you look the part of a young man who has a promising future."

Piro knew it had been the Marchesa Maria Sucretti that had sent him to Henri, but to his credit, the Marquis never let him feel like he was a servant. After a short while, under the direct supervision of the Marquis, Piro was molded into a man of fine tastes. With the introduction by Henri, who always told people that he was his protégé, Piro had made many important connections. Now, thinking back, Henri encouraged him to start the boatyard and make contacts with so many of Paris' high society. Money, influence, and a position of great importance had given the former servant the bravado to start believing he was truly one of them.

With custom tailored waistcoats and shirts of the finest linen the handsome young man quickly became the talk of Parisian society. His long, lean frame and rugged good looks soon led to invitations to balls and galas. Accompanied by the Marquis de Fauntil the striking Italian was much sought after by many of the upper echelon French ladies. Piro was having the time of his life pretending to be a well-bred young aristocrat. It was always a subject of shocked astonishment when an amorous woman discovered his silver streaked back. The red angry ribbons of mutilated flesh had turned a silver color. He had invented a story that a warlord had captured him and nearly tortured to death, only to have escaped by his wits. It did not take too long before that story was circulated among the young and eligible daughters of the wealthy. Piro became a topic of discussion.

Scared, hungry and ill, Piro, escaped to the waterfront. He made his bed along the docks. He wept with great anguish for his betrayal of all those who loved and cared for him. He brought dishonor to himself, the memory of his dear parents and the

Mistresses Sucretti and Lucia. He killed a man whose only crime had been to give him the chance at making something of himself. He thought, "If I were not such a coward I would kill myself and sentence my evil soul to Hell." Piro agonized about turning himself in to the authorities, but, again, he was too much of a coward to face his punishment. He hid during the day and roamed the back streets of Paris at night searching for scraps of discarded food. He was living the life of a criminal. He was better off when he was a servant at Monteforte. One night he had to fight a stray dog for the few scraps of spoiled food he found. Despair was poisoning his mind and eating away at his once toned and muscular body. He reeked of putrid odor and longed for a bath.

His present appearance would not call too much attention; there were many wretches who made the docks their home, he blended in with all the waste of society. On the morning of the fifteenth day after the murder of the Marquis de Fauntil, Piro found himself signing up as a ship's mate aboard one of the many vessels that were making voyages to America. He thought that if he did not get shipwrecked, drowned, or died from the pox he might have a chance at a new life in this foreign country. He was standing in front of a large cargo vessel whose flags bore the registry of the Crown of England.

"Do you know anything of ships?" asked the man who was standing at the gangway of the ship. His harsh toned voice was English to be sure, but his

French was serviceable. The man was powerfully built, with bulging muscles, and inked drawings that crawled up each arm. He was squat with thick legs and a waxed mustache. Had he not been so desperate Piro would have ran from the man whose eyes were black as coal. "Well boy, are you deaf or daft, which is it?" The man now had Piro by the shirt and the spittle was in his face, "I am neither. No, I have no sailing experience, but I am smart and can read charts and I have a good mind for numbers." "Ah, so you think you are smart, well we'll see about that. You can read charts; well that is something of worth. By the looks of you I would guess that you are in some kind of trouble." Piro was shocked at the perception of this man who looked like his mind was as thick as his body. "Why do you make such a statement?" he stammered. Piro was instantly nervous that this man would take him to the authorities; after all, there was a generous reward for his capture. "Don't be shitting in your breeches. I have been a ship's mate my whole life. There are two kinds of men who seek the sea; those who are running from the world and those who wish to discover the world. Which are you?" Piro was not sure how to answer, "I wish to discover a new life," he answered honestly. "Well mate, sign up, we leave tonight" the sailor reached in his purse and threw Piro two coins, "Mate go get a bath and some clean clothes, maybe a good meal, be back early, we leave at high tide. Go, be on with you." Piro was practically running to the bathhouse when he heard the raspy voice call after him "Ah, what is your Christian name?" Piro had not thought to contrive a name but quickly recovered himself "Robere Blanchard". Piro used the name of Henri's head of house, which was Renee Blanchard. There came a roar of laughter from the brash sailor, "Ah, and I'm Henry the King of England. Well, so be it, Monsieur Robere Blanchard. Be back before the tide or I'll come looking for you."

CHAPTER TWO

HEARTBREAKING NEWS

Monteforte

Lucia's letter had arrived a month after the death of Maria Sucretti's oldest and dearest friend, the Marquis de Fauntil. It was a long letter filled with sorrow for the loss of this most beloved man. The contents of which chronicled the events leading to his murder and the identity of his killer. It was with such a heavy heart that Lucia set forth the details of her present condition.

***

It was with great anticipation that Giorgio brought news from Mistress Lucia to her aunt and uncle. So fond was he of his young mistress Giorgio asked Maria Sucretti if he might be privy to the contents of the letter, which he knew just from the weight of it was quite lengthy. Both Maria and Giovanni were seated in the solar enjoying a late afternoon glass of cognac. They were relaxed and jovial "Mistress may I too learn of our Dear Mistress Lucia's progress." Maria who loved Giorgio and knew he had knowledge of all their intimate business replied, "Of course you may, please join us, and take a glass for yourself." Giorgio bowed gratefully "No thank you Mistress, I have much work to complete, I am happy just to hear how she is doing." He seated himself opposite of where they were and the three of them were anxiously anticipating news from Lucia.

Maria held the heavy letter in her hand and commented, "There is much to tell from the weight of this letter. Lucia was always a great storyteller. Let us see what she has to say." She opened the letter with joy and began reading aloud. Maria's voice was light and cheerful and then instantly changed. Giovanni and Giorgio looked at her and then to each other. Giovanni knew something was terribly wrong, "Cara read the letter to us. If something has happened we must know." Maria choked down her tears and cleared her voice, which was filled with anguish.

Dear Zia and Zio:

My dearest family I have missed you so very much these many months that I have been gone from Monteforte. I so truly wanted to be home for the birth of my new nephew. I trust that Antoinetta and Baby Tomaso are well.

So many things, good, and bad have happened while I was away. The good things I shall reserve to share with you upon my arrival home. I have grown in many ways in this short time and have learned many things about myself and those in whom I have laid my trust.

When I came to France to see firsthand the progress of the shipbuilding venture that I had embarked upon with the aid of our friend Henri DeFauntil I was shocked to find the transformation of Piro. He had become a hardened tyrant, but I was hard pressed to let him go. That is when all the trouble started. It is also when I met the Fifth Duke of Northumberland Danford Stevens, in whose company I am presently a guest.

After his dismissal, Piro became enraged at me and tried to capture and kill me. Lord Stevens rescued me and Piro escaped in the process. It was determined for my safety, since Genaro and Mateo, had just left, that I would journey back to England with Lord Stevens. I agreed.

Piro wanted to find me to beg for mercy, to apologize for his mental state of mind. He came in search of me at Henri's apartments in Paris. It was too late; I had already left for England.

It is with the deepest heart that I must write to let you know that our dear friend Henri DeFauntil was murdered. The more worse for this fact is that Piro killed him. Henri bravely fought him to hide my whereabouts and it cost him his life. I cannot express the pain that hangs so heavy in my heart for the loss of this most wonderful man and surely, I know you share that pain. I am so sorry dear ones. My heart is also wounded for Piro, who has yet to be captured.

So much has happened since my brothers left France and I so wish they had been here with me, for I long for the companionship of my beloved family. As you know, I am presently staying with the Duke of Northumberland, His Grace Danford Stevens. The tragedy that has surrounded this magnificent place cannot even be described. Upon our arrival we suffered, the death of the Fourth Duke of Northumberland the father of Danford; which, while anticipated due to his poor health was still a blow. However, that same day his wife, Lady Evelyn died; no more than two days later his brother Jonathan died. All three laid in state for hundreds of mourners.

Lord Stevens was injured severely and I have been caring for him. Upon his recovery, he will escort me back home. I am so anxious to lay my eyes upon all of you and hold my infant nephew in my arms. I will send word when we can make the journey.

Do not fear for me, I am safe. Please keep Danford and me in your prayers.

With all my love,

Lucia

Maria Sucretti was inconsolable at the news that Henri de Fauntil was dead. Giovanni held her tightly in the hopes of bringing her comfort. "Why would Piro commit such a terrible act; Henri was so kind and had written often of the boy's progress. He was so fond of him." Her tears quickly turned to deep wounded sobs that racked her with pain.

Giorgio visibly shaken by the news, contained in Lucia's letter. He had known the Marquis de Fauntil all his life for he was a frequent guest of Mistress Sucretti. He also held great feelings for Piro, whose father had been a trusted and loved servant, along with his wife. His worse thoughts gathered around him as to the telling of these events to Gandolfo who loved this boy, now a man, as his own son. The news will destroy the old man.

His thoughts were broken by the calling of his name, "Giorgio, do not discuss any of this with the staff, especially Gandolfo, at least until we know for sure the outcome of these tragic events." Giorgio nodded "I agree with you. Poor Gandolfo will be destroyed. Every time he received a letter from the boy, he would beam with the pride of a loving father. I can only wonder what happened to Piro. I remember him as a child growing up here under the care of Gandolfo and all the elder servants of Monteforte, into a good young man." His voice was choked at the thought of breaking the news to his old friend.

It was now Giovanni who spoke his own thoughts, "I am truly sorry for the death of such a fine man. While I only knew him for a short time, I sensed he was of the highest character. Cara, I am sorry for your sorrow. On the matter of our Lucia, and from the tone of her letter, it sounds like our dear girl has fallen for this Lord Stevens. She gave him a title; what is he? Lucia called him *The Fifth Duke of Northumberland,* which sounds most impressive. I suspect that our little dove is in love; why else would she go off to England? She should have come home if safety was her primary concern."

Maria regaining her sense of composure, but was still very upset. Giorgio had never seen his Mistress in such a state of emotional upheaval. Thinking about what Giovanni had said she now added her thoughts "I would have to agree with you about Lucia and her new Duke. While I would wish to be happy for her, my fear that Piro will find her overshadows all my joy. I must tell you that I had truly misjudged that young man; and for that tragic mistake, he has killed one of the two men I have loved in my life. Henri was a man so pure of heart that I loved him from the day we met. My only consolation is that he is finally with his beloved wife Auriella. Henri loved her so much and was heartbroken upon her death. May Jesus let them both find their eternal peace."

Both Giorgio and Giovanni were taken aback by the candor with which Maria was speaking. Giovanni had to fight a pang of jealousy for the late Henri, but, quickly shrugged it off for he too had been previously in love; and felt the stab of pain for his beloved Natalie and daughter Rosalie. Giovanni had never really recovered from their deaths even though it was so many years ago. Maria and Giovanni loved each other very much but did hold others also in their hearts.

Giovanni announced, "I shall send word to Genaro and Mateo perhaps they could meet Lucia in France and accompany her and her Duke home. What do you think Cara?" For the first time Maria's face softened "Yes, I think that is a wonderful idea."

Giorgio now joined the conversation "My Lord as soon as you write the letter I shall have one of the stable boys make haste to deliver it. In the meantime may I excuse myself there are many duties still left undone." Before he left Giorgio came to his Mistress' side, knelt down, and kissed her hands, "Mistress, I too am grieving for the loss of Marquis de Fauntil. He was always so kind and generous to the staff and me. Please know that his memory will be long held in my heart." "Thank you Giorgio. Yes, Henri was a special man and I shall miss him." With that said Giorgio stood, bowed deeply to his Mistress, and quietly left the room.

Giovanni came to Maria and embraced her with great love and passion. "I did not mean to expose my deep feelings. I hope I did not offend you?" Giovanni stroked her thick auburn tresses, "I too have loved another, yet, it is in your arms that I have found my soul." They kissed. "Giovanni, make love to me." He did not utter a sound but scooped her up into his arms and carried her to their room where they eased their sorrows through the act of lovemaking.

***

The next morning Giovanni sat down to compose a letter to Mateo. He knew that Genaro was in Rome working for the Holy Father. He was hoping that they would be able to leave and join up with Lucia. He sat to gather his thoughts and compose his letter.

Dear Nephew,

Zia Maria and I have received word from your sister Lucia that our dear friend Henri DeFauntil was murdered at the hands of Piro. Having escaped he is on the loose. Fearing for Lucia's life, Lord Stevens, with whom I believe you are familiar, has taken Lucia to England. Misfortune has followed them, for while there, the Duke and his wife, as well as a son, have all died. Lucia must wait the appropriate mourning period before she and Lord Stevens will be able to leave.

I am writing to ask if you and Genaro can spare some time to meet Lucia in France and accompany her and Lord Stevens back to Monteforte. Zia Maria and I are fearful that Piro, who is still free, will find her and kill her. Send word to us of your answer.

Zio Giovanni

Giovanni having completed his letter called for Giorgio. "Please send this as quickly as we can. I am not sure where Lucia is and with every passing day, I fear for her life. Make sure that whoever you dispatch comes back with an answer." Giorgio took the letter and replied, "Do not worry Master Giovanni I shall send the best stable boy we have and impress upon him the urgency of this letter." Before he left Giovanni withdrew his purse and dug out several coins. "Giorgio, give this to the boy, he will need food and lodging, and there may be a little left for himself." The maître de casa smiled broadly, "That is always a good carrot for the mule." They shared a knowing chuckle.

CHAPTER THREE

BROTHERS TO THE RESCUE

Milan

Mateo was keeping himself very busy with his business. His thoughts always going to Genaro, he missed him a great deal. This was the first time since they had been together that they had been separated. Mateo enjoyed for the first time in his life the feeling of being surrounded by a loving family. His beloved mother had always professed her love for him but he was always alone. He was roaming the beautiful villa he kept, the one in which he lived as a child with his mother, and absently was drawn to the window which faced the church yard where his mother had been laid to rest. The void that her death had brought him was now eased by the love he held for Genaro and his beloved Lucia.

A soft knock came to the door, "Come" he replied. "Lord Rizzo, a messenger has arrived and was instructed to wait for your reply." Mateo was instantly intrigued as to who would be sending a message of such importance that an immediate reply was requested. "Thank you. I will ring for you when I have read the letter. Give the messenger something to eat and drink." His servant bowed deeply and left without a sound.

The handwriting was unfamiliar to him but he knew it was from Monteforte by the distinctive seal. Mateo sat down at his writing desk and broke the wax seal. The letter was from Giovanni Romano. The first thing that caught his eye was how the letter was addressed "Dear Nephew" it was so foreign to him to be part of a family. He savored the feeling of belonging.

As he read, the rest of the letter brought him sorrow and fear. He had met Piro briefly and knew that there was something wrong with the young man. He could see the face of the young man and knew something of his history, and, his association with the Marquis. It was Piro's eyes; they were very troubled. Mateo would never forget their first encounter; Piro nearly beat that poor boy to death. Then his attack on Lucia; and out of spite and revenge he set the shipyard on fire and nearly killed Danford in the process. What manner of evil lurked in Piro's head? He had to be stopped before he killed Lucia.

The memory of the gracious hospitality of the Marquis Henri de Fauntil, and to think that this wonderful man was brutally murdered at the hands of the boy he had made into a man, saddened him. He was angry and hurt. Henri was an old and trusted friend and business associate of the Rizzo family.

Henri loved Lucia and would have done anything for her; even give up his life.

It only took Mateo a few moments to make up his mind that even if Genaro were unable to leave his work in Rome, he would go in search of Lucia and bring her home. He withdrew his finest vellum paper from the drawer and began inscribing a letter to Giovanni Romano.

Dear Zio Giovanni,

By the time this letter is in your hand, I will have already embarked on my journey to meet up with Genaro. Rest assured that we shall find Lucia and bring her safely home to Monteforte. Please convey my deepest sorrow to Zia Maria on the loss of her old friend. The Marquis, while I did not know him for long, I know he was a good and honorable man; all shall miss him. On my honor, I shall avenge his death and safeguard my beloved sister Lucia.

Your nephew,

Mateo Rizzo

Mateo rang for his servant "I am ready to give my reply to the messenger. Have you given him food and drink?" The servant replied, "Yes my Lord." "Good. Now send him in to me." The servant said nothing further but turned on his heels and retreated from the room. In a few moments a young man appeared before him, "I want you to return to Monteforte as quickly as you can. This is a most urgent message. I am giving you this purse. If you get there by sunset within four days, I will double its contents when next I see you." The boy's eyes were wide with amazement, "Yes my Lord. I shall do exactly as you have commanded. I shall ride like the wind until I reach Monteforte." Mateo was pleased. "To show you how pleased I am I shall give you half of that reward now." The servant stood there with his mouth open. "Now that you have rested, drank, and eaten, be on your way, your Master awaits my answer." He bowed deeply and then suddenly turned to face Mateo, "My Lord, thank you, I shall not disappoint you."

As soon as the messenger left, Mateo was already putting his affairs in order. He rang for his valet, Armando, a trusted maître de casa who had been with Mateo for more than twenty years. "I shall be away for an extended period of time. I shall need you to make sure that any important news of my business reaches me in a timely fashion. As always, you know where the cask with the household money is hidden. Use it as you need. Make sure all the servants are well cared for and that we are always stocked with food and wine. I don't know for how long I will be away but upon my unexpected return I wish to find everything as I have left it." Armando, an older man replied, "Of course My Lord, it shall be just as you say. When will you leave?" "I want you to make ready my departure for first light." "Yes My

Lord." Mateo was about to dismiss his trusted servant and then added "Armando, in the event that something should happen, and I fail to return, or you receive notice that I am dead, there are legal documents in the vault in my shop, and duplicates with the avvocato. Lord Genaro Banfi and Marchesa Lucia Banfi are to be notified of my death and given those documents. Is that understood?" The servant nodded, then bowed, and silently left.

The anticipation of seeing Genaro, as well as the anxiety of thinking about Lucia's safety, was so strong that Mateo did not rest through the night. He was up before dawn and ready to leave. It would be several days of traveling, but Mateo was almost thankful for the prospect of being busy and away from the memories of his deceased mother. Now that he held ownership to two villas he would have to come to a decision as to which he would keep. That decision would be made with Genaro.

There was much to see along the roads leading from Milan to Rome and Mateo found that he was enjoying the solitude of making the journey. He would spend the night in an inn on the outskirts of Rome and continue on to the Eternal City first thing in the morning. He found a small inn that appeared to be clean and a room available.

Mateo found himself to be quite hungry and sore from days spent in the saddle. He inquired as to a facility to bathe and told there was a bathhouse a short distance down the road. He wanted to wash the road from himself before he met with Genaro the next morning. After what was a surprisingly savory supper, Mateo made his way to the bathhouse. He paid the sum and made his way in; there were a number of men engaged in lively conversation. Apparently, like with most bathhouses, this was the local gathering place for intellectual discussions.

When he entered, a towel wrapped from his waist, all conversation stopped. He was a stranger, perhaps someone who to be weary. The serving boy was standing next to him waiting to take the towel and offer the basket with soap and a fresh sea sponge. Mateo felt like an intruder and was embarrassed to release the towel. Those gathered continued to stare but resumed their conversation in hushed tones. Mateo took inventory of the others; old men with sagging bellies and tiny, limp, cocks; nothing to spark his libido. "My Lord" said the boy softly, as if prompting Mateo to proceed. Finally, he relinquished the towel and stepped slowly into the tub. He made sure that they spied his well-endowed attributes as he took his time to submerge into the pool. He knew that they were envious, as he was sure that he too would be someday. He turned away from the group, content that he had sparked their gossip, and set his mind to his ministrations.

Mateo was a handsome man, with a finely sculpted body. He had a thick clutch of black hair, which started just below his collarbone and descended to the top of his manhood. His broad unblemished back ended at a narrow waist and high tight ass. His skin was soft and the color of pecans. Truly, Mateo Rizzo was the perfect specimen of the male form. He scrubbed his body with the natural fibers from the sea sponge and paid exceptional attention to his lower extremities. His mind drifted to Genaro and how he could make him come just by the slightest strokes. He kept his lower body submerged in the water and stayed to the farthest end of the pool. He thought that it would have been interesting had Genaro actually been with him. They could have given those old roosters something to crow about. He smiled wickedly to himself. When he felt fully refreshed, he got out, dried himself, dressed and retreated to the inn for a pleasant night's rest.

It was still early the next morning when Mateo left the inn. He decided that he would hold off his morning meal with the hopes that Genaro would share a biscotti and espresso with him. The curia was not far from where he had stayed at the inn. He made his way toward the massive doors, and there greeted by the Papal Guard. Mateo introduced himself as the brother of Genaro Banfi. The one guard left to seek Genaro and inform him of his visitor.

Mateo was left standing in the front vestibule of the Curia. His eyes roaming the opulence of the Palace of the Popes with its stunning frescoes and larger than life size marble statues of various saints, many of which Mateo was sure he had never heard of. The guard returned in a few moments only to inform Mateo that Genaro was at the site of the new cathedral. The guard gave Mateo instructions on how to get there.

It was a pleasant walk from the Curia to the Cathedral of the Bishop of Rome. Mateo was impressed with the grandeur of the structure, which was perfectly balanced; the attention to detail was nothing short of amazing. As he ascended the steps to enter, a feeling of calm came to him. He had been anxious for days since receiving the letter from Giovanni Romano. There were many people in all stages of work around the outside and as he entered the inside of the building.

He immediately noticed the pleasant coolness upon entering. It was very hot and the air was dry outside. He heard elevated voices and directed his attention toward where they were coming. There in the middle of the nave stood a massive scaffold with none other than his beloved Genaro perched on top, Mateo's heart leapt at the sight of him. His thick wavy brown hair was loose and framed his handsome face. His painter's frock stained from the pigments he was mixing. He had streaks of paint smudged across his face. He looked wild, engrossed, and was animatedly speaking to the two young boys that were assisting him. Mateo's mouth suddenly became dry and he had to lick his lips. It had been weeks since they had been together.

Genaro picked up a brush to touch up a small portion of the extensive fresco he was creating. It was magnificent. Mateo thought to himself, "I am a lucky man to have found such a jewel; he is not only handsome and willing, but a great artist as well."

At the bottom, standing just in front of the scaffold, engaged in a heated discussion, was a diminutive priest, and judging from the red color of his robe, a cardinal, who was speaking with a rather tall and elegantly dressed man. The tiny cardinal was flapping his arms and pointing toward the ceiling just above Genaro's head. Mateo hung back to try to hear what they were saying, which was not very difficult since their voices were well carried along by the sheer volume of the space.

"You cannot have that particular fresco placed just above the altar. His Holiness will not permit such a scene. People will be distracted by it." The tall man listening with a grimace on his face, finally answered, "Cardinale Corsi, you are trying to tell me that the Holy Father will not approve this fresco because it will in some way diminish from His presence? That my dear Cardinale is ridiculous." There was a large battered table piled high with sheets of paper, which Mateo, craning his neck and straining his eyes, could see where sketches and drawings. "Cardinale Corsi, see here, we went over all these drawings with your approval. This fresco, which I might add is beautiful, was part of the entire plan for this part of the church. I do not believe that a scene, taken directly from the Holy Bible, will be offensive to The Holy Father." "Yes this is true enough, but those sketches did not reflect the woman Genaro has painted."

The Cardinal was shaking his head from side to side. "It is beautiful and well rendered. Genaro has painted a masterpiece, but it is the subject that I believe will disturb His Holiness. The depiction of the Creation is outstanding; however, the details of Eve are how shall I say, too realistic. She looks as though she is breathing. I ask you, how can His Holiness celebrate Mass with such a scene over his head? What man could keep his mind to the scriptures with that creature hovering overhead?"

The little cardinal's face was as red as the robe he was wearing. "Ah, Alessandro, between you and Genaro, I don't know who will drive me to Hell first. I wash my hands of the whole matter. I have given you fair warning, now, when His Holiness comes down after his midday meal, it will be your undoing." With a flurry of agitation, the tiny red robe scurried out of the cathedral.

Still standing in the back not wanting to disturb the current atmosphere, Mateo continued to observe the drama that was unfolding before him. He heard the voice of the tall man "Genaro, can you spare a few moments and come down?" He could sense the frustration in his lover's face; he threw down his brush, gave a few instructions to his assistants, and started climbing down from the scaffold. Mateo was lusting over the sight of his strong muscular legs and tight ass as he climbed down the rungs.

Now, Mateo finally caught the full impact of what Cardinale Corsi was saying. He looked directly at the depiction of Eve and was shocked at the sight of her. Slowly and with great pleasure, he started to smile. Genaro had rendered the mother of humankind with the face of Lucia. This concept of Eve with her long red tresses flowing in an imaginary breeze, her flawless complexion with just a hint of peach on her high cheeks, her eyes piercing the soul of man; was perfection. Eve with her full breasts and pink nipples, flat belly and soft round hips beckoned every eye to enjoy the pleasures of such a body. Mateo thought that if Lucia were to see this she would be so pleased.

"Genaro, my friend, what have you done? This Eve, if only she were real, I would marry her today. When did you find time to find such a model? I was only gone for a short while and I return to see this breathtaking creature. I must confess that the sight of her fills me with desire. I am afraid that His Holiness may agree with Cardinale Corsi, what man could keep his mind to the scriptures when he is staring at this Enchantress?" Genaro was smiling broadly and did not speak but waited for Alessandro to continue. "Who is this woman?"

Finally, Genaro could not keep his face any longer, "It is my sister Lucia. I painted her from memory, at least the face, I am sure the body is correct in size and proportion. "You have a sister that looks like that?" Alessandro was nearly gasping. "Yes, she is the most beautiful woman I have ever met. She is as kind and intelligent as she is beautiful. Someday I want you to meet her." Just by chance, Genaro caught a movement out of the corner of his eye and turned to see Mateo standing at the back of the church. He stood still to make sure his eyes were not tricking him.

"Mateo" he shouted and the echo reverberated off every wall. Genaro left Alessandro standing there and ran to his lover. They embraced with such love, but was unable to show any more affection than to give each other a manly kiss on each cheek. "It is so wonderful to see you. I did not receive word that you were coming. Is everything well?" Mateo was unsure if he should discuss the issue surrounding Lucia here, in front of a stranger. He decided it would wait until the evening when they were alone. "I missed you," Mateo hissed in his ear. I want you."

Genaro was just about to respond when he heard a polite cough in the background. It was Alessandro, waiting to see who this unexpected stranger was and why Genaro was so excited to see him.

"Come Mateo let me introduce you." They made their way back to where the young architect was standing. It was Genaro who said "Alessandro Galilei may I present my beloved brother Mateo Rizzo." Mateo bowed deeply. "Mateo, Alessandro is the man responsible for creating this splendid Cathedral." Mateo bowed formally to the famous architect "I am familiar with your work Lord Galilei and it is an honor to meet such a brilliant master builder. This is truly a work of art, you must be very proud of it." Mateo was so suave and socially adroit. Genaro was filled with pride, for his lover. Mateo then turned to Genaro "This fresco is the crowning glory of the nave, but, I must confess that I could not help but overhear what the Cardinal was saying. He may be right. This depiction of our baby sister Lucia is too unsettling for the average man. As I look around I see that you have left your imprint everywhere and no finer artist could have graced this magnificent cathedral with such masterpieces." Alessandro smiled and nodded "I have told your brother words to that very sentiment. He is very talented. It will all hinge on His Holiness. I suffer that we must be prepared for his disapproval."

No sooner had they finished speaking when a small entourage entered the church. Flanked on either side by his personal Swiss Guard was the wizened old Pope Clement XII. Straggling behind was Cardinale Corsi and Cardinale Albani. Leading the parade were two young altar boys with trumpets to announce His Holiness' arrival.

All three men fell to their knees at his approach. The Pope, moving slowly came to where they were kneeling and placed a hand upon each of their heads. "Please my sons rise so that I may speak with you." They did as he directed. "Alessandro, Genaro, and I fear I do not know who this young man is?" It was Genaro who bowed formally and replied "Your Holiness this is my brother Mateo, who has come this very day to see me. If you wish he can wait for me outside, if what you need to discuss warrants privacy." The old man, whose eyes were still sharp, appraised Mateo's appearance and remarked, "He bears a strong resemblance to you Genaro. There is no need for him to remove himself. Welcome to the new Cathedral of the Popes of Rome my son." Mateo knelt down on one knee and kissed his ring "It is an honor to be in your presence Your Holiness." He then stepped aside and found a place toward the rear of the nave.

"Alessandro, you have made such great progress. I am told we are nearly complete. You have not only honored me but have brought great honor to Our Lord with this beautiful House of God." "Thank you Your Holiness, we will be ready within two weeks." The old man now sat down on the chair, one of the guards had been carrying, and was surveying the entire structure. "Genaro, I see that you have been working day and night to complete your work for the designated date. Let us take a tour of your labors." No one yet mentioned the fresco above the altar. The old man grabbed Genaro's arm and his gnarled fingers held him firm. Take me around I wish to see everything. They walked slowly, from one side to the other; each wall was done more masterfully than the other was, until finally they came back to the center. "Let me rest for a while." The old man looked up and there in all her glory was Eve. His eyes grew wide and a smile painted his shriveled face. "Cardinale Corsi" he called for the tiny man "Yes Your Holiness." "Why did you not mention this central fresco?" Corsi seemed to have shrunk even further; he was about to open his mouth in reply when Genaro came forward.

Genaro was sweating in anticipation of the Pope's reaction to the fresco. "It is my fault Your Holiness, I shall paint over it. Please forgive me if I have offended you." The old man called him to his side and Genaro knelt at his feet. "I am most pleased with this fresco. The mother of the human race should be beautiful." Cardinale Corsi jumped in, "But Your Holiness she is too beautiful, and all eyes will be fixed on her and not you." There was dead silence and the old man put his head down. Genaro watched and anxiety filled his gut, the bile drifted to his throat, he looked from Alessandro to Mateo with pleading eyes. Finally, the old man raised his head, "I think it will draw men to our altar. If they come for Eve, they will stay for the Mass. The Lord has inspired this great artist to render such a beautiful creature; let it be the Lord to bring worshippers to see it."

Genaro was weak; the color had drained from his face. The Pope rose from his chair and once again latched on to Genaro's arm. "Walk with me my son. The rest of you wait until we are to the door before you follow." They strolled, arm in arm, toward the door. "Genaro, tell me, who was the model for this fresco?" Genaro was going to lie and say it was some young woman from Rome, but then realized to whom he was talking. "Your Holiness the face is that of my youngest sister. Her name is Lucia. The proportions and body I just imagined." The old man, having reached the door, turned to face the artist, "Does she hold such true beauty?" Genaro still holding the Pope's arm patted his hand with gentle affection, "She is that and more. Lucia is beautiful not only of body, but, of mind and spirit." "I should like to meet her someday." "She would be most honored to meet you." "You have pleased the Lord and you have pleased me. Kneel down I wish to convey a special blessing upon you. "May the Lord Jesus continue to fill you with the gift of your talents for His glory, and, may He bless the sister who inspired such a resplendent tribute to Eve."

Mateo was relieved and silently thanked God for this wise old man. Truly, this Pope was one filled with great insight to humanity.

CHAPTER FOUR

ARCHITECTS, ARTISTS AND ANTIQUITIES

Rome

It was as though all those gathered had let out a sigh of relief. Alessandro's eyes followed the artist and the Pope as they walked toward the door, as did everyone. When they saw that Genaro was receiving His Holiness' blessing they started to move in unison. The diminutive Cardinal came to Alessandro and whispered "He is fortunate that this Pope loves beautiful things. His successor may not." Alessandro, who stood nearly a foot taller than the Cardinal made an exaggerated display of bending down, said, "We shall worry when that time comes", and smiled with a sense of victory. Cardinale Corsi tried to stand tall and turned his head in annoyance.

Alessandro found Mateo in the shadows, smiled broadly, and nodded his head and Mateo did likewise. Now that the little entourage was processing toward the door, he was moving slowly toward where the architect was standing. There was a charge of excitement in the air they both felt it. "I am so happy for your brother. Genaro is not only a masterful artist but also a good and kind man. It would have been a sin against humanity if he would have had to paint over this glorious woman." Mateo without even realizing it was staring at the image of Lucia and a warm glow came to him. "She is truly a lovely young woman. You will undoubtedly meet her." They were speaking when Genaro, a slight hint of color returning to his gaunt face, returned. They embraced him congratulating him on winning over the Pope. "Well done Genaro. You see I told you that His Holiness was a man of great vision and an appreciation for splendid art." Mateo could not resist "What did he say to you?"

Genaro just recovered, regained his sense of humor, "He wanted to know who the model was. I was going to lie and say she was a local girl, but then surely I would rot in Hell. I told him she was my sister, his eyes grew wide, and he asked if she was truly so beautiful. I told him that she was not only physically beautiful but possessed a blessed heart and mind." Alessandro could not contain himself any longer "Please I need to meet this woman." They all laughed heartily.

Mateo said, "This calls for a celebration. Alessandro would you do us the honor of joining us for supper?" Genaro also prodded "Yes, you must, we have won a great battle. We shall toast Pope Clement XII for his wisdom and to Lucia for her beauty." Alessandro was visibly pleased to have been invited "Thank you I shall enjoy the company."

They went to Alessandro's favorite trattoria and once seated they ordered up the finest vintage the eatery had. When it arrived, Mateo took the lead, "I wish to propose a toast to the Artist of the Church of Rome and the Architect of the Church of Rome, two more talented men I have never met. Salute!" They took up their glasses and drank deeply for a well - deserved victory. Genaro next proposed a toast "To the finding of a good friend and masterful builder. May you live long and prosper. Salute!" Finally, it was Alessandro's turn, "To Lucia, whose beauty has inspired even the Lord. Salute!" They drank, ate, and laughed for the rest of the evening.

When it was time to leave, it was Alessandro, addressing Mateo, who said, "It has been a most enjoyable evening, I am so pleased that you have come to Rome. I'm sure your presence will give Genaro the inspiration he seeks." He affectionately embraced Mateo and then Genaro "I bid you both a good night. Genaro I shall see you early so that we will put the final touches on everything." "Good night dear friend." Mateo was happy that Genaro had found someone who could understand and appreciate his talents. There was just a slight hint of jealousy that settled in his gut at their apparent friendship. Mateo, when not with Genaro, was lonely.

Genaro did not go back to the Curia that night, but went to the inn that Mateo had taken. It was a spacious set of rooms in an elegant building, which was only blocks from where Genaro had been staying. No sooner did they close the door before Genaro fell into the arms of his lover. "I have missed you so much. You could not have given me a more perfect gift than to appear here in Rome. Thank you for coming." Mateo, caught up in the moment, did not want to stain this great day. He decided that tomorrow would be soon enough to share with Genaro the letter he received from Giovanni Romano regarding Lucia. For tonight, they would bask in each other's joy.

It did not take long before they were satisfying their absence. Mateo had been longing for the touch and feel of this handsome man. He shared his story of the bathhouse with Genaro and they laughed heartily. "What would we have done if we had both been there?" asked Genaro playfully. Mateo with lust-filled eyes said, "Well we can pretend right now that we are in the bathhouse with all those fat bellied gossips watching." Genaro was by now very excited at this role-playing, his creative side was always stoked by Mateo who also enjoyed his imaginative side. "Come let us get in the tub." Buckets of water had been brought and were lined up next to a deep marble bagno. They stripped off their clothes and Genaro said "My Lord shall I fill your bagno?" his voice high as if a young serving boy. Mateo was laughing, the headiness of the wine mixed with the anticipation of his lovemaking were filling his groin with thoughts of fancy. "Yes boy." Genaro took up the buckets and playfully began filling the tub. Mateo said, "Come here boy, I want you to wash me." "Oh yes My Lord," answered Genaro; his erection proceeded him into the tub. Genaro made a flagrant display of pretending to be a dutiful serving boy and elaborately filled his sea sponge with scented soap and was washing his master in all the necessary places much to the delight of Mateo. "My Lord you will need to bend over so that I may do a thorough job." Mateo was very happy to oblige. Genaro's long fingers slipped into the crevice of Mateo muscular backside and a sigh of ecstasy escaped. Genaro worked his magic knowing how to please his lover. "Do you think we have given the old roosters enough pleasure?" he asked the panting Mateo. "I do believe they have been given a good instruction of what their serving boys need to do. Now they will have something to hold in their hands beside the soap." They laughed with such joy.

This banter went on for a short time and then they emerged from the water and found their solace in each other's arms. For now, they could rest and enjoy each other's company.

The next morning Mateo was up and dressed while Genaro was still enjoying the last vestiges of sleep. While he did hear, Mateo roaming around and the serving girl bringing in the tray with breakfast he was so content he hated to get up and face another day of laboring over his work. Mateo finally came in, started kissing him gently at first, and then threw back the covers. Genaro was naked and the sight of him aroused Mateo. He started kneading his buttocks, and then playfully began slapping it, but Genaro pretended to still be asleep. The tattoo became quicker and harder and Genaro was now fully aroused. He began moaning as if in protest to this wicked treatment, but his groin demonstrated his pleasure.

Mateo picked him up, placed him over his knee, and continued his ministrations until they were both ready for more. Genaro slid off, wedged himself between Mateo's legs, and slowly, lace by lace undid his breeches, until the object of his desire was released. His mouth descended upon the erect organ and he gave Mateo his pleasure. They then found themselves locked in a loving embrace and Mateo made sure that Genaro's needs were satisfied. "Ah, what a marvelous way to begin the day" said Genaro. "Get dressed. We shall have our breakfast on the balcony," said Mateo in a serious tone.

Genaro did as he was told and quickly dressed for his work. Finding Mateo waiting for him he came over and kissed him gently on the neck. He sat began pouring the steaming espresso. "Genaro there is something I wish to share with you. I did not mention it last night because I did not want to dampen your spirits." Mateo had the letter out on the table and slid it over to him. "Read this and then we shall talk." Genaro's head was running in every direction imaginable but he said nothing. Taking the letter in his hands, he recognized the seal of Monteforte. He read the letter from Giovanni Romano and then placed it back on the table.

Mateo waited. "We must go to her before something happens. I am filled with pain at the death of Henri. He was a good and kind man and did not deserve to die at the hands of that whoreson." Genaro, who generally was soft spoken and quiet stood suddenly and pounded his fist on the balustrade of the balcony. He was angry and hurt for the death of a dear man and for the fear he held in his heart for his sister. "So help me God, on my oath, if that bastard harms my sister I shall hunt him down and kill him in the most agonizing manner." Mateo was somewhat taken back by this side of Genaro, but echoed his feelings.

"It is settled, we shall go to her, or at the very least we shall join up with them when they arrive in France. I will dispatch a letter to her immediately and tell her to send word when she will be leaving England. I am assuming since Danford is now the Duke of Northumberland he has a small army at his disposal to protect our dear sister." Mateo was once again in charge. "Genaro, how long will it be before we can leave?" There was a look of concern on his face "It shall be at the least two more weeks before the blessing of the new cathedral, for which I must be in attendance." Mateo thought about that and agreed that Genaro must be there, I think we shall be good with that time." Genaro who was so emotionally troubled looked forlorn "Will you stay here until it is time to leave?" Mateo came to him and held him close stroking his thick wavy hair "I realized shortly after we separated that I do not want to ever be too far apart again. I love you and I need you." A broad smile flashed across Genaro's face "I have missed you so much. When I saw you yesterday my heart nearly leapt from my chest. Never leave me again."

***

Alessandro was already in deep discussion with several laborers when Mateo and Genaro arrived at the cathedral. "Buongiorno miei amici." Genaro thought that Alessandro seemed rather lighthearted. "Do you sleep here Alessandro? Never have I come here and not find you buried in work." The architect having given his instructions dismissed the workers "It is an affliction; I do not sleep well. Since I was a young boy, I have suffered from pains in my head. Sometimes it is so bad that I do not sleep for days."

"Alessandro I will be leaving as soon as the consecration of the cathedral is over." The expression on the architects face became sad, "His Holiness has already given you another church to paint?" Genaro, who now wore his own mask of sadness replied, "No there is a family matter that requires urgent attention; that is why Mateo has come here. We must leave for France as soon as possible." Alessandro nodded his head to confirm his acknowledgement of the situation. "Can I help in any way?" Mateo now joined their conversation, "Our sister Lucia, who had tried to help one of the stable servants at Monteforte, was taken, and almost killed by this man. She is now in the protection of the Duke of Northumberland in England, but they will be coming to Monteforte soon. Genaro and I will meet them in France and bring our sister safely home."

"Lucia is she not the sister from the fresco?" he asked Genaro. "Yes it is she." "That is terrible news; you both must be filled with fear for her safety. I wish there was some way that I could help." Again, Mateo said, "If you are completed here and have no other obligations, why don't you join us, and if you wish, you can come home with us to Monteforte." Alessandro seemed shocked by the invitation. "I have not been engaged for any other undertakings, I know that His Holiness has some new ideas for a Vatican Library, but, for now I am free."

Genaro was very pleased "Then you shall accompany us to meet Lucia and then we shall all travel on to Monteforte." Even Mateo was pleased as was evidenced by the smile on his face. Mateo said, "Well then I shall go about my business while the two of you complete your work. We shall all meet up for supper."

***

It was only after they had arrived back at Mateo's rooms in the inn that the subject of Alessandro came up. "Genaro do you think Alessandro knows that we are not brothers but lovers?" He thought about the question and replied, "I am not sure. We have not tried to hide or deceive our feelings." "Perhaps, if you trust him, we should tell him of our relationship since he will be in our company for some time. I would not want him to discover us along the way and feel that we have not been truthful to him." Genaro came over to where Mateo was sitting and sat on his lap wrapping his arms around him. "I trust him, but then you are the better judge of character. Do you trust him?" Mateo did not hesitate "I think Alessandro is an honorable man who would not be offended by our relationship. I also think he is a lonely man who would welcome companionship no matter what their sexual preferences were." "I too agree with all you have said. I am very happy that you like him. You are a good judge of character, for he has shared with me his loneliness. We have all felt the sting of being alone."

With only three days left before the consecration of the new cathedral the happy threesome were out celebrating. Mateo and Genaro decided that it would be this evening that they would share their secret with their new friend. After supper, Mateo suggested they all go back to his rooms for a game of cards. It had been a long, hard day for Alessandro and Genaro who were both putting the final touches to their work.

After a few more glasses or wine, the conversation of relationships came to the table. "Genaro tells me that you have not committed to a woman yet. I would think a man of your talents and money would be a very winning prize for some young woman." Alessandro looked embarrassed but as was his nature, he answered honestly "Yes it is true that I do not have any marriage proposals. My work has consumed my whole life. There is not much opportunity to encounter women when one works day and night under the watchful eye of His Holiness." Mateo grunted, "I see your point. But when you are not otherwise engaged in building do you find time for female companionship?"

At this question, Alessandro flushed "I am ashamed to say that I have never been with a woman. I was raised in a monastery and when I was at universitia there was no time, and, sadly, now I am buried here under my work." There was such lament in his voice. Mateo knew that this was the perfect opening for his explanation of their relationship. Genaro knew it was coming and braced himself for its conclusion.

"Alessandro, Genaro and I, while blood relatives, are also lovers." It was out there, Alessandro would now have to accept or reject their friendship. They were not prepared for his reaction to this news "I suspected that there was something between the both of you. I could see the tension when you brushed against each other. I am no fool. Your secret shall remain within me. But, I do not have an appetite for men simply because I am a virgin." "Good to know." With that, the three of them burst out in raucous laughter. Mateo still laughing said, "Perhaps I can cure you of your affliction. There are many brothels in Rome with girls who specialize in men with your particular problem. Shall I assist you with this?" Alessandro was now serious "How do you know of such places given your preferences?" "When I was a young man it was expected that I learn all the carnal knowledge. It is not that I dislike woman, I just prefer men." The young architect looked to Genaro "Have you also been with woman?" "Yes, many of them, but like Mateo, I have a taste for men." "Can you really help me Mateo, or are you mocking me?" Mateo put on a serious face "One never mocks a man when it comes to sex. Tomorrow we shall make a man out of you. Salute!" They raised their glasses and Alessandro drank deeply, his face burning red, he thought to himself that perhaps he would finally sleep well tonight.

CHAPTER FIVE

A DARK DAY

Wallingston Castle

By the end of the second day, with its endless procession of mourners, visiting Lords and tenants, Danford was truly spent. Lucia had been busy organizing an entire household and was exhausted. She was so tired she could not even find the strength to eat her supper, but she made her way to Danford's rooms. She knocked gently almost hoping he would be asleep, William had told her that he still held on to his fever. "Come" came a raspy voice from somewhere on the other side of the heavy oak door. Lucia gingerly opened the door and stepped in "Danford how are you feeling?" She came to his side and kissed his forehead only to find that he was cool to the touch. "Thanks to you and the potion you made I am much better. I am sore and uncomfortable but I will be fine in a few days. William has told me that you have nearly worked yourself to the bone, and now that my eyes are sharp once again, I can see that you have grown thin and your usual peach blush is pale."

Lucia turned away so that he would not see the dark rings around her eyes. She was tired and miserable "I too will be fine. Tomorrow will be a difficult day for you and your siblings. You will need to be strong and carry them along with you. They have endured much suffering over these many years and tomorrow will be the culmination of all that time. I hope you are strong enough to withstand what will be required of you both in body and in spirit?" Danford did not answer but sat there watching the flames from the hearth lick the darkened bricks. After a while, he said, "I have many things I will need to face over the next weeks. My mind is saying one thing and my heart is saying another. So much has happened in such a short time. I am sure that in many things you are as confused and troubled as I am. We must take our time in making our decisions. I am sure you agree?" Lucia did understand what he was feeling but was uncomfortable as to the tone of his message. Was he referring to their relationship or that of his new position? Either way, the next few weeks would tell the future for both of them. "Did you have your supper?" Danford asked. "No I am too tired to eat. I shall have Sophia bring me some broth and hot biscuits to my room." "Come here." Lucia walked over to where he was sitting and he reached for her wrapping his big hands around her waist "You are getting too thin. Promise me you will start eating." He ran his hands up and down her torso "My God I can feel every rib." She wanted to tell him that much like the English weather, the food was equally grey, and boring, but restrained herself, "I will eat. I promise." He still held her close but she felt a difference in his touch and she thought that perhaps it was because he was feeling so ill. Something had changed in him; something had changed in all of them. "I shall leave now so that we can both get some rest, tomorrow will be grueling. Good night Danford I pray you have a restful night." Lucia bent to kiss him and he did not respond with his usual passion. "Good night Lucia, thank you for all you have done for me and my family." She turned and left, her heart was as tired as her body.

***

When Sophia woke her, the next day she was confused thinking it was still night. The sky was dark and there was the endless drizzle of rain. "I hate this abominable country. I feel like an old lady with pains in my bones." Sophia too hated England for many reasons, the most pressing of which was that the wedding between her and Nicko was on indefinite hold until their return to Monteforte. "Mistress, when will we return to our beautiful Monteforte; to see the sun and the sea?" "We shall return soon, very soon, my dear Sophia, but for now we must do what is necessary and then we shall make haste for our home."

I have chosen this dark navy gown for you Mistress. It is heavy and it will keep the dampness from you. Sophia had brought her a tray of food from the kitchens as well as some gossip. "The servants are all buzzing like bees saying that Lord Danford is not fit to be Duke of such an extensive domain, that he is too young and will take a foreigner for his wife. They say that is the talk everywhere in the province. The rumor is that the older Lords will take advantage of him, and if there is war they will not honor their pledge of loyalty to him." Lucia visibly upset by such information asked, "Does William know of this gossip?" Sophia now very animated in sharing this news said, "Yes he knows all that goes on here. He punishes them for it, but it is also coming from outside the castle." Lucia knew that her presence was a constant source of irritation to the staff and while they would never outwardly disrespect or disobey her orders there was an underlying discontent among them. How would she ever survive being the Mistress of Wallingston, nevertheless the 'Italian' Duchess of Northumberland; it was an impossible situation. She could not finish her breakfast the bile was in her throat.

With Sophia's help, she got dressed. "Mistress I am worried. You have not eaten well in days. Your gowns are starting to hang like sacks of flour." Lucia had lost interest in the food "I am dreaming of Marcello's cooking. I shall eat for days when I return." They hugged each other to console themselves."

***

The castle was filled with people who had come from near and far. Today they would inter the Fourth Duke of Northumberland, His Grace Lord Stevens, The Duchess Lady Evelyn, and their son Lord Jonathan Bayan Stevens. This was more tragedy and drama than they had seen since Queen Anne's War.

The memory of that war with so many lives lost was still fresh on their minds. Lucia even after this short time in this Godforsaken part of the world knew they would never accept a foreigner as their Duchess.

It was only a short ride to the Church of the Holy Family. Lucia had been there when Michael had first taken her on a tour of Wallingston's vast estate. While it technically sat on the Duke's private property, it was used by all the locals not only Sunday services but for weddings, baptisms, and funerals. Lucia thought to herself the blasphemy of the three of them being blessed in a church that was named for Joseph, Mary, and Jesus. The cruel irony of it gave her a shiver.

The weather was particularly nasty. The sky was angry, and the wind whipped around rustling fallen leaves. A steady cold drizzle blanketed the air. Danford with William's help had managed to sit his large horse. The animal, dressed in full regalia, looked as regal as his rider did. Danford wore the colors of his new office and carried the pewter shield with the family crest. He wore a cape with fox trim, another symbol of his family and office. Except for the pain, he carried in his eyes, which she was sure few knew he looked every inch the Fifth Duke of Northumberland. To his right was Michael, another picture of fine breeding; two strong, handsome brothers, leading the procession to the church; their two sisters, driven in a fine coach, right behind them. Lucia opted to ride by horseback and hung back, melding in with the lower lords and merchants, so as not to create any undo gossip.

Out of the misty drizzle came the high-pitched scream of a bagpipe. Lucia, startled by the sound, jumped in her saddle, which caused her horse to lurch forward. Everyone near her gave her a dirty stare. Luckily, she had a tight hold on his reins. From that, single sound there then appeared a troupe of bagpipes. The sound of the mournful tune they blew filled her heart with sorrow. They fell in cadence behind the caisson, the six white horses with their proud stance and elegant step, with four riders who wore the colors of the Duke of Northumberland, solemnly carried the three coffins that were shrouded in black silk. Six pallbearers walked silently on either side of the caisson, they carried the flag and staff of the House of Stevens, the symbol of the red fox emblazoned on them. This, Lucia thought, is quite a spectacle. Hundreds of people lined the path, some throwing flowers, others making the sign of the cross as the coffins went past.

When they reached the church, the priest came to greet the new Duke of Northumberland and gave condolences to the grieving family. Danford keeping up the pretense of a strong leader shielded his wince as he dismounted. He stood erect as one by one the coffins were lifted from the caisson, carried inside the chapel and then placed on the biers. Not being a large building, most of those gathered were left to stand outside, in the rain. Lucia found a pew in the back and squeezed in, sandwiched between two burly, ill smelling men. At the conclusion of the services, the coffins were once again carried to the waiting caisson and the wail of the bagpipes took up their mournful tune. Only immediate family, and select lords and friends were permitted in the family crypt.

Danford caught her eye but did not motion for her to come join him. They both knew that the protocol would not warrant her presence. Lucia thought to herself, is this the way it will always be? She watched as they came to the family mausoleum, a stone structure surrounded by a high iron fence, and the ornate gates held the family crest. Atop the structure was a massive sculpture of a warrior, mounted on his stead, sword drawn and the familiar shield with the red fox forged into its face.

The men who carried the coffins processed into the darkness of the building as shadows fell from the lit torches. Drums were beaten and bagpipes wailed. The priest was the first to enter, the rain hitting the smoking incense, followed by Danford, Michael, their father's brothers, and finally Rachael and Elizabeth. Elizabeth was weeping like a small child, Lucia wanted to run to her side and comfort her but would not dare.

In a few moments it was done. Those who attended came back to the castle and were given a lavish repast. Danford, cold, tired and in pain retreated to his room. Lucia coordinated the serving of the food. It was evening before everyone had left.

Lucia made a silent prayer of thanksgiving that it was over.

William, looking haggard, found Lucia, "Marchesa, His Grace is seeking your company." Lucia felt for the first time more like a servant than the possible wife of the new Duke. She did not say anything but simply nodded. William was still standing there and wanted to speak "What troubles you William?" Lucia asked. The faithful valet spoke in a low soft tone "May I speak freely?" "Yes of course." "You have been a wonderful help since the day you arrived. You have endured physical and emotional abuse and for that, I am sorry. Today, I watched as you found your place among the lower lords and did not go to where you rightfully should have been. You are truly a remarkable woman. These are simple, clannish people, who have little love or tolerance for outsiders. I hope I have not offended you with my forwardness?"

Lucia realized that William was trying to tell her that she would never find favor with these people. "Thank you William, I am well aware of their sentiments toward me. Sometimes love is not enough to forge a bond of marriage. I am carrying a heavy heart. I shall see His Grace shortly. I thank you for your kind words." Lucia would have cried but did not have the strength. She wanted to go home to Monteforte.

She left William standing there with an expression on his face, which said all that had to be said. Quietly she made her way to Danford's room. The hallway was dark and she saw a figure crouched in a corner and the soft sounds of weeping could be heard. Lucia approached cautiously not wanting to startle or intrude on this person. As she neared, her footfalls clicked on the slate floor and alerted the person in the corner. Lucia could now see that it was Elizabeth and went to her. "Dear Elizabeth can I help you?" Lucia said as she knelt by the girl's side. "Mistress Lucia, I am so lonely. I know that they were mean to me but it was, at the very least, someone to know that I am alive. Now there is no one." Lucia said "What about Rachael?" "You mean my beautiful twin. My brothers have already signed a contract for her marriage." Lucia was shocked. "Does Rachael know this?" The dim-witted girl bobbed her head up and down so rapidly Lucia was sure it would roll off her neck. "Oh yes, and she is very happy. They will be married in six months." "Well I suppose they are planning your marriage as well. Did they say anything to you?" At this question the girl began to weep once again, "I heard Michael tell Danford that even though he had pledged a very handsome dowry he could not persuade anyone to marry me."

Lucia was wounded for this young woman, and embraced her lovingly, as if she were a child. "I am sure we shall find a suitable husband for you." A thousand thoughts raced through her head. What shall become of her? She knew she needed to help this poor soul, who had been abused all her life, yet, even that cruelty was better than nothing. It was so sad that Lucia joined in her tears. "Come with me Elizabeth." The sobbing bundle of tears asked, "Where are we going?" "I would like you to come to my rooms for a little while and we can talk. Do you want to?" In her childlike manner Elizabeth jumped up and giggled "Oh yes. Will you read to me?" "Yes, I shall read my favorite book to you, but first I must go see your brother. William said he is looking for me. I shall bring you to my rooms and my maid Sophia will get us some hot cider and a scone." Now Elizabeth was very excited "Can you tell her to get some honey too?" Lucia laughed, "I think we can manage that."

After depositing Elizabeth in her rooms and instructing Sophia to bring some hot cider and scones with honey back from the kitchen, she made her way to Danford's room. His door was ajar and so she softly called to him "Danford, may I enter?" Apparently, he had not heard her, and so she let herself in, sat, and waited. He was in the dressing room. In a moment he emerged stark naked, his long, lean body glistening with moisture. He had not seen or heard her until she gasped at the sight of him. He stood frozen in his place. He began to speak but the words were stammered. "What are you doing here?" he shouted at her. "I am here because William came to ask me to stop by. If you are going to go around naked you should make sure your door is shut." She was embarrassed as well as insulted to think that he was suggesting she was stalking him. "Well, I apologize. Wait I shall but on my dressing robe." "That would be an excellent idea." She was flushed and aroused, and from the looks of him, so was he.

Clad in his dressing robe he came out to find her with her back toward him and looking out the window. He came over to her and put his arms around her "I am so sorry for my outburst. I am quite ashamed that you had to see that." Lucia honest to her bones said, "Why are you ashamed? You have the body of a God and I enjoyed seeing it. I swear to you that I did call out but you did not hear me." He grabbed her and kissed her hard, he would have liked to tear the clothes from her bones and ravage her body. His kiss held no passion, only lust. They both felt it and it made them sad. Lucia pulled away and walked to the middle of the room. He waited.

"I have just met up with Elizabeth. She was weeping in the hall. I understand that you and Michael have contracted for the marriage of Rachael, but that in spite of a rich dowry no one would take Elizabeth." Danford seemed surprised that she knew so many things but answered truthfully "Yes that is all true. We shall eventually find a suitable husband for Elizabeth but given her condition, it will be difficult. Rachael is not sure that Elizabeth can bear children." " I would ask your permission to ask Elizabeth if she would like to come to Monteforte and live with me." At this, he was truly floored "What are you saying? You want me to give you permission to take my sister from her ancestral home and have her live in a foreign country with you." Lucia now annoyed at his tone and insinuation replied "Yes. That is precisely what I said. Will you let me ask her?" Danford walked away, a strange look on his face, "No. She cannot leave here and make her home at Monteforte. She belongs here."

Lucia was stunned that he should take such a position "Here with whom? You, Michael, Who? She is a child and needs someone to care for her. She is desperate for a friend." Deciding that to try to defy his decision would make him even more locked into his answer. Taking a different tactic Lucia said "You are right Danford, I am sorry for trying to help her. You know what is best for her. I am nothing but a foreigner. Please forgive my forwardness. Good night." She turned to leave and in two steps, he was holding a firm grip on her arm "It is I who am sorry. Sorry for everything that has happened. Let me think on it. I should like to discuss it with Michael and Rachel as well." Lucia knew she had won this match "Yes that would be a wise decision for all concerned. I shall abide by your wishes and will not utter a word to her. Once again, I say good night." He let go of her arm but they stayed lingering between the tension-filled air. There was so much to say, so many feelings to be shared, but it would not happen tonight, or any night. She moved toward the door and slipped into the hall, tears of sorrow cascading down her pale face.

Silently she prayed for the day she might leave this wretched place, her heart was a grey as the weather. She closed her tear-filled eyes and envisioned riding Apollo along the cliffs of her beautiful Monteforte, the sun upon her face and the clean scent of lemons in the air. Soon, she must return soon.

CHAPTER SIX

THE BORDELLO

Rome

There was a tension throughout the processional, even His Holiness appeared anxious. So many people had voiced opposition to the construction of this cathedral. Even within the ranks of his own clerics, there had been much dissention as to the need and validity for another church. The talent and personality of Alessandro Galilei thus having won the contest for the best design had charmed Pope Clement XII. Alessandro, having read all the history he could find on this the ancient site, which was the original fort of Constantine, wanted to pay homage to its roots. When the Holy Father instructed all the contestants to submit drawings for the new Palace of the Bishop of Rome to be erected on the sacred site of the Arcibascilica de San Giovanni Laterano Alessandro was astounded to have been chosen. This would be the cornerstone of his career.

Pope Clement XII was born Lorenzo Corsini his pedigree harked from nobility. Clement was a visionary but a poor politician. His love of the arts, antiquities, and architecture met with much opposition. The fact that he also restructured the

Vatican Bank did nothing to endear him to his fellow clerics. With the basis of his papal support coming from the fortunes of his own family, Clement commissioned the construction of the Cappella Corsini, which would become known as the Palace of the Bishop of Rome, and be part of the Arcibascilica de San Giovanni Laterano.

When the designs were submitted Clement, over the strong dissention of his cardinals, chose Alessandro's design. In this rendering, there was a complete shift from the monumental severity of a church or institutional structure to a palatial façade. The Palace of the Bishop of Rome actually looked and functioned like a palace. To his dismay Alessandro's design caused vehement debate and scandal within the Roman artistic circles. Clement was pleased with the design and tonight would be the culmination of years of hard work.

Alessandro, Genaro, and Mateo all sat in the first pew of the newly completed and decorated nave. It seemed like all of Rome, if not, all of Italy, had turned out for the consecration of this magnificent building. His Holy Father, Pope Clement XII, did not spare one scudi on this palace. A processional of priests, bishops, cardinals and finally His Holiness, all led by the playing of trumpets, harps and violins. It was pageantry at its finest. The centerpiece of this edifice was the altar and pulpit from where Mass would be celebrated. All eyes were affixed on the fresco above the altar of the Creation with Eve as the mother of humankind. It was spectacular, sensual, and beautiful. The men did not, could not stop looking at it, the women were appalled, but, more to the truth, they were jealous of this depiction of the perfect female. What a triumph for these two worthy men! Mateo was so proud of both of them but especially of Genaro. Everywhere his eye landed there was no detail, no wall, and no niche that was not imprinted with his brush.

After Mass, His Holy Father, held a reception in the private quarters of the new Palace of the Popes. It was a gala, which included every important member of Italian society. Mateo mingled within the crowd, finding several of his wealthiest clients, and enjoying himself. As for Genaro and Alessandro, they were basking in their well-deserved glory. It would be a night that no one would ever forget. It was the night that forever defined two great artists.

Toward the end of the evening when most of the guests had already left, His Holiness, tired and frail, came to them, "My sons, truly Our Lord has filled the both of you with the Holy Spirit. I can never repay what you both have accomplished, for Holy Mother Church and for me. Thank you. I will keep you both in my prayers always." He motioned for them to kneel and he then placed his hands on each of their heads "Può il Signore Gesù Cristo porterà alla vita eterna e continuano ad ispirare i vostri regali." They rose. "Now that you are finished I believe that you should take a little time to rest and enjoy yourselves." Alessandro said, "Dear Holy

Father, you stood by us when all others would cast stones. You are a man of great vision and courage. Genaro and I thank you for your faith in us."

The old priest, his head trying desperately to hold up his heavy headdress, just nodded. "Go have some enjoyment. Genaro, remember to bring your sister to me when she comes to Rome." They laughed.

***

Even though it was well into the evening, Mateo had arranged with the most discreet bordello in Rome to receive them after hours. They came to a stately home in one of the finest districts in the city. A footman was standing at the gate. He was given their names and they were permitted to enter. They entered into a most refined salon, a servant, dressed in a black waistcoat and wig, showed them to another, even grander salon. He gave them cognac and fine cigars. "My Lords, my Mistress will be with you shortly. If there is anything else you require please ring and I shall come." He bowed formally and retreated from the room.

Alessandro, perspiration glistened his face, did not sit but paced back and forth. Mateo was rather enjoying himself "This is excellent cognac, is it not Genaro?" Genaro was not sure what he and Mateo were going to be doing but went along with the ruse "Yes. I think we should come more often, just to partake of the cognac." They chuckled but Alessandro was in no mood for lightheartedness.

In a few moments a lovely woman, who was past her youth, but elegantly dressed, appeared. "Lord Mateo, so delighted to see you; it has been too long." Mateo rushed to her "Vivianna, you are as beautiful as ever. I have missed you as well. May I introduce Lord Genaro and Lord Alessandro, of whom I had spoken to you about. Do you have everything ready?" Vivianna's eyes drank in Mateo, as she was sizing up Genaro and Alessandro, "Of course My Lord, as you have instructed. All is set, follow me." She embraced Mateo "It is such a pity that your tastes run in the opposite direction of mine. You are a fine specimen of a man." Mateo ever the gentleman answered "Cara, if my appetite were such as yours I would surely ravage your beautiful body. Perhaps, someday, if my pervasions change I will come for you." She threw back her head in a coquettish gesture "I shall pray for the day." Before she left him, her hand came to his crotch and she squeezed him "Oh what a pity." Mateo laughed heartily. "But a pity for whom?" again they laughed.

The trio followed Mistress Vivianna upstairs to the boudoirs. She led them to the first room, knocked softly and the door instantly opened. Standing before them was a petite young woman with a cherubic face. She was dressed in a lovely gown and her long, wavy hair was loose around her shoulders. "Rosemaria this is Lord Alessandro please take good care of him." She stepped aside and nearly pushed the panting architect through the door. As soon as he was fully in the room, she shut the door. "She looks virginal but I wish I had a dozen just like her. She will teach him things even I do not know."

They moved down the hall and came to another door. This time she did not knock but just opened. There to Genaro's surprise were two young men, wearing nothing but a loincloth over their protruding privates. "My Lords may I introduce Dante and Claudio. They will serve your every desire. Enjoy yourselves." She turned to leave but brushed up against Mateo, "Are you sure I cannot persuade you to come to my room instead?" Mateo kissed her on the mouth and fondled her breasts until she gasped. "No I believe I shall stay." "As you wish My Lord Mateo I am sure it will be my loss."

Alessandro was soaked with sweat and embarrassment. The girl was beautiful and spoke to him very softly. She appeared to be intelligent and tried to make conversation with him. "My Lord, please may I take your coat?" Alessandro surrendered his coat. "Please come sit on the settee. May I pour you some more cognac?" He sat with his hands clasped in his lap. He wanted to bolt for the door but was not sure what would be more embarrassing, staying with this beautiful girl and making a fool of himself, or facing his friends still a virgin. Rosemaria came to sit by him "I know that you have not been with a woman before; it is not to be troubled about. I am going to teach you how to make love to a woman. When we are done, you will be a master. My Lord you must relax and put all other thoughts from your mind. Close your eyes, I will do the rest."

Alessandro wanted to vomit. He was afraid that perhaps he would not be able to satisfy this girl. She stood and moved to the back of the settee and began to massage his head; his neck and ran her fingers through his hair. It felt good. He started to breath normally. Next, she stared to loosen his collar. She came back around and kissed his face; his neck, his ear. Her tongue was like that of a serpent. She whispered, "Let me take off your clothes." Rosemaria deftly had him naked in no time. Softly she told him to open his eyes. Seductively, she began to remove her own clothing. When she was naked, she took his hand and led him to the bed.

"Tell me, what you think of my body?" she asked in a whisper. "It is magnificent." "Would you like to touch me? Would you like to feel my full breasts?" He was so excited that his throat was practically closed tight. He managed to squeeze out "Yes. Please may I touch them?" Gently he began to stroke each breast. He cupped them, felt the weight of them, saw the beauty of them. "Alessandro, pinch my nipples like this" and she showed him how. "Roll them like this" he did as he was told. "Now take them into your mouth and suck them until they are hard." He could not believe that he could do this to a woman. Rosemaria was enjoying the role of teacher. He was not handsome, but there was something very attractive about this man, perhaps it was his innocence.

She took his hand and led him to the clutch of black curly ringlets. He was still sucking her tits with fervor. "Alessandro, I want you to take your finger and put it inside my clit." He stopped moved his hand to the mouth of her clit, she was guiding him. "I am going to lie down on my back and you will come next to me; but first I want you to look at me. No, do not be embarrassed, I like when you look at me. I want you to see what I am doing so that you can do it to please me. Yes?" He had always been an ardent student, "Yes. I want to please you. Show me what I need to do."

Rosemaria laid down and spread her legs. "Come stand here, watch what I am doing and then you will do it to me." She began slowly with small circles, and then with her finger went in and out, in and out. "You see, it is not difficult, but it will give the woman much enjoyment. Come lay with me." He was mesmerized by her charms. He did what she asked and she told him "You are a good and gentle lover. A woman appreciates a man who will wait for his own pleasure. Now we will move on to the next lesson. Slide down the bed and come lay between my legs. Take your tongue and do with it what you did with your fingers. Do you understand?" His head already buried in her nest he did not speak but just bobbed his head up and down and went right to his ministrations. She too was enjoying his lesson. He was a very anxious student and took instruction well.

"Ah that was wonderful. Now, it is your turn. Lay down here. She moved over to make room for him. He was savoring her musky taste in his mouth. She was rubbing his nipples and then began sucking. He groaned. She traced the flat contours of his stomach and reached his engorged penis. He was well sized. She repositioned herself and took him in her mouth. He gasped with pleasure. "Alessandro, do not spill your seed, wait into you are inside of me." He was not sure what she meant, actually he was sure he had gone deaf and dumb. It was ecstasy. He closed his eyes and blocked out the rest of the world. She was doing things to him that even in his dreams did not happen. He thought he would explode.

"Alessandro, can you hear me?" she was talking, he knew it, but did not want to stop the dream. "Come on top of me" he thought he heard her say. She was pulling his arm "On top." He came to his senses and said "On top of you? I shall hurt you." She smiled at his sensitivity "No, you will not hurt me. I want you to lay on top of me and put your cock inside me. Don't worry, I shall guide it in." He was not sure of what she wanted but so far, she had made him a very happy man. Obediently, he mounted the petite girl; she grabbed his organ and said, "Put it inside me." He did as he was told. She was hot and wet and her clit swallowed him whole. It felt so good. "Now pump up and down, up and down, push, yes, go deeper, harder, faster, push, deeper, faster." He soon got in the rhythm and found that he was so enraptured with the process. He liked that she was groaning with pleasure. "Alessandro harder; faster; make me come." He was sweating from the exertion but did not want to stop. His heart was pounding in his ears. His cock was growing. "Push, push harder" she was panting in a raspy voice. She let out a high-pitched moan and he felt her back arch. At that moment, he came to his own pleasure and felt his seed spill inside her. He fell onto her in exhausted bliss. After a few moments, she gently nudged him off herself. "Dear Mother of God, if I should die this night, I would die a happy man. Thank you Rosemaria, that was so good. Thank you. I hope I gave you as much pleasure as you have given me." She smiled "You were very good. You will be a kind and generous lover. You will please any woman; look at the size of you. Salute!" He was happy that she thought he had a large penis.

She got up from the bed came to him and said, "Please rest, I will be back in a little while." She picked up a silk throw and covered his naked body. She came to his ear and whispered, "I very much enjoyed myself. Thank you Alessandro." He was already nearly asleep.

Morning came quickly and with it, the noisy sounds of a house filled with people in all stages of morning activities. Alessandro felt a sudden chill as the silk blanket was rudely thrown off him. He opened his eyes to see both Mateo and Genaro standing over him smiling. "Ah, I see what our little bird was talking about; you are generously appointed. Perhaps you would like to come to our side?" Alessandro was still in the fog of rhapsody and did not even feel ashamed for his nakedness. "What did she say?" asked an excited Alessandro. Genaro replied, "She said that you were wonderful. She is certain that you will be a great lover." He was pleased with himself. "Now get up and dressed, after we eat we shall be on our journey to find Lucia." As he was dressing Alessandro asked "And what of your evening? Did you enjoy yourselves?" Mateo with a lustful grin said, "Yes very much so, of course the two men who joined us will be quite sore for days, but I believe a good time was had by all. Don't you agree Genaro?" Mateo then slapped his bottom with a resounding clap and the other jumped from the sting "Yes it was very interesting and delightfully painful." They each gave a knowing grin. Alessandro was confused and still basking in his own pleasure.

CHAPTER SEVEN

AN UNINVITED VISITOR

Monteforte

Maria was enjoying the warm breezes that were sweeping the southern terrace just off the main salon. She put down her book and closed her eyes; she was savoring the scent of fresh lemons that wafted in the air. She heard footsteps and opened her eyes to find Giorgio standing near her chair "Yes Giorgio?" he had an odd expression on his face. "Mistress there is a visitor who is seeking an audience with you. When I inquired as to his name, he simply said he was your nephew, but I have never seen this man before. Shall I ask him to leave or shall I find Master Giovanni before I present him?"

"Yes, ask Master Giovanni to join me, and then show our guest in. I shall be in the library." Maria made her way to the library and Giovanni was already waiting for her "Cara who is this man who claims to be your nephew that Giorgio does not know?" She shook her head, "We will find out who he is when he is presented." "Let us be cautious Cara, there are many things of late that have given me cause for concern." "Yes I agree."

There was a brisk rap at the door and Giovanni said "Enter" and the door swung wide. Giorgio entered and was followed by a tall, muscular man in his footsteps. The maître de casa stepped to the side and with a flourish of formality announced, "Master and Mistress, may I present your nephew." He bowed deeply and awaited instruction. "Giorgio please bring some refreshments." The servant turned on his heels and left.

Maria was looking closely at this visitor "Please have a seat" and she pointed to the chair opposite from where she was sitting. "I am at a loss to know who you are, yet you claim to be my nephew." The man was in his early forties, handsome, with deep auburn hair, which was beginning to turn silver at his temples. He was powerfully built and wore no powder or wig. His beard, of the same hue as his hair, was fashioned in the Spanish style. His waistcoat was of a fine quality and cut. He wore silk stockings and silver buckles on his handmade shoes. Overall, he was a distinguished, fine looking man. She immediately saw the family resemblance and studied him mannerisms. "I beg your indulgence in granting me an audience. I have never been to Monteforte but have heard stories from my grandmother of its magnificence. I can see now the tales were all true. Please forgive my forwardness in presenting myself at your door. We have never met but I am the eldest son of your niece Helena Pugliese. She, as you know, is the daughter of your late brother Mateo Rizzo." He was very calm and spoke with an air of breeding. Giovanni was watching him intently and finally said, "What brings you to Monteforte? Were you passing through on route to another destination?"

At this line of questioning the man, claiming to be her brother's grandson rose from his chair and started to walk around. He was admiring the room and all the objects within it. "This is a grand room. I love to read and so I am thrilled that you chose this room to receive me." He did not immediately answer but when he did, his voice was steady and authoritative "I have come to advise you of my intentions. I am the legal heir of Monteforte not my niece Lucia Banfi. Monteforte is my birthright." Maria could sense, more than see, the anger rising in Giovanni, "How dare you come to this house, a stranger, perhaps even an imposter, and claim such a right?" The man was arrogant and sure of himself; he did not even address himself to Giovanni but focused on Maria. He came to where Maria was sitting and looking down at her proclaimed "I am the sole male heir of my grandfather Mateo Rizzo; upon your death I shall inherit Monteforte and all its holdings. You had no rights to give it to Lucia Banfi. Not only is she a woman but she holds no entitlement to the estate." By now Giovanni, having been slighted by this pompous cock, was ready to fight, but would not overshadow his wife's position.

It was now that Maria stood to address her guest. She came to face the man who called himself her blood. She was tall, but still she had to lift her head to look into his eyes, which were sharp and cold, the deep blue of an angry sea "You will have a long and arduous battle on your hands if you think for one moment that I will relinquish my family estate to a man I do not even know. You come unannounced and uninvited to my home, make all these wild statements, and threaten me. Did you think that I would hand you the keys to Monteforte and quietly walk away? If you did then you are sadly mistaken. You may make any inquiries you wish; you may go to the Supreme Magistrate and plead your cause, but make no mistake, I will see you dead before you inherit what I have given to Lucia."

The man began to laugh heartily "I had heard long ago that you were a woman of great determination and strength. I, unlike the rest of my family, am educated and wealthy in my own right. You my dear aunt presume that I am an ignorant opportunist wishing to make a quick fortune; I assure you that I have paid dearly to have some of the most brilliant legal minds review my petition. It may take some time, but, in the end I will reign triumphant."

Giorgio returned with a tray laden with refreshments and a decanter of wine. Giovanni turned to him "Leave it on the table, unfortunately our guest will not be staying. As a matter of fact, would you make sure he is escorted off the estate." Giorgio bowed deeply "It will be my pleasure; if you would follow me." Jerome Pugliese was a man who was used to getting his own way. He had come to make his intentions known to Maria Sucretti, and would not show his hand. There would be time for that later, for now they knew who he was and what his intentions were; that was enough for the moment.

"Thank you for your hospitality, I am sure we will be seeing each other soon. I bid you both a good day." Jerome bowed deeply and turned on his heels and followed Giorgio out of the room.

Giovanni looked at Maria "What do you make of this? Did you know that Helena had a son named Jerome?" Maria was quiet for a little while thinking about what had just happened. "Yes I knew of his birth. He was named after my brother's first born son Jerome, who died of the plague when he was a very young man. When Helena was with child, she decided to name her first-born son Jerome to honor her brother's memory. The man who came must be that child. I could not help but see the family resemblance. There is much we will have to do now to insure that Lucia's rights are protected." Giovanni was angry "On the soul of my dead child, I will kill that bastard before he will take away what you have given Lucia, of this I vow." Maria knew that Giovanni was more than capable of killing Jerome, and if the circumstances required it she would not hesitate to implement such action; but for now, she would call a meeting of her avvocato to study this man's claims. She prayed silently that Lucia would soon return.

CHAPTER EIGHT

THE DOLL HOUSE

Wallingston Castle

"Lucia, I have been looking for you. Please; will you join me for a few moments, sit with me." Danford almost completely recovered from his injuries, which he sustained at the hands of his dead brother Jonathan. Lucia had been overseeing the collection of honey from the hives for storage for the long winter months. Finding a bench at the end of the garden, both were engrossed in watching the servants carefully using the smoking lantern to distract the bees away from the hives. It was dangerous work if you were not vigilant.

"You are always working and keeping busy. I, we, shall miss you when you leave." It was Lucia's turn "I believe that you will be best served if you place Emma in charge of your household. She is young but very bright and she is organized. But that is only a suggestion, you My Grace, will choose for yourself when you are ready." Lucia was so casual that her tone was not warm or friendly and Danford sensed it "What troubles you Lucia?" Lucia stood to garner a better view of the honey gatherers, her back to him "You are different from the man I fell in love with. Since the day in the dungeon, you leapt from Danford the shipbuilder to His Grace the Fifth Duke of Northumberland. I know that you are trying to find a kind way of telling me that you no longer wish to marry me. Is this not true?" Still she kept her back to him for fear that if she looked at him her heart would break.

Danford came to where she was standing and stood behind her and threw his arms around her engulfing her now too slender figure. "I love you Lucia, I loved you from the first moment I saw you that day in my manor house. But..." he stopped speaking and Lucia seized the chance to finish his thoughts "But yet you cannot marry a foreigner." She suddenly wedged herself out of his grip so that she could face him "I understand that you are no longer Danford Stevens you are the Duke of an extensive domain; your subjects will demand that you take an English bride. I would never fit in and from all the gossip, I hear there is talk that if you were foolish enough to wed me that the older, more strategically located lords would no longer pledge their fealty to you. I do love you, and, I believe that you still love me, but our love cannot survive here. This is the land of your ancestors; this is your right and your duty to rule these people. There will never be a place here for me."

The tears fell from her eyes, as they did from Danford's as well. "I wish it were not so, but I know now that you understand the plight that I am in. I love you with all my heart but it is a love that for both of us will never be. You, like me, are prisoner to your legacy. I am sorry my dear sweet Lucia, forgive me." They held each other tightly and wept unashamed for anyone to see. Lucia thought that she loved him more now than ever. "Danford, please take me home where I belong. I need to get far away from here." " Lucia, I cannot leave yet, there is much that by the laws of the duchy I must see to."

Lucia broke away from him and wiping her nose on her sleeve took a deep breath and announced "Then I shall go by myself. I am in the company of three armed guards and my maid. There is no one who will harm us. I will leave by first light the day after tomorrow." Danford was about to protest this decision when Lucia halted him from speaking "Danford you must move on with your life and your duties. My duties await me in a country far from here. I will ask that for now if you would continue the work you started on my ships, I know that you will find someone who will take over when the time is right. Will you do that for me?" "Of course I will. I shall try to be there always and will move the whole operation to London so that I may have better control over the workings. Actually, Michael has shown great aptitude for shipbuilding, I shall ask him to head things up until I have secured my position with my people."

"It is settled. I shall begin to get things ready for traveling." Danford looked forlorn. "Do not leave so soon." "I must, my heart can no longer withstand the agony of our situation. Before I leave I shall set everything for your household in place." "I cannot thank you enough for all you have done for me. My heart is also broken."

***

At supper that evening Danford announced that, Lucia would be leaving the day after tomorrow. Michael said, "I for one shall miss you dearly. I cannot even begin to measure what you have been to this family. Thank you from the bottom of my heart." Even Rachael, who seemed never truly to have warmed up to her, now had tears in her eyes "I too shall miss you. I wish you were going to be here for my wedding." Elizabeth pushed back her chair and came bounding over to her, "Mistress Lucia, Danford has told me that you want me to come to where you live, far, far, away from Wallingston, to live with you. I want to, but I cannot leave here. This is where someone like me can fit in. Why can't you stay here and be my big sister?" By now Elizabeth was crying like a small child and was clutching onto Lucia who was also crying "Listen to me dear Elizabeth, I, like your brother, have many responsibilities in the land I come from, I was only here for a short while, but now my people need me. I shall make this promise to you, that if ever you want to come to stay with me, even for a short while, I shall send my men to come for you. You must promise to write to me and I will write back to you. We shall always be friends." Lucia, struggling under the weight of the large young woman, stroked her head to comfort her. "I promise Mistress Lucia I shall write to you all the time. I shall remember all the things you showed me and I will be a good girl." "You have always been a good girl. I love you Elizabeth." "Do you really love me?" "Yes, truly I do." Elizabeth stood abruptly and said to everyone at the table "Mistress Lucia loves me. No one has ever told me that before." Turning to Lucia, she said, "I love you to. Thank you." She then returned to her place at the dining table and continued eating her meal.

***

Lucia was not sure who was happier to return to Monteforte, her, Sophia, Nicko or the two guards, she finally decided to call them Brute and Bruto. "Mistress I am almost finished with our packing and Nicko and his men are also ready. I was speaking with William and he has made arrangements for us to have an armed escort to London." Lucia just nodded; her mind was filled with other thoughts.

"Mistress, I know we have not spoken of it, but what will happen between you and His Grace?" "There is nothing to happen. You have heard the gossip; I am a foreigner and they will never accept me. Our love cannot not exist in either of our worlds; we shall be wed to our legacy and suffer our personal loss." Sophia stopped what she was doing and came to embrace her mistress "I am so sorry he was a good man but it is true what you have said. Among the servants, there is so much talk of what the village is saying; the servants are afraid for their master. This is a harsh country that is always at war; if His Grace stands with you, no one will stand with him." Together they held each other for strength and comfort.

"Tomorrow at first light we shall leave this God forsaken land for our home; for Monteforte" but there was no joy in her voice.

***

That night after supper, Danford took her for a walk, the weather was cool and crisp, but there was no rain. They strolled in silence each holding so many thoughts in their heads but afraid to share them. They came to a miniature replica of the castle. "What is this place?" Danford explained that his father had it built when the twins were born, to be used as a playhouse. It was larger than many of the houses in the village. They went inside and it was beautifully detailed. He lit a tapper so that she could see. "This must have been a delightful place for your sisters to play. What little girl does not want to have a castle for her dolls?" He hung his head "I really don't know. I was already gone from Wallingston when they would have been old enough to come here. It is so sad that I know so little of my family and the torment they endured." Lucia went to him and put her arms around his waist "That was the past. You all must look to the future to find your happiness. Please Danford, I know it is not my place, but you must care for Elizabeth with such love. She, more than anyone, needs encouragement. Promise me you will see after her special needs." He kissed her lovingly on the mouth, "Even after all the misery, hard work, and pain you have endured these past months, you can still find love for us. Lucia you are a remarkable woman I will never find anyone to equal you."

Danford took her arms away and dropped to his knees, "I Danford Stevens, Fifth Duke of Northumberland, swear on my honor, that I shall care for my sister Elizabeth Margaret Stevens for the rest of her natural life. I further swear that I shall make provision for her physical and financial comforts in the event that some tragic accident should befall me. So help me God." He took her hand that he was holding and kissed it to seal his oath. "Thank you, I shall rest at night when I pray for you and your family knowing that my dear Elizabeth has finally found someone to love her." Danford, so serious, asked "Lucia you will pray for us?" As if the question was full of folly, she responded, "Yes of course I shall pray for you. I love you. I love all of you."

He stood, his massive body overshadowing her, and took her to himself. "There is one thing that I shall live with all my life; and that is I did not make love to you. I could not bring myself to dishonor you until we were wed." " Danford, please I beg you, do not come down tomorrow to see us off, I do not think my heart could stand it. I shall say my farewell to you here and now." "How could I let you go to leave me forever without saying farewell; not to hold you one last time; my own heart is broken." Lucia was weeping. He was holding her in his strong arms and they went down to the floor and held each other their tears mingling into one. "Shall we ever recover from this tragedy?" "I don't know." They stayed there in each other's arms for what seemed like a long time. They did not speak; there were no words that could make this right. Finally, Lucia said, "We must return I will need to prepare for my journey."

They had nearly reached the castle; the light was gone from the sky and a cold breeze filled the air. "Danford kiss me one last time for I shall not see you again unless you come to me in my country." He took her in his arms and they kissed with such love; with such passion; they were panting from desire. "Farewell my love do not forget me." "Lucia I don't know if I can live without you." "You must. Our love cannot change what is to be our destiny." She broke free of him and ran to the castle her eyes blinded by her tears. She prayed he would not be there in the morning.

CHAPTER NINE

TRAVELING PARTNERS

Paris

This morning, as always, the sky was grey and angry. It was early, yet the kitchen staff was already at work, kneading bread, milking the cows, and churning butter. Lucia and her little troupe sat to a simple breakfast and Emma had made up a traveling basket that Nicko had to strain to lift. They were ready to leave, the horses were saddled, and the wagon was filled with trunks. Emma came to her "Marchesa may I say what an honor it was to have you here. I have learned so much in the short time since you came. I shall miss you very much. May I be so bold as to give you a kiss farewell?" Lucia was fond of Emma, a young woman close to her own age, and hoped that Danford would take heed to what she had told him about the girl's abilities. "Come here Emma, you were a great help during this whole ordeal. I wish you only the best of life." They embraced and kissed each other with tear-filled eyes.

Lucia was looking for Danford but found William instead "Marchesa His Grace said to tell you he will always love you. As you requested he has stayed to his rooms. I will miss you as well. It breaks my heart that you will not be my Mistress. I wish you God's speed and a long and happy life." He knelt down, took both her hands, and kissed them with great love. When he rose Lucia kissed him on each cheek and whispered in his ear "Tell His Grace that I too share that one regret." William looked befuddled at the remark "Don't worry he will know what I mean." The valet just nodded. He bent and gave her a boost up to her saddle. All the servants had assembled outside, stood on either side of the pathway, and waved their white scarves and some of the younger, ones, with whom Lucia had made a special attachment, threw her kisses. They were making their way when she heard someone calling after her; it was Elizabeth "Mistress Lucia, wait, please wait." Lucia pulled up her reins and waited for the plump young woman to reach her. Breathless, she came to her side "I just wanted to say farewell one last time. I love you. I will miss you." Lucia came off her horse to embrace her "Remember what I said, you must write to me and send me news of you and your family and I shall do the same. I will always keep you all in my prayers and in my heart. Tell your brother I love him." By now William was once again, at her side to help her remount "I must be leaving before my heart breaks." As soon as she had fixed herself on her mount, she took off at a gallop and never looked back. She rode hard for a long stretch and those in her party realized that she needed to be alone. Lucia cried for herself; she cried for a life she would never have.

After two days, they reached London and Nicko booked their passage to Calais. They would leave the next morning. Nicko, on the suggestion of one of the men Danford had sent along as an escort told them of a good inn to spend the night. Lucia had them join her for supper and to stay the night at the inn. To her delight the food was savory and the company lightened her spirits, she had only drank ale once before, but enjoyed the taste. After a few pints of ale, she found that she was singing along to the bawdy tunes of the lively patrons. Sophia seeing her mistress enjoying herself was reluctant to stop her from imbibing in the ale and partook of it herself.

It was late and they were booked for the first outgoing vessel. Nicko came to Lucia and Sophia, "Mistress, it is late, we will need to rise early; we will be the first vessel to leave; if we are late in arriving we will have to wait for two more days before the next passage. I will help you both get settled to your room." The two women tried to stand but instantly realized that they were too weak to walk. "Dear Mother of God, how much have the two of you drunk?" They started to giggle and cackle like two little girls. Whispering to each other and laughing. Nicko told Brute, or was it Bruto, she would never know who was who, and to carry Sophia upstairs; he scooped Lucia in his arms, threw her over his shoulder, and carried her laughing and wiggling up the stairs. He put them both to bed. When they came back down Nicko said, "We shall see tomorrow who is laughing. With any luck the water will be rough and they will learn to hold their drink." All the men at the inn were having a good turn at the expense of the two women.

Morning came with a vengeance to Lucia and Sophia. When Nicko came to wake them, they were moaning from pains in their heads. He tried not to laugh but could not control himself "What is so funny?" demanded Lucia "Do you not see that we are ill?" Nicko was now at the point of doubling over from laughter "You two are not ill; you are sick from too much drink. Believe me I have been sick from drink many times. It will take a good part of the day, but you will get better. Now, if you two could hurry so that we do not miss our boat. I will take all your bags down." He gathered up their bags, took a last look at these two sorrowful figures then started to laugh once again as he bounded down the stairs.

After a few minutes, they came down to the tavern area, trying to act as if nothing was wrong. They sat for their breakfast. When the serving girl came with the porridge slathered with bacon grease and butter Lucia promptly vomited into the bowl; followed by Sophia who did the same in her own bowl. "Nicko I forbid you to say one word" growled Lucia. Nicko, the wise and obedient servant, put his head down and quickly turned away and ran to the door but not before, he burst out in laughter. The two women looked at each other for the first time in the light coming through the window; they were a pitiful mess. All of a sudden, Lucia started to laugh; Sophia started to laugh. "I cannot laugh, my head hurts from the banging inside" Lucia said while still laughing. She had needed the release for a long time. The two women hugged each other and then started to laugh and cry all at the same time. Nicko, watching from the doorway just shook his head "Donne, che possono comprendere ciò che vogliono. Ridere, piangere e tutti in una volta. Dio ricambio mi da belle donne." One of the Englishmen that had accompanied them said "Women, who can bloody figure out what goes on in those pretty heads." Nicko just nodded having voiced the same thoughts.

The ride from London to Calais was choppy, much to the chagrin of Nicko who secretly had prayed for rough seas so that his soon-to-be bride and his young Mistress would be sicker than they were. Both Lucia and Sophia hung their heads over buckets and emptied their stomachs. While Sophia's olive skin was pale, Lucia's translucent complexion almost appeared to be a soft green. By the time they reached France, they were spent. They prayed for land.

Lucia, in a state of deep melancholy, remembered that it had been not so long ago that she had made this journey with Danford and her beloved Henri. That she had such mixed feelings for him in the beginning. There was always that physical attraction, the man was handsome and charming, but he also possessed a loving and gentle soul. Her heart sank a little more with every roll of the vessel. She prayed, "Dear Jesus, will I ever find love in the arms of a man?"

Finding enough strength to hold on to the side rail Lucia closed her eyes and tried to soak in the warmth of the sun. She tried to clear her mind of all the events that had happened and to heal her broken heart. Her thoughts were rudely interrupted when the vessel collided with the dock and laid anchor. She reluctantly opened her eyes, almost dreading to face reality; she was searching the dock, when to her surprise she saw her brothers waiting at the pier. Miraculously, she felt better at the sight of them. Her spirits lifted, she started to wave to them. Genaro, so excited to see her, shouted her name "Lucia Bella!" Sophia hearing his voice followed her Mistress' gaze and she too began to wave; the color coming back to their cheeks at the sight of them. Nicko too showed relief at their presence.

It took some time before they could disembark the vessel. Nicko along with Brute and Bruto went with the crew to unload their trunks. Mateo and Genaro greeted him "Nicko, how is everything?" Nicko, having been born and raised at Monteforte was like family and thus he embraced both of them with great affection. "My dear Mistress, she is heartbroken. You must do all you can to lightened her pain. The Duke did not come. I am sure she will tell you everything. I have cried for her sorrow. I can't tell you how relieved I am to see the two of you." They once again embraced Nicko who truly loved his Mistress. "Do not trouble yourself we shall give her comfort."

When it was time, Lucia bounded off the vessel and into the waiting arms of her brothers. She started to cry as soon as she fell into their arms. "My sweet sister do not weep, we shall be here with you" came the soft voice of Genaro. She then went to Mateo who swept her into his arms and spun her around "My baby sister it is so wonderful to see you." He placed her back on her feet and kissed her face all over. "My Dear Lord what has happened, you are a bag of bones; did they not feed you?" Lucia was crying and laughing at the same time, "The food is terrible; grey mushy stuff, just like the weather." Even she had to laugh at that statement. "Well, not to fear we shall fatten you up in no time. As a matter of fact we have a special supper planned for you." Already Lucia was feeling the love and safety of home, even though she was a long way from Monteforte. "I love you both so much, thank you for coming for me. How did you know I would be arriving today?" Mateo grinned in that way that was both charming and devious at the same time, "A little dove has been sending me notes of your wanderings." Lucia knew it could only have been Sophia; she turned around, as Sophia stood just behind her, and hugged and kissed her, then whispered in her ear "I love you."

Lucia grabbed Mateo on her right arm and Genaro on her left and the loving trio made their way to the boulevard. They had a coach waiting for them. "Where are we going?" "Well, unfortunately this is not Paris, so we found the best inn we could, I think you will find it comfortable. Tomorrow we shall leave for Paris and then on to Rome." Lucia looked confused "Why are we going to Rome?" Genaro smiled coyly "I wish to show you my latest work. I have just completed the Palace of the Bishop of Rome and I am most anxious to show it to you." "Oh yes that would be wonderful."

They pulled up to a grand home in the old French style. Several servants came to greet them and take their trunks. The proprietor of the inn came to welcome them "Marchesa Banfi, I am honored to have you stay at my humble home. Please, if there is anything I can do to make your stay more enjoyable let me know." The middle-aged man, with a round belly and white beard, bowed as low as he could, which was not too far since his belly was in the way. He had soft brown eyes and a nice smile. "Monsieur there is one thing that I am desperate for, and that is a hot bath. Can you accommodate me?" asked Lucia in her flawless French. The fat little innkeeper made a grand gesture "But of course, I shall see to it immediately." A woman, who she was sure was his wife, led them to their rooms. It was not luxurious but spacious and nicely decorated. "Mademoiselle, we shall return with your bath." "Merci."

With Sophia's help, Lucia stripped down out of her mourning gown "Sophia I want you to get rid of this gown. I don't care if you have it burned, or give it away; I want to cleanse myself of all these bad memories." Sophia understood, and would ask the innkeeper's wife to take care of it. With a soft knock at the door, there came a small parade of servants carrying a large porcelain tub and buckets of steaming water. Once they left, Lucia immersed herself in the tub, closed her eyes, and thanked her Creator for this blissful gift. Sophia came in and helped her wash her hair. "Sophia while we are in Paris we shall stop by Madame Richaud's to have you fitted for a wedding gown." Sophia's eyes grew wide but she did not say anything and just continued washing her mistress' hair. "Sophia, I see that look on your face and I am disappointed. What troubles you?" Sophia answered honestly, "Mistress, I do not want such a lavish gift. The one thing that I would beg for is to spend two days alone with Nicko away from Monteforte; just him and me." Lucia smiled "You know Sophia; it is possible to have both." Sophia smiled as well "Yes, but the time alone is a gift I shall have forever; a gown of such costs will not last me but a few hours." Lucia grabbed her hand to make her stop and said, "You are the most generous and kind woman I know. You shall have your time in the best inn we can find." Her eyes filled with tears, Sophia said, "I do not deserve such a wonderful Mistress. Nicko will be so pleased when I tell him; but for now, it will be our secret. Also, Marianna told me that she had taken one of your old gowns and had embellished it with lace and pearls, so there is no need for something so expensive." "You will be a beautiful bride even if you were to don a feed sack." They laughed like sisters.

After a long relaxing soak, Lucia was ready for supper; she dressed in a simple but elegant gown, which Sophia had to cleverly pulled in because of her loss of weight. Her hair, now dry, was a mass of curls that crowned her face. Sophia plaited it so that it was somewhat tamed. Regardless of everything that had happened Lucia once again regained a warm peach glow to her lovely face. She finally made her way down to the dining room; it smelled so delicious her mouth was watering. It was a lovely home with a large salon and there she found her brothers engaged in a pleasant conversation with another guest. The three men were drinking wine and smoking cigars.

Genaro spotted her "Ah there you are and looking well rested. Did you find your appetite yet?" Lucia was so pleased to be with them, "I am ravenous. Whatever they are preparing it smells delightful." She took his proffered arm and they came by Mateo and the stranger. "Marchesa Lucia Banfi may I introduce Lord Alessandro Galilei, Master Architect." The man bowed deeply and reached for her hand, which he gently kissed. "You are even more beautiful than your brothers described." Lucia instantly flushed "Do you know each other?" she looked searching at Mateo and Genaro. "Yes" said Genaro smiling "I am sorry Lucia; Alessandro was the architect for the Palace of the Bishop of Rome, we have been working together all this time and have since become good friends." Mateo said, "Well, let us feed this poor girl before she wastes away to nothing."

The innkeeper magically appeared and escorted them to the dining room. Since there were no other guests staying the night, they had the table to themselves. A delicious meal of escargot simmered in wine and garlic; roasted rabbit cooked in shallots and turnips; fresh goat cheese and hot loaves of bread. For dessert there were fresh figs preserved in cognac and miniatures pies with fresh fruit. It was so marvelous Lucia was eating like a sow. "Brothers I am about to burst from my gown; I have not eaten so much in months. I shall have to let Sophia let out my gowns if I eat like this every day." When the innkeeper came to clear the table Lucia said to him "Monsieur, the food was superb, please tell the cook I very much enjoyed it." The man's big belly jiggled with laughter "Ah, you see my predicament. My wife, she is such a cook, when we first wed I was skinny and now I am fat." The man patted his rotund middle. They all laughed. Mateo told the man that they would have espresso and cognac in the salon.

As they settled themselves for a relaxing evening, her brothers told Lucia the story of how their friendship with Alessandro had grown. She could see how they would befriend such a man. He was quiet, intelligent, and handsome in a homely way. She thought that a few more weeks under Mateo's tutelage and he would transform Alessandro just as he had Genaro. After a while, the brothers excused themselves with the excuse of having to walk off their heavy meal, which left Lucia alone with Alessandro.

Lucia could see that he was instantly anxious about being alone with her. She wondered if he shared the same tastes as her brothers. They spoke of her travels and his work for the Pope. They spoke of family. It was then that the subject of her long lost brother Andrea came up. She was pleasantly surprised to find out that Alessandro had gone to universita with him. The architect spoke highly of his genius for mathematics. Lucia was working hard at trying to put him at ease.

"Tell me Lord Galilei what brings you to be traveling with my brothers?" Lucia was trying to draw him out. "Please I am not so formal, I would like for you to call me Alessandro." Lucia smiled pleasantly and added, "Well then you must address me as Lucia, especially if we will be traveling together." "I came with your brothers to find some friendship." Lucia looked at him and directly asked, "I am sure a man as famous as you must garner many friends to himself." Alessandro put his head down "I grew up in a monastery, with no other children; from there I was sent to universita and worked day and night under the thumb of my patron Cardinale Albani. After finishing there, I was sent to the Vatican to work for His Holy Father who is a man of great vision and a thirst for building. While I have travelled extensively, it has only been in the pursuit of my work, going where the Church sends me. I was very lonely and then I met Genaro and found a friend." Lucia sat listening to the man before her, a man who was so famous and whose works will live forever speak with such honesty and humility. She thought to herself, I could grow to like this man very much. He continued, "Genaro has a gift that few men possess, but, he is kind and humble. He introduced me to Mateo and that is when they invited me to join them to bring you home. I am so happy I did, but I hope you do not find my presence an intrusion on your privacy?"

"I am honored to have you join us. My aunt and uncle will be so excited to meet you. My aunt, Marchesa Maria Sucretti is a great patron of the arts and enjoys good architecture. I am so longing to go home." They were interrupted by the reappearance of Mateo and Genaro "I see you two have made yourselves comfortable. I think however, since the hour is late, and we will be starting early, we should retire to bed." Lucia agreed, "Yes it has been a long day and I am tired even though I have enjoyed the conversation. I bid you all good night." She went to her brothers, hugged, and kissed them lovingly "Thank you again for coming for me. I cannot express how happy I am to see you both. I love you." Mateo took her in his arms and stroked her hair taking in the scent "Lucia Bella, we love you." She then went to Alessandro who was standing to the side; he did not want to impose himself into this intimate family moment. "Alessandro, I bid you good night. I hope you don't think me too forward, but, may I give you a kiss as well?" "It would be my honor."

"Come Lucia I shall walk you to your room," said Mateo. She took hold of his proffered arm and they went up to her room. Upon entering Mateo saw that she was a little flushed and asked "What are your thoughts regarding Alessandro?" Lucia was smiling "I think he is a gentle and intelligent man. I enjoyed speaking with him and I am glad for him that he has joined you and Genaro." Mateo knew there was something else lurking in the back of her mind, "Well, I shall say good night once again." He was turning to leave and Lucia came to him "Mateo, does he share your appetites?" "Whatever do you mean?" "You know. Does he prefer male companionship?" "Oh that. No. He likes women very much." Lucia visibly let out her breath "Oh I see; then the three of you are all just friends." "Yes; just friends." She smiled demurely and lowered her lids "Good night dear Mateo. I am so delighted the three of you came for me." She put her arms around his neck and kissed him with great love. "Now go to sleep little one; before you close your eyes we will be knocking at your door to be ready" he lovingly chastised her.

Mateo closed the door gently, filled with a sense of paternity, which he had never known. She was a woman and a child all at the same time and he loved her for it. He thought that he would not object to a union between his new friend the young architect, and his beloved Lucia. Time would be the best judge of what was best for her; but for now, he was just content to be here.

***

It was a cheerful sunny day, perfect for the two-day trek to Paris. After a country breakfast, with beignets and raspberries, and not grey mush, they were on their way. Her spirits were riding high and she was looking forward to Paris. They found comfortable inns along the way each night. The weather was crisp but sunny and the company was fun and lighthearted. By noon of the third day, they had arrived in Paris. Mateo had arranged for them to stay at the Hotel de Crillon, which was the very pinnacle of high society. "Oh, I remember when Henri had taken us here to dine. I fear that whenever I think of that dear man my heart aches. We must go to visit his apartment in Sant Germaine." Genaro replied, "You are right. Perhaps his family has taken up residence there and we can give our condolences."

***

The Hotel de Crillon was a magnificent stone palace that had been originally commissioned by King Louis. It was located on the beautiful tree lined Place de la Concorde, with its striking fountains and monuments. Mateo, so informed of all things beautiful, told Lucia "This is one of two sister palaces that were built and separated by the rue Royale. It had once been occupied by the Duke of Aurmont,

Louis Marie-Augustin, a former client of mine, and a great patron of the arts." Excitedly Lucia asked, "You knew this Duke?" Mateo nodded "Yes. He was a great man, with a keen sense of style and grace. I very much enjoyed working for him." "What happened to him? Why did he give up this grand palace?" "Ah, he was already old when I knew him many years ago. He has since died and his family could not afford to keep such a vast estate. As we go around I shall show you, if they have not sold them, the many objects of art I had acquired for him." Lucia was so excited.

They settled themselves into their rooms and Lucia, aided by Sophia, needed to bathe and get ready for supper. "Mistress, it is always so exciting to be in Paris." Lucia could not agree more. "Sophia, since I will be with my brothers and Alessandro all day tomorrow, why don't you and Nicko take a few hours and go enjoy yourselves? I shall have Mateo give Nicko some money; and I will give you some also, perhaps you may find some small bauble of your fancy." Sophia was dancing around the room with delight.

Dinner was lively and interesting. Alessandro was telling them of his work. He had been commissioned by the Vatican to design churches in Spain, England and in France. It was amazing but Lucia could already see Mateo's influence on his appearance. Tonight he wore a waistcoat that was more tailored to the cut of his body and showed his narrow waist. He had his hair pulled back with a simple leather strap, but his face seemed different. His eyes were brighter and he had a nice flush to his cheeks. Yes; surely, it was her brother's influence, she was seated with the three most attractive men there. Everyone was looking at them. After dinner, they strolled along the Place de la Concorde. It was so pleasant. As it was turning dark men came around to light the street lanterns. A soft warm glow blanketed the tree line boulevard.

Mateo and Genaro stopped to join a chess match while Lucia and Alessandro continued on. "I love Paris it is such a lively place. Sometimes when I think about Monteforte, which is so secluded from the rest of the world, I get sad. It is not that I do not love to be there, for there is no place of more beauty in the entire world, but I cannot experience life behind those stalls. Do you understand what I am saying Alessandro?" The young architect, having spent his whole life, in real as well as imaginary stonewalls, absolutely knew what she meant. "Well you could always build a villa in Milan or Florence and divide your time between the vibrancy of the city and the restful quiet of the country. I could design it for you." Lucia stopped, turned to him, and said, "That is brilliant. I shall talk to my aunt and uncle about such an idea. It is grand." The architect was befuddled as to how such a simple solution could cause her such joy, but he was happy for it. He felt his cheeks flush with embarrassment and cursed himself. Lucia mesmerized him. They stopped and sat on a bench for a few moments. "Lucia" he nearly whispered, "You are the most beautiful woman I have ever seen." She was surprised by the comment and did not know how to respond. Alessandro took her silence as an indication that she was displeased with his forwardness "I am sorry. I did not mean to over step my place. Please forgive me."

Lucia turned to face him and reached for his hand "Dear Alessandro I must confess to you something that has happened to me." He immediately began to stammer, "I have no right to your confidences. You do not need to tell me anything." He was so contrite she felt sorry for him. "I know; yet I feel that if we are to be friends and continue to enjoy each other's company I must be honest with you. I have, just returned from England, as you know. I fell deeply in love with a wonderful man, who through the death of his father had to assume his rightful position as duke of a vast and important domain. We were in love; but there was no hope for it. I was a foreigner and his people would never accept me. He and I are both bound to our legacies, he to Northumberland and I to Monteforte. So you see; at least for now, I cannot, I will not, allow myself the torment of falling in love. Please Alessandro, I beg you just be my friend. Let us just comfort each other and live in the joy of sharing companionship."

Alessandro was stunned at her honesty and appreciated her candor. "Lucia I had no knowledge of the pain you have endured. I am so sorry for the love you lost. Yes, it would be my privilege to be your friend. Maybe, someday, you and I could become more, but, for now, I am content just to be with you, Genaro and Mateo."

Lucia leaned over and kissed him gently on each cheek to seal their relationship. While Alessandro understood, he was also saddened that there would be no possibility to entertain thoughts of anything but friendship with this lovely woman.

They walked back to where her brothers were actively engaged in a heated discussion of the rules of gamesmanship with some other men. When they saw the expressions of both their faces, they abruptly left the game and joined up with Lucia and Alessandro. "The two of you look as if you have received news that someone is on their death bed. What troubles you?" Lucia looked to Alessandro but he would not say of what they had spoken. Lucia said, "I have burdened this poor man and purged my soul as to what has happened since last I saw you. He has bravely listened to my laments and has still agreed to be my friend." Mateo, wise owl that he was realized that Alessandro would have liked a different relationship, but that he would settle for friendship "I too understand. Sometimes in life a good friend is all that we need, at least for a while." The foursome walked back to the hotel engaged in light conversation.

Genaro walked Lucia to her room, and was very quiet. When they reached their destination, he entered with her. "Lucia, did Danford hurt you? You are different than when I saw you last." She sat down on the settee and beckoned him to join her. "He did not hurt or damage me in a physical sense. We loved each other, and I was willing to marry him, but it could never be. As Duke of Northumberland he would, by ancient rite wed a woman of his own country. I was a foreigner and would never have been accepted. Do you understand?" Genaro, tears running down his handsome face took her to his chest and held her tight "Yes my baby sister I do understand. That is why you cannot find yourself in love with another man. For now, it shall take time and love for you to heal. Give yourself time; you will see that it will work out. I promise."

CHAPTER TEN

THE LAND OF STONE TEMPLES

Sardinia

Jerome knew it would not be a simple task to announce his claim to Monteforte. From the day, he was old enough to understand, his grandmother Lucia Rizzo told him stories of the Marchesa Maria Sucretti. Having now met her, even at her advanced age, he could see the elegantly refined beauty, with eyes filled with fire and intelligence. He, as was warned by his grandmother, would never underestimate her power, or her ability to preserve her beloved Monteforte.

He left the estate of Monteforte under the watchful and protective eyes of several of her faithful servants. He had come alone. His horse had been tethered just beyond the high iron gates and stone walls of the ancient fortress. It was just as he had envisioned from all the stories he had been told.

Jerome Pugliese was not a young man filled with piss and vinegar, but a wise and patient intellectual thinker. He was here because he was brought to this place by his fate. He was the eldest son of Helena and Guiseppe Pugliese. Helena was the daughter of Lucia and Mateo Rizzo. Had he lived,

Mateo Rizzo would be the sole heir of Monteforte, but he was killed, and so his sister Maria Sucretti became the Marchesa of Monteforte. It was he, Jerome Pugliese, grandson of Mateo, who should be the Marchese of Montefort ,as it was his blood right.

Lucia Rizzo, his grandmother, had sent her beloved Jerome to Sardinia when he was a small boy. His mother and father protested but Lucia would not be dissuaded from her mission. He was sent to a monastery where Lucia's brother was the Abbot. Jerome was named after the son Lucia had lost to the plague when he was a young man. His resemblance to his deceased namesake was remarkable. It was known that Lucia was a visionary, and could see the future. One day, when Jerome was twelve years old, his grandmother came to him and told him that she had a dream. In her dream, Jerome would become a great man but would have to battle a force much greater than himself. That day Lucia Rizzo decided that he would be sent far away, to a land where no evil could befall him, to a place where he could learn the secrets of how to fight the foes of his destiny.

Lucia called upon her trusted servant Augusto to serve as bodyguard to her beloved Jerome. She knew that the devoted giant, even though slow of wit, would lay down his life to protect the boy, for it was she, Lucia Rizzo, who, when he was of the same age as Jerome, rescued him from the streets of Naples, after his mother had abandoned him to the

Church. He loved Lucia like a mother and would do anything for her.

Armed with a purse full of coins, a bag of clothes, and his grandfather Mateo Rizzo's sword, twelve-year-old Jerome, and his servant embarked on a journey across the sea to Sardinia in search of Lucia's brother, Abbot Sebastian Cioffi. It was a hard voyage, their ship almost being swallowed by the sea, the boy never having sailed before suffered greatly at the relentless pounding of the waves.

After three days, they could see land and their hearts were filled with joy, but as they approached, their spirits sank. The mountains were made of jagged stone that descended with such severity into the sea. Clouds of mist hung at their zenith like a crown. The angry waves which relentlessly crashed furiously against the serrated boulders that protected the shore sent a grave warning to would-be intruders. This was a land, sealed in the past, which would not welcome outsiders to her shores.

Once they landed, they sought out anyone who could point them to the Abbazia di Maria Regine Delle Stelle. The inhabitants were frightened at the sight of Augusto who was a monstrous man with his huge muscular body and asymmetrical features. Women roaming the marketplace made the sign of the cross; mothers drew their children to their side and men narrowed their eyes as the two of them made inquiries. Finally, they were told that it was many days travel over the mountains. They would have to pass through Nuraghe of Barumini. "What is this place that makes you all cower in fear?" asked the inquisitive Jerome. One old man, toothless and shriveled told them to beware of the curse of the unsettled spirits that lived in the stone temple. "There is a temple that remains standing on the sacred grounds that were built by the ancients. It has devoured many men who have dared to pass through her threshold. Walk around it; cover your eyes and ears." " What is the name of this temple?" The old man, making the sign of the cross, answered in an ominous tone "It is the Escala Del Cabirol. The She Devil who lives within will call for you; do not heed her call. If you should venture to her you will be sucked into the mouth of the temple never to be seen again." The boy's eyes grew wide and his mouth dry from fear. By now, a small crowd had gathered around the boy and his giant. The boy was not sure if he had understood all that they said for their language was strange to his ears.

There was within those gathered one of the sailors that had been aboard the vessel that had brought them and the boy approached him. "Did you understand all that the old man had said?" The sailor nodded "I am from this island and so I understand." The boy repeated the story and the sailor confirmed the veracity of the tale.

"I had heard that story many times when I was a small boy. When I was just turning to manhood, I wanted to prove that I was a brave man. I, along with two of my brothers, journeyed to the

Nuraghe of Barumini. It was a difficult route but we made it to the temple. We were so tired we laid down to rest and fell into a deep sleep. I remember that I was so tired and weak that I could not move my body yet I heard the song of a woman calling me. It was strange and exotic and I could not resist. I struggled to get up and when I did, my body was light as a feather. I followed the sound of that beautiful song and was drawing nearer to the temple. Suddenly, I felt arms grabbing me and holding me back; I was fighting to break their hold but I could not escape. Then I felt the sting of a blow across my face and the song stopped. My legs did not hold me and I fell to the ground. When I opened my eyes there were my brothers standing over me. When I asked what had happened they told me that I was under some kind of evil spell and was walking toward the mouth of the temple. We picked up our bags and started running. We ran as fast as we could for nearly a day without stopping until finally we collapsed."

Jerome was bursting with the wonderment of the place, while filled with fear, he also had a sharp intellect, and so his curiosity overcame his anxiety. Augusto did not understand fear of the unknown, he only concerned himself with that which he could see and touch. This was like nothing he had ever known. Having grown up in Naples, a cosmopolitan center, and under the protection of his family the young Jerome never experienced life on his own. Here, on this unforgiving island; in a land steeped in superstition; remote places; and magical traditions, he would become a man.

They found an inn and put up for the night. At first light, fortified with a bag filled with food, wine, and blankets, they began their adventure. True to what the villagers had told them the roads, which were no more than worn paths made by the longhaired wooly sheep that roamed wild across the island, were strewn with rocks and briar bushes. Jerome found that the air was scented with the fresh aroma of citrus and much to his enjoyment, there were lemon trees growing everywhere. There was no argument that this was truly a beautiful but inhospitable land. By day's end, they had travelled far beyond the seashore and were making their way towards the mountains. They made their first bed at the edge of a dense pine forest.

Although he was bone tired, the young Jerome found that sleep did not come easy. He had never slept under the stars and the sounds of wild animals filled his head with frightening images. He looked over to his gigantic companion who was sleeping soundly and rolled over to find some comfort. Eventually, Jerome did fall asleep, only to awake with his clothes damp from the morning mist. He was hungry and went to claim the bag that held the food. He let out a cry that woke Augusto with a start, the big man leapt to his feet, his hand on his dagger. Then he saw what the source of the boy's consternation was. The bag with the food had been torn open and its contents, or at least the scraps of which, were strew all over the ground. "Who would do such a cruel thing?" he said not really expecting an answer. Augusto replied "Not who Master Jerome, but, what?" "We shall go hungry until we come upon another village. Let us get underway."

The forest was thick with undergrowth and the tightly woven canopy of pine trees shrouded the sunlight. The boy's stomach rumbled loudly from hunger, they continued for what seemed like days, but was probably about six hours. By now, they were tired and hunger had claimed them. Augusto said, "Stay here Master I shall go a little beyond this point in search of a village. I will return soon." Jerome by this time was too tired to argue and set out his blanket and went to sleep. He heard rustling and picked his head up with a start. To his utter and blissful amazement, there came Augusto with an armful of nuts and berries. "How did you find them?" "Just beyond this ridge of trees is a clearing and a lake. Tomorrow we will go there and perhaps catch us a fish for supper." They ate their fill and went to sleep.

They continued on, never passing a village or seeing another human being, for days. Crossing over a craggy slope they rounded the top and there sitting in a deep valley was their prize. "Augusto this must be the abbey. I am sure we have found it." The giant, who spoke very little, said "Master let us pray that this is what we seek." They made their way through the thorny undergrowth until they reached level ground. It appeared as if the place was deserted. There were no signs of life and no animals grazing or plants in the garden. They came cautiously to the door, which was covered with an almost impenetrable layer of vines. They knocked at the door; and waited. After a few minutes, they banged at the door; and waited. No one came. Finally, in desperation, they walked around to the back of the abbey; the door was ajar and so they called before they stepped in. No one answered.

Jerome, filled with despair, stood in the middle of what was the most extraordinary church he had ever seen, and wept. He prostrated himself on the nave floor and cried out "Dear Lord is this to be my fate; to die on this God forsaken island. Why have I been sent here? Why? Why? Why?" the boy was now screaming and crying in a state of hysteria. Augusto was for the first time frightened. They had come all this way and now with no money, food, friends, or family, what would become of them. The boy buried his face in his hands and continued to weep for what he saw as the end of his life. The giant, tired and hungry, sat down near him and tears silently fell from his homely face. He silently prayed that God would show them a way.

Off into the distance came a tinkling sound. It was so out of place that at first Jerome ignored it; but it would not go away. The wind was picking up and the tinkling of bells was being carried on its breeze, the sounds getting stronger. The boy could no longer ignore the obvious; he decided to see where the sound was coming from. He lumbered to the door; all spirit and energy had been sucked from his youthful soul. He stood in the threshold of the abbey and became dumbfounded at the sight that appeared before his eyes. He thought he must be near death for this illusion could not be real. Augusto came to his young master and he too was amazed by what he saw.

A caravan of people and animals was parading down into the valley. Longhaired wooly sheep with tinker bells around their necks to announce the arrival of civilization. A small herd of cows, goats, pigs, and cages filled with chickens coming toward the abbey. He could see the monks in their brown homespun robes, shaven heads, and long beards walking with the animals, keeping them in the procession. Mules that were straining under the weight were pulling two large carts that were over burdened with what appeared to be vegetables. It was such a remarkable sight. There at the end of this menagerie of people and animals sitting astride a beautiful stallion was an old man. Three monks, each carryings staffs with flags at their ends, flanked him on either side. One flag bore a cross; another, the image of a saint, the third flag was imprinted with a sun, a moon, and a star. The fourth monk, who was head and shoulders above the others, carried a shield and sword. The boy thought to himself, what is the need for such armament, in three days travel he had not seen another living person.

The boy watched as one by one they arrived; the animals instinctively knew to go to their pens while their handlers watched. Once all the animals were securely in their places, the monks regrouped before the open door. They seemed to have not even noticed the presence of Jerome and Augusto, who just stood there observing. Finally, the old monk arrived. The big monk who carried the shield lifted him off the horse. The rest stood like soldiers awaiting further instruction. The old one, moving slowly came to stand in front of the boy. "Jerome, you have finally come. We have been awaiting your arrival. How is my beloved sister?" The boy had to make a conscious effort to speak "How did you know it was I?" he asked in total amazement. "There are many things you will come to know while you are here. As to my sister, is she well?" Still dazed by how this man knew who he was he replied, "My Nona is well. She sends her deepest love and best wishes to you." I have here a letter of introduction from her. "There is no need Jerome, I know all about you and your large friend Augusto." The boy looked to his companion and they were both struck dumb by what they heard and saw.

***

Jerome rode peacefully transfixed in his memories of his life on Sardinia. He thought 'What will my life be now that I have come to this place?' His first thoughts were to find a suitable inn where he could rest and carry out the plan that had so long ago been laid before him. He was tired and hungry;

it would be a long road to Naples. He remembered passing an abbey on his way to Monteforte; the thought of the abbey filled his heart with vivid memories. He would stop there and inquire as to their accommodations. Surely, a pilgrim in need of lodging would be welcomed, especially one who would contribute to their coffers. His mind was set; he would make his way to the abbey.

CHAPTER ELEVEN

THE PILGRIM

Montecassino Abbey

Jerome made his way to the Abbey of Montecassino knowing he would find food and shelter. He was amazed at the size of the structure. He thought to himself that it was a beautiful country and that he would quickly grow accustomed to living here.

He spotted a monk working on the side of the building and approached. "Pardon my interruption, but I am making a pilgrimage and would ask for food and lodging for a few days. I am able to pay for my stay." The monk, barely a man, was thin as a pike, looked at him, and replied, "Welcome dear brother to our abbey. I am sure it will be no trouble but I must seek permission from our Abbot. Please, come follow me, you can have some refreshment while I search for him." Jerome knew that this was the customary protocol for strangers. He bowed in grateful acknowledgement of the invitation and followed the young monk; he was happy to be out of the blazing sun.

Upon entering the building the temperature immediately dropped by several degrees. The walls were at least two feet thick and solid stone, the floor was made of local granite or marble he could not tell in the dimness of the light. The familiar aroma of incense and candlewax made him instantly feel at home. It was intricately decorated with mosaics and frescoes all of which told a story. "Please wait here while I find Abbot Vittorio." Again, he bowed and said "Thank you."

Captivated by the spiritual energy of the place Jerome's mind wandered back to his life at the Abbazia di Maria Regine Delle Stelle monastery where he had lived for nearly thirty years. He felt the essence of this place fill his soul and he was renewed with his fateful mission. The differences between his own abbey from this one were profound, yet they were so similar, the antiquity of them breathing purpose into his body. He suddenly felt refreshed and more determined than ever to assume his legacy.

Looking down a long stretch of hallway, he saw two monks approaching. The young brother was now walking just a step ahead of his abbot. When they reached him the young one bowed slightly and stepped aside making way for his master. "Good day to you. Brother Emilio has told me of your desire to stay with us for a short while. We are very happy to welcome those who are seeking spiritual solace. How long will you be with us?" Abbot Vittorio was assessing the stranger; from the cut and quality of his clothing, he could see that he was a man of means. The man's deep russet hair and beard and the blue of his eyes struck him. This man was handsome and bore intelligent eyes. Jerome answered honestly, "I am not sure. I am on a spiritual mission that I have waited all my life to fulfill. If my stay takes too long and I become an imposition to you Dear Abbot, I will surely leave. May I introduce myself, I am Jerome Pugliese."

The monk was impressed with the manner of speech and civility of this stranger, yet there was an aurora about him that did not match the physical appearance of the man before him. "I am Abbot Vittorio Fermelli, welcome to our sacred home. Brother Emilio will show you to your cell. We invite you to join us for a simple supper. Please avail yourself of our chapel and library; we ask that you stay to all our public chambers respecting the spiritual privacy of our brothers." Jerome knew very well the rules, he reached into his purse and withdrew a pouch that contained a substantial sum of coins and handed it to the abbot. "Your hospitality is most appreciated; please accept this small token of my gratitude. I shall not be troublesome to you."

Jerome was shown to his cell, which was just as he expected, but it felt like home and for that, he was grateful. Its sparse austerity was an insulation against the outside distractions of the world. Exclusive of a pallet with fresh straw covered by a thread bare blanket and worn pillow there was little by way of creature comforts. A battered wooden table held a ewer and bowl and in a far corner was a piss pot. There was a single window set high into the wall, which let in light and air and covered by a wood shutter. The only visual adornment was a crudely carved wood cross with an emaciated Christ affixed to it. He found comfort in its starkness. The young monk asked, "My Lord is there anything I can get for you?" Jerome looked around and replied "Yes. Please bring me a candle so that I may read." The monk, who was barely a man, bowed and closed the door tightly behind him.

Jerome let out a sigh of relief. He was finally alone, something he had always cherished, the pleasure of solitude. He saw the worn robe hanging from the peg that was stuck into the back of the heavy cypress door. Touching its homespun roughness, he took it from its place and held it tightly to his chest. He brought it to his nose and breathe in its aroma. Quickly he removed his clothing replacing his expensive waistcoat on the peg. Next, he removed his breeches, stockings and donned the familiar brown robe. Its texture was scratchy but the loose fit made him feel free and relaxed. Rolling up the clothes he had come with and placing them in the bag he had brought he laid everything aside in the far corner of the cell.

Exhausted from his travels he decided since he had time before the supper bell would ring that he would take a short rest. He laid down and the smell of fresh straw filled his nostrils with pleasant thoughts, he never remembered falling asleep, but was captured within a reoccurring dream. In his dream, he was facing an opponent, an opponent that he had been warned about his entire life. He could never see who his enemy was yet he knew he was a worthy adversary. He was brave; but his enemy was braver. He was strong; but his enemy was stronger. At every turn, this nemesis would thwart his progress. The two combatants fought; but there were no swords; no arrows; no weaponry that might slay this evil champion. Always in his dream appeared his mentor, The Abbot, who challenged him to keep him strong so that he would one day defeat his foe.

The day came, when he was seventeen years old. Jerome would never forget this birthday; he had been very excited because there had been much secret goings and comings at the monastery. He had never had a celebration for any of the previous birthdays so why was this one so special he thought. He was only mildly surprised when his great uncle the Abbot came for him so early that morning. It was still dark; the sun had not yet risen. "Get up boy; today is your seventeenth birthday; this is the day I have dreamt of for many years. Dress quickly, it is nearly time." The young Jerome was bursting to think what gift would warrant such an early waking and by the Abbot no less. He dressed as fast as he could. The wizened old monk was being carried by his foot soldiers. His bearer, the one who always wore the shield and sword, took up his place just behind him. Jerome was confused; he had never seen the shield bearer not at the side or head of the old Abbot. He followed silently, the procession, which was making its way away from the monastery grounds. He wanted to ask where they were going but thought it was all part of his birthday celebration.

It was a long and arduous walk; the sun was just peeking over the rocky mountaintops; the dew still covered the ground and most of the day light creatures were just stirring. "Where are we going he asked himself?" Finally, just as they were clearing the edge of the dense forest there it was. He had almost forgotten that it was there for he had been warned against going to this place.

Rising up out of the earth, framed by the light of a new sun, was the megalithic Escala del Cabirol, the *deer steps*. It was the site of an ancient stone temple, which over the centuries had been used as a fortress from invading marauders. It was said, that since Sardinians had been sacrificed by those who would conquer the tiny island, and the locals built this fortress and temple, and lured their enemies to its mouth. They say that at certain times, to commemorate the spirits of those poor wretches that were sacrificed, one can hear the screams of the tormented souls, their unsettled spirits roaming the streets of the abandoned village in search of peace. It was surrounded by a labyrinthine village with narrow lanes and steeped in mythical tales of demons and witches; it was said to be inhabited by the high priests of these ancient peoples. The structure, which ascended into the sky, was vertical. There were no doors or window, no gates or bridges to gain access into its mysterious belly. There were however, six hundred and fifty fix steps, each one decreasing in size and width from the bottom to the top until finally reaching the top where there was purported to be an ocular just large enough to let a full grown man pass through. A cold shiver ran down Jerome's supple young body; every muscle tensed and a layer of moisture glistened on his face. His mouth was dry with fear.

The procession halted just outside the perimeter of the sacred area. The monks who were carrying the old one stopped and laid down his chaise. Two of the monks came to the rear and escorted Jerome to be brought before the Abbot. "Master why have we come to this place?" asked the boy. "This, my son, is your destiny." Jerome was confused "Destiny?" "You were sent here to me to prepare you both mentally and physically to face the greatest challenge of your life; but before you can master that which will come to you later in life you must face the Escala del Cabirol." Jerome was weak in the knees "Why Master must I face this challenge? I am strong of mind and body, you have said so many times. I do not wish to go there; I will perish." Jerome was now frightened for his very life. "Come here to me." Jerome was so filled with fear he could barely walk. The boy kneeled before the old monk. He reached into his robe and took out a pouch. Jerome thought what will coins do against demons and witches? The monk handed the pouch to Jerome whose outstretched hand was now shaking. "Do not fear my son; this amulet will guide you and protect you against evil spirits." Jerome felt the weight of the pouch; it was heavy. "Open it" commanded the wizened monk. Jerome, his fingers could hardly undo the silk cord that held it closed. When he finally managed to open the pouch, a brilliant light glowed from within the black pouch. The object within instantly mesmerized him. "Take it out and hold it; feel its healing powers." Jerome did as he was instructed. The instant his flesh encountered the glowing object he felt its power surge throughout his young body. The power that traversed his body was like no other feeling he had ever experienced. After the initial surge of power, the object simmered into a soft glow. "Return it to the pouch," said the monk, a broad smile on his face.

"Jerome, it is time" he heard him say. "My Lord are you ill?" came the hesitant voice of someone just near the periphery of his consciousness. "Are you ill?" there was a hand shaking him back from the darkness. Slowly Jerome felt himself coming back to this world, this time, this place. "No, I am fine. Do not trouble yourself with me. I was just so tired I had fallen into a deep, deep, sleep. I shall be fully awake in just a moment." The young monk stood there staring at the pilgrim. Jerome, now shrugging off the remnants of his reoccurring dream, said, "I am sorry that I did not hear you enter. Is there something you wanted?" "Yes. I came to bring you to join us for supper. I see you have put on the robe." Jerome had forgotten about the robe, "Yes. I hope you don't mind?" The young monk smiled "I am happy to see it. Please come with me. You must be hungry from your long journey. Ah, I almost forgot" he reached into his robe and extracted two candles, "Here are the candles you requested for reading." Jerome was pleased at the young man "Thank you Brother."

After supper when the bells rang calling all to vespers Jerome asked "Abbot may I join in vespers?" The abbot who was used to having pilgrims from all over the world come to his monastery was never asked this question before by someone who was not of a religious order. "Yes. Please feel free to come to the chapel." Jerome found his place at the back of the ancient chapel, which was so different, yet so similar to the one where he grew. When services were concluded Jerome, his head down, was walking toward his cell. He was caught up by the abbot "Jerome may I speak with you a while?" Jerome nodded and followed the monk into the garden. It was a walled enclosure with life size statues, and since it was already dusk, the shadows lent an air that gave them a life of their own. Another monk that was praying at the feet of the Blessed Virgin, his hunched body knelt in adoration. Abbot Vittorio ushered Jerome to the opposite side of the garden where a simple, but beautiful, grotto had been built. They sat on a stone bench and the abbot spoke softly not to disturb the sanctity of the place.

"Jerome, you are not our usual pilgrim. You have donned our robe and joined our prayers. You appear to have true knowledge of our order." The man before him was quiet, his handsome face reflected great intelligence. "Dear Abbot, when I was a child I was sent far from my home to the island of Sardinia. There I became the ward of my great uncle the Abbot Lorenzo Cioffi. I have lived in that monastery all my life and have been taught the ways of a religious life." The monk now understood why this man was so knowledgeable of their ways. "Forgive me if I sound ignorant but I have heard many stories of the monastery of which you speak, as well as Abbot Cioffi. With all due respect, it is said that this man possesses mystical powers and that there are many who come for his healing. Is this true?" Jerome smiled, squared his shoulders, and replied, "Yes it is all true. My uncle is a man of profound faith and spiritual power." Abbot Vittorio was skeptical and inquisitive and wanted to learn more of this famous monk and his nephew, but for now, he would watch his guest closely. "We shall talk more, but, it is late, matins will be here before long. I shall bid you good night. Will you come to matins?" "I was going to ask permission to do so. I would be honored to join all prayer services, as it is my custom to do so." "I will see you then."

e HehhHhh

Several days passed and Jerome was now part of the fabric of the monastery. He was one of them and moved freely among the monks, lending a helping hand in the garden, mending a fence or milking a goat, he had blended into their community seamlessly. Many hours of his day were spent in the library. It was obvious to all that Jerome was a learned man, spoke knowledgeably about ancient manuscripts, and was held in esteem by his peers.

Abbot Vittorio had grown fond of the strange pilgrim and thought he would try to use the man's knowledge to good use. "Jerome, I am told by my Brothers that you possess a great familiarity with archaic language and writing. Perhaps you would like to give me some of your thoughts on a particular manuscript that I have acquired. The language and writing is so old that I am not sure of which century it was written and while it is well preserved, it is ancient. "I am so honored that you, who holds such a reputation as a brilliant translator, would ask me to assist you in this task. Please use me to whatever end I can be of assistance." " Then in that case, follow me to my private writing room. Brother Angelo and I have been working on this particular piece for quite some time and are baffled by its content. Perhaps a fresh set of eyes can uncover its true meaning."

They walked together through the library to a secluded chamber in the back. The heavy cypress door was locked. The abbot reached into his pocket and retrieved the key to open the door. It was a small space with a solitary window that was set high into the wall, much like all the cell windows. It let in some natural light and air but no scenery. Brother Angelo was so engrossed in his work he did not hear them enter. Stacks of scrolled manuscripts surrounded him. The one he was working on was spread on a stone table. Abbot Vittorio said "Brother Angelo?" The monk looked up almost startled "Abbot, I am sorry, I did not hear you enter. Jerome, how nice to see you; Brother Francesco mentioned what a fine job you did with the translation on the manuscript he was working on; thank you.

"Brother Angelo, I would like Jerome to take a look at that one particular manuscript that we have been having trouble transcribing. The young monk's entire demeanor changed, he would have countered his Abbot's orders, but would never disobey a direct command. They were close friends but he still knew his place and the thought of disrespecting his master was out of the question. "As you wish Abbot, but..." then he caught the Abbot's eye and he knew that he should not doubt his decision. " Yes, of course, as you wish Abbot."

The monk scurried about in search of the particular manuscript he was looking for; found it and laid it across the writing table. It was old; Jerome could immediately tell that much, but that much any fool would have surmised. He came closer; he gently fingered the paper and felt the thick, ancient papyrus, he ran his finger over the writing, tracing the symbols that were incised into it. He bent down and breathe in the scent of it. He closed his eyes and placing both his hands just over the surface drew in the essence of the script. Opening his eyes a few moments later he did not speak but withdrew from the table. The man before them grew pale and his eyes began to flutter.

Both monks watched in stupified amazement at Jerome's performance. Finally, Abbot Vittorio, breaking the spell that had descended upon them asked "Jerome that was a rather unusual reaction to a manuscript. What say you?" Jerome had absorbed so much from just that single translation that he felt weak and his head began to spin; in the blink of an eye he was down on the floor having fallen with a thud.

They rushed to his side to assist him, each taking him under the arm and bringing him to a chair in the far corner of the chamber. It was hot and close. The Abbot told Angelo to go fetch some water and rags soaked in white vinegar; he did not hesitate and scurried off. While his breathing was not labored it was still unsettling to see the big man in this state; his face now ashen grey and his skin wet and moist. Angelo returned in a short while, a water skin and wet rags in his hands. He bent down and laid a wet rag on Jerome's forehead and tied one to each wrist. It took a moment, but the unconscious Jerome finally came back. His eyes fluttered open and color was returning to his handsome face. "Jerome are you ill? What happened?" implored Abbot Vittorio. "I don't know. All of a sudden I felt a crushing sensation descend upon me." "Here take some water it will make you feel better." Jerome drank deeply from the skin and did feel better. He made to get up, feeling embarrassed for his weakness, but the monk laid a strong hand on his shoulder "Stay still for a few moments; collect your thoughts before you move again." Jerome obeyed.

They took a collective deep breath and tried to relax. No one spoke for a while. It had been a strange scene that they had witnessed and the Abbot was curious as to its meaning. When he saw that Jerome was completely back to himself he asked "Jerome has that ever happened to you before?" The stranger answered honestly "Yes. Once. It was as if my whole life was sucked from the marrow of my bones. I have only experienced such a feeling once, when I was a boy." They went back to the writing table and cautiously Jerome went over to the manuscript; he was fearful. He felt compelled to touch it once again. As he moved his hand over the parchment is quivered and moved. "What kind of magic are you playing at our expense?" demanded the Abbot. Yet he knew that there was no frivoulous ruse being played; Jerome was interacting with the manuscript; whether by his own doing or that of a supernatural power.

Brother Angelo was in a state of shock "I have never seen such as this; I have touched that manuscript a dozen times. " The young monk, fell to his knees and blessed himself. Abbot Vittorio's voice sounded distant, remote, even frightened "Tell me Jerome, what has just happened here?" "Truly Abbot I do not know; what I do know is that I have seen something ominous from touching this manuscript." "What is it; tell us so that we may be prepared." "I cannot tell you just yet; it will not let me. When the time is ready I shall reveal all to you." He turned to leave the chamber, but then turned around, "I will need to see all the manuscripts in order to solve the parable." "Parable? What parable? Brother Angelo and I have been studying these manuscripts for almost a year, we have not come across any mention of a parable?" "Dear Abbot, it is late, I am not feeling well, I will reveal all truths to you in time. If you will forgive me I need to retire to my cell. Good night." Jerome was emotionally exhausted and needed to lay down.

After Jerome left, both monks stared at the manuscript; fearful to touch it. "This is nonsense I was just working on this earlier today, nothing happened to either me or the manuscript. Abbot what do you make of what we have seen with our own eyes?" The Abbot was walking around the room in circles, which was his favorite method of concentration when perplexed. He made about five laps when he stopped, looked directly at the young monk and said "We must be cautious at all times when in Jerome's company. I have a deep unsettled feeling about this man. I have heard stories of the land from whence he comes; Sardinia is a wild and mystical place. The few people who sustain themselves in its unforgiving wilderness are said to be able to commune with the ancient spirits." The young monk was surprised to hear his Abbot speak so openly about mystical spirits; surely Holy Mother Church would never approve of such heresy. "Abbot are you saying there are unnatural spirits that inhabit that island?" The Abbot, his eyes shrouded by thick black lashes, his posture slightly bent, answered in a low, guarded voice "That my young brother is precisely what I am saying. I believe our new stranger must be watched carefully. He was sent here for a reason; yet I am not sure what that reason is. The one thing that I am sure of is that we shall find out in due time what he is all about."

CHAPTER TWELVE

MARQUISE GIVENCHY

PARIS

"Sophia will you select something for me to wear to go to see the Marquis de Fauntil's family. I wish to pay my respects to them upon their loss." She hesitated "For my loss as well. I truly loved that man" her voice caught on every word. Sophia came to her and embraced her lovingly "Mistress, I know you are very sad, but it was the work of that madman Piro; do not feel guilt, for you have nothing to do with his death." Lucia sulked away to get ready still feeling the aftermath of his death.

"Oh, I nearly forgot, come here Sophia" Lucia was smiling warmly. "Put out your hand," she commanded. The maid was not sure what was to happen but obeyed. Lucia dropped a hefty silk purse in her palm. "What is this for Mistress?" Lucia closed her fingers around the solid bundle of coins "This, my beloved Sophia is a small gift." The maid was still not sure "A gift for whom?" "For you silly girl; I want you to take the day and shop in the streets of this lovely city. I have instructed Mateo to give Nicko the day off as well and to give him a purse. Between the two of you I trust you will find some good use for your time and money." "You mean that both Nicko and I will be dismissed, and that we shall be together for the day; in Paris; with money. It is like a dream. Thank you Mistress. Your kindness never stops amazing me." They were hugging and dancing around the room when there was a sharp rap at the door "Enter" Lucia answered.

It was Genaro. He could see that the two women were having a lighthearted moment and he was happy for them. "I am sorry, if I have interrupted a private moment. Shall I leave and come back when you are ready?" "Oh no dear brother Sophia and I were just planning her day. Where is Mateo?" "He said he had to go speak with Nicko about something and that he would meet us in the dining hall for breakfast. " I shall need to finish dressing; I will meet you there when I am done. I shall not take too much longer." "I hope not, I am hungry." "When are you not hungry?" he left laughing as he closed the door.

Sophia had taken out a simple, but, elegant dark green silk gown that Madame Richaud had custom made for Lucia the last time they were in Paris. It would be appropriate for the occasion. "Mistress I think this gown would be fine to wear." "Oh, I agree Sophia. It is so sad that I remember when Madame Richaud made me this gown; I was so happy then to be here in Paris; now it just fills my heart with sadness." The servant, who was doing her laces stopped and put her arms around her mistress and hugged her tightly. "I am so sorry for all that has happened. Together we will find many more happy memories to share." Tears filled the servant's eyes for she loved Lucia so much.

"Now, I shall go meet my brothers and Alessandro and then we shall not see each other until late this evening. Promise me that you and Nicko will indulge some small trivial desire and purchase something special?" "I promise Mistress; now all I have to do is convince Nicko that it is an order from our Mistress to do so." They laughed.

Lucia made her way down to the dining hall to meet up with her brothers. Lucia was escorted to the table, they all rose; it was Alessandro whose eyes were appraising her from top to bottom. "Good morning Mistress Lucia; as always, you look like a fresh and lovely flower." Mateo chuckled "Ah, you see Genaro he is a romantic poet, in addition to a world famous architect." Alessandro instantly flushed but Lucia jumped in to save him "At least one of the three of you is generous to me; thank you Alessandro."

After finishing their meal, they decided to walk off some of their heavy breakfast. It was too early for a polite call upon Henri's family. "We must walk," insisted Lucia "I did not think it was possible for me to eat so much food in one sitting. I shall become a sow in no time." Mateo came, took her arm "Bella, you need a little extra meat on those bones", and gave her a kiss. "I think you are perfectly proportioned, but a little here and there would not hurt," said Genaro tongue in cheek. Thinking best not to respond, and to save himself some ridicule, Alessandro just shook his head and smiled.

It was a warm, sunny, morning and for the first time Lucia felt comfort in being back in Paris. There were many memories both happy and sad. They walked along the Rue Royale down through the Place de la Concorde. It was such a lovely day, that many people were strolling the boulevard. Little children were frolicking; mothers pushing their babies in carts and old couples out for some exercise. Oddly, the old men whom Mateo and Genaro were speaking with the other day were still at their chess game. "Ah, brother, let us go and have some further discussion with our chess players." It was Mateo, he was such a mischievous troublemaker; yet Genaro was more than willing to join in the fun.

When the two old men saw them coming they called out to them "Have you come again to instruct us? Ah, here they are the two masters of the game." It was said more in jest, for they were laughing. Both Genaro and Mateo acknowledged their greeting and came about to slap them cordially on their backs. "Bonjour, je vois que vous êtes encore à la Commission. Jamais allez-vous Accueil à vos épouses ? Sans aucun doute ils ont trouvé d'autres prêts à prendre votre place."

Lucia was laughing and she said to Alessandro whose arm she was clinging to "Why must they antagonize these poor men. To say that their wives have found someone in their place is rude. Don't you agree?" Alessandro was smiling broadly, "It is all in good fun. I think the old ones like to get attention." Even though his face was filled with humor, it was his eyes that Lucia was watching; they were traveling over the board and were intent on the game.

The old men and her brothers were bantering back and forth, laughing, and taunting each other's ability to win the game that was being played out before them. In one moment Alessandro leaned forward and moved one piece, he said, in a voice so soft is was barely audible over the shouts and taunts of the others "checkmate." Everyone suddenly stopped; it was as if time stood still, they then realized that Alessandro had, in a matter of seconds, executed the one crucial move to win the game.

One of the old men just hung his head in disgust "My God we have been playing this same game for six months; unable to find the solution; now you, a stranger, comes here and in one blink of the eye you end our game." Lucia was not sure if the man was angry or disappointed that their game had ended.

The expression on Alessandro's face was one of contrite horror. "Sir, I am truly sorry. I do not know what came over me to intrude on your game. Please forgive my rudeness." The other man turned to his partner and said, "Well maybe now we can go fishing? This young cock has left us nothing to do with our day." With that said it took a moment for everyone to absorb it but they all burst out into joyful laughter. Even poor Alessandro found the will to smile. Genaro came over and pounded him on the back "Well done. Too bad we did not have some wager on the game."

Lucia felt sorry for the architect. Clearly, he had not meant to cause any trouble. With his face flushed, he looked more like a young boy who had been caught stealing a pastry from the baker's shop, than a world famous architect. It was funny and sad all at once.

Thinking it best to move along, the foursome walked another distance until they came to some benches. Sitting, they decided that it was late enough to make their way to Henri's home. Lucia could not hide her disdain for having to go, but she also knew that she had to go. They made their way back down the Rue Royale, walking this time on the opposite side of the boulevard so as not to have to encounter the old chess players.

Upon reaching the Hotel de Crillon's main entrance, they called up one of the waiting carriages. Mateo gave the address to the driver and they settled themselves in for the short drive to Sant Germaine. Lucia was quiet but her brothers were taunting Alessandro regarding the incident with the old men "How did you know that move so quickly?" asked Genaro. The architect, his head bent on his chest replied, "When I was at universita I would, for a fee, play people. Soon, I realized that chess is just a matter of mathematics. The only opponent who has ever gotten the best of me was your own brother Andrea. One day we were matched against each other. I was desperate to win; I needed the money, so I challenged him to a match. He won handily in just a few strokes. I am embarrassed to say that I tried to accuse him of cheating so that I would get the purse, but lucky for him I did not have the heart to pursue such a lie."

"I did not know our brother Andrea was a chess player, did you Genaro?" said Lucia. Genaro looked sad "there are many things about our dear brother that we do not know. How long has it been since last you saw him? It was while we were still in Naples after the eruption. Our poor mother thinks of him all the time, but he does not write or visit. I tell you Lucia, if, and when, I see him next, I shall give him a much deserved thrashing for hurting our mother."

Alessandro who came to Andrea's defense, "I did not know him well, but this man possesses an intellect that far surpasses anyone I have ever known. He is much sort after for his mathematical skills."

Lucia spoke up finally, "Andrea has always been the different one. Remember when we were small, it was he who would be boarded up in the house seeking quiet, while the rest of us where running around like wild animals. I do not believe, in my heart, that he is a bad man; he is just too consumed by the information in his head. I would love to see him; it has been far too long."

The carriage had pulled up to the stately apartments of the Marquis Henri de Fauntil on the Rue de Sant Germaine. Lucia shuttered at the mental vision of his last hours at the murderous hands of a young man she once loved. Lord Jesus please bring Henri to Heaven and help Piro wherever he may be.

The maître de casa greeted them warmly. To Lucia he said, "Marchesa Banfi, it is so good to see that you are safe and unharmed. My Master loved you so very much." Lucia, her eyes filled with tears said, "I loved him as well. I am so sorry for all of us that he was taken from us at the hands of someone he cared for." The servant took her hand and lovingly kissed it "My Mistress the Marquise Givenchy is expecting you. Please, if you will, follow me to the solar?"

The home held sweet memories of her days spent with Henri, of their long talks, his advice, and most of all his love. They made their way to the solar with heavy hearts. Everything was just as it had been when she left.

The servant poured glasses of cognac and then left to retrieve his new Mistress. A few moments later, a stunningly beautiful woman accompanied him. Lucia guessed she were about her own age. From a distance, she could have passed for her sister Antoinetta. The woman before them was petite of stature, with flawless olive skin and raven black hair, which was plaited on the sides, and the rest left to fall upon her back and shoulders. Her eyes were slanted, almost exotic, and of a depth of color, Lucia had never seen before. She wore a gown that accented her full breasts and narrow waist. It was of a perfect cut for her slender frame.

Her sultry beauty was not lost on her companions, especially Alessandro, who was practically panting at the sight of her. There was an immediate tension as she entered the room. The new Mistress of the Manse glided daintily into the room.

Of course, it was Mateo, with his suave and debonair manner that stepped forward to introduce all those present. "Marquise Givenchy may I introduce my sister Marchesa Lucia Banfi, my brother Lord Genaro, our friend Lord Alessandro Gaileli and I am Lord Mateo Rizzo. Your dear uncle Henri was a dear friend of ours and we have come to express our deepest condolences at his passing."

The lovely Marquise was elegant and poised. She nodded her head and curtsied demurely. Lucia thought to herself that this was a woman of exceptional breeding. Each of the men stood before her; kissed her hand and bowed formally. When it was Lucia's turn, she felt awkward standing next to the petite beauty for she was as tall as any man was, and athletically built; they could not have been in more contrast. Lucia came to her and as she was about to speak the Marquise embraced her warmly "My dear Uncle Henri spoke of you with great love and admiration I feel as if I know you. He had written to me of you many times. He loved you very much."

Lucia was taken aback by this sudden outburst of honest affection. "I too loved Henri; he was a mentor and a special friend. I shall miss him terribly and will never forget him."

The petite mistress waved her hand to indicate that they should be seated. Lucia could not help but see that Alessandro watched her every move; his eyes never left her. Lucia felt a wave of jealousy but quickly put it aside. "I am Marquise Noelle Givenchy; my mother was the sister of Henri's wife Auriella. While it should have been my mother to inherit all of his estate he had made special legal provisions that all should come to me."

"I am here now by myself awaiting the arrival of my mother who was settling her own affairs in Belgium, our family home. My brother will now run our family estate until her death, at which time he will be the new Marquis Givenchy. I am so happy that you have come to visit me; I am lonely here with no family and have not had time to make any social acquaintance."

"Well I do not believe it will be too much trouble for you to be accepted in Parisian society, especially a beautiful woman such as yourself," said Mateo, who was looking at her appraisingly.

Before she sat, the new mistress went to a writing table and retrieved a small box from a drawer. She came to sit next to Lucia "I was given instruction by my uncle that if something should happen to him that I was to give you this box" she said in a voice that was smooth as polished stone.

Lucia held the box in her hand. It was intricately carved wood, which was inlaid with mother of pearl accents. There was a gold clasp on the front, which she opened. To her amazement inside the box, which was lined with red velvet, was the diamond and sapphire necklace that Henri had let her wear the night they went to the opera. It had been Auriella's favorite necklace. Tears began to cascade down her cheeks "Henri gave this to me to wear to the opera. He told me it had been a special gift made just for Auriella. He insisted that I wear it and told me that I reminded him of her. This is too precious; I cannot accept such a gift." The Marquise was also crying her voice now filled with sorrow "Henri was like a father to me. When my own father died in war, it was my uncle who raised me, never having children of his own, he loved me like a daughter. I will not disrespect his wishes and neither must you. Please you must accept this gift in his memory."

The two beauties, as different as night is to day, embraced each other and wept for a man they both loved. Looking around, there were no dry eyes in the room. When they separated, Lucia held the box to her heart as if it contained the man himself.

It took a few minutes but everyone settled down to simple companionable conversation. After a while, Mateo said, "I am sure I speak for all of us; we would be delighted for you to join us for supper this evening. We are staying at the Hotel de Crillon on the Place de Concourse. Will you join us Marquise Givenchy?" The petite heiress could not contain her pleasure at having been asked, "I hope you do not think I am too forward, but I trust the judgment of my Uncle Henri who spoke so highly of all of you that I feel as though we have been friends for a long time. I would be so pleased to get out of this house."

"Excellent, it is now settled, shall we send a carriage for you?" asked Alessandro, who was licking his lustful lips. Lucia was surprised that he had even spoken. "Oh that will not be necessary, I have a driver. Eight o'clock?" "Yes. We look forward to your company." Lucia caught a glimpse of an unspoken communication that had gone from Mateo to Genaro and they were smiling. Lucia wanted to slap their faces; all three of them. Yes, she agreed that Noelle Givenchy was beautiful, but they were acting like dogs in heat. She was angry and jealous; but she did not really know why. Two of them were her brothers and the third, Alessandro; she had told him that she only wanted to be friends. She rationalized all of this in her head but still could not help but feel a sense of envy. Lucia, who was always the center of attention, now found that her new friend took some of her luster; and she did not enjoy the feeling.

They left with the promise of meeting up for supper at the hotel. Lucia was very thoughtful during the ride back and said nothing. She made her excuses of being tired and returned immediately to her room. She forgot that she had given Sophia the day off to roam Paris. She would have to select her own gown and dress herself.

Before she realized it was time for supper. After taking a bath, she chose her royal blue gown; Sophia said it brought out her eyes. For reasons she did not know she was angry with her brothers and Alessandro. Well, to be truthful, she was envious of the attention Alessandro was giving the new heiress. She struggled with her hair, but in the end, the overall picture was quite pleasing.

As she was making her way down to the dining hall, all eyes were fixed on her. She threw back her shoulders and walked with her head up. She felt better about herself. As she was escorted to their table, the three men rose to greet her and Genaro held her chair "You look ravishing this evening dear sister." Alessandro was following her with his eyes and he smiled warmly at her "I must agree with Genaro; that gown compliments your beautiful eyes." Lucia thought to herself 'I must remember to thank Sophia for telling me about this gown'.

Mateo came to her, kissed her on both cheeks, and whispered in her ear "Every man in this room, probably in all of Paris, would like to have you to their bed." "Mateo!" She exclaimed demurely but was thrilled that he said it.

They had just settled down when there was a little hush that descended the dining hall. Everyone focused to the entrance. There in an exquisite white gown trimmed in ermine was the Marquise Noelle Givenchy. Alessandro practically choked on his wine; even Mateo and Genaro were looking lustfully at this vision in white. There was no denying that the new heiress was breathtakingly beautiful in a sensual way.

Alessandro moved so swiftly to get up to greet her that he nearly turned over his chair. "Oh my, she is stunning; don't you agree Lucia?" Mateo licked his lips at the sight of her "I did not think she was of your appetite?" said Lucia sarcastically. "My dear Bella, just because a man eats meat, does not mean that he does not sometimes enjoy fish." "Oh you are wicked!" She was fuming.

When all the men in the room put their tongues back in their mouths, the five of them sat down to a pleasant and delicious meal. The conversation was enjoyable and Lucia had to admit, that even though she tried she could not hate this woman. It was like when she and her sister Antoinette were growing up. She was the tall, pale one with the flaming hair; and her sister was the exotic, olive skinned beauty.

The evening proved to be most pleasant and the Marquise Givenchy was very entertaining. She was born in Belgium but was educated in Austria and thus had many stories to share. Throughout the evening Alessandro's eyes did not leave, her face and he clung to her every word.

After they had finished eating, they retired to the salon where a young man, who was quite talented, was playing a harpsichord. As it was filled with other guests, Alessandro and Lady Givenchy found themselves sitting in a small settee in a far corner, leaving Lucia in the company of her brothers.

Finally, the couple came to where the threesome were seated and announced that given the hour Alessandro was going to escort the Lady Givenchy home. The architect was strutting around with the new heiress on his arm like a proud peacock. Lucia actually felt ill. Once they had left Genaro said to them, "They appear to have become fond of each other. I wonder if Alessandro will be coming to Monteforte after all?"

Mateo who had been observing Lucia during the evening knew that she was upset, it was written all over that beautiful face that could never hide her emotions. "What does it matter? We already have our most treasured prize." He reached for Lucia's hand and kissed it gently. "I believe that you are the most perfect woman. There are far too many olive skinned beauties in this world." He always was able to make Lucia smile. She leaned over and whispered "Thank you Mateo."

Lucia stood, said her goodnights, and retreated to her room. She found a note from Sophia that she would be back late. Lucia was happy for her. She undressed leaving her gown in a bundle on the floor, slipping into her nightshirt she barely had the emotional energy to brush out her hair, but knew that if she didn't she would regret not doing so in the morning. She sat on the side of her bed and begrudgingly took out the braids she had managed to weave earlier. Her hair was particularly unruly this evening. She thought of Sophia and wished she had been there; she needed someone to comfort her.

As she was trying to brush through the tangled mass of wild curls the brush passed over her breast; the sensation excited her. She continued brushing her hair and each time the brush stroked her breast she tingled. Finally, unable to control her desires she laid on the bed; her nipples were taut and erect. She pinched them and gasped; she pulled and pinched until her clit was aching to be touched. She pulled up her nightshirt and her hand traveled down her flat belly until it found the sacred nest. Lucia lingered there for a few moments trying to forestall the gratification she so desperately needed. Making tiny circles her finger slipped between her hot, wet lips. She tried to let it last, longer; her desire, her lust was so strong she could no longer control herself. Her mind envisioned Danford with his massive hands caressing her skin. He used his powerful fingers, at first teasing; and then punishing, relentlessly driving further and further into her sex. His mouth wet with desire; suckling like a newborn babe her hard pink tits; until she would scream with ecstasy.

Lucia was soaked with sexual desire, she drove her finger deep inside until her back arched and her muscles tightened and her clit released its musky perfume all over her finger. With the tears running down her face and the thoughts of the man she loved, she took her finger to her mouth and sucked the lust from it. Remembering with sorrow so deep the passionate scent of Danford's manhood as his seed flowed through her fingers.

In her pain, she called out to her God "Lord why have I been so cursed? Will it ever end? Send me a man I can love forever."

She did not even bother to wipe the tears from her eyes, but rolled over and wept until she fell into a deep sleep.

CHAPTER THIRTEEN

THE TEST OF MANHOOD

Sardinia

Abbot Vittorio and Brother Angelo were suspicious of their guest. "I do not believe it is by chance that Jerome comes to us?" said the Abbot. "We must try to find what it is that he is seeking. From his reaction to the manuscripts I think it may have something to do with them." Brother Angelo was sure that Jerome Pugliese was not who, or what, he said he was.

After morning prayers, the three of them went to the secluded chamber behind the main library. Brother Angelo opened the door, which was always locked. Everything in the room was in disarray. The two monks stood there in utter amazement "Brother did you come here during the night?" The younger monk, dazed by the sight of the place, replied "Of course not Abbot. When I left last night, everything was in order and I, as always, locked the door behind me. Who would have done such a thing?"

Jerome stood there surveying the room; his face was painted with concentration. He cautiously moved about the space looking and moving like a general inspecting his troops. The monks were watching his every movement. He finally said, "This is the work of angry spirits." Abbot Vittorio was not sure what he meant, "What say you? You believe there are evil spirits in this sacred place?" Jerome turned to face him directly "There are forces beyond all our reasoning afoot here. I have been sent here to find something of supreme importance. I have lived my life in pursuit of this final piece in a struggle for good and evil. You must trust me?"

Abbot Vittorio was now angry at what this man was saying, "How dare you come to this holy place in the guise of a pilgrim and claim to be our savior? Be careful, you are speaking in the voice of a heretic."

Jerome was furious "You live in the safety of these stone walls. What do you know of the evils that plague this earth? I have seen the face of the Devil himself. You will not believe me, or trust me, until I show you my powers. You, my dear Abbot harbor a dark secret within your heart of a forbidden lust for a woman who is very much part of this sacred quest." Abbot Vittorio was stunned that he should know about his love for Lucia. "Again, how dare you assume to know me and what my desires are?

Jerome reached into his robe, pulled something out, and threw it to the stone floor. It glowed brightly in the dim light of the small chamber. "What trickery is this?" demanded the Abbot. Jerome looked at them, he was standing tall with his arms folded over his chest "This is what I came in search of, and you know where it is." They looked at each other in total surprise. "What do you seek Jerome; the glowing crystal or the manuscripts?" asked the Abbot with clenched teeth. He was trying to control his anger at the man who so defiantly stood in their midst. It was as if this stranger was holding them captive and the Abbot did not appreciate the feeling.

Jerome's body language changed as he saw the anger build within his host "I am sorry Abbot Vittorio, I had no right to speak to you in such a manner. Please do give me." While his words asked for forgiveness his body was still tense, yet he was making an effort to calm himself.

"May I tell you both a story; perhaps once I am finished you will both understand, and even assist me in my quest." He went to the stone floor and sat, crossing his legs like a Buddhist monk, and then he beckoned them to do likewise. Joining him on the floor, they waited for him to begin his story.

"I shall start at the beginning so that the two of you will understand all that I am about to reveal. As you know, I was sent to Sardinia to live with my great uncle in the monastery. All the tales that you have heard regarding his powers are true. He taught me many things but none of what I learned had prepared me for the greatest test of my life.

When I was seventeen years old, in point of fact it was on the actual day I had been born, my uncle came to my cell before the sun had risen and leading a procession of monks brought me to the Escala del Cabirol or what is known as the *Deer Steps;* the Barumini, the Stone Temple. The only way into this temple is through a sky door. It was still dark when we arrived, and the wind carried the cries of those souls within the stone temple. I was frightened and did not want to go, but my uncle told me I had no choice.

He handed me this crystal and said it would light my way in the blackness. I begged for forgiveness for whatever sin I had committed to warrant this punishment, but again he told me I was destined to fulfill this quest. Knowing that if I refused to go I would be either killed, or cast from the monastery, I did as I was commanded. "Go my son, I have lived my whole life for this day, keep your heart, and mind pure and you shall survive this ordeal. I will wait here for three days; if you do not emerge within that time I shall presume you are dead." He took his knurled old hand and made the sign of the cross on my forehead."

Jerome stopped in the telling of the story to catch his breath, it was as if he were reliving that day. Brother Angelo asked, "Jerome, if you lived there for years prior to that day why was this day so important?" "I asked my uncle the same question and his answer was very simple: there are six hundred and fifty six steps that lead to the sky door. " Yes but why seventeen?" be persisted in his curiosity. It was now the Abbot who answered "Brother Angelo is it a simple formula 6+5+6 =17."

It was very simple; so simple they would have lost the meaning. Jerome seemed pleased that his audience was so intelligent; it would make the rest of the telling easier.

He began once again. "I left the caravan of monks and animals, who by now had made their camp. Even though it was early morning the sky over the Nuraghe was dark as night. As I drew closer, the wind subsided and a noiseless calm fell upon the place. I looked back and could see the camp but it was as if they were in a dream. I stood back to try to encompass the whole of the stone temple but it was so tall its peak sat in the midst of the clouds.

With legs so weak from fear, I could barely climb the first step. It was so high off the ground I had to reach up with my arms and pull myself up over the edge of the first step. It was wide and not truly flat. It took a number of steps for me to reach the second step, which again I had to pull myself up to reach.

As I ascended the massive structure each succeeding level grew shorter and the steps more narrow and the incline more severe. I was about half way to the top when I decided to rest. I was tired and thirsty; my belly growled from hunger. I began to cry out of fear and frustration; I was going to die. After all this hard work I would, in the end, fail. Why did my uncle not just kill me and be done with it? I asked myself.

Looking around I spotted some vines growing through the cracks in the wall. I went to see how this was even possible and to my delight, there was an abundance of berries. I ate ravenously, gathering some to fill my pockets. When I was full, I proceeded on my journey. As I continued the trek upward, the stone steps became narrower, covered with slick dew.

I was now near the last steps from my goal. The thoughts of what, or whom, lay ahead engulfed my ability to think. The mist from the cloud cover hung eerily in the air that surrounded me. I became disoriented nearly falling to my death. My head was spinning from the altitude and my legs were growing weak. I was mentally and physically exhausted. Unable to go on, I laid down; the step was so narrow even my slender form was challenged to stay in place. I remember feeling cold; a bone chilling dampness filled my very soul; and then I slept. I am not sure how long I slept but it was dark when I woke.

Paralyzing fear encircled me; I could hardly breathe. I was fighting the demons inside me that told me to run. I knew I could not run for surely I would perish. This was a darkness the likes of which I had never seen. There was no wind, no external sounds, just complete and utter blackness. I wept.

For some reason I felt compelled to pray. I struggled to control my fear and managed to get on my knees. I reached in my pocket to remove my rosary beads and my hand felt the crystal that my uncle had given me. The moment my hand enclosed the object it became warm and I could feel it quiver in my cold hand. I slowly pulled it out and a soft but brilliant light filled the space around me. Instantly I felt comforted; my spirit was renewed. I looked around me and saw that I was now very close to the top. I reverently laid the crystal on the step and began praying. "Dear Jesus, I do not know what I am to do, please guide me in this holy mission. Give me the strength and wisdom to face my enemies and to seek that which is for Your honor and glory." I was calm and found a sense of serenity. I placed the crystal back in my pocket; once again, I was in complete blackness; but this time I was not afraid. I took some of the berries I had saved and sat quietly and ate a few. I then took out my rosary and prayed until I once again fell into a deep slumber."

Jerome was visibly exhausted and the Abbot and his assistant were completely absorbed in the telling of the story they had not realized that they too were exhausted. "Jerome, I see that you are tired. Let us go and refresh ourselves with some food and wine. We shall continue after we have fed ourselves and then we shall stop in the Chapel of Relics to ask Our Lord for his guidance. I must confess that I am apprehensive; I am not sure of what is to come and the road we must follow. I will ask for wisdom in all things and the courage to accept the Lord's direction. I ask that you both do the same." Brother

Angelo and Jerome were grateful for the invitation to retreat for refreshment.

After they had eaten their fill, they retreated to the somber quiet of the Chapel of Relics. A small structure, which had been left in its original state, and succeeding appendages, were added over the centuries. There was something that Abbot Vittorio always found inspiring about this place. Whenever he was troubled, he came here for encouragement and guidance. He was praying and his thoughts were interrupted by the memory of Lucia; she loved to come to the Chapel of Relics and said it gave her hope. The Abbot chastised himself for thinking of Lucia; she had been the one and only blemish on his clerical life. He was also replaying the words of Jerome in the inner library "You, my dear Abbot harbor a dark secret within your heart of a forbidden lust for a woman who is very much part of this sacred quest", how would he have known of Lucia.

The monk was both captivated and frightened by this stranger; yet he knew that he would become very much a part of the quest for what Jerome claimed he was sent to Montecassino to complete.

They left the Chapel of Relics; the Abbot was more confused than before; he would have to try harder to see the Lord's vision for the three of them and to find out where Lucia fit into the conclusion of this adventure.

Leading the way the trio found themselves back in the inner chamber of the library. Jerome took up his place, as did the monks. Brother Angelo, the youngest of the three, was excited, his young mind filled with dreams of fancy. "Jerome, please tell us the rest of the story." The storyteller was aware that the young monk was thrilled at the telling of the story; yet he was wise enough to know that the Abbot, a highly intelligent man, had many doubts as to not only its validity but as to his part. He also knew that his love for Lucia, the current Mistress of Monteforte, would cloud his decisions when the ultimate end came. He would have to watch the good monk closely; love and lust were too strong a force to be taken lightly.

Jerome settled himself into a comfortable position on the stone floor, took a deep breath, and once again resumed his tale. "I awoke the next morning; some of the fog had lifted; leaving a clear sight to the top. I braced myself, ate the remaining berries, said a pray and continued upward. At this point, the steps were so narrow that I barely had a foothold. There I was, now at the very last step, standing on a stone threshold half the length of my foot, holding desperately to a jagged protrusion on the rock face. The sweat falling like rain into my eyes; my vision was blurred and my hands were wet with fear. This was it; I was here; now what was I to do?

When I reached the top, I was able to stand up and saw that it was a large flat area. Carefully, taking small steps I went toward the center, but just before reaching the edge of an opening large enough for a full grown man to enter I dropped on to my belly and crawled the rest of the way. Finally, I came to the edge and cautiously peered over the side. It descended straight down into a large expanse that was divided into many lanes and alleys with what appeared to be small buildings. It was very detailed and the pattern was organized. I had seen such planning in books and the design was called a labyrinth, which are used to confuse and capture unwanted visitors.

Observing from this uppermost view, I could clearly make out an opening to an extremely complex maze of corners and turns, all of which, led to a central building surrounded by trees and water. It all looked so peaceful and benign. I thought to myself that I must try to remember the design for surely, if I survive the decent to the bottom, I will need to get to that central building. I tried to capture all the turns and corners in my mind; when I thought I had it commit to memory I began formulating a plan.

I crawled around from side to side to see different views of what I might encounter when I ever reached the bottom. My most pressing thought was how was I to reach the bottom? There were no stairs to climb down. Searching for a way to transport myself I reached into the opening; carefully running my hand all along the side. First, I went to the north side, there was nothing; then to the west side, again nothing; now I moved to the south side, still no means of getting down. I moved to the east side and slowly moved my hand along the inside praying that I might discover something that would help me get down.

My fingers found something protruding through the stone; none of the other sides had this. Gingerly I tried to make out the shape of the object; thinking it was just an irregularity of the natural contour of the stone. Exercising great care I leaned a little further over the edge and tried to see what it was but it was dark. I then remembered the crystal in my pocket and took it out, holding on to it with all my concentration. I crept as far beyond the edge as I dared; holding on to a deep crack in the stone with one hand and using the crystal as a torch in the other I shined the light into the opening.

To my complete and utter amazement, it revealed an iron handle. It was ancient and rusted from exposure to the elements; its surface, which had once been smooth, was now rusted and pitted. Now that I knew what it was, do I dare to try to use it? I pulled back off the ledge, put the crystal back in my pocket, and tried to catch my breath. My heart was beating so rapidly I was sure it would run out of my mouth. As I always did whenever I was scared or unsure of what to do, I went to my knees; made the sign of the cross, looked to the Heavens and said "Lord Jesus, you have brought me this far, if I am to do your bidding you must show me the way."

Within a second of my prayer the crystal began to pulse inside my pocket; was it a sign from Jesus or some other reason, I did not know; but I decided that I would try the handle and see what would happen. By the placement of the shadow I was casting from the sunlight that peaked through the cloud cover I could tell it was midday. I did not know if it was hunger or fear but my belly was growling; perhaps it was both. I needed to make a move, which would either reveal a way down or lead to my death.

I got down on my now empty belly and reached over the side for the handle. I made the sign of the cross, took a firm grip, and pulled as hard as I could. Nothing happened. I cursed. Moving a little further beyond the edge, I now used both my hands to grasp the rusted steel and with every muscle in my body, I pulled as hard as I could. It moved ever so slightly. It did not take long for me to determine that at the pace I was going it would be yet another day before I would be able to make any headway. I was feeling lightheaded from lack of food and water. I stepped back and sat there for a few moments trying to devise a better method for moving the handle. Then it occurred to me that I might try to use my more powerful legs to push it open. The only problem was that I would lose all safety because my body would be extended further beyond the edge. I had no choice I had to try.

With great courage, I laid down on my back and with my legs, dangling over the side used them to push the handle. I could feel it give way, it moaned and groaned until finally with one swift movement it released, and I nearly plunged into the hole. The stone block which I lying on, began to separate itself from the rest. Half of my body was perched over the hole and the other half was moving along with the block, before I knew what was happening I dropped into a shallow well. I was not hurt; but I was overcome with fear. Slowly I let my breath out, and opened my eyes; I could see it was stairwell into which I had fallen into. I scrambled to my feet and once I got my bearings, I started down. I was surprised because it was not dark inside even though there were no windows or doors to let in light.

Using great caution, I descended hundreds of steps until finally I reached the labyrinthine village with its maze of narrow lanes and dark empty houses. The air was stagnant and dry as dust. It looked like the former inhabitants disappeared into the ground."

The monks were enraptured with the story, but their reverie was shattered by the call to evening prayer. The monks shook the fog from their minds and the Abbot said "Jerome we must leave for evening prayer; will you join us?" "If you do not prohibit me I shall stay here and get some work done. I have spent the entire day in the recitation of my life's story; now the time is approaching for me to complete my mission. May I stay; I promise that I shall not in any way harm any of these precious manuscripts?" Brother Angelo looked with wide-eyed anticipation at his superior "Yes Jerome you may stay; after services I shall come back; perhaps I may even be of some help to you." The young monk chirped in "I will come back as well." Jerome smiled and nodded his head. When they left, he was sitting on the floor.

CHAPTER FOURTEEN

A SHOPPING EXPEDITION

Paris

When Lucia awoke the next day she was greeted by the pretty face of her beloved servant Sophia "Good morning Mistress; when I arrived back last night you were already asleep and so I did not bother to announce my return. Is everything fine?" Lucia wanted to tell Sophia what happened the night before with the Marquise Givenchy and Alessandro but did not want to sound jealous.

"Everything is fine; why do you ask?" Sophia said, "I see that your gown was left in a bundle and your eyes are all puffy as if you had been crying." Lucia was amazed at her maid's powers of observation and with no ability to lie; she hung her head upon her chest and whispered, "It was awful. I was so lonely and sad. I miss him; I miss Danford." She began to weep and Sophia clutched her to herself and stroked the wild strawberry curls. "Do not weep my dear Mistress; you will find the love of your life soon; very soon." They stood like this for a long time; then Lucia gently pushed her away and looking at her asked, "Did you have a grand time in Paris yesterday?" "I did; truly I did. Thank you so very much; yet, now I am sorry that I was not here for you. You must have been in so much pain. Please forgive me." Lucia took her by the shoulders "Do not say these things. You have the right to your own happiness; it gives me joy to see you happy; I love you Sophia. My pain is not your fault; it is the curse of my birth. I pray that someday it will be lifted, and I will enjoy the love of a man. For now, I must be brave and accept my lot in life. Help me get ready I want to go shopping today."

Sophia helped her mistress to dress and while she was getting ready, she ran down to the kitchen galley and put a potion together to smear on Lucia's tear soaked face. When she returned Lucia was just finishing a letter to Abbot Vittorio.

Dear Abbot Vittorio,

I will be leaving Paris for Rome in two days. We will stay in Rome for only one week. I hope to be at Monteforte within three weeks. When I arrive home, I shall send word before I impose upon your hospitality. I have many things to tell you. Please keep me in your prayers.

Your devoted friend,

Marchesa Lucia Banfi

"Sophia, please make sure that this letter is sent out today." "Yes mistress. Now can I try to do something with those curls; did you not brush them out last night?" Lucia did not even want to think of last night but replied, "Yes I tried."

Once she was done, she made her way down to the dining hall to find her brothers and Alessandro. She was escorted to their table but the young architect was absent from the table. "Where is Alessandro?" asked Lucia in as nonchalant a voice as she could muster. "Ah, our young friend spent the evening with Henri's niece at Sant Germaine." Lucia was astounded "So soon; they just met." Mateo laughed heartily "Do I denote a tone of jealousy baby sister?" Lucia was flushed "NO" she nearly shouted; the couple at the adjoining table turned to stare at her rude tone. Genaro shrugged his shoulders "Was it not you who told Alessandro that you could give him nothing but friendship?" Lucia was about to launch a protest when Alessandro appeared at their table "May I join you?" Mateo who seemed surprised to see him just nodded.

"I did not believe we would have the pleasure of your company this morning Alessandro" stated Mateo with a lustful smirk on his face. Alessandro grew crimson at the insinuation of any intimacy involving the Lady Givenchy. He picked up his glass and took a long draught to cover his embarrassment.

Genaro seized the moment to change the conversation "Lucia where are you going today?" She wanted to spare Alessandro from any further distress "I would like to go shopping. Mateo do you think we might be able to stop at Madame Richaud's today? I should like to have her send me several of her magnificent creations." Mateo mercifully took the architect off his hook and gleefully said "But of course; anything for you Bella. We shall leave after our breakfast." In one swift movement, he was calling over the serving boy "I want a messenger to be sent to Madame Richaud's shop. Tell her that the Marchesa Lucia Banfi and her brothers will be by this morning; if she could make some private time for us." He reached into his waistcoat and extracted two coins; the value of which was more than the boy would make for a year. "Yes, My Lord Rizzo, I will run there myself." Mateo was pleased, as was Lucia.

Lucia leaned over to speak with Alessandro "Will you be coming to Rome with us; or will you be staying with Marquise Givenchy?" The architect did not hesitate "I shall be coming with all of you; that is if you still want my companionship?" Lucia was smiling broadly within herself, but her outward appearance was mildly composed, "Yes, dear Alessandro, why would we not want your company?" The expression of relief was written all over his handsome face. Lucia thought to herself that he looked more attractive than he had before. "We leave the day after tomorrow; then we shall stay a week in Rome and finally home to my beloved Monteforte. I cannot wait to see everyone."

The shopping expedition proved to be exactly what Lucia needed. Upon entering the shop, Madame Richaud came running over to them. Mateo embraced her warmly, while Genaro and Alessandro were polite. She then came to Lucia, "Marchesa they are still talking about you at Versailles. Apparently, you made a great impression upon His Majesty as well as the Queen. I have had twenty orders for the gown I made for you; yet I will never replicate the special color I created for you; and you alone." She curtsied deeply and finished by saying "A woman with your beauty must never be copied."

Lucia's ego, which, up to today, had become fragile, was now infused with renewed hope. "Thank you Madame Richaud, I did truly admire that creation; and thanks to you, I enjoyed my time at Versailles. Please send my most sincere regards to His Majesty and the Queen."

Madame Richaud was dancing all around Lucia "Marchesa, you have lost too much weight. I shall have to alter all your gowns; that is unless you intend to put a little more meat on those bones?" Mateo stepped up "You see, I told you that you had gotten too thin." Lucia smiled, but behind that smile was sadness "I know. I was far too long in England; it is a country of grey weather and grey food." They all laughed "You poor child; I too have been there and know exactly what you mean. Dreadful food!" "Madame, leave my gowns as they were; I shall be home to Monteforte within a few weeks and my chef will make it his mission to fatten me up; that I can assure you."

The men settled themselves to the salon and were treated to delicious confections and cognac. They chatted companionably amongst themselves. Madame Richaud waited on Lucia and came to her with a most magnificent red velvet gown. The fabric was of such high quality and the cut was so complimentary to Lucia's curvaceous figure. Madame was whispering, "I had this piece reserved for Her Majesty, but since you are here I will fit it to you instead and make her a different one." They helped Lucia into the gown and when she emerged for her fitting Alessandro, who caught her image in the mirror nearly choked on his pastry. He spoke to no one but said, "Dear Mother of God, she is a vision of beauty!" Mateo and Genaro turned to see Lucia standing on the dressmaker's podium and her beauty too mesmerized them. Mateo got up and walked over to where she was "My beautiful baby sister, you are a vision of divine femininity. I shall buy this gown for you as a gift." Lucia's cheeks were the same color as the deep red gown "Thank you dear brother." By now the drooling architect who was speechless, only his eyes were able to talk and Genaro joined him. "Bella, you are breathtaking. We must invent a special gala so that you may wear this fabulous gown. Bravo Madame, you have outdone yourself." Madame Richaud was beaming with pride "It is only fabric dear sir; it is this lovely woman who gives it a life all its own."

Finally, Alessandro found his tongue "Lucia I am trying to find the words that can express how beautiful you look, but there are no words that can tell you how I admire you." It would have been comical had he not been so sincere; for both he and Lucia's faces were now in competition with the deep, rich hue of the dress. Even Mateo the jokester left that as it was; it was too special to fool with.

With promises from Madame Richaud to have the gowns prepared and sent on to Monteforte they took their farewell with warm wishes and left to spend a quiet afternoon strolling the streets and shops of Paris. "I will miss all the fashion and high society of Paris," she said while walking arm in arm with Alessandro. They made a handsome couple. "I am not one for such excitements but I can see that it pleases you; and I am happy for it." There was something about this man that Lucia enjoyed; perhaps it was his simple ways. In comparison to the handsome giant Danford, with his flamboyant personality, Alessandro would not stand out in a crowded room, unless of course, it was a room he had designed.

Lucia could not resist any longer and decided to be bold "Alessandro, I must confess that I am surprised that you are not spending your last days in France with Lady Givenchy." At first, he did not answer and she could see from his face that he was searching for a proper response. "I am sorry, that was inappropriate of me; please forgive me. I shall tend to my own matters." Alessandro stopped abruptly and turned toward her; she turned to face him. "I will also make my confession; I am in love with you Lucia. Yes, I will admit that Lady Givenchy is beautiful and I could desire her but only in a physical sense. It is you, your mind, your heart, and your body that I want."

There they were in the middle of the Rue Royale and this man was confessing his love for her. Lucia was dumbfounded; her penetrating eyes the color of the sea, were wide with amazement. Mateo and Genaro who were walking several paces behind them were witnessing what was unfolding and were stunned at the scene. They were not sure if they should approach or stay back. They stood back and watched.

"It is now I who am sorry for my forwardness. You have rendered me incapable of social civility when it comes to my feeling for you. An aura surrounds you, and it transcends your physical beauty. I cannot find any fault with you Lucia. If you do not wish me to pursue your affections I shall leave your company at once; for if I stay and you reject me I shall do something terrible." The young architect hung his head in supplication. Lucia had blocked out all of her surroundings and had focused her attentions on this man who stood before her; she was not sure, if she loved him or if she was desperate for someone to love. The one thing she was sure of was that he loved her...

AFTERWORD

The first two novels in this series, which chronicle the life and adventures of Lucia Banfi, Mistress of Monteforte, have been a labor of love. The next novel entitled, **Lucia and the Gypsy's Prophecy**, which will be released in a few months, continues the love affair.

In the upcoming book, we will join our beautiful young heiress as she faces many challenges. We will be transported to distant lands, encounter evil in the most unsuspecting characters, find love, and loss.

It will be in this, the third book in this series, that Lucia truly comes of age. Forces for both good and evil will challenge her beyond her limits. Destiny has set in motion events that are so strong that not only her mind, body, and soul, but also her very life will be held in the balance.

Lucia and the Gypsy's Prophecy is